Acclaim for K[...]

"Kelly Irvin's *With All Her Heart* is a tender journey that explores friendship, second chances, and finding unexpected love. It reminds us that God's grace and mercy is ever present, especially when we're uncertain of His plan for us. This story will captivate readers who love the Amish culture and an endearing romance and leave them wanting more."

—AMY CLIPSTON, BESTSELLING AUTHOR
OF *THE HEART'S SHELTER*

"Kelly Irvin's *Matters of the Heart* is wonderfully written and paints a complete picture of the joys, trials, and tribulations of the average Amish community. It is filled with beautifully flawed characters you will laugh with, cry for, and then rejoice in their happiness when they finally find love."

—AMY LILLARD, BESTSELLING AUTHOR

"I do love a quick-paced, entertaining novel, and *The Heart's Bidding* is just that. I was immediately drawn into Toby's and Rachelle's stories and found myself rooting for them page after page. Kelly Irvin's latest belongs on the everyone's keeper shelf."

—*NEW YORK TIMES* AND *USA TODAY*
BESTSELLING AUTHOR SHELLEY SHEPARD GRAY

"Strangers at first, Maisy Glick and Joshua Lapp find solace in their unhappy circumstances in Kelly Irvin's *Every Good Gift*. Joshua, full of sorrow and doubt. Maisy, full of regret. Together, they forge a path forward in ways that will surprise readers. Irvin's knowledge of the Plain people shines in this endearing tale of love and redemption."

—SUZANNE WOODS FISHER, BESTSELLING
AUTHOR OF *A SEASON ON THE WIND*

"A beautifully crafted story of mistakes, redemption, healing, and grace. Kelly Irvin's *Every Good Gift* will captivate readers and tug on the heartstrings as characters brimming with real human frailty try to work through the consequences of their lives and choices with love and faith."

—KRISTEN MCKANAGH, AUTHOR OF *THE GIFT OF HOPE*

"Just like the title, *Warmth of Sunshine* is a lovely and cozy story that will keep you reading until the very last page."

—KATHLEEN FULLER, *USA TODAY* BESTSELLING AUTHOR OF THE MAIL-ORDER AMISH BRIDES SERIES

"This is a sweet story of romance and family that will tug at heartstrings. It is another great story and great characters from Irvin."

—*THE PARKERSBURG NEWS AND SENTINEL* ON *LOVE'S DWELLING*

"*Peace in the Valley* is a beautiful and heart-wrenching exploration of faith, loyalty, and the ties that bind a family and a community together. Kelly Irvin's masterful storytelling pulled me breathlessly into Nora's world, her deep desire to do good, and her struggle to be true to herself and to the man she loves. Full of both sweet and stark details of Amish life, *Peace in the Valley* is realistic and poignant, profound and heartfelt. I highly recommend it!"

—JENNIFER BECKSTRAND, AUTHOR OF *ANDREW*

"With a lovely setting, this is a story of hope in the face of trouble and has an endearing heroine, and other relatable characters that readers will empathize with."

—*PARKERSBURG NEWS AND SENTINEL* ON *MOUNTAINS OF GRACE*

"Kelly Irvin's *Mountains of Grace* offers a beautiful and emotional journey into the Amish community. Readers will be captivated by a heartwarming tale of forgiveness and finding a renewed faith in God. The story will capture the hearts of those who love the Plain culture and an endearing romance. Once you open this book, you'll be hooked until the last page."

—AMY CLIPSTON, BESTSELLING AUTHOR
OF *A WELCOME AT OUR DOOR*

"Irvin's fun story is simple (like Mary Katherine, who finds 'every day is a blessing and an adventure') but very satisfying."

—*PUBLISHERS WEEKLY* ON *THROUGH THE AUTUMN AIR*

"This second entry (after *Upon a Spring Breeze*) in Irvin's seasonal series diverges from the typical Amish coming-of-age tale with its focus on more mature protagonists who acutely feel their sense of loss. Fans of the genre seeking a broader variety of stories may find this new offering from a Carol Award winner more relatable than the usual fare."

—*LIBRARY JOURNAL* ON *BENEATH THE SUMMER SUN*

"The second entry in Irvin's Amish Blessings series (after *Love's Dwelling*) delivers an elegant portrait of a young Amish woman caught between two worlds . . . Irvin skillfully conveys Abigail's internal conflict ('How could Abigail put into words the longing that thrummed in her chest? The sense of loss, of missing out, of missing it all,' she reminisces about Amish life). Fans of Amish romance will want to check this out."

—*PUBLISHERS WEEKLY* ON *BENEATH THE SUMMER SUN*

"A moving and compelling tale about the power of grace and forgiveness that reminds us how we become strongest in our most broken moments."

—*LIBRARY JOURNAL* ON *UPON A SPRING BREEZE*

"Once I started reading *The Bishop's Son*, it was difficult for me to put it down! This story of struggle, faith, and hope will draw you in to the final page. . . . I have read countless stories of Amish men or women doubting their faith. I have never read a storyline quite like this one though. It was narrated with such heart. I was fully invested in Jesse's struggle. No doubt, what Jesse felt is often what modern-day Amish men and women must feel when they are at a crossroads in their faith. The story was brilliantly told and the struggle felt very real."

—DESTINATION AMISH

"Something new and delightful in the Amish fiction genre, this story is set in the barren, dusty landscape of Bee County, Texas . . . Irvin writes with great insight into the range and depth of human emotion. Her characters are believable and well developed, and her storytelling skills are superb. Recommend to readers who are looking for something a little different in Amish fiction."

—CBA RETAILERS + RESOURCES
ON THE BEEKEEPER'S SON

"The Beekeeper's Son is a perfect depiction of how God makes all things beautiful in His way. Rich with vivid descriptions and characters you can immediately relate to, Kelly Irvin's book is a must read for Amish fans."

—RUTH REID, BESTSELLING AUTHOR
OF A MIRACLE OF HOPE

WITH ALL HER
Heart

WITH ALL HER
Heart

AN AMISH CALLING NOVEL

KELLY IRVIN

ZONDERVAN

With All Her Heart

Copyright © 2025 by Kelly Irvin

This title is also available as a Zondervan e-book.

Published in Grand Rapids, Michigan, by Zondervan. Zondervan is a registered trademark of The Zondervan Corporation, L.L.C., a wholly owned subsidiary of HarperCollins Christian Publishing, Inc.

Requests for information should be addressed to customercare@harpercollins.com.

Library of Congress Cataloging-in-Publication Data

Names: Irvin, Kelly, author.
Title: With all her heart / Kelly Irvin.
Description: Grand Rapids, Michigan : Zondervan, 2024. | Series: Amish calling novel | Summary: "Bonnie is successful in her crafts shop but fears no man will see past her disability to her strong and loving heart. Elijah dreams of leaving the family business to focus on his carvings. Can they find a new path together?"—Provided by publisher.
Identifiers: LCCN 2024034315 (print) | LCCN 2024034316 (ebook) | ISBN 9780840709486 (paperback) | ISBN 9780840709516 (epub) | ISBN 9780840709561
Subjects: LCSH: Amish—Fiction. | BISAC: FICTION / Amish & Mennonite | FICTION / Small Town & Rural | LCGFT: Christian fiction. | Romance fiction. | Novels.
Classification: LCC PS3609.R82 W57 2024 (print) | LCC PS3609.R82 (ebook) | DDC 813/.6—dc23/eng/20240726
LC record available at https://lccn.loc.gov/2024034315
LC ebook record available at https://lccn.loc.gov/2024034316

Zondervan titles may be purchased in bulk for educational, business, fundraising, or sales promotional use. For information, please email SpecialMarkets@Zondervan.com.

Printed in the United States of America

24 25 26 27 28 LBC 5 4 3 2 1

To Tim, for taking those vows—especially the one about in sickness and health—so seriously

Pride goes before destruction,
   a haughty spirit before a fall.

Proverbs 16:18 (NIV)

Those who know your name trust in you,
   for you, LORD, have never forsaken those who seek you.

Psalm 9:10 (NIV)

Featured Families

Lee's Gulch, Virginia

Silas and Joanna Miller (grandparents)

Charlie and Elizabeth Miller (parents)

Toby   Jason   Elijah   Declan   Layla   Emmett   Josie   Sherri   Sadie

Toby and Rachelle (Lapp) Miller

Declan and Bethel (King) Miller

Nathan

Micah and Layla (Miller) Troyer

Selah

Marlin (deceased) and Jocelyn (Baumgartner) Yoder (widow)

Bonnie

Uriah and Frannie Baumgartner

Tammy   Rose   Rodney   Carter   Thomas   Serenity

Theo (widower) and Ellie Beiler (deceased)

Noah

Aaron and Katherine King

Bethel   Enos   Claire   Robbie   Judah   Liam   Melinda

Karl and Cara Lapp (grandparents)

Adam and Leah Lapp

Rachelle John Dillon Mark Steven Kimmie Emma Mandy DeeDee

Jonah Sean Sam Michael Darcy

Atlee and Hilda Schrock (nursery owners)

Ben Harriet Hannah Nan Amos Kendell Lulu

Luke and Deana Beachy

Andrew Christine Ryan Corrine

Bartholomew "Bart" (bishop) and Miriam Plank

David Henry Nyla Hannah Matthew Timothy Esther

David and Opal (Coblentz) Plank

Tucker

Martin (deacon) and Cindy Hershberger (grocery store owners)

Bella Sophia Justin Harry Finn

Jedediah "Jed" (minister) and Martha Knepp

Sarah Carol Isaac Will Thomas

Menno and Patience Coblentz

Opal Leo Kathryn James Gabriel

Noah and Mary Eash (parents' committee member)

James Melanie Catherine Robert

Glossary of Pennsylvania Deutsch*

aamen: amen

ach: oh

aenti: aunt

bewillkumm: welcome

bopli, boplin: baby, babies

bruder, brieder: brother, brothers

bu, buwe: boy, boys

daadi: grandpa

daed: father

danki: thank you

dat: dad

dawdy haus: attached home for grandparents when they retire

dochder, dechder: daughter, daughters

dumkopf: blockhead

eck: corner table where newly married couple sits during wedding reception

eldre: parents

Englischer: English or non-Amish

enkel: grandson

eppies: cookies

es dutt mer: I am sorry

faeriwell: good-bye

Glossary of Pennsylvania Deutsch

fraa, weiwer: wife, wives

froh gebortsdaag: happy birthday

fuhl: fool

gaul: horse

Gelassenheit: a German word, yielding fully to God's will and forsaking all selfishness

gern gschehme: you're welcome

Gmay: church district

groossmammi, groossmammis: grandmother, grandmothers

Gott: God

guder mariye: good morning

gut: good

gut nacht: good night

hallo: hello

halbgscheit: cracked, rattle-brained, crazy

hochmut: pride

hund, hunde: dog, dogs

hundel: puppy (little dog)

jah: yes

kaffi: coffee

kapp: prayer cap or head covering worn by Amish women

kind, kinner: child, children

kinnskind, kinnskinner: grandchild, grandchildren

kossin, kossins: cousin(s)

kuss, koss: (noun) kiss, kisses

maedel, maed: girl, girls

mamm: mom

mammi: grandma

mann, menner: husband, husbands

Mennischt: Mennonite

mudder: mother

narrisch: foolish, silly

nee: no

onkel: uncle

Ordnung: written and unwritten rules in an Amish district

rumspringa: period of "running around" for Amish youth before they decide whether they want to be baptized into the Amish faith and seek a mate

schweschder, schweschdre: sister, sisters

sei so gut: please (be so kind)

suh, seh: son, sons

wittfraa: widow

wittmann: widower

wunderbarr: wonderful

---

*The German dialect commonly referred to as Pennsylvania Dutch is not a written language and varies depending on the location and origin of the Amish settlement. These spellings are approximations. Most Amish children learn English after they start school. They also learn high German, which is used in their Sunday services.

A Note from the Author

With All Her Heart is book three in the Amish Calling series. It continues the exploration of mental and physical developmental disabilities as well as the debilitating diseases experienced by many Amish people because of a limited gene pool, resulting in what geneticists call the founder effect (thoroughly explained in the story you're about to read). These challenges are viewed through the lens of the Amish characters and their corresponding worldview begun in *The Heart's Bidding*. As I mentioned in the author's notes for those first two books, I want readers to know I'm keenly aware of the tender issues that may be raised by the disability community when encountering the Amish term "special" children and their view that these children are "gifts from God."

As a writer, I know better than most the power of words to hurt, demean, make one feel less-than, and perpetuate stereotypes. First know that I'm a Christian writer living with a disability. I came by my disability later in life. My struggle to accept this disability is ongoing. I don't see it as a gift from God. However, I respect and value the Amish perspective as Christlike and beautifully loving. Readers will see that Amish believe all children are gifts from God. They employ the term "special" for these babies as a term of affection and love. Therefore, I use it in the context of my Amish characters' points of view. These are their views, not mine, as I walk a narrow path between what the "English" world finds acceptable and representing an authentic Amish voice.

I say all this to respectfully ask readers to honor the Amish view as loving, kind, and so much more Christlike than the worldly view of some would-be "English" parents who hold the belief that bringing a child with disabilities into the world is a choice that can be rejected. I have no doubt that Amish parents agonize, worry, and even shed tears over their "special children." But they choose an attitude of gratitude.

Many of you might disagree with the premise that women should only aspire to be wives and mothers. Others will want to argue that there is no disputing that people with disabilities can excel at any task in the same way that people do who don't have those disabilities. I personally agree. But this is an Amish romance, not an English one. If I'm going to write about the Amish, I must honor and respect their values and faith. They take great pains to not only disengage from the electrical grid but also from the world's value system. That's how they live their faith. This story reflects that desire.

I hope you will read and enjoy *With All Her Heart*, along with the other two books, in the spirit in which the Amish Calling series is offered—to edify, provoke thought, and shed Christ's light in the world. God bless.

Chapter 1

$\mathcal{H}$umming "Amazing Grace," Elijah Miller stuck a box filled with wooden toys into the back of his buggy next to a rocking horse, a doll's cradle, a tiny table with four matching chairs, and a child-size wooden push lawn mower toy. The humming and that particular hymn took his mind off what was coming. He brushed his hands together. "That'll do it."

Slowpoke barked once and proceeded to race around the buggy. The gangly pit bull mix, who seemed certain he was still a puppy, had a serious case of the zoomies.

The dog knew how to make Elijah laugh just when his owner needed it. Chuckling, Elijah shoved his straw hat back. He clapped twice. "Hey, are you going with me or what?"

Slowpoke, who was anything but slow, flung himself into the buggy. Panting, his pink tongue hanging out, he plopped down on the passenger side of the bench and smiled at Elijah as if to say, "Ready when you are."

"I guess that answers my question." Slowpoke's company would help. His antics would keep Elijah from obsessing about the reason for his trip to Lee's Gulch. He'd practiced his speech at least a dozen times in the workshop he built for himself behind his family's house. All he had to do was drive into town, park in front of Homespun Handicrafts Shop, walk in, show the owners his wares, and convince them to sell his pieces on consignment.

A walk in the park. For anyone in the world except Elijah. Despite a brisk breeze this cool April morning in Virginia, his palms were damp at the thought. So were his armpits underneath his blue work shirt.

The owners were three Plain women he'd known most of his life. His brain's thoughtful reminder didn't help one iota. Talking to women was even harder. Sweat ran between his shoulder blades down his spine.

He had to do it. Now or never.

Elijah heaved a breath and put one foot up to climb into the buggy.

"Elijah! Elijah, wait!"

Ducking his head, Elijah closed his eyes and opened them. He settled his boot back on the ground, turned, and faced his father. Charlie Miller's cheeks were red and his usual smile missing. "Didn't you hear me calling you, *Suh*?"

"I guess I was thinking."

"Daydreaming more likely." His father tromped across the gravel road until he reached the buggy. "Toby says you told him you're not going to Richmond with us tomorrow."

"I thought I'd pass on this trip." Elijah forced himself to straighten and meet his father's gaze. His brother Toby was in charge of the day-to-day tasks of running their auctioneering business that covered five states. That included what he called staff scheduling. "I'm trying to get my business up and running."

His business. His father had agreed to the artisan wood-crafting business as long as it didn't get in the way of the family business. Miller Family Auctioneering needed all its menfolk to make it work. His grandfather Silas had started the business as a young man. When he retired, Dad took over. His strong suit was working with his hands, not reading, writing, and numbers. He'd learned pretty quick to delegate the scheduling and such to his sons. He expected all five of them to share the load. "Why did you wait until the auction season kicked off to do that?"

Being on the auction circuit all of March had encroached on the time Elijah needed to build up his inventory. But that wasn't the real issue. It had taken him that long to summon the nerve. "I wanted to have my best work to show to the shop owners in town. My very best work."

"I understand you don't feel like you're suited for auctioneering. You're twenty-six. It's long past time for you to get over it." His tone softening, Dad treaded closer. "You took the classes and got certified. You've practiced. Once you're on the platform, it'll come to you. You'll get over the stage fright. I did. Your *brieder* did. You'll see."

Toby loved being center stage. He loved auctioneering. So did Jason. Declan had too, until his throat cancer took away his most important tool—a strong voice. Emmett was eighteen, and he was chomping at the bit to have his turn.

The images whirred in Elijah's brain. *Walk up the steps. Walk across the platform. Pick up the microphone. Face the crowd.* A wave of nausea washed over him. His throat went dry. His heartbeat surged. His hands shook. "I can't," he whispered. "I wish I could, but I can't."

That was a white lie. Fine, a lie. *Forgive me, Gott.* No way Elijah's father would understand. Working in the shop, taking a piece of wood and turning it into a horse or a herd of cattle or a wagon. Birds, possums, foxes, raccoons. No audience. No noise except the robins chattering outside the open windows, the leaves rustling on the maple, redbud, and white oak trees, and the crickets serenading him—that was enough. More than enough.

"With Declan not able to call auctions anymore, we really need you." Dad jerked his thumb toward the road that led to the highway and Lee's Gulch. "Go. Take your toys into town. See what you can get for them. But when you get back, you best pack your bag. You're going with us tomorrow."

Elijah's toys. Like making toys and children's furniture didn't amount to a suitable occupation for a Miller son. Not really a job. Elijah could make full-scale furniture. But seeing his nieces and nephews playing with their little farm animals, pretending to be farmers, happy in their make-believe, it was the best job ever. *"Dat—"*

"We need you to spot bids and help with the inventory if you're not going to get on the platform."

Dad might be trying to hide his disappointment, but he wasn't doing a very good job.

"Understood."

Whistling tunelessly, Elijah's father strode toward the business office down the road from the house.

Message delivered.

"Well, that's that." Elijah climbed into the buggy and picked up the reins. Slowpoke had curled up on the seat with his snout resting on his mammoth paws. He opened one eye, closed it. Elijah snorted. "A lot of help you were. Some friend you are."

Slowpoke yawned so widely that his tonsils wiggled. Dogs had tonsils, didn't they? His stinky doggy breath rolled over Elijah, along with the pungent smell of something that had been dead awhile.

"Ach, you stink. If I didn't need you to listen to my spiel, I'd leave you here. Wake up, sit up, and make yourself useful."

Slowpoke's good ear, along with the one that had been torn half off when Elijah found the dog, ribs showing, snout bloodied, shivering in the cold as he scavenged for food in the family's trash barrels, perked up. He had slunk away when Elijah yelled at him but paused on the road, head down, tail wagging. Now Slowpoke unfurled his long, muscular body and sat up on his haunches.

Declan claimed that Slowpoke was the ugliest dog he'd ever seen. Who could look at that ugly face and not feel bad? Slowpoke might be a cross between a German shepherd and a pit bull. It was impossible to say. He had grayish-brown short fur, long legs, and a pit bull–shaped face. Kids were scared of him at first. But his insistence at joining their play—whether it be basketball or hide-and-seek—won them over.

Slowpoke had never met a person he didn't like. He made a good friend.

"Here we go."

For the next hour, Elijah practiced his sales pitch. Toby had said he needed a sales pitch. Elijah couldn't simply stroll into a store and expect them to gaze upon his made-with-love toys and fall for them. Store owners were businesspeople. They made decisions based on existing inventory, customer demographics, and proven sales records. Since taking over managing the family business, Toby had acquired a vocabulary that boggled the mind.

All too soon Elijah arrived in downtown Lee's Gulch, a town of about seven thousand that swelled to three times that size with college students in the fall and spring. In the summer months, tourists swarmed local Civil War–era attractions that included a museum and a thirty-one-mile trail that followed the path of Confederate General Robert E. Lee during the war. It was a busy place, which boded well for local artisans like Elijah. Hopefully.

At the moment, the three-block stretch of Main Street dotted with Plain-owned businesses and tourist-driven English businesses was quiet. Only a few cars occupied the angled parking slots. Elijah pulled the buggy into the space designated for it and stopped in front of Homespun Handicrafts Shop.

The sweat under his arms was back. His hands were slick on the reins. "Maybe I should wait until I have more doll cradles. They sell a lot of Plain dolls and Raggedy Anns here." Elijah glanced at Slowpoke. The dog's ears went up, then flopped down. The doggy version of a shrug. "I know. I'm not a coward." Even if his dad might think so. "What if they say no?"

What if they didn't? His dad would never be convinced that Elijah could earn a living making toys and kids' furniture. "Here goes nothing."

Elijah hopped down and headed to the back of the buggy. Slowpoke joined him. "Are you going in with me?"

The dog trotted up the long wheelchair ramp that led to the wood-frame-and-glass door, turned, and glanced back with an inquiring face. A wreath of bound straw, daisies, sunflowers, and purple asters covered the window under a painted wood sign that said WELCOME! And underneath it BEWILLKUMM!

"I'm coming, I'm coming."

Elijah gathered up the box of toys and headed for the door. It swung wide just as he attempted to balance the box on his knee so he could open it.

"*Hallo, hallo*, bewillkumm. It's nice to see you, Elijah." Bonnie Yoder, one of the shop's co-owners, had one hand on the door, the other on her walker. Her smile grew as Slowpoke pranced in ahead of Elijah. "And you too, sir. I assume you're with Elijah."

Slowpoke woofed softly and kept going.

"I hope it's okay if Slowpoke comes in. He sees himself as my business partner."

"Mr. Slowpoke is certainly welcome, as long as he minds his manners. I suspect he'll do a better job than some of our two-legged customers." Smiling, Bonnie pointed toward a basket of baby quilts. An enormous, cream-colored, fluffy cat slept in it. The cat raised its head, opened one eye, then went back to snoozing. "Puff is officially employed here as a mouser, but she likes to think she owns the place. As long as Slowpoke doesn't bother her, she won't bother him."

"Slowpoke's indoor manners are better than a lot of people's. That's for sure and for certain." Elijah shifted the box and leaned his shoulder into the door. "I've got the door. I don't want you to fall."

"My balance isn't that bad." Bonnie's smile faded. "My legs aren't so weak I can't hold the door for a customer."

"I'm not a customer." Elijah cringed inwardly. If he was bad at making conversation with people in general, he was at his worst with women. Even ones like Bonnie whom he'd known since first grade. Especially pretty, soft-spoken Bonnie, who didn't have a mean bone in her body. She would never tease a shy kid. And she had warm caramel eyes and chestnut curls that often refused to stay under her prayer covering. Not that he'd noticed. "Wh-what I mean is, I mean, it's, these are . . ."

Stutter, stumble, stuck. That was him.

Bonnie grabbed her walker, which had wheels, which meant it was probably called something else, and moved away from the door. "Regardless, it's always nice to see a familiar face. What brings you by?"

"I . . ." Elijah's sales pitch, so earnestly memorized, disappeared. Frantic, he searched his memory. The overwhelming scents of

Kelly Irvin

cinnamon, blueberry, vanilla, lemon, and a potpourri of other smells emanating from homemade candles and soaps assailed him. His head hurt. Slowpoke woofed from the spot he'd commandeered as his own near the window display of Plain dolls. *I know, I know.* Heat billowed. Elijah's face burned. "I . . ."

His mind had gone blank.

Chapter 2

*E*lijah Miller's stricken expression sent a flaming arrow straight to Bonnie Yoder's heart. She angled her rollator between him and the door to keep him from making a run for it. "That box looks heavy." She gentled her voice, talking to him the way her father used to talk to the stray cats he fed scraps to on the back porch after supper on frigid winter nights. The thought of her father's kindness didn't hurt as much as it would've only a few months earlier. "Why don't you set it on the table over there where we have the craft classes?"

His head bent as if studying the box's contents, Elijah didn't move.

Okay, that was okay. Bonnie waved at Hannah Plank, her part-timer, who'd been straightening and dusting merchandise on the displays by the floor-to-ceiling windows at the front of the shop. "Hannah, can you handle the cash register while I talk with Elijah?"

Hannah's big grin signaled her delight at the added responsibility. The seventeen-year-old had worked at the shop for about six months, mostly cleaning or helping customers and artisans carry packages. "No problem."

With only one customer, an English lady from nearby Nathalie, in the store, she was probably right. "*Danki*. Just call out if you have any questions."

Taking advantage of an aisle made extra wide to accommodate wheelchairs, Bonnie passed Elijah and took the lead past displays of leather goods, jewelry, birdhouses, candles, soaps, ceramics, pottery, paintings, scarves, totes, baskets, and handmade greeting cards, all created by area artisans. Then bookshelves filled with books written by Plain authors and even some Amish romance novels written by English authors followed. Bonnie and her co-owners did their best to give local and regional artisans, specifically ones with disabilities, a place to sell their wares.

If Elijah noticed the carefully curated displays, he didn't say anything. Bonnie's earliest memories of him were of a boy who rarely spoke and never raised his hand in class. If his older brothers hadn't insisted on including him in games during recess and after church, he probably would've sat them out. He was too shy to ask to join in.

Big brothers Toby and Jason also took care of anyone who dared to pick on a Miller kid. They were a close-knit family. A person always knew when she was seeing a Miller boy, too, because they were all cut from the same cloth: tall, lean, blond hair, blue eyes, and dimples. Elijah was shorter and slighter but still had the trademark dimples and sky-blue eyes. If he knew he was a handsome man, he surely didn't show it.

What made a child in a family of boisterous, loud, outgoing kids so painfully shy? Maybe it was exactly that. He couldn't compete. Bonnie had no way of knowing. She was an only child who often longed for a noisy bunch of siblings, especially a sister.

It never happened, much to her parents' sadness. "*Not Gott's plan,*" Bonnie's mother had always said. Instead His plan somehow involved allowing their only child to be born with a rare disease called type 3 spinal muscular atrophy, or SMA3 for short.

Now wasn't the time to noodle the nature of that unfairness or the others that seemed to follow. Like her dad slipping away, his heart giving out while he slept after a hard day's work at a barn raising almost two years earlier.

"Two or three times a week and every Saturday, we offer customers the chance to learn some of the crafts represented by our artisans." Maybe her prattle would help Elijah relax and keep her mind off what couldn't be helped. "Last week Sophia led a class in watercolors. Even though it's not tourist season yet, we had ten ladies participate. All English, mostly from around Lee's Gulch. I call that a success."

Sophia Hershberger was one of Homespun Handicrafts' three co-owners. She'd been in a buggy accident at age eleven that resulted in paralysis of her legs. She used a wheelchair to get around. A talented artist, she created greeting cards, postcards, and small framed paintings that regularly sold out.

Bonnie glanced back to make sure Elijah still followed. He did, along with Slowpoke, who panted as if he'd been chasing a possum across an open field. He surely felt his owner's nerves and wanted to make sure no one gave Elijah a hard time. Such a good dog.

Bonnie stopped at one of the long wooden tables used for the classes. After locking the brakes on her rollator, she balanced herself with one hand and used her other one to quickly move aside skeins of yarn, knitting needles, sewing kits stuffed with embroidery threads in bright colors, needles, tomato-shaped pin cushions, and small scissors.

"For the next three months, Carol is teaching classes twice a week in crochet, embroidery, and knitting. We have a ton of women signed up. It always interests me to see trends that bring back crafts that were once skills all women were expected to have. So many of them remember their grandmas and great-grandmas making quilts or embroidering dresser scarves and knitting mittens and shawls. Most of them can't darn a sock or reattach a button."

Carol Knepp, the shop's third co-owner, was born with a mild form of spina bifida that she never let slow her down. She handled her crutches like extensions of her body. A person should pray for anyone who got in her way, but when it came to their customers who wanted to learn to sew, Carol had an unending wealth of patience.

The kind of patience a person needed to coax a shy person from his shell. Her co-owners loved what they called "helping the underdog." Elijah definitely fell in that category. "Sophia and Carol will be here in a bit. They come in later and stay later so we can have extended store hours." Bonnie patted the table. "You can set your box right here."

Elijah obliged. Bonnie restrained herself from peeking. Elijah's mother, Elizabeth, and his sisters always talked about how talented he was, but Bonnie had never seen his work. Unless they were a member of the Millers' massive extended family, most people hadn't. Instead, she inhaled the enticing scent of fresh coffee and cocked her head toward the nearby coffee and pastry bar. "Would you like some *kaffi*? We have cinnamon rolls and banana-nut muffins if you're interested."

The complimentary offerings kept browsing customers in the store longer, which frequently led to more sales.

Elijah rubbed his clean-shaven face with both hands. His Adam's apple bobbed. "*Nee*, but danki."

Likely he was too nervous to think about food or drink. "Maybe later, after we're done with business. I don't know about you, but I could drink kaffi all day long. I do, in fact. My *mamm* baked the pastries so I can vouch for them being mighty tasty." Elijah heaved a breath. A little less tense now? Bonnie tapped on the box. "I'd loved to see what you've brought us. May I?"

Elijah nodded. Slowpoke woofed in obvious agreement.

"*Wunderbarr.*"

It was hard to know where to start. Elijah had filled it with handmade flannel bags. One contained a set of miniature farm animals, all painstakingly painted in realistic colors. Another held forest animals. Deer, raccoon, fox, rabbits, frogs, squirrels, and a wolf, all whittled by hand. A third featured zoo animals. "Lions and tigers and bears, oh my." Bonnie bestowed her most encouraging smile on him. "These are beautiful. Almost too beautiful to let *kinner* play with them."

"Nee. Toys." Elijah touched the rooster with an oversized red crest. "For kinner to have fun."

Now he was talking. Bonnie nodded. They would make an arresting display next to the dolls, stuffed animals, and puppets she and her friend Opal Plank created—when Opal, who was married and had a baby now, had time. The usual pesky envy twinged in Bonnie's chest. Smaller than it had been when Opal confided that she and David would marry. Hard work kept the ugly envy at bay.

Focus on the shop. The shop gave Plain folks like herself, with disabilities, a way to earn their keep when traditional Plain tasks couldn't be accomplished. More importantly it gave them a sense of self-worth, a sense that they contributed just as their abled family members did.

Elijah didn't have a physical disability, but his shy nature might be considered a disability by his family of outgoing auctioneers if it kept him from fulfilling their expectations that he, too, be an auctioneer. Maybe he never wanted that life. Maybe his craft fulfilled him.

"We've been wanting to expand our toy section. These beauties will make great birthday and Christmas presents." Bonnie smoothed her fingers over a horse pull toy and admired its regal bearing. "Even the *Englischer* shoppers will want them so they can display 'Amish-made' knickknacks in their homes next to their quilt wall hangings. You do beautiful work."

"Danki." He ducked his head, making it hard to see his face under his straw hat. After a second, he reached into the box and pulled out a sheet of paper. Without looking at her directly, he held it out. "Lots to choose from."

Indeed. "Yo-yos, tic-tac-toe games, Noah's ark with two dozen animals, wooden tractor and wagon, alphabet boards, a barn with farm animals, a corral with horses, a wooden piggy bank." Bonnie ran down the inventory list on which each item was meticulously described. "And that's just a start. I see you have kinner's furniture as well. Did you bring any of those for me to see?"

Elijah's head came up. The beginnings of hope mixed with obvious surprise flitted across his face. "I can get them if you really want to see them. They're not much. I mean, I try to make them nice . . ."

"If they're anything like what you've shown me so far, they'll be just what I've been wanting." Bonnie popped the rollator's brakes, wheeled around, and pointed it toward the door. "I'll come with you."

"Nee, nee, I'll bring them to you."

"If you're going to do business here at Homespun Handicrafts, the first thing you have to learn is not to treat us like we're not able to do for ourselves." Bonnie silently berated herself. She could've been more diplomatic about it, but this was her number-one pet peeve. "I know you're just trying to help, but the best thing you can do is ask if I need help first. If I do, I'll let you know."

His face red as a candied apple, Elijah nodded jerkily. "Is it all right if I get the door for you?"

"That would be great." She reached for her most conciliatory tone. Mom was always telling her she was way too prickly. Mom didn't have everyone trying to wait on her hand and foot. She probably wished she did sometimes. "One day I'd love to install one of those doohickeys that opens the door automatically, when we can afford it."

They had electricity in the store, but it was bare bones and needed to be upgraded. They had to be careful not to overtax it. First priority was keeping the air-conditioning working, which the English customers expected. Ceiling fans weren't enough during the summer months. They wouldn't browse if they were sweating, and if they didn't browse, they didn't buy. Plus the automatic door mechanisms were expensive themselves.

Slowpoke led the way to the buggy. He hopped into the back as if he would do the show-and-tell himself. He really was a good friend and business partner. Bonnie hung back to give Elijah a chance to gather his thoughts. "Whenever you're ready."

Elijah leaned into the buggy and pulled out an old-fashioned rocking horse with the ease of a man who did heavy lifting. His biceps strained against his shirt's faded blue cotton sleeves. He set the horse on the sidewalk. He nudged the head and set the horse rocking. The woodworking was beautiful. Bonnie ran her hand over the padded leather-covered seat and examined the yarn mane and tail. "This is really nice. Beautiful work. Is it walnut?"

"Oak with a medium walnut stain." He ducked his head, his face darkening to a scarlet hue. The man had a hard time taking a

15

compliment. "My *schweschdre* helped me with the yarn. Josie and Sherri help with painting the animals too. What they do, Sadie has to do, of course."

Elijah's sister Sadie was born with Down syndrome—not that she let that stand in her way.

"Opal Plank helps me with a lot of the fine sewing needed for my dolls and sock puppets and my stuffed animals." Bonnie's fingers weren't nimble enough for the fine work. "It's *gut* to have help, especially family. They must be excited for you to start your own business."

If that was what this was. Someone as talented as Elijah could go a long way toward earning a living with his skills. Bonnie studied his face. His expression had gone wooden. His calloused fingers smoothed the horse's mane. "Some of them," he mumbled.

Some of them. But not all. *Don't you worry, Elijah, we'll win them over. In time.* Just as Bonnie had won over her parents when they'd objected to three young, single, Plain women, all with disabilities, opening their own business. It hadn't been easy. But that was a story to be shared at another time. "What else did you bring?"

Next came a child-size table and four chairs. Then a child's footstool and a wagon big enough for two kids. Followed by a child's desk and chair. And then a child-size push lawn mower with moving parts.

"This is wunderbarr. How fun." Bonnie rolled closer. She gave the mower a gentle push. The inner workings made a *clink-clink* as the barrel turned. "English kinner will have fun with this too."

They wouldn't know what it was used for since their own parents likely used gas-powered or electric mowers. Plain children didn't have to wait long before they were enlisted to cut the yard with a real push mower. "These will make great nostalgia pieces for older English shoppers."

"You think so?" For the first time, Elijah seemed to forget his awkwardness. "You're really interested in selling them?"

"Of course we're interested. Do you know how consignment works?"

"I make the toys. You sell them. We split the proceeds." Simple as that. "It's a sixty-forty split. Does that sound fair?"

"I get forty. You get sixty. That seems fair."

"Nee, nee. You get sixty. We get forty."

"Ah, ah."

"Why don't you bring them into the shop? Then we'll fill out the paperwork. It's important to get everything in writing."

The beginning of a smile blossomed into a full-fledged grin. Her grip tightening on the rollator handles, Bonnie paused, suddenly breathless. She racked her memories. Surely she'd seen Elijah smile during their school years. Maybe not. She would've remembered that knock-your-apron-off smile.

"I'm right behind you." Elijah blessedly didn't seem to notice her sudden disorientation. "Do you want me to get the door first?"

He learned quicker than most. Bonnie settled the lawn mower on the rollator seat. "Sure. If you'll put the doorstop in front of the door, I'll get Hannah to help you bring in the other items. She'll show you where to put them in the storage area. Once that's done, you and I can talk business. After we set the prices, she'll help you create the inventory tags and attach them."

"I would like to talk business." Elijah's tone held undisguised surprise. "Very much."

"Gut." Bonnie trudged back inside. Her brain wanted to run. Her weak legs would never cooperate. It was ridiculous to be so aware of a man like Elijah. He was here on business. He wouldn't think twice about a woman like her.

Disability made no difference to Plain folks when it came to family. They loved every child, abled or disabled, equally. But Plain men needed wives who could take care of the house, bake, sew clothes, plant and reap gardens, and take care of babies with little or no help.

The thought of babies brought with it the memory of Dr. Newcomb's question during her last appointment at the Center for Special Children. A searing heat swept over Bonnie.

"Are you dating, Bonnie? As we've discussed before, there's no reason you shouldn't."

Dr. Newcomb had sat Bonnie down years earlier to explain that she could have romance, marry, and bear children. Her life expectancy, praise God, was the same as any other woman's. Childbearing would be harder and might cause her muscle weakness to progress more quickly, but women with SMA did it.

Maybe English women with their electric appliances and bounty of conveniences, but how could a Plain woman with limited mobility cook, clean, bake, can, garden, and take care of children when she didn't have the strength in her arms to pick up a baby, let alone carry him around or bathe him? Because of the titanium rods that guarded her spine against further progression of her scoliosis, she couldn't bend over to pick up a toddler, even if she had the strength. She couldn't run after a wayward child who decided to toddle too close to the road or deep water. She couldn't keep him safe.

Dr. Newcomb's question had been salt in the wound. As if to say, "What are you waiting for?"

Waiting for someone to ask me to take a buggy ride.

Waiting for someone to see past the rollator. Waiting for someone to see beyond my limitations to my potential.

"Men see the rollator first. Old ladies use walkers. Not the kind of woman a man wants to court," Bonnie had told the doctor.

Her expression so full of kindness it hurt Bonnie's heart, Dr. Newcomb had patted Bonnie's arm. *"Any man worth his salt will look past that rollator and see a beautiful, smart, funny, hard-working woman he'd be blessed to have as a wife."*

"Would he be blessed? The honest answer seems to be no, not really."

"Don't sell yourself short."

"I'm not. I'm trying to be realistic."

Having pie-in-the-sky dreams didn't help Bonnie. It created longing, discontentment, and a peevish desire for things she couldn't have. Better to seek contentment and count blessings.

That was Mom talking in her ear. Mom, who sought to be content in her new life as a widow.

Most of the time Bonnie tried to take a page from that same book. She was happy with the life she'd carved out for herself. She loved her store and her job. But sometimes, like today, it hurt to think a kind, sweet man like Elijah wouldn't give her a second thought.

To him, Bonnie was likely just business.

Chapter 3

No spiel necessary. All that worry for naught. God's Word advised against worrying. Yet Elijah couldn't fathom how a person stopped. How long had he been holding his breath? He exhaled, wiped his sweaty palms on his pants, and followed Hannah into the shop's storage room, which had a desk complete with a computer monitor to one side, a round table and chairs, and a mini refrigerator. Beyond that, under a bank of four windows, stood an electric-powered treadle sewing machine next to a long worktable covered with all manner of cloth, felt, dolls, stuffed animals, and puppets in various stages of completion. This space did quadruple duty—storage, office, workspace, and break room. Even so, they kept it clean and well organized, and it smelled of a forest air freshener.

"We'll keep your items in the box for now until you get your tags on them. You can't do that until you and Bonnie agree to a price for each one." Hannah set the rocking horse she'd taken from Bonnie's walker onto the floor in front of an open section of wooden shelves that reached to the ceiling. She pointed to an open spot above the horse. "Take that space near the middle. It'll make it easier for you to put the tags on and for me to reach them when it's time to build the display."

Elijah squeezed past her. If Hannah had any qualms about making conversation with a Plain man she hardly knew, she didn't show them. He racked his brain for something to say. "You design the displays?"

"Nee. Bonnie does all that. She has an eye for it. I just carry everything to the front and do any heavy lifting needed."

When Hannah smiled, which she seemed to do a lot, she was the spitting image of her father, Bishop Bart Plank. The hair around her prayer covering was the same golden blonde, and she had the same inquisitive pale-blue eyes and wiry build. Still grinning, as if tickled by the idea that she might do display design, she turned to the cart that held the remainder of Elijah's bigger items. "Sometimes I get to help customers if they're busy. I like that too."

"It's a gut job." Glad to have something to do with his hands, Elijah slipped his box onto the shelf. The task of making conversation with a girl he knew only because she was friends with his sister Josie wore him out worse than a day working in the family's alfalfa fields. "How long have you worked here?"

"Six months." Hannah retreated toward the door. "It's fun because Bonnie and the others like to tease each other and talk and laugh. It's not all business all the time. I do work, though. I dust, sweep, mop, and I also clean the bathroom. I earn my pay."

"I never doubted it." Heat ran through Elijah. Had he suggested otherwise? "Josie works in the auction office now."

"Josie's good with numbers like your *schweschder* Layla. Me, not so much."

Lots of numbers swirled in Elijah's head at that moment. He did okay with numbers. Not great, but not bad. He'd been an average student. Good enough to get by. A sixty-forty split. It was more than equitable, but now Elijah needed to calculate and set his prices to cover the cost of materials, his own labor, and a fair profit. How much would he need in order to buy more supplies?

Thoughts, ideas, and a surge of almost overwhelming hope swirled inside him. He could do this. A Miller man could start a new business, one that had nothing to do with auctions, stages, microphones, and chatty customers who wanted to know all about this bed set or that table and chairs. Nothing to do with sleeping in hotels and eating in restaurants, facing an unending gauntlet of strangers.

His toys on display in a store. The thought didn't fill Elijah with pride so much as determination. Determination and hope. He could make his own way.

"Help yourself to a soda pop from the fridge if you're thirsty." Hannah dusted off her hands and headed for the door. "There's a pitcher of water too."

"Danki," Elijah muttered, still thinking about sixty-forty commissions. "For the help too."

"Bewillkumm to the store."

Elijah sank into a chair at the table. He needed a pencil and piece of paper to make a list of supplies he'd buy from the lumber hardware stores. His hands itched to get started. He pulled his pocketknife and a small piece of wood from his pocket. The fox with a bushy tail had taken its time revealing itself. He smoothed his fingers over its thin snout and pointy nose. His fingers shook. Maybe not the best time to whittle.

But whittling would calm his nerves.

"Sorry for the wait." Bonnie rolled into the room. She paused at the desk, where she grabbed a sheaf of papers. "A customer waylaid me wanting to talk about custom-made quilts. I don't do quilt consignments. I don't want to cut into the Kauffmans' business. Quilts are their bread and butter at their store. Some people are just too lazy to drive out to their farm."

Elijah nodded. Made sense. Not much more needed to be said. A quilt lover could find bed-size quilts, crib blankets, lap quilts, doll-size quilts, and pot holders, plus everything needed to make quilts at Kauffmans' Store. Plus quilting frolics and classes. The Miller womenfolk had quilts on consignment there. They loved the store too.

Bonnie laid the paperwork on the table. She then turned her walker around and used it as her chair. "The padded seat is more comfy than the chairs," she said as if by way of explanation. "That's a cute fox. You do such fine work. How did you learn to whittle like that?"

He hadn't learned so much as it just happened. Elijah shrugged. "The wood talks to me."

She would think he was nuts, but he'd simply spoken the truth. He didn't know how else to explain it.

"I love it." There was that smile again. How could a person not smile back? Bonnie turned the top sheet of paper so it faced Elijah. "Now that you've had time to think about it, are you okay with the sixty-forty split?"

Elijah nodded again.

"Wunderbarr."

Her caramel eyes warm, Bonnie held out the contract. When some of the boys had teased Elijah at recess, she'd shoved her way through their cliques, using her walker—in those days it had been a silver metal contraption with neon tennis balls on the front legs—to get to him. She told the boys she needed Elijah to carry her books to her buggy or return her lunch box to the schoolroom.

The truth was, Bonnie really hadn't needed anyone's help when she was younger. She drove herself to school in a pony cart and never let anyone help her unhitch or hitch her pony. Buttercup— that was the pony's name. She couldn't play baseball or volleyball, but she played a mean game of cornhole. And she always won the English spelling bees.

It didn't matter what time of day it was, her prayer cover neatly hid her hair's bun. Her dress and apron were clean and unwrinkled.

It was obvious her disease had progressed from her legs to her arms, making them weaker, but she still had the same neat appearance and kind voice.

"Elijah?"

Bonnie's dark brows had risen. The paperwork still hung in the air. Heat scalded Elijah's face. His ears burned. She'd surely caught him studying her high cheekbones and pretty, perfectly shaped nose. Some might call what he did woodworking or whittling, but it was more like art, and he had an eye for what was symmetrical and beautiful. Bonnie was beautiful. Elijah accepted the document. *"Es-es-es dutt mer,"* he stuttered. "I was thinking."

"Thinking hard. I know how that is. I get lost in thought sometimes. Mamm gets irritated with me."

Same with Elijah's mom, but more so with his dad. "Same here."

"Go ahead and review the contract. Read the fine print. In the meantime, I'll make a list of what I'd like to have in the first order."

The room was quiet except for the scratching sound of Bonnie's pencil on paper. The contract was detailed. They would set the price for his items together. They would keep a written inventory of what sold and when. He would be paid once a month. If an item or category of items didn't sell in six months, those items would be returned to him.

"Do you have any questions?"

Elijah looked up to find Bonnie studying him. He shook his head.

"Are you sure? You seem . . . concerned."

"Nee." He glanced around. "I don't have a pen."

"I'll get you one." She started to rise.

"Nee. Let me."

"I told you I can do for myself." She sounded peeved.

"It's not about you being able or not." Elijah searched for words that wouldn't offend her more. It would be easier to let it go, but her being mad at him didn't set right. "Isn't it polite for a man to offer to help a woman—any woman—no matter what the world says about equality and such?"

"You're right." Her cheeks reddened, which only made her prettier. "My *mudder* says I'm prickly as a desert filled with cacti, but I don't like people to think I can't take care of myself."

"I would never think that." Not in a billion years. "Can I get the pen?"

"Of course. *Sei so gut.*"

Now they were both being polite. Elijah didn't need a please or a thank-you. Finally he had the pen in hand and the contract signed.

"Here's my list." Bonnie handed it over in exchange for the contract. "I'm not sure how fast you can turn these items around, so I'm not setting a deadline, but sooner rather than later would be gut. The tourist season seems to arrive earlier every year. In the meantime, I can sell the items you brought today, if you like."

Five corrals with horses, wood tractors, alphabet boards, and children's stools each. *Each!* A dozen wooden yo-yos. Five Noah's arks with the animals. Four more push mowers. Four more rocking horses. A child's desk and chair. A checkers set. A wooden toy box to use in the toy display. The display of Elijah's toys. "That would be great."

"I know you have up-front expenses for your supplies." She tapped the table with one finger. "I can give you a down payment against sales if need be."

Elijah had a nest egg from his auctioneering salary. As an unmarried brother still living at home, he didn't pull down nearly what his married brothers did. Which was only fair. He was able to save most of it, except for what he spent on workshop supplies. "Not necessary."

"Gut. Then let's set prices for what you've brought me today."

This would be hard. The more he earned, the more he could save toward opening his own business. With an employee who would handle the front end—dealing with customers and taking orders. Still, he didn't want to price himself out of sales. "I think twenty-five dollars for the rocking horse. I know that's a lot—"

"A lot?" Bonnie hooted. "Seriously?"

"I could go down to twenty—"

"Elijah! You truly don't get how in demand well-made, handcrafted Amish toys and furniture are." Shaking her head, Bonnie clasped her hands together. "Fifty dollars would be on the low end."

"Seriously?"

"I can show you some in an Etsy store that they want ninety-five for."

"What's an Etsy store?"

"It doesn't matter. The point is, we want you to get enough to recoup your costs and still make a nice profit for both of us."

Agreed. "So what you think, then?"

"I'd say sixty-five, ninety-five."

His mom would likely faint. She'd talked about selling them in the combination store for thirty dollars. "If you think they'll sell."

"They'll sell."

Down the list they went, setting prices that seemed far too high. Bonnie assured Elijah if any item didn't sell initially, they could reduce the price before withdrawing it from the inventory. "Sometimes it's trial and error to hit the sweet spot for consumers."

She sounded like the English men who came to the auctions to buy furniture that they would resell on the internet as "authentic Amish furniture." They had to know just how much to pay and still be able to sell it for a profit.

"You're sure these prices are—?"

"Elijah, your *bruder* is out front!" Panting as if she'd run a race, Hannah dashed into the room. Slowpoke hopped to his feet and barked at her. "Hush, *hund*. He says come quick."

"Which bruder?" Like it mattered. Elijah stood. Leaving the paperwork, he ducked past the girl and raced toward the door. "Es dutt mer. I have to go."

Slowpoke's bark grew louder.

A clatter sounded behind Elijah.

"Ach, ach, Slowpoke!"

Elijah whirled. Bonnie lay flat on her back, her rollator lying on top of her.

Chapter 4

"Nee, nee." Elijah rushed to where Bonnie lay on the storage room's tiled floor. He knelt and thrust the rollator aside. "Slowpoke, back off, back off now."

"It's not his fault." Wincing, Bonnie raised her head. Her hand touched her prayer covering. "He wanted to go first. I understood. He didn't want to get left behind. I tried to back up to get out of his way. I'm not supposed to do that—not in a hurry, anyway. I lost my balance and fell backward. Like a *dumkoph*, I didn't think to let go of the rollator."

"Are you hurt?" Elijah took her arm, then released it. He shouldn't touch her without her permission. Or maybe even with it. "Do we need to call 911?"

"I'm fine. I'm gut." Her face bright red, she struggled to sit up. "I never fall down anymore. I'm always so careful."

"A dog underfoot doesn't help." Embarrassment flooded Elijah. He should never have brought Slowpoke into the storage room. He'd taken the man's-best-friend pact too far. "Can I help you up?"

"What's going on in here?"

The voice tinged with anger and concern didn't belong to a man. Elijah glanced over his shoulder. Jocelyn Yoder swept into the room, followed by Elijah's brother Toby. Jocelyn didn't wait for an answer. She pushed past Hannah and Slowpoke and dropped to her knees. "Why are you on the floor, *Dochder*? What is Elijah doing in here with you?"

A fresh wave of mortification threatened to drown Elijah. "I was . . . We were . . . we just—"

"Elijah is our newest vendor, Mamm." Bonnie grabbed her mother's hand. "Help me up. It was just a little fall. It's not his fault. I'm fine. Everybody's fine."

Toby had an arm around Slowpoke, holding him back. The dog whimpered. "Elijah, Jason is on his way to the hospital in Richmond. The paramedics think his appendix ruptured."

Elijah stumbled to his feet. "I have to go, Bonnie. If you don't want to do business with me—"

"Because I fell down? Don't be *halbgscheit*." Bonnie grasped both her mother's hands. Jocelyn tugged her into a sitting position. "Start bringing in your inventory as soon as you can."

"He'll have to get back to you on that." Toby nudged Slowpoke toward the door. "Let's go, Bruder."

"Es dutt mer." Saying the same phrase over and over wouldn't change the result. If only it could. Elijah swiped the contract from the table and stuffed it into the folder on his way from the storage room. He raced to keep up with Toby, who was halfway to the front door.

"What's going on?"

Sophia Hershberger pulled her wheelchair into his path. Behind her Carol Knepp swung to a stop on her crutches. The two presented a united front, their expressions fierce. "What happened?"

"Bonnie fell, but I think she's okay. She says she is." In his haste, Elijah stumbled. He knocked into a display of sewn goods. Two sweaters tumbled to the floor. He paused to scoop them up. "Es dutt mer, es dutt mer."

"Out of the way." Sophia bulldozed past him. "Let us through."

Elijah squeezed into the next aisle. The two women left him standing there without a second glance.

"Don't worry about Bonnie. They'll take care of her. They take care of each other. They're the three musketeers." Hannah popped up next to him. She took the sweaters from him. "You go take care of your family."

"That's gut. It's gut."

Elijah heaved a breath and shoved through the door. Outside Toby had already climbed into his buggy. He held the reins. His heart still slamming against his rib cage, Elijah paused at his buggy. "Is Jason going to be all right?"

"The paramedics were talking about infection. If the appendix burst, pus and bacteria leak all over your insides." Toby's expression was grim. The muscle in his jaw pulsed. "He's so *narrisch*. He's been throwing up and complaining of a stomachache for two days. He insisted it was food poisoning."

Calling his brother stupid was Toby's way of saying he was worried. "But he'll be okay?"

"It's in Gott's hands." Toby wrapped the reins around his hands. His broad shoulders hunched. "*Dat* hired a van. He and Mamm and Caitlin are on their way to the hospital. She was beside herself, not being able to go in the ambulance with her husband, but she needed someone to watch the kinner. Josie is doing it. Dat will call when they know something."

"So we're not going to Richmond?"

"Not to the hospital, nee. We have an auction tomorrow, re-member? We have a contract. We can't let those folks down."

Elijah's heart revved. Hands shaking, he untied the reins from the hitching post. They dropped to the ground. A low whine rumbled in Slowpoke's throat. He thought he was in trouble. Elijah picked up the reins. "It's okay, buddy." He climbed into the buggy. "Why do I have to go to Richmond?"

"Because we need you to call an auction. Jason was supposed to handle the furniture and household goods. Who knows how long he'll be out." Stress lines carved lines around Toby's mouth. "*Daadi* is coming along as backup, but he wants you to call it."

Dad had to stay with Jason. No question about that. Still, dread careened through Elijah. His stomach rocked. His sweaty palms were back. "Ach, it would be better for Daadi to do it. He's experienced."

"His arthritis has gotten worse. His joints hurt if he stands too long." Toby snapped the reins and clucked at his horse. "See you back at the farm. You can help us finish loading the trailers and then pack your bag."

Elijah smoothed the folder for a second. God's plans always came before man's best-laid plans, Mom would say. He climbed into his buggy next to Slowpoke. "They're called accidents for a reason." He patted the dog's head. "Bonnie said it wasn't your fault."

Slowpoke lowered his head and settled onto the seat.

"I'm not sure how fast you can turn these items around, so I'm not setting a deadline, but sooner rather than later would be gut. The tourist season seems to arrive earlier every year." Bonnie with her head for business and a sweet smile that made it almost easy to talk to her.

Five corrals with horses, wood tractors, alphabet boards, and children's stools each. Each! *A dozen wooden yo-yos. Five Noah's arks with the animals. Four more push mowers. Four more rocking horses. A child's desk and chair. A checkers set. A wooden toy box to use in the toy display.* The display of Elijah's toys.

He could still work on the smaller items between auctions. It was only until Jason got back on his feet.

Sure.

"Elijah!"

He glanced up. Toby had pulled into the street, headed for home. "Don't just sit there, Bruder," he called over his shoulder. "Get a move on. We need you."

The family needed him. Family came first.

"Right behind you, Bruder."

The dream would have to wait.

Chapter 5

hat's enough, all of you, I'm fine. Really, I am." Bonnie used her braked rollator on one side and her mother's hand on the other to heave herself to her feet. Falling was awful. But getting up was impossible without help. She wavered on unsteady legs. Her mom's hand tightened on her bicep. "I'm okay, I'm fine."

"Are you sure?" Mom didn't let go. "You're shaking."

"Legs just don't want to cooperate." The muscles were too weak to allow Bonnie to use them to stand, and she didn't have enough strength in her arms to push herself up. It was incredibly frustrating. "Give me a minute."

Bonnie inhaled and straightened. One step, two steps. She stuck her hand on the desk, worked her way around it, and sank into the chair. She shoved her loose bun back under her crooked prayer covering and straightened it. Her back still ached from the jolt of the tile floor. Her head throbbed. Her right arm twinged where she'd flung it into the desk, flailing as she tried to right herself.

The three women gathered around her. Mom brought her a washcloth for her head. Frowning, Carol hovered to one side while Sophia set a glass of cold water in front of Bonnie. "Really, stop staring at me like that. Nothing's hurt, except I think I sprained my dignity."

"You know better than to back up in a rush." Mom pulled up Bonnie's sleeve to inspect her arm. She was fifty years old but looked much younger. Only a few silver strands streaked her dark-brown hair. A person had to study hard to spot age lines around her mouth and eyes. More likely laugh lines. "You're going to have a big bruise where your arm hit the desk. That hund doesn't belong in here. It's no wonder you tripped over him."

"I didn't trip, Mamm." For the third time. Her mom didn't listen, mostly because she was busy worrying that something would happen to her only daughter. Losing Dad had worsened her tendency to cling to Bonnie, to treat her like she was still a child. Not her disability. Mom had never treated her as less than grown-up as the years passed—even when she didn't act like it. "Don't blame Slowpoke."

"It's better than blaming you, I reckon." Carol rolled her pale-blue eyes. At twenty-four she was too old for eye-rolling, but sometimes she fell back into old habits. "Or Elijah. Why was it necessary for him to bring a hund into the store?"

"You know how folks have comfort animals—that's not the right name." Bonnie racked her brain. She snapped her fingers. "Emotional support animals, that's it. I think Slowpoke is Elijah's emotional support animal, if a Plain man could have such a thing. He's super shy. Slowpoke is his friend. He helps him with situations that make him uncomfortable."

No doubt turning around to find Bonnie sprawled on the floor hadn't done much for his comfort zone. The memory of the horror on his face sent embarrassment cascading through her every time she replayed the scene in her head. Falling to the floor like a clumsy oaf, Elijah's dash to help her, and then Hannah, her mother, and, of course, Toby. Not one but two Miller brothers had seen her flopping on the floor like a baby just learning to walk.

Sophia and Carol, she didn't mind. They'd seen her at her worst plenty of times, and her, them. Might as well let the whole world see her lying there. Or all of Lee's Gulch at least.

Not Elijah, though. Why? Now wasn't the time to dwell on that question.

With a squeaky meow, Puff jumped into her lap. She perused Bonnie like a doctor examining a patient. Her heartbeat slowing, Bonnie stroked the cat's long hair. Her purr ramped up. "Speaking of emotional support animals." She kissed Puff's nose. "You're mine, aren't you, kitty?"

"Are you sure you shouldn't go to the clinic?" Pushing her dark-blue-rimmed glasses up her nose, Mom muttered something else. It sounded like "crazy hund" and "what was he thinking."

"We can all hear you, Mamm. Stop muttering like a grumpy old woman, sei so gut."

The *please* was an afterthought. Bonnie almost said "grumpy old grandma." But Mom didn't have any grandchildren, and at this rate, she never would. This reality probably caused her heartache, but if it did, she never let on.

Just like she never admitted to feeling sad at not being able to have more children. Just like she never uttered a word of self-pity or complaint about Dad's sudden, inexplicable exit from their lives. *"God has a plan. God will provide. God can bring good from all things."* Mom held her Scripture close. She hadn't even shed tears at the graveside service.

Only Bonnie knew when her mother cried. Because lying awake

late at night, staring up into the darkness, trying not to question God's plan for two women now living alone, Bonnie couldn't help but overhear her mother's muffled sobs coming from the bedroom she'd shared with Dad for twenty-six years.

A "hmmphfft" greeted the command. Followed up by a "tsk-tsk." Mom opened a first aid kit and extracted a small tube of antibacterial ointment. Despite her testy frown and irritation in her dark-brown eyes, she employed a gentle touch while bandaging the scratch on Bonnie's wrist. "You haven't fallen in forever. Dr. Newcomb will be disappointed."

Not just disappointed. Every time Bonnie fell, she came a day closer to the next phase of her progression—the wheelchair. Dr. Newcomb would order tests to determine if there had been progression in her muscle weakness. She would explain all the reasons why it was a good "option" as she liked to call it. Bonnie would stare at the floor and reject it as no option at all.

Mom would twist her hands in her lap and pretend not to fight tears.

Bonnie was no longer a child eager to get gold star stickers and lollipops after her doctors' appointments. "It doesn't make me happy either, but it was a fluke accident." Not a sign that her muscle weakness had progressed. Dr. Newcomb would insist on more physical therapy as an alternative—for the time being. Bonnie didn't have time for that. "No harm done. I'm fine."

"You keep saying that, but you have a knot on your noggin, and you'll probably have a bruise on your arm. Not to mention you're bleeding."

With a plaintive meow, Puff nudged Bonnie's hand. Bonnie resumed petting her. "A tiny little dab barely worth mentioning."

Another disagreeing grunt. "Elijah is a grown man. He should be past his shyness by now. No wonder he hasn't married."

Ouch. Sometimes Mom didn't think before she spoke. "He's my age, Mamm. I haven't married."

Mom's face flushed. "I didn't mean—"

"Or me." Sophia crossed her arms over her skinny chest. "Maybe he hasn't met the right woman."

Her cornflower-blue eyes lit up in her pale face. Sophia had always been a tiny girl. Now she was a waif who looked no more than sixteen instead of her twenty-two years. Her wheelchair dwarfed her as did her unruly blonde curls that required a massive time commitment to tame into a bun each morning. Grinning, she cast a sly glance at Bonnie. "Until now."

"*Jah*, because toppling over on the floor is the way to impress a man." Bonnie scoffed. "He probably wonders how I manage to co-own a store."

"We were all in school at the same time." Sophia's tone was soft, remembering. "Elijah might've been shy, but he was always nice. He pushed my chair for me when I came back to school after the accident."

If Sophia still had heartache for the changes in her life wrought by a moment of carelessness by her older brother that resulted in a runaway buggy rolling on its side and spilling her onto the highway, she didn't show it. "He pushed me out to the benches by the ball field and sat with me while the other kids played. It was nice to not sit alone."

"I remember him being nice too." Bonnie plucked a memory from a store of more painful ones that centered around learning the many ways she didn't get to participate in recess activities. "We played cornhole a few times after church. His brother Declan dragged him over to the boards. I don't think he looked at me a single time. He still has trouble looking at me. He had a hund then too, a shaggy gray one called Mutt."

Mom tucked the first aid kit back on the shelf. She dusted her hands off as if to say "done with that." "You know what Dat always said—"

"'*Hunde* are better friends than most people.'"

They spoke the words in unison. Bonnie waited for the tsunami of grief to drown her. Instead, a gentle wave of sorrow lapped against her heart, making it ache rather than the fierce pain that had once threatened to drop her to her knees.

"You have your dat's heart for animals. You always did." Mom pulled out a chair from Bonnie's worktable and plopped into it. "People can be nice too, you know?"

"I *know* that."

"Now who's the grumpy old lady?"

"Am not." Lately it seemed as if they bickered like sisters more than like mother and daughter. "Ach, I'm embarrassed. Which makes me grumpy."

"Why? Because you fell?" Carol waved one of her crutches in the air. She was tall and round to Sophia's short and thin. Her pale-blue eyes flashed with mock scorn. A strand of her thin black hair had escaped her prayer covering. "Do you know how many times I've fallen? Besides, people who don't have SMA fall. Kids fall. Adults fall."

"Jah, at least I don't have to worry about that," Sophia said airily. "I'm snug as a bug in my chair."

"I think Gott wanted to take me down a peg or two."

"Why? You're not full of yourself, Dochder." Mom shook her finger at Bonnie. "You're one of the most humble people I know."

"I'd just finished telling Elijah not to try to help me, that I could help myself just fine."

"And then you fell."

"Jah. A big splat on the floor."

Mom pressed her lips together. She smiled. Then she chuckled. She snorted. Then she let out a huge belly laugh.

Sophia and Carol giggled. Then they laughed. No one could hear Mom guffaw and not join her.

"It's not funny." Bonnie couldn't help herself. She giggled. The giggle turned into a laugh. Tears gathered in her eyes and her nose ran. "Okay, it's a little funny." She gasped. "Okay, a lot funny."

Apparently Puff didn't think so. Either that or she'd determined her ministrations weren't needed anymore. She hopped from Bonnie's lap and trotted from the office, tail and head held high.

Mom grabbed a tissue from a box on the worktable and wiped her nose. She handed the box to Sophia, who took one and passed it to Carol. "Pride does go before a fall, or so they say."

"Whoever they are, they should know I'm doing my best to hold my own in this world. I wasn't trying to be prideful."

"That's the thing you'll never understand." Mom tossed the tissue in the wastebasket. She rose and picked up her canvas bag. "Everyone knows that. It's obvious how hard you work. The three of you started this business. You give people like yourselves a place to sell their wares and another way to earn their keep. Families are thankful for that. This store is a blessing for our special children."

"People like yourselves."

Mom didn't mean it in a bad way. Plain folks loved their children with physical and mental developmental disabilities with a fierceness that couldn't be denied. They treated them like the rest of their children. They also made sure a family member would step in and take care of them, if need be, when they were gone.

Did Mom worry about what would happen to Bonnie if she suddenly died the way Dad had? Bonnie had aunts, uncles, and cousins who would step up if she didn't marry.

I don't need to be taken care of.

Pride goes before the fall.

When would she learn that?

Tucking the bag's strap over her shoulder, Mom trotted to the door, then paused and turned. "It's too bad you won't go to the singings. I reckon you might see Elijah there."

"I'm too old for singings." She'd gone a few times as a naive sixteen-year-old. After being left behind to be driven home by one cousin or another after her friends hopped into buggies with this boy or that boy, she'd stopped going. "And I reckon Elijah figures he is too. Plus he's too shy. Plus what difference would it make?"

"Hmm." Mom was good at pretending she didn't hear a question. "You're sure you don't want to come home? Sophia and Carol can handle the store. You should take a hot bath before your muscles get sore."

"Absolutely," Carol chimed in. Her crutches thumping on the tile floor, she followed Mom to the door. "I need to get out there and take over. Hannah's bruder will be here to pick her up shortly."

"I need to finish a few more animals before I go. Margie wants them by the end of the week." Margie Joens owned a day care in town. She was replacing her stuffed animals, worn by time and toddlers with tummy upsets and runny noses. "Besides, Chet will be upset if he comes by and has no one to pick up."

"Jah, he mentioned you were next on his schedule when he dropped us off." Sophia wheeled her chair around. "He's in fine form today. He sang tunes from the musical *Oklahoma* all the way into town."

Chet Danner was a retired language arts teacher who ran a taxi service for Plain folks "to make himself useful." His shiny white twelve-passenger van was equipped with a wheelchair lift. "This morning it was songs he said were written by a man named Gershwin." Bonnie laughed at the memory. Chet had an amazing baritone and a limitless supply of songs to go with it. Some days he preferred to recite poetry, act out passages from Shakespeare's plays, or tell stories from his days teaching school in Washington, D.C., Arlington, and Baltimore. His passengers could expect a show with every ride. "Yesterday he recited a poem called 'Ozymandias' and then explained what it meant."

"Once a teacher, always a teacher." Mom's tone said she approved. "I'll have supper ready when you get home. I'm making sandwiches with the leftover pulled pork."

"Sounds gut."

Mealtime was the hardest. Evenings the longest. Dad's absence left a gaping hole ripped in the fabric of their family. In such a small family, silencing one person's voice made a void that couldn't be filled by reading, puzzles, sewing, or even working on the store's books.

"Love you, Dochder."

Those last words were uttered softly as she slipped out the room.

"Love you, Mamm."

Sophia and Carol chorused the words with Bonnie. Somehow her friends knew. Plain folks didn't proclaim their feelings. They didn't wear them on their arms like bracelets. But since Dad's death, Mom had taken to saying it whenever they parted. She felt the need. A person never knew when the last time would be. Had she said those words to Dad before she closed her eyes that last night?

Probably not.

Dad never said them to Bonnie. Nor Bonnie to him. They didn't have to. They'd simply known it.

Don't think about it. Bonnie put one hand on the rollator and her other one on the desk so she could hoist herself to her feet. "I'd better get cracking. I want to finish the lion and the panda bear before I leave."

"Are you sure you're all right?" Sophia wheeled so she sat next to Bonnie. "You seem kind of punk."

"Punk?"

"Margie says that when the *boplin* don't feel good, they feel punk." Sophia picked up a piece of black cotton cut in the shape of a panda leg. Her expression absent, she rubbed her fingers over it. "With you it's more like sadness. Are you still thinking about your dat?"

"Nee. Well, jah, but not like before." Not like she was drowning in an ocean of salty tears. Bonnie slid onto the chair and picked up her scissors. She bent her head over a pattern of tissue she'd already affixed to a piece of white cotton material. "You and Carol are both courting. I'm older than both of you, yet I don't see any *mann* or family in my future. I love the store, but I always hoped there'd be more."

"You're the smartest, the kindest, the funniest, the prettiest of all of us." Sophia ticked off the qualities on her fingers. "You just have to open yourself up to the possibilities. Be ready. Gott brings good things to those who wait and those who love Him with all their hearts."

Sophia could say that. She and Matthew Schultz had been courting for more than a year. The two had met when Matthew, who had a partial hearing impairment, came into the store to offer his leather goods for sale. He lived south of Lee's Gulch in another *Gmay*, which meant they hadn't grown up together. Amid a conversation interpreted by Matthew's friend over purses, wallets, belts, key rings, and jewelry, something had clicked. Even though Matthew's hearing aids gave him the ability to hear much of what was said, he still employed American Sign Language with his family and friends. Nowadays, Sophia was likely to use American Sign Language when she spoke without realizing she was doing it.

Bonnie raised her head. She swiveled to observe her friend. Sophia smiled, but sadness resided there as well. "Your words are positive, but I see something else in your face."

"Matthew wants to get married."

"What? Why didn't you say anything? That's so wunderbarr. That is such gut news. I'm so happy for you." Except Sophia didn't appear ecstatic. "What's the matter? Why aren't you over the moon?"

"Because I haven't said jah. By marrying me, Matthew is resigning himself to never having kinner." She sniffed and swiped at her face. "I've always known that, but I love him so much, I couldn't bring myself to stop seeing him. I feel so selfish. If I say no, I'll hurt him. If I say jah, he'll never be a *daed*. I don't know what to do."

"Ach, Sophia. I'm such a selfish friend." Bonnie was so busy feeling sorry for herself, she didn't see that it was her friend who felt "punk." She struggled to her feet and swept Sophia into a fierce hug. "What does Matthew say about all this?"

"He says I'm being narrisch. That he wouldn't have asked me if he wasn't willing to make that sacrifice." Sophia's smile was watery. "He has six older brieder and schweschdre. He says we'll never lack for kinner in our lives. He also mentioned adoption."

"See there. He's a smart man."

"Do you really think an adoption agency will let a man with a hearing impairment and a woman who's a paraplegic adopt a *bopli*?"

"You won't know until you try, will you? Just be you and they won't be able to resist."

Never were truer words spoken. Sophia was a bulldozer when she wanted something.

"Ach, now who's being eternally optimistic?"

"Gott gave you Matthew. Who are you to argue with Gott?"

43

Sophia's hug was just as fierce. She smelled of lavender and mint and friendship. "Just between you and me, sometimes I ask myself where Gott was when my bruder drove onto the highway in front of a pickup truck."

Bonnie leaned back to get a good view of Sophia's face. Her friend never referred to that day. She always put on a happy face. Maybe that was all it was. A happy face. "He was there to make sure the ambulance came. He guided the doctors so they could save your life."

"There were times when I wished He hadn't, but now I think about all the things I would've missed. Seeing my schweschdre and brieder get married and have boplin. Opening this store with my best friends. My first buggy ride with Matthew. My first kiss. I'm content. Then every once in a while, I start wanting what I can't have. Then I have to give myself a talking-to." Sophia grinned. The happy face was back. "Did Carol tell you Ryan Beachy came in the store yesterday to pick up a package for his mudder?"

"Nee." There was nothing unusual about that. Ryan's mother had purchased one of Bonnie's teddy bears for her new grandbaby. The Beachys belonged to the south Gmay as well. "The baby was born last week. It's about time."

"While he was here, he asked Carol if she wanted to go for a buggy ride."

"Oh my! Wunderbarr!" Joy bloomed in Bonnie. God answered prayers. Not always the way she wanted and always on His time, but when He did, it was worth the wait. "She used to talk about running into him at keggers during her *rumspringa*. I think she liked him even then."

"She did. She says there's just something about him. She's happy but nervous. I told her not to be nervous, to just be herself."

"Is that what you did?"

"Of course not. My armpits were wet. Matthew could probably smell me."

"He was too relieved you said jah to even notice. I reckon I'd be nervous too." But mostly happy. Not if Ryan asked her, of course. Ryan was a nice man and a hard worker. But she'd never thought of him like that. "I can't believe she didn't tell me."

"She didn't get a chance, what with your big scene today."

Bonnie faked a laugh. "You're so funny. Big scene. Let's go tease her."

Sophia wheeled her chair around. "Giddyup, giddyup. Let's!"

The stuffed animals could wait.

Chapter 6

eftovers were the scourge of human existence or a bountiful blessing—depending on whom a person asked. Jocelyn pulled open the refrigerator door, hauled out a plastic-wrapped bowl of pulled pork, and set it on the counter. When would she learn to stop making such large quantities? Two women didn't eat nearly as much as two women and a hardworking man with a big appetite. She and Bonnie would be eating leftovers until they had sandwiches running out of their ears. Jocelyn didn't even like pulled pork that much. It had been Marlin's favorite. With pickles, onions, and spicy barbecue sauce on homemade sourdough buns.

Served with corn on the cob, roasted potatoes, and peach cobbler.

"Bringing in the sheaves, bringing in the sheaves . . ." Jocelyn warbled the first hymn lyrics that came to mind. "We shall come rejoicing, bringing in the sheaves." The louder she sang, the quieter the house seemed.

The taste of Marlin's kisses warmed her. His smell of earth and hard work enveloped her. She closed her eyes to lean into a fierce hug borne of sinewy muscles honed in the fields.

You're not here. You're gone. Gone in the time it took her to drift off to sleep, dream of babies she never had, and wake up to his cooling body at her side. For two years.

Shivering, Jocelyn opened her eyes.

"'Get thee behind me, Satan.'" She grabbed a wooden spoon and smacked it on the counter so hard it splintered. "Es dutt mer, Gott, es dutt mer."

It had to be Satan who needled her forty times a day, trying to make her question God's plan for herself. And for Bonnie. Especially for Bonnie. "Bringing in the sheaves, bringing in the sheaves . . ."

Songs had become Jocelyn's weapon of choice in this battle against loneliness. Against self-pity and the sin of worry. The louder Satan flung his barbed questions at her, the louder she sang. "We shall come rejoicing—"

"Hey, hey, hallo!" Whoever spoke interspersed pounding on the back door with the words. "Hallo!"

Heat suffusing her face, Jocelyn dropped the spoon in the trash can. She rushed to open the back door. A man she'd never seen before stood on the porch. It was evident he'd heard her singing . . . and her conversation with Satan. "Hallo."

"You sing pretty." He cocked his head and smiled a big toothy grin. "I hated to interrupt."

"I don't sing hymns for prettiness."

"I reckon not." This strange Plain man had eyes the lightest shade of brown Jocelyn had ever seen. If she had to put a name to it, she'd say teak. His silver beard matched the silver hair not covered by a straw hat that had seen better days. He was tall and rangy, and had the leathery brown skin of a man who'd worked outdoors for many years. "No offense meant."

"None taken."

"I'm Theo Beiler. I'm your bruder Uri's new hired hand."

That explained who he was but not why he stood on her porch at the end of the day. Surely her brother Uriah, known as Uri to his friends and family, would've seen the propriety of coming along to make an introduction to a stranger. "Uri sent you, then?"

"I reckon you're Joci."

Only her family and friends called her that. "I reckon I am."

Theo glanced over Jocelyn's shoulder, then back at her, his expression tentative. "I heard you talking, but it looks like you're alone."

He had heard her. Jocelyn's cheeks burned. She raised her chin and straightened her shoulders. "I'm sure Uri told you I'm a *wittfraa*. My dochder is still in town working."

"Jah, he did." Theo seemed to contemplate something on the porch ceiling. "Maybe you could come outside, and we could talk."

At least he was sensitive to her being a woman alone on the farm. He didn't want to enter the house unchaperoned. Funny that Uriah hadn't thought of that. Jocelyn nodded. Theo stepped aside and she slipped past him. Motioning to the canvas lawn chairs lined up under the kitchen windows, she moved in that direction. "Have a seat and tell me why Uri sent a strange man to my door."

Theo eased into a chair and stretched his long legs out in front of him. "I may seem strange, but really I'm not. I'm pretty average."

Jocelyn shooed away a momma cat and her two kittens so she could sit in the chair next to him. She'd have a backside covered with cat hair, but no matter. "I meant strange as in unknown."

"I know you did." He chuckled, a rich baritone sound. "Do you always sing like that?"

"Nee. Not always."

"You're not much for making conversation, are you?"

Marlin would've said she couldn't be hushed. "Under the right circumstances, I talk."

"I can take a hint. I'll get to the point."

"Apparently not." What was it about his breezy attitude and eyes that said he was searching for a reason to laugh that sent her prickles into overdrive? "Or not so I've noticed."

This time he laughed outright. "You, on the other hand, do get right to the point. Uri wants me to see what needs to be painted, repaired, and slash or replaced. He's made me crew leader for the frolic next week. I'm to make a list of supplies we'll need."

"What frolic? My mann left everything in tip-top condition," Jocelyn sputtered. She sucked in a breath. Uriah had no right to suggest otherwise. "Marlin was the handiest man I know. He kept this place in gut order."

"No need to get your dander up." Theo raised both hands as if under arrest. "I meant no offense, and I know Uri didn't either."

Of course not. Mama cat—who really needed a name—meowed from the spot she'd taken in the third chair—Marlin's chair. She recognized a dustup when she heard one. "My dander's not up. I just don't think we need a frolic."

"How long has your mann been gone?"

"Two years."

His merry air had evaporated into evening air turning cool and crisp as the sun faded on the horizon. "Two years. Long enough for the paint to fade, but not necessarily the pain."

It sounded like the voice of experience. He was probably in his early fifties. He had a beard, which meant he was married. Or had been married. Jocelyn studied his face. Lines that hadn't been there a few minutes earlier took up residence around his full lips and expressive eyes. It was none of her business. "Jah."

"I looked around before I knocked. The house could use a coat of paint. The second step to the front porch needs fixin', and you got some corral fence that needs replacing. The gutters need cleaning.

Several trees need trimming. You haven't started your spring garden, so I reckon a rototiller might come in handy. The solar panel has come loose up yonder." He pointed to the roof above them. "I suspect your porch light hasn't been coming on. And that's just a quick survey."

"Marlin planned to repaint the house. He'd just bought the paint." Two days before he died. Jocelyn cleared her throat. She forced her hands to relax in her lap. Two years were plenty long enough to grieve. Her sisters and brothers said so. The bishop said so. Even her mother, who'd lived through losing Jocelyn's father in a freak boating accident, thought so. "It's in the barn."

"I don't mean no disrespect for your late mann."

Jocelyn breathed in the scent of mud from the previous evening's rain. A robin called to its mate on a nearby dogwood, already plush with white blooms. Blue jays and chickadees chattered. A titmouse hopped from branch to branch in the red maple tree. What had Bonnie just been saying about pride coming before a fall? Jocelyn should be thankful to be blessed with family and friends who wanted to help her. God provided.

Also, God giveth and God taketh away.

Satan knew Scripture as well as the next fallen angel. Better even.

"I know that. Es dutt mer. I'm a cranky old woman. Danki for being willing to lead this frolic crew."

"No apology necessary, nor thanks."

"Did you want to look around some more?"

"If you don't mind."

"I don't mind." She did, but that was just Satan again, whispering in her ear that having this stranger poke around the farm was somehow a betrayal of Marlin. Her husband had been nothing if not a practical man. He'd scoff at the idea. "Do you want a cup of kaffi first? Or some cold tea?"

"Maybe when I'm done." He stood and stretched his arms over-head. His fingers nearly touched the roof. "You know what you need?" Theo's tone indicated he was about to tell her. "You need a hund. Cats are well and good, but hunde are better protectors."

"We don't need protecting."

"Just like the farm don't need fixin'."

How full of pride she must sound. "I have Plink."

Theo let his arms drop. He cranked his head from side to side. "Plink? So you already have a dog?"

"Nee. Plink is Marlin's shotgun."

"Interesting choice of names." His expression was dubious. "A BB gun plinks."

For the first time, Jocelyn had the urge to smile. "Plink was Marlin's little joke—not that he thought guns were funny. The shotgun can do plenty of damage."

Not that he or she would shoot anyone bent on stealing what wasn't theirs. No Plain person would. Material goods weren't worth taking the life of another human being. The rifle, used for hunting, was intended to scare off unwanted guests without the need to resort to actually using it.

Theo smiled back. He had a good, honest smile. "Gut to know. Then I'll stick my nose back in my own business where it belongs."

It *was* a long nose, but not so long that it kept him from being easy on the eyes. He clomped down the steps and headed toward the barn. After only a few steps, he paused and turned back. "I happen to know hunde are gut company and the right hund will run off a bad guy without you having to worry about the guy taking Plink away from you and using it to shoot you."

"Your nose just won't stay where it belongs, will it?"

Theo threw back his head and laughed. "I reckon it won't. I'd apologize—"

Jocelyn couldn't help but join him. He had that kind of laugh. "But you're not sorry."

"Not even a little bit." With that admission, he resumed his trek to the barn.

"Mamm?" Jocelyn glanced back. Bonnie stood with the screen door pushed half open, her rollator keeping it from shutting. "Who's that man?"

Jocelyn returned her gaze to Theo's retreating back. "Someone *Onkel* Uri sent our way."

She explained about the frolic.

Bonnie edged onto the porch. She parked her rollator in front of the chair Theo had vacated and eased herself into it. "So that's the new hired hand. *Aenti* Frannie was in the store last week. She mentioned they'd hired a *wittmann* who just moved to town from Berlin, Ohio."

A widower.

Bonnie chuckled.

"What's so funny?"

"I thought it would be Aenti Frannie who did the matchmaking." Bonnie's smile held an extra heaping helping of bittersweet. "Onkel Uri beat her to it."

Surely he knew Jocelyn wasn't ready. That, whatever the expectations of her community, she might never be ready. "Ach, he wouldn't."

Her smile widening, Bonnie shrugged. "We'll see, won't we?"

"We will indeed."

Chapter 7

You can do this.

Sei so gut, Gott. Help me do this.

The rain a fine cooling mist on his face, Elijah clomped up the steps to the auction platform. Like a man facing his executioners, he turned in seemingly slow motion to face the sea of people clothed in raincoats and muddy boots, some hidden behind umbrellas. It wouldn't be a mud sale without mud. Holding fundraising auctions in April invited people to spend the day in the rain. Meaningless details captured his mind and wouldn't let go. An English woman's bright pink boots. A polka-dotted rain poncho. Baby strollers with attached umbrellas. A man sipping a tall coffee shop drink. Plain twins seated on the bleachers eating plates of grilled chicken, potatoes and gravy, noodles, bread, and strawberry shortcake.

His stomach turned at the thought of food. His breakfast of sausage and biscuits threatened to reappear. No, not in front of this crowd.

The crush of folks grew with every passing moment. The chatter rose and surrounded Elijah. The household goods and furniture portion of this mud-sale auction was about to begin.

You can do this.

If Grandpa, Dad, Toby, Jason, and Declan could do it, so could Elijah. Three generations of Miller men were auctioneers.

The auctioneering school instructor, who always appeared as cool as a snow cone, like he'd never had an iota of stage fright in his life, had briskly suggested picking a focal point in the back of the room or crowd and "flinging your fear at it."

At the moment, Elijah's fear weighed more than a team of Percheron horses. There was no flinging it anywhere.

All Elijah had to do was pick up the microphone.

He'd rather take Jason's place in the hospital, recovering from surgery to remove a burst appendix, in pain, and being pumped full of antibiotics to treat something called peritonitis that could kill him if not treated.

No such luck.

Elijah glanced up at the dour sky. Gray clouds hung low. A cold wind whipped rain droplets across his cheeks. Just enough to get him wet. Not enough to cancel the auction. *Gott, now would be a gut time to send a deluge, sei so gut.*

"Are you ready?" Dillon Lapp clapped Elijah on the shoulder as he walked by, headed toward the platform corner where he'd be spotting bids. He seemed thrilled to have accepted Toby's offer to serve as a spotter while the Millers were shorthanded. Toby being his brother-in-law probably helped. "The crowd sure is. They're chomping at the bit."

"Jah."

The single syllable likely didn't reach Dillon's ears. Elijah's mouth was too dry to repeat it. Yet his hands were slick with sweat despite being icy cold. His heart clanged in a rib-bruising beat. Any minute it would break through bone, muscle, and skin, and flee. Any second his knees would give out and he'd sink to the floor. Elijah closed his eyes and tried to summon his instructor's words.

"The more you focus on not making a mistake or embarrassing yourself, the more likely you are to crack under pressure and do just that. Focus on your intention."

His intention was to call the auction to the best of his ability.

"Loosen up. Do a dance. Shake out your muscles. Breathe mindfully."

Not helping.

Elijah tried to summon the cadence he'd learned more than five years ago. A cadence he'd heard thousands of times growing up. Most of the other students only had the benefit of eight days of class, eighty-three hours of instruction. Not Elijah. He had a lifetime of on-the-job training.

Who'll give me $10? Bid 10. 10. 10. Bid. Now 15. 15. Got 15. Bid. Now 20. Bid 20.

That was it. Elijah reached for the microphone. His jaw muscles ached. How would he unlock them enough to open his mouth? The microphone was in his hand. It slipped from his fingers.

"I've got it." His expression puzzled, Dillon materialized next to Elijah. He scooped up the mic and held it out. "You're a Miller. You've got this. Remember, it's for a gut cause. Do it for the volunteer firefighters. They need new equipment."

If only it were that simple. Knowing that the fire department received a percentage of the proceeds from the consignment auction, however worthy, didn't help in the least.

"You're a Miller." That didn't help either. Maybe Elijah was adopted. Maybe Mom and Dad didn't want to tell him.

This time he tightened his grip. He stared out over the vast crowd, so vast it seemed never-ending. Thousands upon thousands of people. It couldn't be that many, could it?

His stomach cramped.

Sei so gut, Gott, don't let me vomit in front of all these people.

The murmuring died away. Faces stared up at him. Waiting. Expectant.

Start. Just start. Just open your mouth.

Elijah pried his mouth open. No sound came out. He stared down at the mic in his hand. How had it gotten there? His entire body was encased in ice. An iron belt tightened around his chest. He couldn't move, couldn't breathe.

"Elijah."

Bony, age-spotted hands took the microphone from his.

He looked into his grandfather's eyes, still sharp and steely blue behind thick, dark-rimmed glasses. "Daadi."

"I've got this. You go on, now."

The ice melted. His heart beat again. "Es dutt mer," he whispered.

"No need, and, *Enkel*, head up, shoulders back."

In other words, this wasn't shameful.

If only he were right.

Grandpa turned and faced the crowd. "My grandson has a touch of the stage fright. Let's give him a hand, show him he's got no worries."

And they did. A big round of applause echoed around Elijah as he forced himself to walk slowly down the steps. Fiery heat singed his face and neck. He didn't deserve applause. He'd failed. He'd let down Grandpa, Dad, and his brothers.

The crowd parted for Elijah. A hulking man in gray overalls, a red bandanna around his neck, clapped Elijah on the back with a heavy hand. "You'll get it next time."

"No worries," his companion hollered. "Your gramps needed a workout."

Elijah managed a jerky nod. Grandpa was retired. The last thing he needed was a workout.

He gritted his teeth and plowed forward. His boots threatened to stick in the mud. Muck, muck, a sucking sound loud in his ears. The crowd faded into a sea of blurry faces, mostly strangers. For that he was thankful. Finally he made it to the enormous canopy where the auction items were inventoried and prepared for sale. He stumbled to the far end, behind a curio cabinet. There he vomited the breakfast Grandpa had insisted he eat at daybreak into wispy spring grass.

Danki, Gott, for answering my prayer not to hurl in front of a bunch of people. He didn't dare blame God for his shortcomings. Or question why God chose to answer one prayer but not others—at least not the way Elijah had wanted. If it was part of a bigger plan, why not let Elijah in on it?

He must seem so prideful, so full of himself.

Es dutt mer, Gott. Why am I like this? Why can't I do it?

"Feel better?"

The gravelly whisper was unmistakable. Declan.

Elijah straightened. He wiped his mouth and turned. "Nee."

Declan held out an oversize travel bottle.

"Danki." Elijah took it, drank, swished the water around in his mouth, and spit. "What are you doing here?"

"Took the day off from the nursery." Declan rubbed his throat. He did that sometimes, as if it still hurt even though it had been more than a year since he finished treatment for the cancer that had partially destroyed his voice box. "In case you needed more hands."

Hands, not voices. Cancer had taken Declan's beloved occupation as an auctioneer, but he never complained—at least not to Elijah. Did he think about how unfair it was that Elijah had the ability to call an auction but didn't do it? Couldn't do it? "Es dutt mer."

"Sorry for what?"

"You wanted nothing more than to be an auctioneer. Now you can't, and I'm too much of a coward."

Kelly Irvin

Declan's expression darkened. He shook his head. "Don't ever let me hear you say that again."

"It's true."

"Nee. There's a difference between being shy and being a coward. Not everyone is cut out for the spotlight. In fact, the bishop would remind you we're not to seek the limelight. We're to avoid it."

"The Gmay has made an exception for auctioneers for gut reasons. And that's not the issue. The issue here is that my family needs my help. I should step up and help, whether I like it or not."

Declan eased onto a glider rocker covered with plastic that crinkled under his weight. "So you're going to throw up your hands and have a pity party?"

"Nee. I tried. I really tried."

"I saw you trying. Daadi and Toby and Emmett, we all saw you trying. That's all a person can ask, that you try. If it's not in your wheelhouse, so be it."

Elijah heaved a breath. Bile burned his throat. He sucked down more water. "That's not the way Dat sees it."

"Dat seems to forget he's the one who refused to admit he couldn't read until Toby finally pulled it out of him." Declan leaned forward, elbows on his knees, hands clasped. "We all have our stuff we need to work on."

"You don't think it's unfair that I have the voice to call auction but not the personality?" Elijah pulled up a three-legged pine stool and sat across from Declan. "While you have everything an auctioneer needs except the voice?"

"You know what they say about fair."

"I do. It's stupid. I just don't know how else to say it." Elijah contemplated his younger brother. He'd never looked healthier with his light spring tan, his solid build, and his face devoid of the dark circles and haggard lines brought on by the cancer treatment. He still had to have CT scans and blood work every three months, but no one who didn't know him would guess at his health challenges—until he started to talk. "You should be calling auctions. You loved being on the platform. You loved an audience. You loved telling jokes and teasing customers."

That was an understatement. Declan was a born comedian. His smile held a trace of sadness. "I also love Bethel and my bopli and running the nursery. Not everyone gets to live to do these things. I'm blessed to still be here. I have no complaints."

"Really? None?"

"Do I miss the microphone and my smooth-as-a-bopli's-behind vocals? I do." He cleared his throat and rubbed it some more. "But cancer teaches a person to focus on the good in the here and now, instead of stewing over the past and what might have been. I'm alive. I get to love my fraa and my suh. That's a blessing. Gott willing, there will be more boplin to love, more memories to make."

The Millers' world wouldn't be the same without Declan's bad jokes and sunny view of life. Elijah stood and paced. He pulled open the curio cabinet's top drawer. Nothing but a few specks of dust on a red felt interior. He closed it. His family needed him. He'd let them down.

"Didn't you ever question Gott's will for you, even a little?" Elijah lowered his voice as if whispering the words made them less heretical. "Didn't you ask Him why you had to give up calling auctions, why you had to go through the treatments and the not knowing and the fear of dying before you could marry Bethel and have a family?"

"I did." Declan's gaze shifted over Elijah's shoulder to some faraway place. "But I learned Gott was the one I could depend on through it all. Only Gott. Whatever happened, whatever happens now. It's not over. With cancer it's never over. It could come back.

It could already be back. I have a CT scan in three weeks. I could be fine—until the next scan."

"And you'd be okay with that?"

"Nee. I'm not that stalwart a believer, much as I'd like to be. But whatever happens, Gott will be there." Declan the clown had disappeared. In his place sat a man who'd been honed by life's experiences. "Scripture says He holds my right hand. I can rest in Him."

It was the most serious conversation Elijah had ever had with Declan—or any of his brothers. Any of his family. Ever. Why hadn't he asked Declan how he felt when he was in the throes of the cancer treatment? Why hadn't he offered Declan words of comfort?

Because it wasn't their way. Not the Plain way. Not the way of men. A multitude of excuses. Or because Elijah didn't have the words. Or the guts to say them. Such a shallow faith.

"It's okay, Bruder." Declan laid his hand in the vicinity of his heart. "I can see you beating yourself up from here."

"I want to believe the way you do. But I don't. When I prayed for Gott to help me just now on the platform, He didn't answer."

"Maybe He did, you just didn't like the answer."

"I don't like that one either."

"You're honest. Gott loves an honest man." Declan's chuckle was rueful. "All I know is, I can't do it on my own. I learned that from the cancer. So what do you want to do now?"

A dull throb pulsed at Elijah's temples. His mouth tasted like sour milk. He wanted to drive back to the farm, go to his workshop, and lose himself in making toys that gave children happiness. "I want to call an auction. Nee, that's not right. I need to call an auction. I need to pull my own weight. I need your help."

Declan's mouth fell open and hung there.

"You'll have flies in your innards if you don't watch it."

His brother closed his mouth. "You want my help to call an auction?"

"If I don't do this, I'll always feel like a failure." Elijah knew how to call an auction. What he didn't know was how to overcome the fear that ensnared him every time he stood in front of more than two people. "I know people see me as the other Miller brother, the one who's afraid of his own shadow—"

"No one said anything about being afraid—"

"They may not say it, but they're thinking it. I'm the one who can't make the grade."

"Who cares what other people think?"

"I know, but I want to be the brother you can rely on when you need help—whatever the need is." Like now with Jason in the hospital fighting a life-threatening infection, Mom and Dad at his side. "Will you help me?"

"I can try." Declan fingered his sandy-blond beard. "We'll need some mock audiences."

"With our big family that shouldn't be too hard."

"Not our family. That wouldn't count. But Bethel's would, I reckon." Declan rubbed his hands together. He stood. "I guess I still have some pointers on how to get rid of the jitters."

"It doesn't involve imagining them with no clothes on, does it?" One of the instructor's suggestions—offered in jest.

"No way. Daadi and Dat are in the audience—"

"And Toby's fraa and yours."

"And kinner."

The laughter felt good. But Elijah still had to face Dad. And tell Bonnie he would have to postpone filling her order. Bonnie. Another person Elijah would have to face after the fiasco in the store the previous week. The Lee's Gulch grapevine's efficiency also would make sure she heard about his performance on the platform today. His heartbeat hitched at the thought.

Maybe Declan could teach him a thing or two about talking to women.

Especially pretty, smart, kind women who could take care of themselves.

"When do we start?"

"First things first." Declan picked up an inventory rundown on a clipboard and held it out. "It's all hands on deck. We might not be calling, but we can still help."

Elijah accepted the board and the challenge. He squared his shoulders and led the way back into the fray.

Chapter 8

*T*he *clickety-clack* of the rototiller blades couldn't be heard over its small gas-powered engine's rumbling floating through the open window in the kitchen, but it was there. The sound promised the goodness of nature to come in the form of fresh vegetables all summer long.

Bonnie leaned against the counter in front of the sink and inhaled the mingled scent of fresh earth and not-so-enticing gas. The sounds and smells signaled the final day of April, dwindling spring, and a prelude to summer despite a cool northern breeze.

Josie Miller handled the rototiller in the easy manner of someone who'd tilled gardens all her life. Her sister Sherri pushed the old-fashioned—in the English world—reel mower, adding the sweet aroma of fresh-cut grass to the outdoor medley.

Bonnie had never done either. Shaking an imaginary finger at the pity party in her brain, she picked up a bowl from the soapy dishwater and scrubbed it down. Inside the kitchen, the aroma of baking chocolate chip–pecan cookies perfumed the air. At Plain frolics, everyone had a job to do suited to their abilities. She could make cookies. She could wash dishes as long as she didn't rush. She had to make sure she had a good handle on each slippery-when-wet dish.

She hadn't said anything to Mom, but it seemed certain her grasp had become weaker in recent months. Getting the lid off her pill bottle had become a chore. Making her sweet panda, monkey, elephant, and giraffe stuffed animals had become more difficult. But not as hard as the faceless dolls the English tourists loved.

"Anytime now."

Bonnie blinked. She glanced at Opal. Her friend held up her dish towel. "You're gathering wool while I'm waiting to dry. At this rate we'll never finish. What are you thinking about?"

"Nothing in particular."

"That's not what the sigh says."

"What sigh?"

The other woman rolled her eyes. "The one that says you were thinking about how you'd rather be out there tilling the garden or cutting the grass than in here baking cookies or washing dishes with me. Danki, by the way."

Her best friend knew her far too well. "Sorry. I'm in a funk today."

"Because your mamm insisted you come to this frolic instead of going into the store on your day off."

The store was closed on Sundays, and Mondays were Bonnie's day off. Sophia and Carol piloted the ship. By Tuesdays, Bonnie was eager to get back to work. She'd work seven days a week if Mom would let her. "It was convenient of them to schedule the frolic on my day off so I could be here." She forced a smile. "And I like washing dishes just fine."

As a child she'd longed to run the bases after a hit between the center and left fielders, spike the volleyball, and dunk a basketball. She'd wanted nothing more than to help Mom prepare the earth for the vegetable and flower gardens and then do the planting. Being outside was more fun than being cooped up inside, learning to sew, cook, and clean—as important as those tasks were and as limiting as her mobility was.

As an adult she'd put aside childish wants and learned to do well those tasks God had prepared her to do. Like run a store.

"Liar, liar, pants on fire."

"You're such a *kind*. Okay, so I'm resigned to doing the jobs I'm able to do."

"More truthful." Opal's smile faded. She put both hands on the counter, lowered her head, and closed her dark-brown eyes. "Ach."

"Are you all right?" Bonnie tugged the towel from her friend's grasp and dried her hands. "Sit down."

Fearful that Opal might faint, Bonnie stayed close to her as they walked to a chair at the kitchen table. Her friend sank into it. "I'm fine. Just morning sickness, you know, morning, noon, and night."

"Again? Already?" The response flew from Bonnie's mouth before she could register it. "I mean, congratulations. That's wunderbarr."

"You were right the first time." Opal patted her belly, still round from carrying now four-month-old Tucker. "We were surprised too."

"But happy."

"Jah. Always. Boplin are such blessings." A squawk from the playpen situated next to the table punctuated her remark. Tucker was awake. "That was a short nap."

The pity party was back in Bonnie's brain. If only she could pick up Tucker for Opal. She could hold him for her friend, play This Little Piggy, and carry him around the house, like any person who loved babies would do. Have tummy time on the rug with him, help him learn to crawl, then hold his hand as he learned to walk. "I wish I could—"

"I know you do." Her face pale, Opal rose. She tucked a loose lock of chestnut hair under her covering. "It's okay. I'll get him."

"I'll take the *eppies* from the oven. I reckon you'd rather have crackers right now." A poor substitute, but the best she could do. "I think Mamm has some ginger ale in the refrigerator from when I had the flu."

Opal held her hand to her mouth. Her words were muffled, but Bonnie caught the gist. She didn't want to hear about food.

Bonnie took care of the cookies. Then she brought the crackers and a glass of ginger ale to the table. By that time Tucker was in his mother's arms. They had settled into the chair at the table.

The spitting image of his daddy, he stared up at Bonnie with sleepy brown eyes. His dark hair stuck up all over his head, leading his family to call him "Spike."

"He recognizes Aenti Bonnie." Opal smiled. She cooed at her baby. "Don't you, Tuck? You know your aenti."

Aunt. Never mother. Try as she might, Bonnie couldn't swallow the ache in her throat. Being an aunt was a good role, an important one, but being a mother stood head and shoulders above it. She cleared her throat. "You started feeling better pretty quick with Tucker. I reckon you will with this one too. Maybe this one will be a girl."

"We'll take either." Opal rearranged her clothes so she could nurse Tucker. "This poor guy will have to learn to drink formula from a bottle soon. My milk is about to dry up." She glanced up. "Don't look so forlorn. You'll have your turn. I know you will."

"Maybe. If it's Gott's will." Bonnie returned to the sink and her dishwashing duties. That way Opal couldn't see the tears that threatened. "If not, I'll be content with the store and my work."

"That's your mamm talking." Opal's tone turned scoffing. "Or the bishop. Don't give up on love. It hasn't given up on you."

"How do you know?"

"I heard about your accident at the store. I heard Elijah was there when it happened."

Despite the lack of technology, the Plain grapevine was every bit as powerful as any found in the English world. "So."

"So." Opal chortled. Tucker squawked. "Oops. I need to sit still. So Elijah is your age, he's single, and he's a nice man."

Yes he was single, her age, and nice. As if that was all that was necessary to make Bonnie happy. The man for Bonnie—for any woman—had to be much more than that. "Elijah was there because he wants to sell his wares in the store. That's the only reason."

"A perfectly gut reason. And perfect timing. It'll give you two a chance to get to know each other again."

"Have you spent any time around Elijah since we were in school?"

"Nee. So?"

"He's every bit as shy as he was in school. Maybe worse."

"Ach. That explains what happened at the auction over the weekend."

"What? What happened?"

"My aenti told my schweschder who told my mamm that they wanted him to call an auction in Richmond on account of Jason being in the hospital. Elijah froze. He couldn't do it."

"Ach. Poor thing."

"Who's a poor thing?" Mom traipsed into the kitchen, a large-mouthed thermos swinging from both hands. Opal's mother, Patience, followed close behind. "And why is he poor?"

"We were just talking about Elijah—"

"I heard what happened to him at the auction." Mom settled the thermos on the table. "After the incident at the store, he must be beside himself."

"It wasn't an incident—"

"Whatever you call it, I'm sure he was upset and worried about it." Opal sat Tucker upright, adjusted her bodice, and began to pat the baby's back. A burp much too large to come from such a small baby bellowed. "Goodness, I reckon you feel better." She turned him around and continued to feed him on the other side. "Freezing up in front of a big crowd couldn't have helped him feel better."

"He and Declan are redoing the corral fence. That north wind is chilly despite the sun. Winter refuses to give up and let spring take charge." Mom proceeded to place some of the cooled cookies from an earlier batch into a plastic bag. "You two should take them some coffee to warm them up. And some of these eppies. Your eppies are mighty tasty."

Now who was matchmaking? "We haven't finished washing the dishes. The mixing bowl and cookie sheets pans are still on the counter."

"Your mamm and I'll take care of them." Patience opened the refrigerator and removed a small pitcher of fresh milk. "Those young men would rather see you than us old ladies on a fine day like today."

More matchmaking. "Opal's feeding Tucker."

"I'll be done in the time it takes them to make more kaffi." Opal patted Tucker's cheek. His dreamy brown eyes widened, but he didn't stop eating. "This little glutton will spit up everywhere if he doesn't stop soon."

More matchmaking. "I thought you didn't feel gut."

"A walk outside in the fresh air will make me feel better."

"Ha."

"Don't ha me."

"Jah, don't ha her." Mom grabbed the coffeepot from the stove and began filling the thermos. She added milk and a liberal dose of sugar. "You're stuck inside the store all week long. You need fresh air and sunshine. It's just what the doctor ordered."

"And you might be just what the doctor ordered for someone else." Opal grinned at Bonnie. "You just never know."

Elijah had enough challenges without a woman like Bonnie sticking her nose where it didn't go. "We'll see about that."

"Gott's will be done," the other three women chorused together.

"You're narrisch. All of you." Bonnie dropped a few large Styrofoam cups into her rollator's pouch, along with the bag of cookies. "You'll see."

"Jah, we will."

Chapter 9

*B*id $1,000. 1,000, 1,000. Bid 1,000. Now 1,500?" Elijah picked up the pace and his volume. It was easy to capture the cadence, standing next to the corral fence in the middle of the Yoders' farm, hammer in one hand, a nail in the other, a light breeze carrying to him the scent of coral honeysuckle and the stink of horse manure in equal measure. He had only two horses, a smattering of birds, Declan, and Slowpoke as his audience. Repairing the fence in the midst of a work frolic seemed as good a time as any to hone his auctioneering skills. "Bid 1,500, 1,500. Bid 1,500. You up front. 2,000? Who'll give me 2,000? Bid 2,000? Bid 2,500. 2,500. Who wants in? Now 3,000. 3,000. Bid 3,000 . . ."

Jason's stay in the hospital had extended to nearly a week with no end in sight. The infection refused to abate. When it finally did—God willing—it would be weeks before he could return to the auction circuit. They needed Elijah to sub for him.

So sub for Jason he would. Even if the mere thought made Elijah's skin flush, itch, and burn.

"See, you can do it. You have a nice, clear voice and an easy rhythm." Declan clapped to punctuate what had been a steady stream of encouragement. "Just keep easing the bid up. You can get four, five thousand dollars for a solid oak, five-piece handcrafted bedroom set. Especially if you sweet-talk them as you go. Switch to *Deutsch* now and then. For a guy who hasn't actually called an auction, you've got the cadence down."

Slowpoke raised his head and barked twice from his resting spot in the shade of a white oak. He obviously agreed.

"Sure, when it's you, Slowpoke, a couple of horses, and a pair of robins who could care less as an audience." Elijah nailed the rough-sawed, untreated one-by-six oak plank replacing the rotted one into its spot with more force than necessary. "Maybe I could stand behind a curtain to do the calling. Maybe if I couldn't see all those people staring at me, I'd do better."

With an exaggerated grunt, Declan picked up the next one-by-six and handed it to Elijah. "Maybe, but would that accomplish your goal of facing your fears and overcoming them?"

Leave it to Declan to be right once in a while. Elijah groaned. "You're smarter than you look, Bruder."

"Danki, Bruder." Declan bowed with an elegant flourish. "I'm also funnier. Would you like a joke?"

Declan knew humor was powerful medicine. It sure couldn't hurt. Elijah nodded. "A joke would be gut."

"What does corn say when it gets a compliment?"

"I don't know. What does corn say when it gets a compliment?"

Declan hung his head and kicked at the dirt with his work boot. "Aw, shucks."

Elijah groaned again, but then he laughed. "Smart and funny."

"Danki." Another elaborate bow. "I'm here for two shows a night. Tips welcome."

"It's nice to see two brieder getting along so well."

Elijah swiveled at the sound of a familiar voice. *Don't let it be her. Sei so gut, don't let it be her.*

It was Bonnie. Opal accompanied her. Elijah had seen Bonnie serving sandwiches at lunch, but she hadn't looked his way. Intentionally? Or was she just busy? Not that he'd sought her out either. Was she offended that he hadn't said hello?

Round and round went the hamster on the wheel in his brain.

Slowpoke hopped up and trotted in a beeline for the women. Bonnie let go of her rollator with one hand long enough to give the dog a good pet. "Slowpoke, my old friend. Danki for helping keep these worker bees in line." She scratched in that favorite place behind his left ear. His tail wagged faster. "If I'd known you were out here, I would've brought you some water to go with the kaffi and eppies for the men."

"Woo-hoo. Kaffi, eppies, and gut company." Declan pumped his fist and then clapped. "You two are the best."

Bonnie and Opal acknowledged his praise with modest bows.

Bonnie didn't hold a grudge against Slowpoke for tripping her up. Not against the dog. What about his owner? Her face was flushed from the brisk northern breeze. She was so pretty. Did seeing him remind her of falling flat on her back in her storeroom? Elijah forced his gaze to Slowpoke. "I brought water and a bowl."

Why couldn't he sound more relaxed and welcoming like his brothers?

"You're the gut pet owner, for sure and for certain." Opal cocked her head toward Bonnie. "Bonnie thought you could use some kaffi to warm you up and some of her chocolate chip–pecan eppies, fresh from the oven. Isn't that right, Bonnie?"

The scowl Bonnie shot her friend wasn't all that friendly. "Mamm actually thought of it, but jah, it seemed like a gut idea."

"Wunderbarr." Declan laid aside another one-by-six plank. "Elijah was just saying he could use another cup of kaffi, and he had a hankering for chocolate chip–pecan eppies. Weren't you, Elijah?"

How could he answer that without either lying or turning his brother into a liar? Elijah glared at Declan. "Both sound gut." How was that for threading the needle? He laid the hammer on the closest fence post. "My hands are cold."

"I heard there's a new batch of kittens in the barn. I want to check them out. They're so cute when they're little. I'm thinking about taking one home." With that Opal traipsed toward the barn without so much as a by-your-leave to Bonnie.

Storm clouds gathering in her face, Bonnie stared after her friend. "Opal—"

"My fraa loves kittens too." Declan slid his straw hat back on his head. "I reckon my suh would be head over heels for one. I should check them out too."

Off he went, leaving Elijah to stare at the ground and contemplate all the ways he'd get even with his brother in the near future.

"Well, that wasn't obvious at all, was it?"

Not daring to ask what was so obvious, Elijah forced himself to look up. Slowpoke at her side, Bonnie had moved closer. She pulled a thermos from her walker's bag and held it out. "I reckon it's up to you and me to drink the kaffi and eat all the eppies. They get none. Would you mind pouring?"

"Nee, not at all."

Elijah concentrated on pouring the beverage without spilling it, despite hands that didn't want to cooperate. Bonnie said nothing when the coffee sloshed over the side onto his fingers. Steam billowed from the cup. The rich aroma steadied him. He handed a cup to her and poured one for himself.

"Danki. How's Jason doing?"

"He's been better. His body isn't fighting the infection the way it should. They're trying a stronger antibiotic."

"He's a strong man."

Young and strong. A husband and father with so much life to live. God willing. Why wouldn't God be willing? What plan did He have to hone character through a painful trial such as this? Painful for Caitlin, for the children, for Mom and Dad. For Jason's brothers and sisters. "Jah."

"He'll be okay." Bonnie plucked a cookie the size of his palm from the bag and handed it to him on a napkin. A man had to appreciate a big cookie. "I like to make them big." Her soft tone invited him to agree. "That way I can say I just had one."

"I like the way you think." He took a big bite. They were still warm, the chocolate chips gooey. Just the way anyone in his right mind would like them. "Gut."

"It's Mamm's recipe."

Slowpoke was too well-mannered to beg, but he did inch closer, his nose in the air, sniffing, on alert. "Sorry, friend, no chocolate for you." Instead Elijah laid his snack on the napkin Bonnie had provided so he could dig the hound's favorite chew bone and a doggy biscuit from his nearby duffel bag. Then he poured him some water. "There you go. You'll like that much better, I promise."

"You are a gut friend to him." Bonnie watched, her expression appreciative. She took a sip of her coffee. "There's nothing better than hot kaffi and warm eppies on a cold day."

Nice, safe topic. Elijah nodded. "Jah."

"But I must say I'm looking forward to warmer weather when we can have watermelon and lemonade and fresh tomatoes from the garden."

Again safe. "Every season has its perks." Elijah closed the lid on her walker. "Would you like to sit?"

She shook her head. "It feels gut to stand."

Had he messed up again? "Did I do it again?"

"Do what?"

"Act like you need special treatment instead of treating you like everyone else?"

Bonnie set her cup on the seat. She smiled. "I know I came off as prickly last week. I tend to do that. You were trying to be nice. I shouldn't take offense when people are nice. And kind. So many people aren't these days. And just now, you showed gut manners and kindness."

"Gut." Elijah's heart slowed. Maybe talking to Bonnie could be easier than talking to other women. Not harder. Maybe. "Is it possible to treat someone as special and have it be a gut thing?"

Her eyes narrowed. Her smile faded.

He'd done it again.

She pursed her lips. Her forehead wrinkled. Finally, she nodded. "I see what you mean. I care about my mom, so I ask her if she wants to sit while I make supper because I know she's tired. Not because she's weak, but because she's special to me."

Elijah exhaled. "Jah."

Bonnie picked up her cup and toasted him. "Gut point."

"So this . . . walker . . ." Elijah pointed to the contraption with its wheels, pouch, and seat. "Is it still called a walker?"

"Nee, it's called a rollator." Bonnie patted one handle. "It's so helpful to be able to cart around things I need. Plus I take my own seat wherever I go. If I get tired, I can sit. If the waiting room is full, I can sit. It's handy-dandy."

"I can see that."

"Danki."

"For what?"

She ducked her head and stared at the handy-dandy rollator. "Most abled people like to pretend it's not there. Like they don't see it. Or they see me and get confused and don't know what to say because I'm not old. Danki for asking."

"I like knowing things."

"Me too."

What now? If Declan were here, he would tell a joke. Contemplating the void in his brain where small talk should be, Elijah took his cup to the fence. The horses, a beautiful roan and a sorrel, trotted over to meet him. With his free hand, he took turns patting their muzzles. "Sorry, I don't have any treats for you today."

"I fed them apple slices this morning. They just like to beg." Bonnie had moved to stand next to him. "They're not as well-mannered as Slowpoke."

Elijah glanced at the dog. He was blissfully occupied with his bone. "Are you all better?"

"I'm fine. I had a little cut, that's all, and it's already healed. And it wasn't your fault." She scratched between the roan's ears and murmured sweet nothings to him. She had such a calming voice. "It wasn't Slowpoke's either. It was all my fault." The flush on her face deepened. She shrugged. "That's what I get for being prickly toward you. Punishment for being prideful."

"You don't deserve to be punished." Not ever. Elijah couldn't take his gaze from her long, slim fingers. She had a delicate touch. What would it feel like to hold her hand? Was her skin as soft as her touch? Warmth that had nothing to do with the coffee rolled over him. His wool jacket was suddenly itchy and hot. He cleared his throat. "I'd better get back to work."

"Jah. Jah, me too."

An emotion flitted across her face, hard to identify at first. Then it made itself clear. Sadness. She was sad. Elijah's heart wrenched in his chest. The last thing a woman like Bonnie should have to feel was sad. She deserved to be happy. Not everyone did, but Bonnie did.

Elijah searched for words to make that sadness go away. None came. Words were not his friends. "Slowpoke's break is over too."

He picked up Slowpoke's bone. He stuck it in his duffel bag. His back to Bonnie, he heaved a breath. What if he told her he liked hearing her laugh? What would she say then? "Go on, 'Poke, find Declan, tell him to stop slacking off. Time to work."

A dog in the barn with a new batch of kittens was bound to get his brother moving.

"My mamm and I appreciate everyone pitching in on the repairs." Bonnie pushed her rollator closer. She took Elijah's cup. Their fingers touched for a scant second. Hers were warm. The desire to hang on to them flooded him. Her gaze on the cup, she smiled. "We haven't kept the place up the way Dat would've wanted."

"He'd understand."

The sadness returned, making her brown eyes darker. She nodded. "I suppose. I guess it felt like making the repairs meant we finally accepted that he's never picking up a paintbrush or a hammer again. Never coming through the back door, growling like an old bear coming out of hibernation about what's for supper, and kissing my mamm when he thinks I'm not looking."

A hard truth to accept. Words of comfort eluded Elijah. "I always liked your dat."

"He was the best dat a *maedel* could ask for."

If only he had a way with words. If only he could drive away the mourning that lingered in that sentiment. With a kiss. The warmth turned into a searing heat. Elijah swiveled back to the roan, who had stuck his head over the fence, still begging for attention. "He's a beautiful *gaul*."

"He is." Bonnie reached for her rollator. She paused, those long, thin fingers gripping the handles. "If you're auctioneering, will you still have time to make the pieces we agreed on?"

Here we go. "I don't know how quickly I'll get to them, it's true."

"But you're still planning to fill the order?"

If it meant spending time with her, he'd find a way. "I hope so."

A tiny wrinkle appeared between her eyebrows. "Have you changed your mind?"

"My family needs my help."

Her gaze seemed to assess him and find something wanting. "I thought maybe you didn't want to be an auctioneer after . . . what happened."

She'd heard. Probably everyone in the tristate area had heard about Elijah's fiasco. "I don't. I never have, but my family needs me and family comes first."

"I understand that."

Her words said one thing, but her tone and her eyes said something else entirely. Elijah stepped into her path. "I still want to . . . sell at the store."

I want to work with you. I want to see you, to see if there's something more there.

"It won't take long for the pieces you brought in to sell. Just so you know. If you decide you can't make more, I'll tear up the contract."

Tell her why. I can't. I don't have the words.

Far too many words were needed. "Danki."

"No need to thank me. Your toys are lovely. Their sale will benefit the store." She rolled around him and started for the house. "I'm hoping to sell many of them in the future."

If only she would turn back. Maybe her expression would reveal if she simply wanted his toys because they were good for business. Or did she want to see him too?

A few yards away, she stopped and pivoted. One hand still on the rollator, she gave a tiny wave. "See you at the store. I hope."

"See you at the store." Elijah waved back. "I hope."

Not just at the store, but anyplace, anytime.

Chapter 10

*W*hoops."

The exclamation registered just before the sensation of something wet dripped down Jocelyn's forehead. She touched her fingers to the spot and examined them. Paint. Snowy white. She glanced up.

Theo Beiler stood on a catwalk set up on scaffolding not far from Jocelyn's brother Uriah. Theo held up his paint roller. "I tried to stop it, but I was too late." His expression amused, he nodded toward the catwalk under his feet. "Just your luck to pass by when a gust of wind whips up."

"I didn't feel any gust of wind."

In fact, the chilly breeze had stilled for a few minutes, which was surely nice for the men who'd been standing out in the cold painting her house most of the day. It was so like Virginia weather this time of year. Cool and springlike one day and summery hot the next. Which was why she'd brought out two more thermoses filled with hot coffee, along with cookies.

"Huh." Theo rested the roller on the paint pan, wiped his hands on a rag, and hopped down from the catwalk. "Is that fresh kaffi?"

"It is."

"Let me carry the thermos for you."

"I can manage."

"Don't be such a grumpy old woman, Joci." Uriah climbed down with more agility than a man five years her senior should have. That was the second time in a week someone had called her a grumpy old woman. She wasn't, was she? Uriah wiped his paint-speckled hands with a faded blue bandanna. "Letting people help you is as much a blessing for them as it is for you. I keep thinking you'll learn that lesson anytime now."

He was right. The district had rallied around Bonnie and her after Marlin's death in a hundred small and big ways. "I do know that. I appreciate everything you do for me."

"I wasn't fishing for appreciation."

"I know that."

"That lesson also applies to small things." Theo tugged one of the thermoses from Jocelyn's hand. He strode ahead toward the picnic table that held the snacks and drinks she had laid out earlier. "I'm feeling a little peckish. I could use an eppy."

"I do appreciate you and your fraa organizing this frolic." Jocelyn stepped into Uriah's path. They paused in the shade of an enormous oak tree several yards from the picnic table. "I'm just surprised you sent a strange man to my door to tell me about it." Jocelyn kept her voice low. "Knowing I was probably here alone."

"I reckon I didn't think about him being a stranger to you. He's not to me and Frannie, and the kinner like him. He's quite the storyteller." Uriah craned his head side to side. He buttoned the top button on his black wool jacket. He and their dad could be twins twenty-five years apart. Tall, broad-shouldered, wiry gray hair and beard, and skin marked by years of sun. "Theo's been working for me since February. He's handy, a hard worker, and smart. He fits right in."

Why didn't that sit well with Jocelyn? "Gut for him."

"There you go, being a grumpy old woman again."

"Am not." Now they sounded like the teenagers who had bickered endlessly while doing their chores, annoying their mother so much. Bless her soul for putting up with five children born in ten years' time. "I mean, I'm glad you found an extra set of hands, but don't you think you should've told me about the frolic yourself?"

"You would've insisted it wasn't needed. I figured it was better to just go ahead with it. You'd get on board in the end."

So she had.

Was that a flicker of amusement in his walnut-colored eyes? "Plus I wanted you to meet Theo."

"Why?"

"You have a lot in common. He's a wittmann. He farmed in Berlin, but he has family in Lancaster County, same as us. He has just the one kind too, but his is a boy. After his fraa died, he decided he needed a fresh start. Came here to Lee's Gulch to stay with his cousin."

A few things in common, true, but what did that matter? Then it hit Jocelyn. Her brother was matchmaking. "Uriah Baumgartner. You should be ashamed."

"Of what?" He had the audacity to appear astonished and even hurt. "What did I do?"

"Time's wasting. You should get back to painting."

Uriah hitched up pants a little too big for his lean body. "It's time, Joci, and you know it. The bishop even said as much after church last Sunday."

A bunch of men sitting around talking about something

none of them knew squat about. Not a widower in the bunch. "You must've been hard up for conversation if you were talking about me."

"Hey, we just want what's best for you."

As if they knew. Jocelyn ducked past her brother and strode to the picnic table where Theo had taken a seat. He had a cup of steaming coffee in one hand and a cookie in the other. He held up the cookie. "This is a mighty fine eppy. Reminds me of the ones my fraa used to make."

His smile didn't waver, but something in his voice gave him away. Jocelyn lowered the thermos. A person who'd lost a spouse couldn't simply walk away from someone with a shared experience of such excruciating pain. It would be uncompassionate. Inhumane. "How long has she been gone?"

"One year, six months, and twenty-three days." His Adam's apple bobbed. His faint smile was wry. "But who's counting?"

"My dochder made the eppies." Her throat suddenly aching, Jocelyn had to clear it. She sat across from him and nudged the plate in his direction. "She's my only kind. Uri mentioned you have one kind as well, a *bu*."

"Jah. Noah. Named for his daadi. He's twenty-three."

"I wonder if we'll ever stop counting the years, the months, and the days. If I'll ever stop wondering why I didn't see that my mann's heart was bad. How I missed it."

Theo laid his cookie on a napkin. His gaze bounced from her face to a spot over her shoulder. "Ellie had cancer. She waited too long to go to the doctor. She was like that. Too busy taking care of others to take care of herself. I should've made her go."

"Maybe if I'd had served less fried food, less red meat, more vegetables and fish, maybe Marlin would still be here."

Jocelyn had never shared that gnawing sense of guilt with

Kelly Irvin

anyone else. Her family would poo-poo the idea to make her feel better. Theo simply nodded. He nudged the snack plate in her direction. She selected an oatmeal raisin cookie but didn't take a bite.

The conversation teetered, stopped, but it felt comfortable, as if there were no need for words. They both understood. Momma Cat trotted up to the table. She stopped, one paw suspended in air, tail swishing, and peered at its occupants, then resumed her journey. A mourning dove cooed in the red maple that shaded the table. It was the sound of summer coming, of long childhood days spent playing outdoors, a sound of contentment hard to achieve as a grown-up. Jocelyn closed her eyes, listened, and heaved a breath. The longing to get it back was so strong that the hurt in her heart spread and filled every crevice of her being. *Why, Gott?*

God probably wondered why she still asked this infernal question after two years, two months, and twelve days. *Let it go, Dochder.*

God's plan was God's plan. *Thy will be done.*

Even when it was incomprehensible. Even when it hurt worse than any physical pain she'd ever experienced. Even when dragging herself from the bed she'd shared with Marlin every day of their married life was a monumental—almost impossible—task.

"Are the elders pushing you to remarry?" Theo's voice had gone soft, barely above a hoarse whisper.

"Not directly to me, but my brieder and schweschdre seem bent on doing some matchmaking."

Uriah and her brothers wouldn't approve of their sister having this conversation with a man she barely knew—or any man at all. But Uriah had opened the door and shoved her through it.

Theo shook his head. He grinned. The change lit up his face. Lines disappeared. He shed years of pain and hurt. It would be

84

miserly not to return the gift. Jocelyn summoned her best smile. It was rusty from lack of use.

"Fortunately for us, we're adults used to making our own way in this world." He finished his cookie, dusted crumbs from his beard, and drained his coffee cup. "I better get back to painting before your bruder fires me."

"He wouldn't do that. He likes you."

"I'm glad he does. I'm starting to really like living in Lee's Gulch."

His expression, an invitation to share something singularly theirs, sent a tingle up Jocelyn's spine. A feeling she hadn't had in a very long time came along for the ride. A sense of aliveness. Of creating a connection with someone that wasn't there before.

No, no, no. That couldn't be. None of that.

Marlin had been the only man for her. It didn't matter what the elders thought or wanted or felt. It didn't matter what her brothers and sisters thought was best for her. She wasn't a teenager on her rumspringa.

Guilt, like boiling water, scalded her skin. Jocelyn hopped up from the bench. In her haste she knocked against the table. The open thermos toppled over. Hot coffee spread across the table and dripped on Theo's pants. He sprang up. "Whoa!"

Jocelyn backpedaled. "I didn't mean to do that."

"I didn't think you did." Looking puzzled, Theo snatched up a napkin and dabbed at the coffee spots. "No harm done."

Jocelyn whirled and fled.

"Don't you want to take the thermoses?" Theo's voice calling after her held a hint of laughter.

What was so funny?

Chapter 11

*T*he long kitchen table seemed unusually crowded. Elijah squeezed past his brother Emmett's chair and plopped into his seat next to Dad's at the end. After a day working outside in the cold at Bonnie's house, his brain wasn't chugging as fast as usual. He'd been the last to finish washing up and head into the kitchen for supper. His stomach rumbled at the heavenly scent of beef gravy and homemade bread. He eyed the large platter of sliced roast beef just within his reach. As soon as his dad prayed, he'd grab it. He glanced across the room. Kathryn Coblentz, seated between Josie and Sherri, smiled at him.

What was she doing at the Millers' supper table?

Elijah let his gaze run around the room. No wonder the kitchen was crowded. Mom had added a card table to one end of the table that seated as many as twelve Miller family members at a time. Kathryn's three brothers occupied seats on the other side of Emmett. Menno and Patience Coblentz were also at the main table. Elijah's younger sisters sat at the card table. They undoubtedly pretended not to notice that Sadie had Matilda the Cat on her lap. The cat liked to eat whatever the eleven-year-old ate.

Mom and Dad had been going back and forth to the hospital

all week, using the time at home to do laundry, check on the children for Caitlin, and sleep in their own bed. Yet with the girls' help, Mom had managed to invite guests and fix this big spread. No one multitasked like she did.

Kathryn had been a couple of grades behind him in school. She used to hang around the ball field, watching the baseball games, watching him at bat. She wasn't one of those girls who liked to play sports. She played a lot of hand-clapping with her friends or sat on the swing, but mostly she watched the other kids play. Meaning Elijah.

"Elijah, did you say hallo to our guests?"

Before he could answer his mom, Dad cleared his throat.

They prayed silently. Another clearing of the throat and Dad handed him the platter of sliced roast beef. "Did you hear your mamm?"

"I did." Elijah stabbed a few slices of beef and dropped them on his plate. He passed the platter and then forced himself to look at the Coblentzes again. "Hallo."

The elder Coblentzes nodded and waved from either side of the table farther down.

"Kathyrn started working at our store today." Mom made the announcement as if it were the hottest news to hit Lee's Gulch in a decade. "Tourist season will be here before we know it."

Elijah concentrated on dumping mashed potatoes onto his plate.

"I saw some of your handiwork too." Kathryn had a chirpy voice reminiscent of a happy robin. "Your toys are really cute. And the children's furniture is adorable. Englischers will like both, for sure and for certain."

Had she been in his workshop? In the middle of doing laundry, fixing meals, and checking on the store, Mom had had time to take

Kathryn to his workshop? Elijah hazarded a glance in her direction. She was a sturdy girl with light-brown hair and eyes to match. At the moment her cheeks were red. She looked as awkward as he felt. When would Mom give up on the matchmaking? Never. Not until all nine of her children were married and giving her a barn full of grandkids. "Where?"

"In the store. Your mamm wants me to be familiar with all the inventory."

"My toys are in our store?" Elijah dropped his napkin in his lap and laid his fork down. "What's that about, Mamm?"

"I figured since you're not selling them at Homespun Handicrafts, we should put them on the shelf here." His mother slid into a chair next to Patience. "At least you can recoup what you spent on supplies, if not your time, for the stuff you've already made."

Bonnie's disappointed tone echoed in Elijah's head. And those last words . . . what did they mean? *"See you at the store. I hope."*

A challenge? Of course he did. He wanted to sell at Homespun Handicrafts for several reasons, but he also wanted to do the right thing. "So you went into my workshop and helped yourself to my work?"

"What was there, which wasn't much." Mom helped herself to a roll. She picked up a knife and scooped up some butter. She'd bypassed the part where she addressed his unspoken concern over not having asked him first. As his mother, she likely didn't feel she should have to. Dad might be the property owner, but Mom kept the household organized, the store running smoothly, and still managed to plant and reap a vast vegetable garden. She was in charge most every other way. "You'll have to get back what you left at the shop."

"What makes you think I won't be able to sell them at Homespun Handicrafts?"

Squinting, Mom peered at him as if he'd suddenly transported himself to a spot three farms away. "If you're on the auction circuit, you won't be making new pieces. You won't be able to fill the shop's orders."

The homemade bread had turned to cardboard in Elijah's mouth. He chewed and strained to swallow it. "I won't be on the circuit forever. Just until Jason gets back."

A shadow danced across Mom's face. Suddenly, she seemed old and tired. "Jason will be fine. But this is an opportunity for you to help out with the family business and contribute to the family store. Tourists who visit our store will love the toys."

As much as they would at Homespun Handicrafts. The remainder of her sentence hung in the air. Only the people who came to her store usually bought produce and fresh canned vegetables from the Millers' garden. It wasn't a gift store. English folks from the area who didn't want to go into town shopped there. "We'll see."

"Declan told Bethel who told Layla who told me that you've been practicing." Josie jabbed her fork in the air. "And I told Mamm. He said you're doing gut. He said you shouldn't freeze up again and run off the stage like you did in Richmond."

"Jah, and why would you do that if you're not going to call?" Sherri chimed in.

"Jah, why?" Sadie might not understand the nuances of every conversation, but she always participated. Matilda the Cat meowed. So did she. "Why, Bruder?"

Elijah's hand froze, fork halfway to his mouth. His gut lurched. Heat seared his cheeks and neck. Those practice sessions weren't a secret necessarily, but Declan knew Elijah didn't want Dad getting a whiff of them until they were sure he could actually do it.

Declan couldn't be blamed for telling his wife. Husbands told wives everything. At least Elijah assumed they did. But plunk a bunch of Plain women in a kitchen together fixing lunch after church and all nuggets of news were fair game. Likely they were commiserating about the fiasco in Richmond and Bethel felt the need to reassure Layla that Elijah wasn't a lost cause. Declan to the rescue.

"Now, Dochders, no sense in bringing up Richmond." Mom flapped her napkin in front of her face like a fan. "That won't happen again. Elijah likely had a touch of the flu that day."

More like a touch of the nerves. Mom's fixed smile reflected her determination to convince the Coblentzes—mainly Kathryn—that Elijah wasn't a nervous Nellie or, worse, a coward.

"I'm not bringing those pieces back. I plan to become a vendor at the store." Elijah pushed his still half-full plate away. "I've signed a contract. I'm committed to starting my own business, just like I told Dat before."

"We don't need to talk business at the table." Dad picked up a bowl of green beans and helped himself. His gaze steely, he handed it to Elijah. "It's bad for the digestion. Especially when we have company. Eat your vegetables, Suh. Menno, how's the hog business?"

Menno took the opening and ran with it. The conversation turned to hogs, mud sales, summer vacation plans, and frolics.

"Eat your vegetables." Like a good boy. Like a good son. Dad hadn't meant it that way, but the Coblentzes couldn't know or understand that. Elijah handed the beans to Emmett. He'd eaten plenty of vegetables.

The rest of the meal passed slower than August at the end of a long hot summer. The one time Elijah glanced up, Kathryn was staring at him. She immediately looked away. Finally, Mom served strawberry-rhubarb pie with whipped cream. Elijah polished off his in four bites. It tasted of nothing, of empty air.

Getting out of the kitchen wouldn't be easy. He stood, sucked in his gut, squeezed through the narrow aisle between the chairs and the wall, and plunged out the other end. A few more strides and he was out the back door. Slowpoke popped up from his usual spot on an old rug reserved for his naps whenever Elijah was inside. Mom didn't cotton to the idea of having dogs in her house.

Which was fine with Slowpoke. He didn't cotton to the idea that Mom didn't like dogs. Especially considering Matilda the Cat was allowed in. Made no sense whatsoever. He barked and trotted down the steps as if ready for whatever came next. "Whatever" not being anything here. "Just give me a minute."

Slowpoke huffed and sat, his ears perked.

"It's nothing. I just needed to breathe." Elijah inhaled the dusk's cold air. A gust of wind whistled through the live oak tree branches over his head. He raised his face to it, letting it cool his nervous heat.

"What was that all about?"

He swiveled. Dad pushed through the screen door and let it slam behind him.

Elijah turned back to the back porch railing. His hands tightened around the painted wood. "Nothing. I just needed some air."

Slowpoke whined deep in his throat. He settled down, head on his paws, with an exaggerated air of long-suffering.

You and me both, buddy, you and me both.

"Don't go too far. I want to talk about your plan." The way Dad emphasized *plan* suggested he didn't think much of it.

"I'm just stretching my legs."

Dad grunted and went back in the house.

Stretching came in the form of walking himself back to his workshop. In the aftermath of the noisy supper scene, made noisier by six guests, the space welcomed Elijah with the open arms of quiet. He and his brothers built the 100-by-150-square-foot building with reclaimed wood he bought at an auction four years earlier. The pitched roof was covered with solar panels with the exception of the two large skylights. What he'd given up in shelf space, he'd gained in natural light by covering two walls with large windows. Most days he didn't need artificial lighting. He could open the windows to allow breezes to cool the workspace in the summer.

To make up for the loss of wall space normally used to hang tools, they'd built a counter along an entire wall with a series of drawers underneath where he could store his hand tools. In the center, facing the east, he positioned the workbench he'd built from scratch. He even bought a used bunk bed and set it up in one corner. If it got late and he was tired, he could slip off to sleep in his favorite place. If he simply had had enough of people, he could do the same thing.

Of course, Slowpoke thought the bed was for him, which was why he headed straight to it as soon as Elijah let him in. He curled up on the faded Lone Star Cabin quilt and sighed in obvious pleasure.

"Bum." Elijah went to the workbench and picked up a piece of sandpaper. He could use the buffer, but sanding by hand soothed him. He settled onto his stool and went to work on the pieces of walnut that would eventually become another small rocking chair.

"Home sweet home," he whispered.

Slowpoke snored in response.

Elijah chuckled. How could life go from crazy hard to sweetly calm from one minute to the next? If he could live in this moment, not peeking over his shoulder at the past, not digging himself into a hole in the future, life would be good. The scents of raw wood, varnish, and mechanical oil mingled in the best perfume in the world. It was surprising no one had bottled it.

His mind hummed with silly and sillier thoughts. Declan would find a joke in there somehow, someway. Declan needed a course correction. Telling Bethel about the auction lessons. And Bethel telling Layla. That was like telling a gossip columnist. Or a town caller like they had in olden days.

His mind traipsed around and around in circles, avoiding the one topic he needed to address. Homespun Handicrafts. Tomorrow. Bonnie. Vendor. Maybe if he worked early morning until late at night, when he was home, he could get a good start. The smaller, simple items took only a few hours. A table and four chairs, longer.

"May I come in?"

Poof. The calm dissipated. The chirpy sounds didn't belong to a robin. They belonged to Kathryn. His stomach clenched. Neck hot, Elijah leaned into the steady swipe, swipe of sandpaper against wood. "Jah. Sure."

"My mamm and dat are still yakking with yours." She stepped inside the door and lingered on the well-worn welcome rug. "We finished cleaning up. Josie had some paperwork to do at the office, so I decided to take a walk."

"Uh-huh."

Kathryn sashayed along the counter, running her fingers along the edge like she was checking for dust. Despite Elijah's solar-powered vacuuming system, there was plenty of that. "I didn't know that you didn't know your toys were in the store. I assumed—"

"Don't worry about it. I would've thought the same thing." Kathryn was not at fault. His matchmaking mom was. Elijah stood. He lined up the pieces of wood one by one. Orderly. Ready to become a chair that a child would love. So much easier than talking to a woman he barely knew. He cleared his throat. "Mamm has a reputation as a matchmaker, especially for her own kinner."

Kathryn's forehead wrinkled. Her gaze dropped to the floor.

Kelly Irvin

"Are you saying she didn't hire me because she thought I would be gut at working in the store?"

Red spots glowing on her fair cheeks, she whirled and trotted toward the door. "Mamm and Dat are probably ready to go."

"Wait. Sei so gut." Elijah strode around the workbench. Kathryn paused at the door, one hand on its frame. Elijah halted still several feet away. They shouldn't be having this conversation, all alone, in his workshop. But what Mom had started he had to finish, for this poor woman's sake. *Not fair, Mamm.* "She did hire you because you are a gut fit. She wouldn't hire someone who isn't."

"But?"

"But sometimes she gets carried away with her schemes." Elijah crossed his arms. He studied the sawdust on his boots. He forced himself to meet her gaze. "She just wants her kinner to be happy. It doesn't occur to her that I might be able to sort that out on my own."

"And she thinks . . ." Kathryn pointed at Elijah, then at herself. The scarlet on her cheeks spread across her face and down her neck. "And you think . . . ?"

"I don't know."

"I see." It was her turn to cross her arms and study her sneakers. "Margie Joens asked me to work at her day care. I might be better at that job. At least until you *do* know."

"Es dutt mer."

"You didn't do anything."

"Which is why Mamm did what she did."

"For what it's worth, I think you should sell your toys at the gift shop." Kathryn cocked her head toward the rocking horse sitting on the counter. "A person only has to see your work to know it's your calling. Not the other auctioneer kind."

94

People on the outside of a situation oftentimes could see the circumstances better than the ones up to their eyeballs in the miry clay of dissension. Kathryn was wise beyond her years. She would make some man a good wife.

But not Elijah. His thoughts couldn't be so occupied with Bonnie otherwise. Kathryn seemed nice, but he didn't give her a second thought upon saying hello to her at church or a frolic. He didn't wonder what it would feel like to hold her hand or touch her cheek's soft skin. He didn't think about her before he closed his eyes at night or opened them in the morning.

He didn't hope to see her again. Soon.

Kathryn had been gone only a few minutes when Mom stomped into the workshop. She marched up to his workbench, stopped, planted her feet, and stuck her hands on her hips. "Seriously, Elijah. That has to be a world record. You almost drove off a store employee after one day. One day!"

"What do you mean, *almost*?"

"I talked Kathryn into staying on. It took all my powers of persuasion, but she finally agreed. Why would you want to drive off such a kind, sweet, hardworking girl?"

Mom's powers of persuasion *were* legendary. "I didn't want to drive anyone off. You embarrassed me. You embarrassed her." Elijah rubbed his temples. "I know you think you brought Toby and Rachelle together. And Layla and Micah. And Declan and Bethel. But you didn't—"

"I don't think that. Gott brought them together according to His plan." She raised her chin. "I just nudged things along a bit."

"I don't need anybody nudged."

"Kathryn is a nice maedel. She'll make a gut fraa."

"She's not . . ." Elijah stopped. He clamped his mouth shut. This conversation was over. Parents weren't supposed to meddle in their children's pursuit of a husband or wife. That his rumspringa hadn't produced a wife was his own business.

Elijah picked up the sandpaper, then laid it down. No point in taking his frustration out on a poor piece of wood. "I need to work. We're leaving for Charm on Wednesday. I want to finish a few pieces tonight so I can take them into town tomorrow."

"She's not what?" Mom was a hunter who'd spied her prey. "Or who is she not? That's it. She's not who?"

"Mamm."

"Hmm. Uh-huh, uh-huh." Mom stalked around the bench. She patted Elijah's shoulder. "Don't stay out here too late. And don't sleep here. You want to be well rested when you go into town to do business."

To do business. "Mamm, sei so gut."

She paused at the door, much in the same way Kathryn had. "If you decide to never call an auction, your dat will get over it. He'll understand."

Not so a person noticed. *"Gut nacht."*

"I won't nudge Kathryn toward you again. I promise."

Elijah almost said thank you. The glint in her eyes stopped him. Mom had moved on to new prey.

Chapter 12

*W*hat difference did it make? Bonnie adjusted the lamp to see the pink cotton material that would be a bunny ear she was about to feed under the needle on her sewing machine, a Singer treadle that had been adapted to run on a battery. It didn't make the lovely pumping sound of a treadle, but at least it sat in the carved wooden case that had belonged to her grandma Eva. It was Bonnie's favorite piece of furniture.

Unfortunately the lamp didn't cast a better light on her muddled thoughts. Either Elijah decided to push through with his plan to sell toys in the store or he didn't. If he did, she would see more of him. If he didn't, she wouldn't. It would be a loss for the store, that was all. It bothered Bonnie for no other reason. Really.

A pin holding the two pieces of material together pricked her finger. "Ouch." Bonnie sucked on the tip. She grabbed a tissue and held it against the tiny spot of blood so it wouldn't get on the material. "That's what happens when you lie, maedel, even to yourself."

After her conversation with Elijah, she'd stayed inside the rest of the afternoon, helping the women make new curtains for the living room. The frolic had ended before dark, which was fine by her.

No more temptation to march back out to the fence and apologize to Elijah for her cryptic remark. He had enough pressure on him. He had to do what was best for his family. Faith, family, and community. That was the Plain way of life.

He and Declan had been among the last to leave. Bonnie knew that only because Opal had kept her informed of all his movements as if she needed to know. In a day or two he'd leave again, this time for auctions in Pennsylvania.

Fine. So be it.

She should go to bed. Mom had turned in early, after a quick dinner of leftover vegetable beef stew and buttered sourdough bread. She said she was tired, but she didn't sleep a lot. Not anymore. She was probably reading.

One more piece and Bonnie would follow suit. She ran the ear under the needle, careful to keep her fingers clear. The machine hummed, making its own unique music. The needle pumped. Her head cleared. At the end she stopped, turned the material around, and double-stitched so the seam wouldn't come undone later. Then she flipped the lever, cut the thread, and held up the ear. The line of stitches was crooked. It would be so obvious stuck up over the sweet bunny's face.

She sighed and picked up the thread picker—her name for the implement used to pull out thread in situations such as this—and began removing the stitches.

Nerve pain flashed through her index finger and thumb. She laid the piece on the case and rubbed her fingers. How could a person have nerve pain in fingers that were numb? The doctor couldn't explain her neuropathy. She called it "idiopathic," which was a big word for "I don't know." Bonnie picked up the piece and went back to work.

"What are you doing still up?"

Bonnie jumped. The ear fell to the floor. "Ach." Bonnie swiveled. Clad in her long cotton nightgown, hair flowing down her back, Mom stood in the doorway. "I thought you were asleep."

Mom held up a Vannetta Chapman cozy mystery. "Reading. My eyes are tired, but the rest of me won't give up and go to sleep."

"Do you want me to make you a cup of tea?" Bonnie grabbed one of the grippers she kept in every room and used it to pick up the ear. She laid it next to the bunny's body, ready to be attached the next day. She tugged her rollator closer, snapped on the brakes, and used it to stand. "Chamomile or Sleepytime?"

"Neither. Tea will just make me have to go to the bathroom, as if I don't do that often enough during the night." Mom grimaced and fanned herself with the book. "Besides, it'll only make me warmer. Is it me or is it hot in here?"

Bonnie hid a smile at her mother's disgruntled tone. "It's you. Sit with me while I make myself one."

"You shouldn't be drinking tea this late either."

Mom lived in fear that Bonnie would get up during the night and fall in the dark. Even though Dad and her uncle Uri had remodeled the house so her bedroom was next to a new bathroom that had doors wide enough to get her rollator through, a shower with zero entry, and bars by the toilet and in the shower, which even had a seat. It was fancy for a Plain home, but the elders agreed it was necessary for a family member with her disease. Bonnie had a propane lamp next to her bed within easy reach and a railing to help her get out of the bed. A person ought to be able to do that much for herself. "Mamm."

"I know, I know." Mom's expression brightened. "But you do have to work in the morning."

"You know me. I've never needed much sleep."

Or been able to sleep. Migraine headaches often kept Bonnie awake as she grew older, which made concentrating at school harder. And when she didn't have a headache, she simply couldn't get comfortable. Many nights she gave up and read her favorite mysteries—she preferred Colleen Coble or Carrie Stuart Parks—with the help of a flashlight after her parents went to bed.

Had life been different, she would've had the perfect sleep schedule for courting. Friends had picked her up for late-night jaunts during her rumspringa, which had been fun but no more fruitful than the singings when it came to courting. Which brought her right back to Elijah. "Grrrrr."

"Now who's growling like a grumpy old woman? You're chewing on something mighty grisly." Mom headed to the kitchen in front of Bonnie. She swept her hair behind her shoulders, twisted it in a knot, and let go. Even at fifty she still had thick, shiny dark-brown hair. "It stings, whatever it is."

Mom might forgive Elijah for bringing Slowpoke into the store, but she still wouldn't include him on her favorites list. Bonnie had plenty of other concerns to plumb. "I'm determined to finish a dozen stuffies this week, even if Opal can't help me."

"She was definitely puny on Sunday."

"More like worn-out." Bonnie settled the teakettle on the stove and turned on the flame. "Tucker is just getting over the croup. Now he has an ear infection."

"And her with morning sickness."

"I have an order for stuffed animals for Margie's day care." Bonnie took her favorite mug, handcrafted and fired by a friend she met at the clinic, from the cabinet. She added a Sleepytime tea bag. "The sheriff's department wants a stash of my animals to give to kinner when they're victims or witnesses to crimes."

"It's nice that they want your animals for such a worthy cause."

Mom plopped a few pieces of ice into a glass and carried it to the table. Her usual hot flash remedy. "You're blessed that business is gut."

"Very blessed." Bonnie picked up her mug. A second later it shattered on the pine floor. "Ach, nee." She stared at the pieces of fired clay, then at her empty hands. What just happened? How could she have dropped it? "I don't understand it. I really don't."

"It's okay, Dochder." Mom trotted across the kitchen. "I'll get it."

"Nee, you're barefoot." Bonnie pushed her rollator to the shelves where she'd left her gripper. "I'll get the big pieces, if you can grab the broom for me."

"Teamwork." Mom hummed "Bringing in the Sheaves" under her breath. "I don't mind helping. It makes me feel still needed."

Such bittersweetness haunted her words. Such longing. She would always be needed. If only it wasn't to pick up this keepsake mug.

"I'll always need you, Mamm." Maybe not in the ways she'd needed her as a child, but to navigate adulthood as a woman with disabilities who had to prove her abilities twice or three times more than people with no disabilities. "For your advice, for sure and for certain."

"You'll marry one day, don't think you won't." Mom stooped to position the dustpan. She made quick work of the remaining shards. "You just need to get out of your own way."

"Mamm, did you even see what just happened?" Bonnie shook the gripper at her. "I dropped the mug for no good reason. None at all. It just . . . slipped."

Humming once more, Mom emptied the dustpan and returned it and the broom to their rightful places. She went to the cabinet and retrieved another mug, which she immediately handed to Bonnie. "You dropped a mug. It's like falling. It happens."

"Say that all you want, but it's not the same and you know it." Bonnie set the cup on the counter next to the stove. She turned off the flame. "It's getting worse."

The ache in her throat made it impossible to continue. Bonnie made her tea and set the cup on her rollator seat, along with honey and a spoon. She rolled to the table without another word.

"Have you been taking your medication?"

"Of course I have." Studies had shown the drug was effective in slowing progression in all three types of SMA, Bonnie's doctor had assured her. And it had. For three years. "I'm a grown woman who knows how important it is."

And it was getting harder to get the lid off the pills' container. That had to be the definition of irony.

"If it's progressing, we'll deal with it."

"So stop talking about marriage as if it's part of Gott's plan." The quiver in her voice shamed Bonnie. Her mother had dealt with enough pain in her life. Bonnie always endeavored not to add more. "I'm blessed to have the store, gut friends, and family."

"You have your four-month appointment coming up next week. I'll call tomorrow and confirm it." Mom tugged a piece of ice from her glass. She rubbed it across her cheeks and down her neck. "They'll run tests. It's better to know than not know."

"I agree, but you're missing my point."

"I'm not missing it. I'm ignoring it." Mom popped another chunk of ice in her mouth. "It's not just Gott's plan but also His timing. I plan to keep praying. That's what we're supposed to do."

Yes, it was. But by the same token, she shouldn't blame Bonnie for choosing to be realistic rather than setting herself up for disappointment. Of course, the elders would call it a serious lack of faith.

"You don't believe Gott can bring you a man who will love you exactly as you are?" Mom's frown shot a quiver full of disappointed arrows at Bonnie. "I can hear Him now, *Oh ye of little faith.*"

Bonnie lifted her bent right leg up onto her left knee. Taking her time, she undid the Velcro that held the brace—which her doctor called an ankle-foot orthotic because all medical stuff had to have difficult, mysterious names—to her calf. She untied the sneaker and pulled it off her foot. Her toes wiggled their relief. "I believe. I also believe He has better things to think about."

"He knows how many hairs you have on your head. He knew your name before you were born." Now Mom was getting fired up on her favorite topic. If Plain women could preach, she would surely draw the lot. What would Bart say about such a thought? A wild flight of fancy, no doubt. "He will bring you through this season. And if your SMA is progressing, He'll make sure you're surrounded by family and friends who'll take care of you."

I don't want anyone taking care of me. Bonnie bit back the mulish sentiment. What twenty-five-year-old woman did?

"That includes me. I'm in gut health. Gott willing I'll be around a bit longer." Mom rolled the glass with its melting ice across her forehead. Suddenly she plunked it on the table. "In fact, I can help you right now. I can take Opal's place doing the fine sewing for your stuffies."

A smile of triumph lined her face, and she popped another piece of ice in her mouth and crunched.

Bonnie worked on the other brace. The left leg was harder. The severe spasticity made it more difficult to get her leg propped up on her right knee. Mom's idea had merit. So why did it feel like a step back? No pun intended. "We pay Opal for her work. It's not much—"

"I work for free. See, even better than having Opal do it."

"Are you talking about coming into the store to work?"

"Why not? Not every day, of course. Only when you have work for me to do. You have a great workspace in the back. It's a perfect way for me to help with the store's bottom line. Plus I can drive us into town in the buggy on the days I come in. It'll save you the cost of the van."

And she could take care of her only daughter. What would it be like to have her eyes and ears—however well meaning—overseeing Bonnie's every move at home and at the store? Plain families worked together all the time. Why should Bonnie's be any different?

Because I want to be treated like a grown-up.

"Do you not want me at the store?" The excitement faded from Mom's voice. She pushed her glasses up her nose with her index finger. "Because if you don't, I can do the work here just as well."

"Of course I do." Maybe this wasn't about Bonnie. It was about her mother being lonely and alone in this house without Dad coming and going from the fields each day. A small garden. A bit of laundry. No need for a lot of baking. Meals for two. No grandkids. *Don't be selfish.* "Of course you'll come into the store. The more hands, the better."

"Wunderbarr. Be sure you take your socks off before you walk back to your bedroom." Her glass of melting ice in one hand, Mom stood. She handed Bonnie the gripper. "You know how slick socks can be on these wooden floors."

Bonnie didn't need to be reminded, but that's what moms did. She accepted the gripper and used it to work off the sock so she could plop it on the rollator seat with her sneakers.

Mom picked up her book and tucked it under her arm. "We're having a canning frolic at your aenti Frannie's tomorrow. I'll plan to come to the store on Wednesday. For now, we really do have to go to bed. Chet will be honking his horn at the crack of dawn. I'll make waffles and bacon. Waffles sound gut, don't they?"

"Waffles sound great." Bonnie squeezed her tea mug on the rollator seat with her shoes. She pulled herself up on her bare feet. They felt deliciously cool. "Danki for offering to help. It'll be gut."

"Jah. And I'll be right there to help you up if you fall again."

Such a well-meaning sentiment. It came straight from her motherly heart.

All the same, part of life was learning to pick up oneself all on her lonesome.

Mom paused at the door once again. "Don't worry; I won't forget to confirm your appointment for next week."

If only they could both forget. Instead they were reminded every time Bonnie dropped something, every time she picked up a needle, every time her hands refused to do the simplest task. "Of course you will."

Chapter 13

Putting on a happy face took far more energy than simply letting your true face hang out for all to see. Jocelyn heaved a sigh as she turned to go back into the house. Chet's van left a trail of dust and gas fumes behind as it disappeared down the dirt road that led to the highway. The driver was in fine form today with his "Top of the morning to you," hat-doffing, and smile that seemed to spread from east to west as far as the eye could see. Maybe he would cheer up Bonnie.

Likely tired from staying up so late the night before, the girl had been as mum as a monk practicing a vow of silence at breakfast. She'd hardly touched her waffles. Jocelyn had been tempted to take her temperature to see if she was coming down with something.

Only that would be classified as coddling a grown woman. Jocelyn snorted. She grabbed a plate sticky with maple syrup and plunged it into soapy water. Bubbles and a lemon scent arose, lightening her mood for a second. Bonnie might be a grown woman, but she often acted like a child when it came to taking care of herself the way her disease required. Maybe Jocelyn did bug her about it too much. "How am I supposed to know when enough is enough, Gott?"

No answer. God probably wasn't happy with Jocelyn's less-than-placid mood today. "Es dutt mer, Gott."

Momma Cat meowed at the screen door. "Jah, jah, I'm coming." Drying her hands as she went, Jocelyn trotted to the back door and let the feline in. "This is our little secret, missy. Don't be telling Bonnie I let you in the house. She'll get a big kick out of it. Don't take your sweet time either. I have to leave for Uri's as soon as I wash the dishes. All the other chores are done."

Bonnie had fed the chickens and collected the eggs while Jocelyn took care of the horses and their two dairy cattle. Milking them always made her feel closer to Marlin. He loved fresh milk with his fresh over-easy eggs in the morning, fried potatoes, thick slabs of bacon, and homemade toasted bread slathered with her strawberry preserves. *"I'm a growing bu,"* he would say with a grin when she added another piece of toast to his plate and topped off his coffee mug. Jocelyn was lucky if Bonnie wanted a single slice of bacon with her toast smeared with apple butter.

Those trips down memory lane didn't hurt the way they once had. A twinge of guilt grew and rippled through Jocelyn. Was she forgetting him already? No, simply learning to live without him. That realization felt like a bandage ripped off with no allowance for the skin it took with it.

Momma Cat wound herself around Jocelyn's ankles. Her purr filled the quiet kitchen. "I know, I know. I get distracted easily, don't I?"

A sign of impending old age. Or of a person who slogged around in the miry pit of worries instead of taking them to the throne and leaving them there like a good Christian believer.

Jocelyn filled a bowl with water and set it on the welcome rug in front of the door. She opened a can of salmon-flavored food from the stash she kept behind the canned goods on the bottom shelf. It smelled almost good enough to eat herself. Almost. "Here you go. You're queen of the cats for the day, aren't you?"

Momma Cat didn't deign to respond. She was too busy chowing down.

A sudden knocking quickly turned into pounding. An impatient someone was at the front door. Maybe it was Theo. What reason would he have for turning up on her doorstep now? The frolic had left the house and grounds in tip-top shape. Plus surely he knew Jocelyn was due at Uriah's today for the canning frolic. Past due.

She strode down the hallway to the door. "Coming, coming." She swung it open. "I'm here."

A tall English man—a stranger—stood on the porch. He wore tan slacks, a crisply starched long-sleeved white shirt, and a thin red tie. The scent of spicy aftershave wafted from him on a humid breeze that felt like summer. It was only nine o'clock and already warmer than the previous day. In one hand her visitor clutched a leather briefcase. "Hello, ma'am. Would you be Jocelyn Yoder?"

"We don't need any insurance. We bought books from the salesman who came through last month, and we're stocked up on smoke alarms." Jocelyn moved to close the door. "But thanks for thinking of us."

"I'm not selling anything. I'm buying, and I think you'll want to hear me out." His smile, full of unnaturally white teeth, brought out deep dimples. He sounded so sure of himself. "I promise if you don't, you'll kick yourself later."

"I doubt that. I don't have anything for sale."

The stranger swept his free hand to his left, then his right. A ray of sun caught the gold watch band on his wrist. It sparkled. "Oh, but you do. I'm Logan Knox. I'm a real estate agent, and I'm authorized to make a very substantial, significant offer on your farm, Mrs. Yoder."

"It's not for sale—"

"Please hear me out, Jocelyn. Can I call you Jocelyn? Such a pretty name. I'd love to sit down with you over a cup of coffee and talk about the terms my client is willing to offer you."

Irritation welled in Jocelyn. The man knew how to gab, but he didn't seem to use his ears for much. "My farm is not for sale." She hung on to her manners by the hair on her chinny chin chin— yes, they were there and no amount of plucking kept them at bay. "My husband left it to me and my daughter. I wouldn't dream of selling it."

Nor would she invite an unrelated man into her house for coffee or any other beverage. The man knew nothing about Plain people if he didn't know this simple edict.

"It's just you and your daughter, isn't it? A good piece of farmland, a hundred acres that haven't been planted in two years. You're paying taxes on a piece of nonrevenue-producing property. It's obvious it's too much for you and your daughter alone to manage. Your daughter is disabled, isn't she?"

"That's none of your business, Mr. Knox." Her manners flagged a tad. How dare he bring Bonnie into this? She was a hard worker. She co-owned a business. Any faults in the management of the farm were Jocelyn's alone. "Thank you, but this conversation is over."

Jocelyn almost had the door shut. Mr. Knox squeezed a white card through the crack—his business card. Jocelyn took it. She turned and leaned against the door. More to prop herself up on shaking legs than to make sure he didn't try to breach her house. The fancy script told her Virginia Realty was located on Third Street, not far from Homespun Handicrafts. Not interested in buying or selling real estate, she'd never noticed it. Why had he zeroed in on her property? How did he know it hadn't been planted since Marlin's death? How did he know about Bonnie? Had he been spying on them?

All questions she couldn't answer. It didn't matter. She'd said no and that was the end of the conversation.

An hour later the conversation started all over again when she told Uriah about it the minute she hopped from her buggy parked in front of his house.

"How much were they offering?" Her brother tied the reins to the hitching post, but his gaze stayed on her. "Who's his client?"

"What? Why does that matter?" Jocelyn held out the offending business card. Uriah took it, read it, and instead of handing it back, stuck it in his pants pocket. Why? "The farm isn't for sale, obviously. Why are you keeping his card?"

Uriah craned his neck side to side. He swiped at a horsefly that buzzed near Jocelyn, then took aim at another. "The man's not wrong. It's a nice piece of property sitting idle. We haven't had the workers to farm both my place and yours. I'd hope to do it this year, but I'm not sure we'll have enough workers in the district."

So many of the Plain men now worked in other occupations as family farms became harder to sustain. Some farmed hogs or chickens and didn't have time to work her land.

The money she and Marlin had saved over the years had tided her over so far. Bonnie earned her keep with the store, but her income wasn't enough to cover all the bills. "I'll farm it myself."

"Just you with your bad back and Bonnie with her rollator."

"I'll hire a couple of workers."

"A couple won't be enough, and with what money?" Uriah smoothed the Morgan's silky withers. Buster responded with an appreciative neigh. "I'm not trying to discourage you, Schweschder. I'm trying to be realistic. If they offer a good price, you'd have a nest egg. We have room for you and Bonnie here. Or you could stay with Nan or Luke or John."

Passed from sibling to sibling with no place to call their own. How had this suddenly become a thing? Just because some stranger showed up at their door. "Why hadn't you brought this up before?"

"We agreed to wait until you had time to grieve. It didn't seem right to spring it on you so soon after Marlin's passing."

As if there'd ever be a good time. Then it hit Jocelyn. "So you've actually been talking about this for a while?"

"The topic came up." Now Uriah had the good grace to look uncomfortable. "You and Bonnie shouldn't be living there alone, especially with her health being what it is. You'd be better off with family."

"I'm capable of taking care of Bonnie and myself."

"For now. But what about later when you're older?"

"One minute you're trying to fix me up with a man I don't even know. The next you've got me living with brieder or schweschdre because I'm older than dirt and not able to fend for myself. Which clearly makes no sense because you're older than I am. So which is it?"

The difference being that he was a man.

The sound of a throat clearing filled the pause necessary for Jocelyn to draw a breath. Startled, she glanced over her shoulder. The usual faint amusement on his face, Theo approached from the direction of the barn. It was hard to know if he'd heard her tirade or just found life that humorous.

"I'm older than both of you. I guess that makes me older than two tons of dirt." He brushed hay from his pants with hands big enough to hold a watermelon in each one. "I'm feeling it today after planting corn all morning."

He'd heard.

Heat scalded Jocelyn's cheeks. Her neck burned. Words refused to behave and line up so she could gloss over her earlier statement. *"Fix me up with a man I don't even know."* "It's just, I was, I'm, someone's trying to buy my farm."

"It's a sweet piece of property, for sure and for certain." Sweat darkened the band on Theo's straw hat. He tugged a bandanna from his pants pocket and wiped down his face and neck. "I wouldn't sell it for less than seven hundred thousand."

"You think? That seems high." Uriah walked past Jocelyn like she wasn't even standing there. "I've seen some properties in Cumberland County go for as little as five thousand an acre."

"You have to figure in the location, plus the house, the barn, the other outbuildings, the farm equipment. I may even be low-balling it."

"You can stop selling off my farm out from under me right now." Jocelyn grabbed her sewing basket from the buggy. She needed to get inside before she said something she regretted. "I don't see either of you talking about selling *your* farms."

Because they were men.

"I did sell my farm." Theo's voice turned low. "Right after my fraa died. They say you shouldn't make any big decisions in the midst of grief. They're right."

Caught by the pain he tried to hide, Jocelyn swallowed against a sudden lump in her throat. She gripped the basket handle so hard it hurt her fingers. "You regret it, then?"

"I wanted a fresh start. I got one. But I wasn't thinking of my suh. He's farming with his special friend's father, so I don't get to see him much. It pains me to know I hurt him by not consulting him first. He grew up in that house. Worked the fields with me. Now it's gone to a nice English couple who don't know anything about farming."

The lines around Theo's eyes and mouth deepened, making him look older than his years. His face was red with heat and humidity. His gaze met hers head-on, the teak eyes so full of veiled emotion. She swallowed hard. "But you got your fresh start?"

He shrugged. "I did. I paid a price, but I did."

"I don't need a fresh start, so I'd thank you to keep that nose out of my business."

There was that big nose again.

An odd, undefinable emotion flitted across Theo's rugged face. His shrug was almost imperceptible, and this time he didn't smile.

"No need to be rude." Frowning, Uriah stuck his hands on his hips. "Theo knows a lot more about this stuff than you do."

"She's right, though. It's none of my business." The emotion was gone, replaced with a neutral tone that matched his blank stare. "I keep sticking my nose where it don't belong."

It had been funny that day at the house. Not so now.

"I better get inside and get to work."

"We'll talk about this later." Uriah's voice followed Jocelyn up the steps to the door. "When you're not so wound up about it."

Wound up? Her brother hadn't seen wound up. Not yet. In the end women had to submit to the men in their lives, but that didn't mean she couldn't speak her piece first. Good thing, or she might blow an artery trying to contain it.

Chapter 14

*B*onnie never went into Fabrics and Notions alone. She had a pact with Sophia and Carol. Sophia always accompanied her. Otherwise Bonnie would blow Homespun Handicrafts' profits on a rainbow of materials and "just one more pattern." If she had an addiction, it was sewing notions and fabric. That addiction was on full display. Maybe because it was getting harder and harder to use her hands.

She shrugged off the melancholy thoughts that had plagued her after Chet picked her up earlier in the day and entertained her with a rousing rendition of "Up from the Grave He Arose."

The man had a great voice, he was a good people-reader, and he had good intentions.

But he couldn't fix her hands.

The first day of May was a dreary one that promised rain, but it delivered a measly hit-or-miss sprinkle that only served to increase the humidity. It was supposed to be approaching summer, yet finicky spring weather continued to plague the area, making it impossible to know whether to wear a coat, a shawl, a sweater, or none of the above.

No pity parties allowed. Instead Bonnie had permitted herself thirty minutes in her second most favorite store behind Homespun Handicrafts. Simply walking through the door to see shears, thimbles, needles, and threads lifted her spirits. Not to mention the scent of industriousness. That was how sewing felt: industrious. "Look, Soph, at this cute purple-and-lilac paisley." Bonnie held up a bolt of cotton material. "Wouldn't this make the cutest cat? I saw a new pattern—"

"Easy, maedel." Sophia reached up to tug the fabric from Bonnie's hands. "We agreed. Three kinds of material. Three patterns. You already have a sloth, a flamingo, and a unicorn."

How could she limit herself to three fabrics when the store had row upon row of bolts—cottons, denims, polyesters, blends, flannels, jerseys, rayon—in every color and print imaginable? Not to mention the six five-foot-high spinning racks of patterns. Women's clothes, men's clothes, children's clothes, doll clothes, stuffed animals, dog beds. Even dogs' coats. "Jah, but—"

"No buts. You can use the pink polka-dotted material for both the flamingo and the pig."

"Nee, the flamingo needs to be hot pink. I saw some on the clearance rack."

"Well, if it's on sale, of course." Sophia's eye roll coupled with her sarcastic tone said she wasn't buying that logic. "It's on sale because it's ugly, and no one wants a hot-pink flamingo. Go with the pink polka dots."

"What do you know about material? You're a painter."

"With an eye for color." Sophia laid the bolt in her lap. She wheeled her chair around to the row from which the bolt had come. Without an iota of pity on display for Bonnie, she stuck the bolt back on the shelf between a big sunflower print and a too-stretchy maroon jersey material. Next to it was a darling white flannel with kittens and puppies on it that would make cute pj's for the English dolls. Sophia must've seen the desire on Bonnie's face. "Don't even think about it. Hey, isn't that Patience Coblentz and Mary Eash? Let's say hallo."

This would be a lot better medicine for the blues if Sophia would give an inch on Bonnie's purchases. Trying to distract her wouldn't work. Still, Bonnie tore her gaze from the flannel to see two women standing side by side at the pattern racks. Most Plain women could make pants, dresses, shirts, and such in their sleep. They didn't need patterns. They could even make doll clothes from the scraps without patterns. But it was still fun to browse. Or make stuffed animals for their children. In these women's cases, their grandchildren.

"On second thought, you go say hallo. I'm going to visit the restroom. My bag overfloweth." With a wry grin, Sophia cocked her head toward the back. "I love that Miriam remodeled the restroom to make it more accessible."

"Take your time."

"Just remember, I plan to check your basket when I return. No sneaking purchases."

"Like I can sneak a bolt past you."

"Go say hallo. I'll be right back."

Mary and Patience stood with their backs to the store. They chattered as they spun their racks to check out patterns for doll clothes, teddy bears, bunnies, lions, and more. The lion pattern had called Bonnie's name, but Sophia nixed the idea. Not until Bonnie used every pattern she'd bought the last trip to Fabrics and Notions.

"Kathryn really likes the idea of working at Millers' Combination Store. She says Elizabeth and the girls make it fun." Patience held up a boa snake pattern. Mary shook her head. Patience returned the pattern to her rack. "Of course, it doesn't hurt that Elijah will be around when he's not auctioneering. She says they're selling his toys and such in the store now. He'll be in and out of the store bringing in new inventory."

The unspoken words *if all goes well* ended her sentence.

At the mention of Elijah's name, Bonnie paused. Not eavesdropping. Simply surprised. So he did plan to call auctions. He had to bow to his father's wishes. Any good Plain son would.

Mary spun the rack until it stopped at doll clothes. "Did he seem interested?"

"Who can tell with that man? He hardly says a word. The cat didn't just take his tongue; he hid it somewhere permanently."

"But Kathryn's interested?"

"She doesn't say it, but it's obvious. I'm pretty sure she visited his workshop last night while Menno and me talked with Charlie and Elizabeth. She had the strangest look on her face after she supposedly went for a walk. She told Elizabeth she'd changed her mind about the job."

Patience sighed. "Fortunately, Elizabeth talked her out of it. She needs a job since the Englischers moved their grandmother to assisted living. No more cooking and cleaning for her. I'm hoping this will be the last one, though. She'll be twenty-four in a few months. Maybe Elijah will wake up and notice her if she's around every day."

Over for supper. Visited the workshop. Working there every day. Why would Elizabeth choose to matchmake with Kathryn if she hadn't seen a spark of interest from Elijah? Why did any of the mothers in the district matchmake? They pretended to let nature take its course during rumspringa, but everyone knew they were on pin and needles—sometimes for years.

Enough. Bonnie retrieved her manners. "Hallo, ladies. Fancy running into you here."

117

Patience turned first. "Ach, Bonnie, we were so busy jawing, we didn't hear you come up. How're you doing? How's your mudder doing?"

That question asked with that certain tone of honeyed concern shouldn't grate, but it did. No doubt Patience really wanted to know. By the same token, Bonnie's health shouldn't be the first order of business in every conversation. "I'm gut. Really gut. Mamm is gut. Did you find some fun patterns?"

As usual it was her job to steer the conversation toward more interesting topics. In this case, Kathryn's new job. How did she get there without revealing that she'd heard more than her share of the women's conversation?

"Just browsing." Mary waved at the racks in dismissal. "Why go to the trouble of making stuffies for the grandkids when we can buy them from your store?"

Because it would be cheaper. Bonnie didn't voice that thought. The Plain women in her district thought the shop's prices were high. They were. She and her partners set prices according to their primary customer—tourists who could and would pay more. Neither Mary nor Patience would buy from the shop. They made birthday and Christmas gifts just like everyone else. "I thought I heard you say Kathryn got a job working for the Millers."

"Jah, in the store. Today is her first full day." Despite her early comments, Patience managed to appear happy about it. "I think it'll be a nice change after spending so much time caring for Mrs. Danforth. Taking care of all her needs was rewarding, but watching her health decline was hard. I'm hoping this will be Kathryn's last job before she marries."

Bonnie thumbed through packages of buttons. Every color, round, square, rectangle, metal, plastic, glass, vintage, two holes, four holes. A woman couldn't have enough buttons. Of course

Bonnie had two fruitcake tins full of buttons at the store and another one at home.

Still, the red ones shaped like stars would make cute eyes. She touched their smooth surfaces. So small. Threading a needle and then pushing that needle through the tiny holes on the back—it would be hard for adept sewers. Impossible for Bonnie.

Stop feeling sorry for yourself. You have a mudder who wants to help, who's happy to help.

So true. She was blessed. Bonnie slipped them in her basket. "Kathryn has a beau, then."

Just the right touch of disinterest in her voice.

"You probably know more about that than I do."

Bonnie glanced up. Patience's face was full of innocence. That hadn't been a dig, even though they likely knew Bonnie didn't go to singings. She didn't run around. She hadn't done much of that even before her baptism. They couldn't help but know of Bonnie's perennial lack of a suitor. Women talked. Just as Patience and Mary had been talking while browsing. A perfect time to gossip *and* solve their children's problems. "I don't."

"I heard Elijah Miller is selling his toys at your shop." Mary adopted the same tone of disinterest. "I'd love to see some of his toys. Kathryn says they're nice. They must sell well in your store."

"We don't have his toys and furniture out."

Her business dealings were confidential.

"Then I guess it's true he's really going to try again to call auctions." Patience perused a pattern for a dog bed, then discarded it. Plain dogs slept on old rugs or in the barn. "His dat wants that, so I reckon he'll have the last word. Any woman who marries a Miller better be prepared to stand on her own two feet six months out of the year."

"If he doesn't freeze up again." Mary picked up a basket sitting on a nearby pile of fabric remnants stacked on a clearance table. "I better skedaddle. Lunch isn't going to make itself."

"I reckon he will. I've never met a man so tightly wound into himself. I'd better go too." Patience dropped the lion pattern in her basket. Her cheeks turned pink. "I need to make a birthday present for James's youngest. He'll be one next month."

So she was thinking of how Kathryn would adapt to such a life. Putting the horse before the buggy.

"He's not tightly wound. He just doesn't like being the center of attention," Bonnie blurted out. Such a quality was supposed to be an admirable one, one to which Plain folks aspired. "He's quiet because he thinks before he speaks."

Something to which these ladies could aspire.

Patience wrinkled her nose in a frown. Probably wondering how Bonnie knew so much about Elijah's qualities. "He probably doesn't listen to conversations that don't involve him either."

Ouch.

"Have a gut day."

"You too."

"Her face was the color of steamed eggplant." Sophia wheeled to a stop in the next aisle. "What did you say to her?"

"I may have called her out for gossiping."

"About what?"

"If I told you, I'd be gossiping."

"You're no fun." Sophia led the way to the cash register. She took it upon herself to move Bonnie's items to the counter. The star buttons stayed, but the lion pattern went into the cashier's return-to-shelf cart.

Bonnie pretended to pout while the cashier held the door so they could both exit. "You're no fun either."

Out on the street, a soft sprinkle dampened her face. Bonnie put her hand to her forehead and squinted. Several cars were parked across the street at the shop. Good. Again, she was blessed.

"Looks like we've got a full store." Sophia wheeled down to the accessible curb cut. She stopped and peered both ways. "Even Slowpoke showed up. Elijah must've made him stay outside."

One buggy sat between two SUVs with Pennsylvania tags. Slowpoke did occupy the seat. Which meant Elijah couldn't be far away.

"We'd better hustle." Sophia wheeled into the street in the crosswalk. "With Hannah off today, Carol will need our help."

"You go on. I want to stop into the bakery."

"Your mamm sent blueberry muffins."

"They'll be gone by now."

"What's with you? You've been dying to see if Elijah would come back."

She hadn't said a word to her friends about Elijah. Now they were stopped in the middle of the street in downtown Lee's Gulch, and Sophia brought it up. Bonnie set her bag in her friend's lap. "Have not. Tell Carol I'm right behind you."

"I can read your face better than anyone else." Sophia flapped her arms. "Chicken. *Bawk, bawk, bawk.*"

"I'm not a chicken—"

"Are too."

A familiar bell dinged. Elijah poked his head out the shop's door. "Carol says to get out of the street before you get hit by a car."

He closed the door.

"That wasn't embarrassing at all." Sophia wheeled forward. "Now you have to go in."

Bonnie followed. She might have to enter the store, but she didn't have to like it.

Or Elijah.

Chapter 15

When two grown, wind-blown Plain women argued in the middle of a damp street, jabbing index fingers in the air, something was up. Elijah studied Bonnie and Sophia. Sophia held their Fabrics and Notions bags in her lap. Bonnie had one hand on her prayer covering to keep it from blowing away. Their cheeks were red, but that was probably from the chilly wind that once again refused to acknowledge that May had arrived. A car slowed and honked. Finally, they rolled out of the street.

Sophia entered the store first. She waved at Elijah and kept on going toward Carol, who was deep in conversation with a customer interested in her embroidery classes. Bonnie rolled through the door, into the store, and past him without a wave—in fact, with barely an acknowledgment. What had he done? He followed in her wake.

She glanced back and kept going. What was her hurry? Elijah quickened his pace. "I brought a few items—not everything we agreed to, but a few until I can make more."

Bonnie stopped so suddenly, Elijah had to detour around a greeting card rack to avoid colliding with her. She made a U-turn. "You're not here to pick up your merchandise?"

So she'd assumed the worst. That didn't seem like her. "Nee."

"I heard your wares are on sale at the combination store."

How did she hear that? The Plain grapevine could choke the life out of a person. Elijah took off his hat. He held it in both hands. It gave them something to do. "Is that a problem? My mamm did it without asking me. I can take them out."

No change in her expression. Did she find it strange that his mom did this without asking him? She chewed on her lower lip. She shrugged. "How will you keep up with demand if you're on the road?"

"It's temporary. Until Jason comes back."

Bonnie didn't crack a smile. She didn't seem pleased. She definitely wasn't the woman who stood next to him at the corral eating cookies and drinking coffee the previous day. "I see. It's up to you if you sell in two locations, but you can't sell your items for less at the combination store. You'll undercut your sales here. Which will affect our bottom line as well as yours."

Business. Strictly business. "I'll talk to Mamm when I get home."

Mom didn't need his stuff in the store. He would get it out and bring it to Homespun Handicrafts.

"Bring in what you have, price your merchandise, and then you can be on your way." Bonnie resumed her trek to the workroom. The air was so frigid that a man might think it was midwinter and all the doors and windows had been left open. "I'm sure you're eager to get back home."

Far from it. Declan would be waiting for him to practice some more while Elijah washed the trucks to get ready for the road trip. Elijah had practiced so much that he dreamed he was calling auctions. Loudly, in Deutsch. Sometimes it went well. Sometimes he stuttered and couldn't speak English. Sometimes he couldn't remember how to talk at all. He'd wake up in a cold sweat, trembling, his heart pounding. "We leave tomorrow for Charm."

Head bent, Bonnie scooped up a folder from her desk and laid it on her rollator. She slipped around the table and faced him. "Have a seat." The oomph had gone out of her voice. Dark smudges spread under both eyes. She wasn't sleeping well either. "How long will you be gone?"

Three weeks. Too long. Too many opportunities for him to try and fail. Too long when he could be in his workshop creating toys kids would love. Instead of sitting, Elijah went to the work-table along one wall. A panda bear still lacking his face lay next to Bonnie's sewing machine. Elijah picked it up. The material was soft in his calloused hand. The stuffing was spongy, just right for hugging, just right for a child to cuddle while falling asleep at night. "I like pandas."

"I do too." Bonnie didn't sit either. She followed him. He held out the panda. Her expression softer, she took it. "It's funny, isn't it, how we both make animals but in different media? You with your wood, me with my material and my sewing machine."

"Kinner like them both."

"Do you think about the kinner who will play with the toys you make?"

"All the time." Elijah touched the tissue pattern pinned to a piece of floral cotton. It appeared to be a bunny ear. "I have lots of time to think while I measure, saw, sand, stain, and finish pieces, or when I'm just whittling a little animal the size of my palm. I hope the kinner find joy in riding the rocking horse or pretending to be on Noah's ark with all the animals coming in two by two. I hope they pretend to be farmers with the corral and the horses and cows and pigs."

That had to be more than he'd ever said to any woman ever. Each time he saw Bonnie, it became a little easier to talk to her.

Her expression pensive, she stroked a piece of felt. "I hope a little girl instantly loves my bunny rabbit. She takes it with her to bed every night. When storms and the thunder crashes so loud outside her window, she cuddles it close and finds comfort. She carries it around for so long, it gets ragged and faded. Finally, when she's ready to go to school, she leaves the bunny on her bed, an old friend but one she doesn't need with her all the time anymore."

Her imagination matched Elijah's. "Did you have a bunny friend when you were growing up?"

"Not a bunny. A lamb. It was just me and my little lamb. I played by myself a lot. So Baa was my friend. She followed me around just like Mary from the nursery rhyme. We ate our meals together. I read to her. When I learned to sew, I made clothes for her. I fed her eppies when Mamm baked."

"It's hard for me to imagine being an only child."

"I'm sure it is, what with all your brieder and schweschdre."

"Are you mad at me?" Elijah hadn't meant to ask the question outright. Somehow it slipped between the bars and escaped.

"Nee, not at you. Of course not." Bonnie straightened the tomato pin cushion, shears, and seam ripper. Her head bent, she tossed a few scraps of material into a bin next to the table. "I'm just turning into a grumpy old woman like my mamm."

"You're not old."

"It's a figure of speech. We'd better get you squared away." Her rollator's wheels squeaking on the vinyl floor, she headed back to the table used for shop business. "You never did say how long you'll be away."

"Three weeks." He settled into a chair. She might be in a hurry to conclude their business, but he wasn't. He could listen to her talk for hours. "Two auctions in Charm, one in Sugar Creek, and one in Millersburg." But for now, he was here with Bonnie. "Can you help me decide how to price them?"

"I'm happy to do it." She shuffled the papers together. "Would you like to practice calling while we price the toys?"

The lack of segue between the two sentences stumped Elijah for a second. She wanted to help him practice? It didn't make sense. If she supported his desire to start his own business, why would she want him to succeed at calling?

Besides, he couldn't call in front of her. The idea summoned a cold sweat on his face and under his arms. "I don't think so." His throat had gone dry. His tongue swelled—or was that his imagination? "It takes all my concentration to do arithmetic. I was never gut at it in school."

"I'm a friendly audience. I thought that might help."

"Danki, but I don't think I can."

Her frown was back. No matter what Elijah said after that, Bonnie kept the conversation focused on pricing his toys and furniture. It took more than an hour. Finally he placed the tag on the push mower and set it back on the shelf. "That's that."

"That's that." She stuck a bag of blank tags in a cabinet next to the storage shelves. The black felt-tip markers went into a pencil holder on the desk. "You can come back at your convenience when you return to Lee's Gulch. We'll have a sales report for you, and we can discuss whether to replace inventory."

So formal. The warm, chatty Bonnie had been replaced by shop owner Bonnie again.

She couldn't know she'd landed squarely on Elijah's greatest conundrum. If he overcame his fear of calling auctions, should he still want his own business? Should he abandon his dream in favor of his family's business? Even Elijah hadn't really considered the possibility of this result. Or at least he hadn't admitted it to himself.

No matter what happened with auctioneering, as long as he had merchandise at Homespun Handicrafts, he had an excuse to come to the shop. In other words, he had an excuse to see Bonnie again.

"Will do." He tipped his hat to her and scrambled from the office before he told her as much.

Chapter 16

*I*f Bonnie could've tiptoed, she would've. Past Sophia and Carol, out the front door, and down the street. The shop usually served as a place where she could take her mind off her troubles. Today her troubles visited her at the store. Instead of fleeing, she went to the clearance shelves closest to the shop's front windows. This would be a perfect spot to build the new display of Elijah's toys.

"Hey, what's with you and Elijah?" Sophia must have eyes in the back of her head. She wheeled around by the coffee bar so she faced Bonnie. "He ran out of here looking like a wet towel that somebody just ran through the wringer."

"He brought in a few more of his toys." Bonnie lifted the seat on her rollator. She laid some spice-scented candles in its pouch. Winter and the time for cozy scents and warm candles had passed. "Then we priced his merchandise. That's it."

"Sure it is." Carol swung on her crutches to a table usually reserved for customers who decided to take a break from shopping to have a pastry and a cup of coffee. "Soph told me how you didn't want to come into the shop when you saw Slowpoke outside. Was he—Elijah, not Slowpoke—at the frolic? What happened? Did you two talk?"

"I took him and Declan some coffee and eppies. That's all." The hand-fired clay candle holders could go to the storeroom as well. Along with the embroidered hand towels with their sledding themes. Their vendors could take them home the next time they came into the store. "Nothing the least bit interesting. Not like your buggy ride with Ryan, Carol. Tell us everything in minute detail. Don't hold back."

"Jah, tell us, tell us." Sophia was easily redirected. For now. "What did you two talk about? Did you hold hands? Did you—?"

"Hey, hey, hey, hold your horses." Carol held up both hands. Her fair cheeks turned a deep scarlet. Her eyes shone. "That's kind of personal, don't you think?"

"Oh, come on. I've told you everything about me and Matthew. Your turn." Sophia wheeled to the table. She tugged the plate holding Carol's blueberry muffin out of the woman's reach. "I'm holding your muffin hostage until you spill the details."

"Jah, and there aren't any more, as I'm sure you noticed." Bonnie pushed her rollator to the bar so she could pour herself a cup of coffee. "I wanted to pick up some pastries from the bakery, but Sophia wouldn't let me. Just so you know."

"Okay, fine." Smiling, Carol took a sip of her coffee that was more milk and sugar. She knew exactly what she was doing. Prolonging the suspense. "He drove us out to the stand of pines on his daed's farm, the deep one that runs along the fence on the dirt road—"

"We know where it is, and then?" Sophia nibbled on Carol's muffin. "This sure is a tasty muffin."

"Stop eating my muffin. We pulled into a clearing and parked. Then we talked and talked. That's all."

"Talked about what?" Bonnie set her coffee on the table. She turned her rollator around and sat on the padded seat. "Was it hard to think of something to say? That's what I always worry about."

"Not with a talker like Ryan Beachy. With men like him you just have to ask a question and they run with it. We talked about his daed's health. Luke's better after the quadruple bypass. About working the farm with his brother Andrew. Corrine and Henry expecting triplets—what a blessing that will be." Carol sucked in a breath. "Can I have my muffin back now?"

"Wait a minute." Sophia held the plate away from her friend's reach. "Surely he asked about you. What questions did *he* have? Did he say anything about the crutches or the spina bifida?"

"Nee. It's old news. Boring news." Carol's nonchalance matched her grin. "It's like he doesn't even think about it. He sees me, not the crutches. Like I see me."

"You're right." Bonnie stirred her coffee. She stared into the murkiness. Her SMA was old news too. Did Elijah see it that way? Or did he have reservations that kept him from asking her out? Or did he simply not see her as more than a business owner? "Is he coming by again?"

"He is. Next Saturday." Carol clapped. Then she paused, hands lifted. "And guess how we sealed the promise?"

"Nee."

"Yep."

"He kissed you?" Sophia beat Bonnie to the answer. "Wow. On your first date. Matthew didn't kiss me for almost three months. I was beginning to think he never would."

"We kissed each other," Carol corrected. "I might have been the one to lean in first."

"Have you no shame?" Sophia put both hands to her cheeks in mock horror. "Shameless hussy, that's what they would call you in a romance novel."

Carol took a pretend bow. "Guilty as charged."

"So?"

"So what?"

"Was it as gut as I said it would be?"

"Again, that's personal."

"Come on, turnabout is fair play. I couldn't stop talking about Matthew. Your turn." Sophia clasped her hands and held them up as if begging. "It's wunderbarr, isn't it?"

Carol and Sophia were so happy, so excited. They were having fun with it. Sophia as much as Carol. They were good friends who wanted wonderful lives for one another. Bonnie swallowed the sudden lump in her throat. She was thrilled for Carol, just as she'd been thrilled for Sophia. It was the first step in what could be a long or short road of courting. But taking that first step was everything.

Bonnie didn't need a kiss—not immediately, anyway. Not really. It would be nice. But the closeness, the feeling of being with someone special, a man who thought she was special, that would be amazing. It would be everything she could possibly want. To share in the possibility of happily ever after. To share in the inevitable trials along the way. To share in the winter season as well as the spring.

"Why so quiet?"

Carol's question broke Bonnie's reverie. "Just thinking, wondering."

"Do you think I should've waited to kiss him?"

"Nee, I think it's wunderbarr." Bonnie picked her words carefully. "Now that you've spent an evening with him and kissed him, do you still feel the same way about him? Was it everything you imagined it would be?"

"Better." Smiling, Carol captured her muffin and plate. "Before, I was nervous. I kept imagining myself freezing up. I imagined that he would turn out to be dull or big on himself, even though I've talked with him plenty of times. I imagined tripping and falling on my face. Once we actually started talking, it was just two people chatting about ordinary things, but time flew by. We talked for two hours."

"And then you kissed."

"And it felt like a dream. Then it felt like we were the only people in the whole world who'd ever done it. It felt like we made a pact."

Her expression beatific, Carol stared into space.

Carol had a chance at her dream. Her tomorrows held brighter, more hopeful, more certain promises.

That didn't mean Bonnie's couldn't be just as bright and hopeful. She had the store. She had a purpose in life—to give other folks with disabilities a place to earn their keep. That was a worthy purpose. Such a life would be good. Better than good.

Different than she'd expected, but still good.

Time to get back to that purpose. Bonnie rose.

"Hey, you're not getting off that easy." Carol touched Bonnie's arm. "You still haven't told us why you and Elijah were arguing."

"We weren't arguing."

"Why didn't you want to come in the store, then? Why were you giving Elijah the cold shoulder?"

"I wasn't giving anyone the cold shoulder." Bonnie sank back onto her rollator. "Besides, it's stupid."

"Let us be the judge of that." Arms crossed, Sophia leaned back in her chair. "What happened?"

"Nothing happened."

Carol adopted a pose similar to Sophia's. "We're waiting."

"Elijah's mudder had the Coblentzes over to the Millers' for supper Sunday night."

"How dare she!" Sophia elbowed Carol. Both women giggled.

"She also hired Kathryn to work in the combination store."

"Ah." Carol pursed her lips and shook her head. "Kathryn will be at the Millers' farm several days a week."

"Jah, but Elijah will be on the road auctioneering," Sophia pointed out. "Plus it's not Elijah's fault. Elizabeth is prone to matchmaking. Everyone knows that."

"And everyone knows she's gut at it." Bonnie swept crumbs from the table into her hands. She deposited them on Carol's plate. "Toby and Rachelle. Micah and Layla. Declan and Bethel."

"You honestly believe she brought all three couples together?" Carol snorted. "No one is that gut. Except Gott. His plan. His timing. He doesn't need a mudder to meddle in His business."

All true. And yet . . . "Patience told Mary she thinks Kathryn likes Elijah, and she'll be right there under his nose."

"The question is, does Elijah like her?" Sophia thumped on the table. The coffee mugs rattled. "Oops. My point is Elijah came here to the shop instead of opting for the combination store where Kathryn is working. Which means he'll come here regularly. Maybe that's because he wants to see you."

"It's because he wants to sell more toys faster and for more money. It's a gut business decision, and he wants to have his own business."

"All true, with the added attraction of you."

If only. "He's never shown any interest in me."

"Can you say *shy*? Shy doesn't even begin to cover it. He's so shy, he shakes when he talks to a stranger. Yet he manages to talk to you."

He had managed. Quite well at the farm. "I suggested he practice calling an auction in front of me. He got all prickly about it."

"He's afraid of freezing up in front of you the way he did with the crowd." Sophia's tone suggested Bonnie was a silly goose if she couldn't see that. "He doesn't want to be embarrassed again, but especially not in front of a girl he likes."

Wishful thinking on Sophia's part. "Hogwash."

"Nee, it's not. And what is hogwash, anyway? Hogs don't wash themselves."

"Stay on track." Carol frowned at Sophia. "Bonnie needs to apologize to Elijah."

"Why? For what?"

"For pressuring him. For acting like you'd rather he call auctions than follow his heart. For embarrassing him when he had to say no. Besides, you always get prickly about people wanting to help you. Maybe he feels the same way. You don't get to be irked that he doesn't want your help."

The bell over the front door dinged.

Bonnie swiveled. A swarm of girls whose sweatshirts signaled they were from the nearby college chattered their way into the store and dispersed around the jewelry and hand-embroidered blouses. They would eventually make their way to Matthew's leather purses, billfolds, and jewelry, followed by candles and soaps. The noise increased fourfold.

Bonnie stood. Carol snagged her arm. Bonnie glanced back and said, "I know. Apologize. Don't give up."

Carol smiled up at her. "One date doesn't make me an expert on love. But I do know Gott's timing is perfect. That one date was enough to convince me. It's not about romance; it's about sharing your life with someone who loves you and who you love back."

"I know."

"Do you?"

Carol and Sophia knew Bonnie better than anyone in the world except—maybe—her mother. "Danki for sharing your night with us, Schweschder."

"You also have to believe you're worthy of his love."

"I do."

"Nee. You think no man will marry you because of the SMA."

Bonnie couldn't deny it.

"You're wrong."

"We have customers."

Carol let go of her arm. "There's so much of you to love. Gott made you in His image. Think about that. Remember that."

What would Carol think if she could read Bonnie's thoughts? The mighty, powerful, omnipotent, omniscient, and all those other *O* words, God wasn't traversing the universe pushing a rollator. Maybe He made Bonnie in His image on the inside, but the rollator thing, that was the result of a fallen world in which there was disease. *Thanks a lot, Adam and Eve. Mostly Eve. Or mostly the serpent.* Plenty of blame existed to go around.

What remained in the end? Questions Bonnie shared with no one. What was God thinking, letting Adam and Eve run amok in the garden? Why didn't He kick that serpent out before he changed the entire course of human history?

"I see the wheels turning. What are you thinking about, friend?"

"Nothing worth saying."

Nothing that wouldn't get her sent to hades for all eternity.

Chapter 17

Would the other women canning in her sister-in-law Frannie's kitchen mind if Jocelyn ripped off her glasses, her prayer covering, her apron, her black sneakers, and her matching socks? Probably. Jocelyn settled for sticking her head through the kitchen's open window. The breeze did little to cool her sweaty face. Everyone kept talking about how spring refused to give way to summer, but so far May had been plenty hot for Jocelyn.

"Hot flashes?" Elizabeth Miller joined Jocelyn. Her round face was as red as Jocelyn's felt. "I think I may be the first case of human spontaneous combustion any day now."

Her comical tone made Jocelyn laugh. Her children had inherited their blue eyes and dimples from Elizabeth and possibly their sense of humor. "I'm not sure if it's hot flashes or the heat in the kitchen." Or the discussion she'd just had with Uri followed by a surprising conversation with Theo. Or all three.

Canning required a huge rectangular steel canner filled with boiling water. A dozen Mason jars filled with chopped pork had been in Frannie's canner on the wood-burning stove. The steam hung in the kitchen like fog. "I guess I should be glad we're not doing this in August."

Plenty of Englischers would argue meat canning should be done with a pressure cooker, but Plain folks had been using the hot bath method—even for low-acid foods—for generations. It was a matter of knowing how long to bathe the jars at high temperatures. And paying attention to foods that didn't pass the smell test later down the road.

"True. One advantage to using a pressure cooker is it goes a lot faster, but Frannie prefers the hot bath. Anyhoo, I brought a gallon of my hot-flash tea." Elizabeth held up a glass of murky liquid. "It's made with sarsaparilla, shatavari root, red clover, licorice root, sage, raspberry leaves, and lemongrass for a nice citrus twist. I grew most of them myself. It's gut for hot flashes, depression, low libido, bloating, mood swings, being tired—you name it. I even brought ice."

Elizabeth was known for her herb garden, along with her love of native flowering plants. And matchmaking. Successful matchmaking, if the grapevine tidbits were true. What did she think of Elijah's plan to sell his toys at Bonnie's shop? Moreover, how would she feel about a daughter-in-law with SMA?

"I'll help myself. Danki." Jocelyn turned away so Elijah's mother couldn't see her expression. Bonnie would be a good wife and mother. She would need some extra help, but Jocelyn stood ready to offer it. Grandchildren would be such a blessing after her inability to have more children. Elizabeth, with her nine children and multiple grandchildren, surely understood the joys of both. How did a person broach such a delicate subject? If Jocelyn were Elizabeth, she'd jump in with both feet. Or an open mouth. "I better see what Frannie wants me to do."

"I helped chop the pork and filled the jars for the next batch." Elizabeth followed along behind Jocelyn. "I reckon this batch is ready to come out of the bath."

Frannie confirmed Elizabeth's observation. Using long rubber-tipped tongs perfect for the job, Jocelyn transferred the jars to a towel spread on the cabinet. Sweat dripped down her forehead into her eyes. She stood back as far as she dared from the steam. If the jar slipped back into the canner, it could splash her with scalding water. The first jar made it safely to the towel. Eleven to go. Number two came out of the water without a fight.

"So I think my Elijah has a hankering to court your Bonnie."

Jocelyn let go of the jar. It plopped back into the canner. Water splashed. It sloshed on her hand and forearm. She jolted back. "Ouch! Ouch!" The tongs clattered to the floor. Jocelyn danced around like a kernel of popcorn in hot oil. The burning sensation intensified. "Ouch."

"Me and my big mouth!" Elizabeth took Jocelyn's arm and guided her to a chair by the kitchen table. "Es dutt mer. I didn't mean to startle you."

"Nee, you didn't." Jocelyn cradled her arm against her chest. "It was my fault."

"I'll get my B&W ointment." Frannie rushed to the shelves that lined one wall of her spacious kitchen. "I keep it handy. Uriah is the most accident-prone man I know."

"Ice first." Elizabeth busied herself wrapping a bag of ice in a dish towel. A contrite look on her face, she handed it to Jocelyn. "I had no idea the thought of Elijah and Bonnie together would startle you so much."

"It didn't. It doesn't." Jocelyn pressed the cold compress against her red skin. She cast a glance around the room. Sophia's mom had retrieved the tongs and taken over the job of removing the jars from the bath. Everyone was back at their stations. "In fact, I was wondering how to bring it up myself."

Elizabeth put the reading glasses she wore on a chain around her neck on her long nose. She took the B&W from Frannie. "I'll take care of her. With nine kinner, I'm practically a board-certified doctor."

Jocelyn joined in their laughter. Elizabeth had no idea Jocelyn longed to have that many kids. Still, God had given her one child with needs that far outnumbered those of other children. Maybe He'd been thinking of that when He chose not to open her closed womb despite her incessant cries in the form of prayers.

Frannie went to retrieve more Mason jars from the basement. Jocelyn shifted the ice pack to her forearm. The stinging eased. "How do you feel about Elijah being interested in Bonnie?" She fought the urge to hold her breath. "Things being what they are."

"What'd you mean?"

"The SMA."

"Ach, that." Elizabeth opened the B&W jar. The sweet scent of honey mingled with comfrey root and aloe vera. "Your dochder works as hard as the next woman. As far as housekeeping, gardening, and such, she'd have plenty of help. I have *kinnskinner* running out my ears."

Any remnants of worry melted away. Some people were simply smart. Elizabeth and Charlie had so many kids because they loved children. They had their own special child, Sadie, a beautiful, energetic, funny girl with Down syndrome. That love extended to their grandkids and to other people's kids. Jocelyn had underestimated them. "Gut to know. Now to convince Bonnie of that."

"She doesn't want to marry?" Elizabeth's gaze darkened. "Or she's not interested in Elijah."

"Nee, nee, she wants to marry," Jocelyn hastened to clarify. "She's definitely interested in Elijah. She thinks he could never be interested in her. Truth be told, he's never really shown her that he is. How do you even know?"

Kelly Irvin

"I know my suh." Elizabeth tugged the ice pack from Jocelyn's arm. She offered her a dish towel. "Pat it dry and I'll put on the ointment. Of all my kinner, Elijah is the most sensitive. Strange thing to say about a bu, I know, but he's different. In a gut way, though. Hard as it is for my mann to see it.

"He has been shy since he was a tiny thing. He always hid in my skirts when strangers came around. Once, when Elijah was about ten or eleven, the bishop came for dinner, and I found Elijah hiding in the barn." She gently dabbed the B&W on Jocelyn's wounds. "The older kinner took him with them to school on his first day. He turned around and ran all the way home. Charlie had to take him back. I wanted to do it, but Charlie insisted that would only make it harder."

"It's funny how kinner are. Bonnie was eager to go, but she was worried her friends at home would be lonely without her."

"Friends?"

"Imaginary friends. I had a hard time convincing her they'd be fine with me. That I would feed them lunch and make sure they took their naps while she was gone."

Smiling, Elizabeth leaned back and wiped her hands on the towel. "I miss those days sometimes, don't you?"

"I do. They're so sweet. You're blessed to have kinnskinner to fill up your house."

"I didn't even think . . ." Elizabeth plucked at a loose thread on the towel. "I assumed. Can Bonnie . . . ?" Her face, already red from the heat, grew darker. "Not that it's my business."

"She can. She's worried about how she'll take care of them." Jocelyn's face likely was just as red. "Her hands are weak and she can't run after a toddler."

"She'll have more help than she knows what to do with. You know me, I can't wait to get my mitts on my kinnskinner. I reckon you're the same."

140

"I would be. I'd move in if they'd have me." Jocelyn shifted in her chair. The B&W helped with the burns, but there wasn't a salve for her embarrassment. "Here we are talking like Elijah and Bonnie are married with kinner when they're not even courting."

"Yet. Never you mind that." Smiling, Elizabeth wiggled her index finger in the air. It was easy to see where the Miller children got their dimples. "I have experience in this area. You nudge from your end, and I'll nudge from my end. We'll get it done; you just wait and see."

Chapter 18

*N*ot staying for supper?"

Theo had a way of sneaking up on a person that was disconcerting. Jocelyn turned from her buggy to face him. His face was even redder than it had been earlier in the day. Dirt decorated his faded shirt. Mud caked his boots and the bottom of his pants. He looked tired. His scent of sweat and dirt wafted on the cooling evening breeze. It reminded her of Marlin. She dug for the apology Uriah claimed she owed Theo. "About what I said earlier—"

"Don't worry about it. You were right." The words seemed to come easily to him. "I'm always sticking my nose where it doesn't belong. You said so yourself the first time we met."

"I didn't have to be so nasty about it. Sometimes I forget my place."

"I imagine it's hard to adjust to having a bruder run your life after your mann did it for so long."

"Bart would say I should submit. It's a woman's lot to submit. Gott loves an obedient believer. Gott forgive me for being so full of *hochmut*."

"I wondered sometimes why Gott gave my fraa a mind of her own if He didn't intend her to use it." A full-fledged smile accompanied

Theo's chuckle. He, too, was beginning to meet happy memories halfway, it seemed. "She had a way with words, that woman. And the staying power of a Percheron. I got an earful when we disagreed."

"I'm sure she'd say it was for your own gut—or the gut of your family."

"I'm sure she would. I reckon that's your excuse as well. It was one of the many things about her I liked." He scraped at dirt on his sleeve, smudging it more. "I always knew where I stood with her. I also liked the fact that once the decision was made, she accepted it. She stood by it and me, whether she liked it or not. I suspect you did the same for your mann."

He liked this thing about his wife. Which meant, by association, he liked it about Jocelyn. Why did that revelation make her want to wiggle like a child about to enjoy an ice cream cone?

Grow up. Get over yourself. Jocelyn was out of practice at giving herself a talking-to. It had been twenty-six years.

Jocelyn had spoken her piece on every occasion, but Marlin had the last word. He was the head of the household. Occasionally he was wrong. When he was, he said so and changed course. She loved him all the more for it. Tears gathered behind her eyes.

None of that. Focusing on the past served nothing for either of them. "To answer your question, I'm not staying for supper because my dochder and I try to eat together when she gets home from the shop. I don't want her to eat alone."

It only served to remind her of her loss. It reminded Jocelyn of the inability to give her dochder a bruder or schweschder.

"Because you're also a gut mudder as well as a gut fraa."

He was determined to compliment her. No need. She simply did what a Plain woman was expected to do. Plain women performed these roles every day. "I better get going. Bonnie will wonder where I am."

Theo scratched the bridge of his offending nose. Truth be told, it wasn't so big. "Before you go, can I just say I spoke out of turn? I shouldn't have sold my farm when I did, and you shouldn't sell yours if it doesn't feel right. Of course, I reckon I could still be speaking out of turn, what with my tendency to stick my gigantic nose where it doesn't belong."

Jocelyn dropped the reins. It took a lot for this man who hardly knew her to admit that not only had he said the wrong thing, but he also regretted it. A page from Marlin's book. "Danki for saying that. I'm sorry you didn't have someone there to help you see that it was a mistake."

"I did. I just wouldn't listen."

"You were hurting." Jocelyn glanced at the house. The curtains lifted in the breeze. Frannie had opened the windows to release the heat generated by the canning—and a bunch of women chattering nonstop. No one had come to see what she was doing standing out in the yard, yakking about deeply personal topics with the farmhand. Uriah had started this. He had no business objecting. When was the last time she had this kind of unguarded exchange with anyone? Not since Marlin.

Not exactly what Uriah had intended, no doubt. Her brother was the last person she'd expected to be a matchmaker. This wasn't that kind of connection. Not at all. Nope. More misery loved company. "I'm the opposite. I still haven't let go of Marlin's things."

The admission was jagged glass on her tongue.

Plain folks were expected to give such items to folks who needed them. They shouldn't go to waste sitting in a drawer or hanging on a hook. Jocelyn had failed in her duties. Marlin's black woolen jacket he had worn to church every other Sunday glared at her from its hook every time she entered the room. Giving away

Marlin's clothes would be tantamount to letting go of the last little piece of him.

"My schweschdre took it upon themselves to do that after the funeral. She was barely in the ground." Theo's voice faltered. He cleared his throat. "They served the meal and cleaned up afterward. When I went to bed that night, everything was gone."

"It's something women do, I reckon." Had her family done such a thing, could Jocelyn have forgiven them? "They thought they were helping by taking care of a hard thing."

Theo nodded. He shifted his feet and stared over her shoulder at something likely long gone and far away. "I know. They meant well. They also told me not to sell the farm. I did it anyway. Turns out they were right about that too."

It hadn't even occurred to her to sell the farm Marlin loved, that they loved together. That Bonnie loved. "So you don't think I should sell the farm?"

"Not unless you want to." Theo had a small scar over his left eye, standing white against his red forehead. How had it happened? "Not unless you want a fresh start."

"It wouldn't be a fresh start like the one you've had. Bonnie and I would have to move in with Uriah or one of my other breider or my schweschdre."

Women didn't get to strike out on their own. They didn't get to leave everything behind. Not that Jocelyn wanted to leave Bonnie behind. Her daughter needed her. She was the only person left who did. Being needed gave Jocelyn a reason to rise in the morning. To plan for the next day before she lay down at night.

"Fresh starts aren't as great as they're cracked up to be." His smile was lopsided, faint. "Ask my suh."

"You mentioned he wasn't happy about it."

"Noah and me should be farming the land together, land he

would inherit one day." Theo plucked a piece of straw from Buster's mane and let it drop to the ground. Buster tossed his head and neighed as if offering his thanks. Poor horse, caught in the middle of a personal conversation for the second time in a day. "Instead he's working for my bruder. He'd likely be married by now if he had the farm."

"Have you tried talking to him about it?"

"Jah. He's not much interested. I'm not sure how long it'll take him to get over it. If ever. He'd lost his mudder. Now he feels like he's lost the farm and me. He's bitter."

Consequences of a decision made in the murky, endless dark night that followed the loss of a person loved like no other. "You can't buy it back?"

"Some mistakes can't be undone."

"I wish Uri could see that."

"He just wants to do what's best for you. Try talking to him when you've had time to simmer down."

Good advice. The voice of experience. "I'm sorry about your suh."

"I'm praying Gott softens his heart."

"I'll pray that too."

"Danki. I need all the prayers I can get."

"Have you thought of going back to Berlin? At least then you'd be close to him."

"I have. I left a message at his phone shack last week. He called me back yesterday. He told me not to bother."

"In those words."

"Nee, he said there were no jobs for farmhands up that way. They've already been filled earlier this spring. There might be some need come harvesttime."

"That sounds like he's saying not now, but not never."

"It was the way he said it."

"Es dutt mer."

"I deserve it."

"Nee. As he grows older, he'll learn that *eldre* make mistakes too. That you can't hold them to a standard of perfection. We all fall short."

"Kind words."

His voice had gone hoarse. His gaze caught and held hers. A need she recognized filled his teak eyes. He longed for a human connection a person didn't get at a frolic or sitting on the church bench or eating supper with people he was just getting to know.

Joceyln's breath caught in her throat. Her heart fluttered. Tiny petals of knowing, of touching something so intimate it boggled the human mind, opened and brushed against her skin.

"Truth." Her own voice trembled. "I should go."

Right now, before his need collided with hers and neither were able to back away.

Theo ducked his head. "Safe travels."

The longing had receded, replaced with the usual niceties a person offered to a mere stranger.

Jocelyn climbed into the buggy. She looked down at Theo. Somehow they'd turned a corner during an unexpected walk together. "Gut nacht."

He nodded. Jocelyn snapped the reins. Buster whinnied and took off with a jolt.

She couldn't help herself. Halfway down the road she swiveled. Theo hadn't moved. He waved.

The gesture held promise. She hadn't dreamed that small, sudden moment in time. It had happened. He'd felt it too. Jocelyn

Kelly Irvin

faced front. A scalding wave of embarrassment, as if she'd been caught eavesdropping on a private conversation, drenched her. *Wave back.*

I can't.

Jah, you can.

Just do it.

She swiveled. Theo had already turned away.

Chapter 19

Toothpicks were great for picking teeth. How would they work for propping up eyelids? Elijah slipped into a chair at Charm's Pizzeria and Pasta Restaurant. He grabbed the toothpick holder and rolled it back and forth on a table covered with a red-and-white-checked cloth. The aromas of oregano, garlic, onion, and baking bread made his mouth water. His eyes burned under heavy eyelids. After a long night staring at the motel room ceiling, listening to his grandpa snore, Elijah might finally be able to sleep—from sheer exhaustion. On the other hand, every time he stopped working, all he could think about was Bonnie.

Smart. Hardworking. Faithful. Pretty. Very pretty. Kind. His brain liked to pair the words up with pictures of Bonnie at the store. It was like the kaleidoscope he had as a kid. The images fell into different patterns each time, but they were always beautiful.

Did she ever think of him?

"I do love the smell of garlic breadsticks baking." Toby dropped into a chair on the other side of the two tables the server had kindly scooched together for the Miller men—most of whom hadn't shown up yet. Toby's boot smacked into Elijah's. "Sorry. I needed to stretch my legs. Did you order? I'm starving."

"I did. This place is crowded. It'll take a while to get the order out. Where is everyone?"

"Daadi isn't coming. He said he's more tired than hungry." Toby tapped a rhythm on the table with one finger from each hand. "It's not like him to pass up eating his favorite spaghetti and meatballs. I hope this trip hasn't been too much for him. Don't tell *Mammi* I said that. Her meatballs are plenty gut."

If their grandfather got sick, it would be Elijah's fault. Grandpa had come along only because Elijah had an aversion to auctioneering. "I guess he's not getting a restful sleep if he's snoring all night long. It's so bad they can probably hear him three rooms down either direction."

"It starts out like a bullfrog with a sore throat and works its way up to a wood chipper chomping up a tree trunk. They can hear it in the next county." Grinning, Toby stole Elijah's glass of iced water. He gulped down half of it. "It's gotten worse. That's why no one offered to share the room with you two. So what were you thinking about when I came in?"

"Nothing."

Nothing Elijah wanted to share with a brother who seemed to have few faults, little self-doubt, or even fears. Toby was married, he had kids, and he took over the administrative side of the family business when Grandpa retired. On the auction circuit, he was the favorite Miller auctioneer. To be fair, Declan, the jokester, had people eating out of his hands before cancer took his voice, but Toby had a charisma that couldn't be denied.

It seemed when God was handing out qualities to the Miller brothers, He'd shorted Elijah. Even Emmett, who came along afterward, was more outgoing and determined to be the best Miller auctioneer yet.

"Come on, Bruder. You were so deep in thought, I figured I

needed to send in a search party to find you. You're still doing it." Toby paused while the server set a glass of water and a basket of breadsticks in front of him. He thanked her and helped himself to the bread. "Let your big bruder help you solve your problem. Is it about auctioneering? Dat agreed not to put you back on the platform until you say you're ready. I told him you'd be scarred for life if it happened again."

"Danki for sticking up for me."

"You're my favorite bruder." Toby pointed the breadstick at Elijah. "You don't talk too much. You don't tell corny jokes. You let me boss you around."

He probably told Jason, Declan, and Emmett that they were his favorites too—but with a different list of reasons why. Toby was a good big brother. He didn't get married until he was thirty. He had plenty of experience with women. Elijah squirmed in his chair. "It's not the auctioneering."

"Then what? Come on, you can tell me. I won't laugh. I promise."

Elijah helped himself to a breadstick. He broke it in half and dropped both pieces on a saucer. "You talk to everyone. Even women."

Toby threw back his head and laughed a deep belly laugh that startled the elderly couple at the next table. The man frowned, but the woman laughed. The Toby effect. "I do my best. Half the people in the world are women, in case you haven't noticed."

"How do you do it?"

"I talk to them like people."

"I know, but I don't talk much to people either."

Toby tore off half the breadstick and stuffed it in his mouth. Chewing, he wiped his hands on the red napkin. Finally, he swallowed. "Is there a particular woman we're talking about?"

"Maybe."

"Spill the beans, Bruder."

"Bonnie. Bonnie Yoder."

"Ah, Bonnie from Homespun Handicrafts. No wonder you were so wound up after she fell. Not exactly a great start." Toby took another bite of bread, chewed, and swallowed. He smacked his lips. "Everybody says Bonnie does a gut job with her shop. She doesn't let that walker slow her down much. She's nice."

"It's called a rollator."

"What is?"

"The thing she uses to get around." For some reason it seemed important to clarify that. And easier to talk about than his feelings for Bonnie. "It's a rollator."

"Got it. So you talk to Bonnie like you would Josie or Layla or my fraa or Jason's fraa. Say hallo. Comment on the weather. This beautiful spring weather lasting well into May is a blessing. Bonnie probably thinks so too. She has a shop. Ask her how the shop's doing."

"You talked about the weather when you took Rachelle for a buggy ride?"

"Ah. So we're to the buggy ride stage." Toby dropped the breadstick and clapped softly. "Gut for you. Rachelle and I talked about a lot of things, but we had a lot in common. Both families have special kinner. She was a teacher. We needed someone to teach Dat to read. She loved teaching. I love auctioneering. Neither of us wanted to give up what we loved. We had plenty to discuss. Just figure out what you and Bonnie have in common. When are you taking her for a ride?"

"I haven't asked her yet."

"Well, what are you waiting for?"

"To get off the auction circuit, for one thing." Elijah's leg jiggled of its own accord. He stuck his hand on his thigh to still it. "Trying to figure out what to say, for another."

"You've never courted, have you?" Astonishment flitted across Toby's sunburned face. "How old are you?"

"You're not helping."

"It isn't that hard. Really it isn't. I promise. You make toys. She's makes stuffed animals and dolls." Toby shoved his straw hat back on his head. He scratched his forehead. "Talk about making things. Be sure to tell her she's pretty."

"You're supposed to say that?"

"You think she's pretty, don't you?"

"I do."

"Then why not say so?"

"Looks aren't supposed to be important."

"You're saying something nice to a girl you like. We're allowed to do that. Bonnie doesn't seem like the type to let it go to her head."

"Maybe I should tell her a joke."

"A joke? I've never heard you tell a joke, ever." Toby grunted. "Leave the jokes to Declan."

"I can tell a joke."

"Okay, fine, lay one on me."

Elijah searched his brain for one he'd heard Declan tell Sadie a million times. She never failed to laugh. But she was eleven. "What does corn say when it gets a compliment?"

Toby rolled his eyes. "What does corn say when it gets a compliment?"

"Awww, shucks."

More eye rolling, this time accompanied by head shaking. "Like I said, leave the jokes to Declan. Just be yourself."

"Should I, you know, should I . . . ?" Heat scorched Elijah's face. He grabbed his ice water and gulped it down. "Where is that server? I need more water."

"Are you asking me if you should, what, hold her hand?" Toby pursed his lips as if trying not to let his laughter escape. "Maybe kiss her?"

"Stop laughing! How am I supposed to know?"

"When the time is right, you'll know. I promise. It'll be like you jumped on a runaway Amtrak train and there's no slowing it down. Just follow her lead."

"I don't think she has much experience either."

"Because of the rollator thing?"

"Jah."

"Everybody has disabilities. Some show. Some don't. I think Gott allows them so we don't get too uppity for our own gut. Like the verse says, so no one can boast. In our weakness Gott is strong." Toby stuck his arm in the air and waved wildly. "There they are. It's about time."

Elijah swiveled and craned his neck. The Miller men tromped through the restaurant toward him. Emmett's hair was still wet from a shower. Dad was even more sunburned than Toby. Grandpa had decided to come after all. "Don't tell them what we were talking about."

"I wouldn't do that to you. Our food is here." Toby moved the bread basket so the server could place two deep-dish pan pizzas on racks she'd placed on the table. A helper followed with pasta dishes, side salads, and more breadsticks.

"What are you two jawing about?" Dad plopped into a chair next to Toby. "Seemed pretty serious."

"Nope. Elijah was just giving me some pointers." Toby winked as he picked up the tongs lying next to the extra-large Canadian bacon, mushroom, green pepper, and black olive pizza. "On life. You want the first piece, Dat?"

"I'll take two. I'm starving."

Elijah silently telegraphed his thanks to Toby as the conversation around him quickly diverted to which pizza place had better pizza and the day's auction.

No more messing around. In three weeks, he would march into the store, stride to the counter, and ask Bonnie to take a ride with him.

Three weeks was a long time. Somebody else could ask her out before then.

He should've asked her before he left.

He could write her a letter. Nah, she'd think that was weird.

Could You do me a favor, Gott? Don't let anyone else get a hankering to ask her out before I get a chance.

He should add, *Thy will be done.* But somehow he couldn't. Let God's will coincide with Elijah's. Just this once.

Chapter 20

*T*he incredulity on Sophia's face came as no surprise. Bonnie took Elijah's push mower from her coworker and placed it on a scrap of artificial turf Declan Miller had so kindly saved from the nursery dumpster and donated to the shop instead. The display next to the tall front windows was coming along nicely. "I needed someone's help with needlework and she offered."

"I love your mudder, and we are coming up to our busiest time of year with summer just around the corner." Sophia lifted a box of Elijah's toys from her lap and set it on the table next to the display. "I do, but don't you think the two of you would get along better if she did the work at home?"

Bonnie chuckled to herself. Sophia was nothing if not diplomatic. Everybody loved Bonnie's mother—in small doses. In larger ones, she could be a little much. She had no qualms about sharing her opinion on everything from the weather forecast to best names for new babies—related to her or not—to the most effective way to advertise the shop.

"I'm sorry I didn't ask you and Carol first. I should've. But she was trying so hard to lift my spirits, when honestly, I think it's her spirits . . ." Bonnie cast a glance over her shoulder. Carol was busy at the register, checking out a customer who'd bought Elijah's pull-duck, his horse and buggy, and a Noah's ark before they'd made it into the display. Mom had disappeared into the back room after an inspection of the displays, a chat with the postal carrier, and a thorough cleaning of the coffee bar. No sign of her in the last half hour. "I think she's the one who needs help. Being alone at the house isn't gut for her. There's not enough cleaning and cooking to keep her busy. Now that spring is in full swing and summer is coming, she'll have gardening and the yard to take care of, but still . . ."

"She's lonely." Sophia tut-tutted and shook her head. "Poor thing. I should've thought of that. Of course she should work here at the shop."

"Jah. She's bound to be lonely after all those years married to Dat." Bonnie faced the display so her friend couldn't see the sadness that seeped into every nook and cranny of her own body. They were supposed to accept the circumstances of their lives, come what may, but nobody really explained how to do that. "Sometimes I think that's the silver lining."

Bonnie stopped. She clutched Elijah's oversize wooden pig in her arms. The wood was polished to a smooth sheen. The chubby animal had an exaggerated long snout and squinty eyes. Exaggerated like her feelings today. A toddler would love playing with this chunky pig. Bonnie's mind's eye immediately conjured up a scene with a little girl lugging the pig out the front door, down the steps, and toward the actual pigpen. Her dad would delight in the make-believe and lead the way, oinking and squealing. A dog who looked an awful lot like Slowpoke followed with an occasional bark of encouragement.

Where was Bonnie? Standing at the screen, watching the small parade. Smiling.

"Silver lining in what?"

The concern in Sophia's voice burst the dream's bubble. "In me not getting married. I'll be around to keep her company."

"Don't be narrisch. You could get married and stay at the house. It's already been remodeled to suit your needs." Sophia scooted her chair closer. She tugged the pig from Bonnie's arms. "It would be practical. Or your mudder could move in with you and your mann."

She rolled past Bonnie and settled the pig into an open spot near the boy doll and his mower. "Everything in its place. Everyone in their place."

"I suppose."

"It'll happen."

"And if it doesn't, Mamm and I have each other."

The bell that hung over the door dinged. Good, a customer. They needed more customers. And less talk.

"I'll get him." Sophia held out the box. "You keep working on the display."

Bonnie took the box. That didn't keep her from peeking at the customer. It was a man. They didn't get a lot of male customers on their own. Something about Homespun Handicrafts didn't resonate with a man unless he needed a gift for a wife who liked handmade scarves, homemade scented soaps, one-of-a-kind jewelry, or hand-painted bird feeders.

She stepped back, cocked her head, and reviewed what she'd done so far. One of her Plain dolls sat in a buggy. Another stood next to a corral that held three wooden horses of various colors. A boy doll sat with a miniature baseball and bat in his lap, his straw hat at his side. An alphabet board sat on top of a child's school desk. Each letter was beautifully carved. The lawn mower and the rocking horse took up the area closest to the windows. Mixing her dolls with Elijah's toys worked out perfectly.

"That's some good stuff you got there."

Bonnie turned. The newcomer was a man in a long-sleeved white shirt and navy tie, carrying a briefcase. Definitely not a typical customer.

"Mr. Knox said he wanted to talk to you." Her curiosity evident in her expression, Sophia brought up the rear. "No one else could help him."

"Pleased to meet you, Bonnie. I'm Logan Knox with Virginia Realty. Call me Logan." He held out his hand. "Your mother probably told you about me."

She had not. Bonnie automatically shook his hand, which turned out to be a bit sticky. "I'm sorry. My mother didn't mention anyone named Logan Knox."

His long, skinny nose—too big for his round face—wrinkled for a second, but he hid his dismay quickly. "You and your mother are the only ones who reside at the Yoder farm off Lakeside Drive northwest of town?"

"That's us."

Mr. Knox glanced around. "Maybe we could have a chat over a cup of coffee."

"Mr. Knox—"

"Logan."

"Logan, I'm working right now, and I can't imagine what a real estate agent would want with me."

"Your mother didn't mention that I have a buyer for your farm?"

"A buyer . . ." It took his meaning a few seconds to sink in. "No, she did not." Bonnie whipped her rollator past her visitor and headed for the back room. The *click-clack* of dress shoes on the pine floor told her that Mr. Knox followed. She stopped at the counter. "Wait here, please."

For a second it seemed he would ignore her wishes. He offered a smile. A fake smile. "Yes, ma'am."

Kelly Irvin

His tone oozed insincerity. Bonnie left him standing there.

Her mother was seated at the worktable. She had a small piece of black felt in one hand and a needle in the other. She'd left the angry red burns on her right hand and arm open to the air after applying B&W before they'd left the house. An almost-finished stuffed bunny lay in front of her. It just lacked one eye and a mouth. She looked up. "I found a sloth pattern in the basket on the desk. I'll start on one as soon as I give this little guy a face. Sloths are big right now. The tourists will love them. The college girls will want them for their dorm rooms. They can hang them from their bunks—"

"Mamm, why didn't you tell me someone wants to buy the farm?"

Mom frowned. Her shoulders hunched. "Because I told the man no and I meant no. No need to waste air talking about it."

"Apparently he didn't get the message." Bonnie jabbed her thumb toward the door. "He's out there and he wants to talk to me about it."

"Apparently he doesn't understand how a Plain family works."

"Meaning the decision is yours."

"With your dat being gone, jah, it is. I own the property. Whatever your onkels may think."

"What does that mean?"

"It means I told Uri about it, and he thought I should consider it."

"You told Onkel Uri and not me? I've lived in that house my whole life."

"And one day you'll move into a house with your mann. I'll be alone there." Mom said it without the slightest tremor in her voice, but her shoulders sank a little more. "Uri thinks I should sell so we have a nest egg. We can move in with him or one of your other

160

onkels or aenties. He says they don't have time to work our land. It's valuable, and it's sitting fallow."

"He said all that and you didn't tell me?" Was it her pride or her feelings that were hurt? Bonnie picked up a paisley-print elephant Mom had finished. Her stitches were so neat, so perfect. Even better than Opal's. Bonnie fought the urge to clutch the soft, huggable animal to her chest like the sad five-year-old who hadn't wanted to go to school because she would miss her imaginary friends. They didn't notice her walker and always let her pick the games they played. They never left her out. "Why wouldn't you talk it out with me? I thought we talked about everything."

Hadn't they become more like friends as Bonnie grew into adulthood? Especially since Dad's death. Hadn't caregiving become a two-way street?

"I didn't want to worry you." Mom laid her needle on the table. She returned the spool of black thread to its spot with its matching bobbin on the enormous wooden rack hanging on the wall above the table. A hundred-plus colors arranged in alphabetical order made life a little easier for the seamstress. "You already worry about the weakness in your hands. I did confirm your appointment for Monday. That way you won't have to miss too much work. It's our Sunday off so we can go to Strasburg Sunday and come back on Tuesday."

A shudder ran through Bonnie. The doctors, nurses, and all the staff at the clinic were wonderful, kind, caring people. Yet dread foreshadowed every visit. Dr. Newcomb said it made Bonnie human. The truth was, it surely made her ungrateful in God's eyes. *Forgive me, Gott, for being so weak and disrespectful of Your gifts.* "It's a sin to worry."

An automatic response. Everyone did it instead of addressing their sin.

"Gott forgives our trespasses as we forgive those who trespass against us."

The familiar words of a prayer said by Plain people everywhere daily. "In the meantime, Mr. Knox is still loitering out there saying who knows what to who knows whom."

"You take care of your customers. I'll send him on his way." Mom stood. Her face tight with determination, she brushed past Bonnie. "Nicely, of course. There's never an excuse for being rude."

Chapter 21

*R*egret was a bitter cup of tea. Jocelyn couldn't get the taste out of her mouth. She should've told Bonnie about Mr. Knox's visit. Hoping he'd taken her strongly worded refusal had been wishful thinking. Time to nip this unwanted attention in the bud. Shoulders back, head up, she strode down the hallway to the shop's main floor.

Marlin would've handled it better. Marlin wasn't here. The ever-present voice that blared in her ear was famous for stating the obvious. Not to mention Mr. Knox would never have approached her front door if Marlin still lived there.

Mr. Knox wasn't by the front counter. Jocelyn surveyed the shop. The real estate agent had taken a chair by the front window. He shared the table with a salt-and-pepper bearded man wearing faded jeans and a western-style, pearl-snap blue shirt that had long sleeves despite the fact that the May weather had finally decided to warm up. He wore cowboy boots and a Massey Ferguson cap. The two men were drinking coffee and eating the lemon-raspberry whoopie pies she'd made the previous evening after a long, hard day. For some reason, that last fact irked Jocelyn.

Those treats are for customers, the voice in her ear insisted.

They can go down to the coffee shop instead of mooching off my girl's coffee bar.

Not a Christlike attitude. There it was. The voice in her other ear. The one that sounded just like her mother.

She heaved a sigh. Counted to ten. Slowly. Jocelyn took her own advice. Or her mother's. It was hard to say. She pinned a smile to her face and approached the table. "Mr. Knox—"

"Logan."

"Logan—"

"This is Clyde Steadman from Charlottesville. He's the farmer who's interested in your property."

Both men stood. Clyde Steadman smiled and offered his hand. Jocelyn had no choice but to accept it.

"Nice to meet you, ma'am." Steadman had a firm shake and a kind face. "I'm sorry for your loss. I know it's been two years, but I can't imagine ever getting over losing my Lucy Lou, God forbid."

He had one of those disarming voices, like warm maple syrup on a cold December morning.

Jocelyn's pique disappeared in a puff of who-could-be-mean-to-a-person-so-bent-on-being-nice? Genuinely nice. Not smarmy nice like Mr. Knox. "Thank you. Please don't stand on my account. Your coffee's getting cold."

"I'll get you a chair." Mr. Knox hustled to another table and returned with said chair. "Please sit with us. I know you said no, but I thought it would be a good idea to hear from Clyde before you make a final decision."

"I'm sorry, but my decision *is* final." Jocelyn eased into the chair. Not sorry, not really. Were white lies sins if told to soften a blow? All lies were sins. Jocelyn groped for a better response. "Honestly, I'm not sorry I said no, but I am sorry if my refusal to sell puts a crimp in your plans."

"Let me get you some coffee. Sugar? Milk—that milk is delicious, by the way. I bet it's from the cows I saw on your farm," Mr. Knox babbled. "The whoopie pies are delicious. Did you make them?"

"It is and I did. None for me, thank you. Please sit down." So they could get this over with. "I don't want to waste any more of your time."

"I don't consider it a waste of time." Clyde sipped from his still-steaming coffee. His smile had disappeared, replaced by weariness. No, not weary—sad. "I didn't think it was right to ask Logan to plead my case for me. It's personal. I should do it myself. I would truly appreciate it if you would do me the favor of hearing me out."

Jocelyn intertwined her fingers and settled them in her lap. "Of course." *When you put it that way, it would be churlish to refuse.*

"Last year my wife and I lost our youngest son to leukemia. Todd was fourteen."

"I'm so sorry." The least helpful words in the universe. Personal experience had taught Jocelyn that lesson. No words existed to encompass what people wanted to say when they confronted the heartbreak, grief, and sorrow billowing from a person devastated by the loss of a loved one.

It didn't matter—although of course it should—what Scripture said about the number of days God intended for a loved one to be on earth. As much as Jocelyn had faith in the living hope of Jesus Christ, the merest whiff of the thought of losing Bonnie still produced a paralyzing pain that reduced her to tears. "I know those words are hollow, but they seem to be the best language can come up with."

"Thank you." Clyde dabbed at his eyes with his napkin. "I find working hard gets me through each day, but Lucy Lou's not doing so well. Our older boys are out of the house, one married, another one in college, living their lives. Her nest is empty before it was supposed to be."

"The chair is empty at the supper table," Jocelyn said. "There's not enough laundry to do. No birthday to celebrate. No one to scold for not wiping his shoes on the rug." The scenes spun themselves out in Jocelyn's mind's eye. Familiar tears pressed against her eyes. "No bed to make up. No one to surprise with his favorite dish. No one to play a little joke on."

"The voice of experience." Clyde picked at a few remaining whoopie pie crumbs. "She's wasting away. The doctor says it's melancholy. He wants to prescribe pills. He don't know my wife like I do. She wouldn't take pills if she was dying."

"She feels like she's dying every day."

"She does."

"Can you tell me what this has to do with my farm?"

Clyde raised his head. He peered directly into Jocelyn's eyes. "Your farm is my prescription for a fresh start. Todd still lives in every corner of our house and our land. He said his first words there, took his first steps, lost his first tooth, learned to ride a horse there, learned to ride a bike, learned to push a mower. He learned to drive the tractor. He loved to fish in the pond on the south forty. He mucked the stalls in the barn and gathered the eggs from the chicken shed. It would be easier to name the places he's not been because there aren't any."

"Ach, I do understand. I truly do." Marlin's earthy scent enveloped Jocelyn the same way it did when she slid under the sheets at night even though they'd been washed many times since he left this earthly realm. "It's a hard season. Are you and your wife believers?"

"We are. Me more than her, I reckon." He scooted his chair away from the table, leaned back, and crossed his arms over the beginnings of a paunch. "I know what you're getting at. We take comfort in knowing we'll see him again, but it's this side of heaven that's the challenge."

"Why *our* farm?"

Jocelyn swiveled. Bonnie stood behind her. She'd returned without a squeak of the rollator to give her away. She took a seat on her rollator.

"There's not much good farmland on the market in this area." Clyde spread his calloused hands. "Yours is just the right size, the land is fertile, the house and outbuildings are in good shape. It's close to Lee's Gulch and far enough from Charlottesville to give us that fresh start we need."

"Each person grieves in their own way." Bonnie stared at her hands, then raised her head to gaze at Clyde. "I know that, but I would think sorrow would follow a person wherever he went. The absence would be felt regardless. Plus, won't your wife miss her family and friends there in Charlottesville? Your church family? It seems as if they would've been the ones to stand by you in your time of need."

Bonnie spoke from her experience, her life. Would an English woman see it the same way? Jocelyn started to speak. Clyde held up his hand, the one with a thin silver band on the ring finger.

"I suppose you're right in some respects, young lady, but I've seen how my Lucy Lou perks up when I talk about starting over in a new place. We've talked about going to estate sales and auctions to buy farmhouse antiques. New wiring and plumbing throughout the house, a coat of fresh paint and wallpaper in the bedrooms, remodeling the kitchen to make it state-of-the-art for two people who like to cook, making the place our own." Clyde nodded as if agreeing with his own words. "Her only concern is being so far from Todd's grave. She's afraid he'll be lonely."

His voice broke. He cleared his throat. "I remind her Todd's long gone from that earthly body. But I also tell her we'll ride out for a visit to the cemetery as often as she likes. It's only an hour and a half's drive. We could go every Sunday after church."

The elders would frown on Jocelyn's monthly habit of visiting Marlin's grave rain or shine with a picnic basket containing his favorite Reuben sandwiches, homemade potato chips, fruit salad, and double-fudge brownies. Afterward they would share a cup of extra-strong coffee laced with fresh milk and too much sugar—just the way he fancied it. He wasn't there, but it was the last place they'd been together. The oak trees gave shade to his plain marker. She would kick off her shoes, sit cross-legged on an old quilt after her lunch, and offer Marlin a soliloquy on life in the district since her last report. If anyone saw her jabbering to herself, they'd be certain she needed her head examined. Maybe she did. Or maybe she'd found a way to comfort herself when no one else could.

The Plain cemetery was only five miles from the farm.

"I feel for your wife. I truly do, but I don't need a new start. My Marlin put years of sweat and muscle into that farm. I like knowing he's in every nook and cranny." Jocelyn liked getting under the comforter on a cold winter night and imagining she could tuck her cold feet under Marlin's. His arm would come around her and tug her closer, keeping her warm all night long. Plain women didn't share those intimate details with anyone, let alone two English men. "I can't imagine living anywhere else."

"Let's not be hasty," Mr. Knox piped up. He reached for the briefcase sitting on the floor next to his chair. "We haven't talked money."

"Hold your horses, son." Clyde shot the other man a frown. "The lady said she's not interested. We'll just have to keep searching."

No self-pity marred the words. Yet they hurt. Defeat lurked in the slump of his broad shoulders. Jocelyn glanced at Bonnie. Her daughter inclined her head a fraction. Her shoulders moved a tiny bit. She, too, felt for Clyde, but not enough to give up the only home she'd ever known.

With a grunt, Clyde hoisted himself to his feet. He nodded at Jocelyn and Bonnie. "I better get back. I told Lucy Lou I'd be home before it gets dark, and I have a couple of other stops to make. It was a pleasure meeting you both." He picked up his coffee cup and paper plate.

"Nee, nee, we'll get that for you." Jocelyn collected Logan's trash and added Clyde's to it. "Godspeed to you both."

"I'm going to visit the little boy's room."

Mr. Knox hadn't moved. "I'll meet you at your truck, Clyde."

The older man nodded and kept going. The real estate agent waited a beat. Then he opened the briefcase and pulled out a manila envelope. "I just think you should know what you'll be missing out on before you make a final decision." He laid the envelope on the table, then stood. "You have my card, Mrs. Yoder, and my office is just a hop, skip, and jump away."

Without using the facilities, he made his way to the door and was gone.

"He has a lot of gall." Bonnie shook her head in disgust. "Clyde seems like a gut man who wants to do right by his fraa, but not at the expense of a wittfraa and her dochder."

"That's likely what makes him a gut real estate agent. He doesn't take nee for an answer."

"I guess he didn't grow up around here. I don't remember seeing him, and he surely doesn't know how Plain folks think." Bonnie smoothed her fingers over the envelope. "As if money could make you change your mind."

"Plain folks like a little pocket change as much as the next person." Jocelyn moved the envelope beyond Bonnie's grasp. "Shouldn't you get back to work?"

Bonnie got to her feet. "You're not taking the offer seriously, are you?"

"I feel as if I should at least read the offer eventually, but first I need some air. I'm going to walk over to the diner and bring back Cobb salads for us and whatever Sophia and Carol want. Could you ask them for me?"

"Sure." Bonnie put the men's mugs and trash on her rollator seat. "You don't want some company? You might not be able to carry everything."

"I'll be fine."

Carrying lunch orders was the least of her problems.

Chapter 22

A few minutes later, the envelope tucked into her canvas tote hanging by its strap from her shoulder, Jocelyn strode toward Terri's Diner, a staple lunch destination on Lee's Gulch's Main Street. Why did Clyde Steadman have to be such a nice man? So courteous. So fair-minded. So sad. It would be far easier if he was an arrogant jerk trying to pull the farm out from under them.

Nothing's ever simple.

There will be trials in this world—

I know, I know.

Had she just interrupted the voice in her head in mid-recitation of Scripture? God surely would smite her with lightning on this sidewalk on a sunny mid-May day in small-town USA.

If taking sandwiches to her dead husband in the cemetery didn't get her committed, surely talking back to the voice in her head would.

"You really are lost in thought." Theo loomed over her. A step or two more and Jocelyn would've smacked into him. He wore his usual lazy, amused grin. "I thought about letting you bulldoze into me, but that seemed rude, here on the street for all of Lee's Gulch to see."

"Danki for saving me from that embarrassment." Even so, heat flamed through Jocelyn's body. At least she hadn't talked aloud to herself. "What are you doing in town?"

The question was the first thing to come to her mind. Why would she care what her brother's employee was doing in town? Why did her words sound like a criticism? "Not that it's any of my business."

His grin growing, Theo lifted his hat and settled it farther back on his head. All the better to see those teak eyes. His silver hair was a thick, unruly mess. Somehow that made him even more handsome. That smile. It was almost as if he knew what she was thinking. "It's okay to make conversation with someone you see on the street. A person could even say it's polite to inquire."

Handsome? Handsome! Where had that random thought come from? Jocelyn's heart fluttered. She patted damp palms on her apron. She shouldn't be standing on a public sidewalk, talking to a man she hardly knew. Her feet refused to move. "I'm . . . I'm g-getting lunch for the girls." Now she was stuttering like a teenager on her rumspringa. "I better— I mean, I should get going."

"I'm sure they're starving." He didn't move either. "I'm pretty hungry myself."

"Didn't you have an errand to run for Uri?"

"It'll wait long enough for me to pick up something to go at Terri's Diner. That's where you're heading, isn't it?"

Jocelyn studied a dandelion that had worked its way through the cracks in the sidewalk with a half dozen buds ready to burst into yellow blooms. The weeds were always the first to announce that spring had sprung. They were impossible to get rid of. Kind of like a certain handyman.

Did she really want to get rid of him?

"Jah. I had a hankering for Terri's Cobb salad."

Theo did an about-face. "I'm more in the mood for a club sandwich with a side of curly fries. With a double-fudge brownie to finish it off."

"So you have a sweet tooth?" Marlin used to tell Jocelyn she made the best brownies in the tri-county area. As if he'd sampled them all. Her heart didn't twinge. Her throat didn't tighten. Not even a threat of tears. Guilt sidled up her spine and curled around her neck. Why? Marlin wouldn't mind. He would be happy for her. He was that kind of man. "I prefer carrot cake myself."

Idle chitchat about cookies and cakes took them another block. The conversation dwindled, but not uncomfortably so. The sun shone. Shoppers chattered as they threaded their way past Jocelyn and Theo. Banners advertised the weekly farmers market in the town square. It was a nice day for a walk, especially when the company was good.

"Did you need to go to the post office first?"

"Hmm?"

Theo tapped the envelope sticking from her tote bag. "Were you supposed to mail this?"

Theo's presence had knocked any thought of Clyde Steadman and his sad story from Jocelyn's mind. Theo had regretted selling his farm. Maybe he could help her sort through the tangled morass of her emotions about this offer.

She had finished her explanation by the time they arrived at the diner. His expression unreadable, Theo held open the door. "I think it'll take the walk back to the shop to unwrap this package."

Chewing her bottom lip, Jocelyn inhaled the cornucopia of aromas that included frying chicken, hamburger, sausage, and bacon—a paradise for those who loved fried meat. Nope. A nice salad to go would be fine. "The grapevine will shoot up to the heavens."

"If people don't have enough of their own business to mind, I'm sure Gott will find something for them to do."

Good enough. After they placed their orders, Jocelyn took a seat in the row of mismatched wooden chairs designated for to-go orders along the wall next to the double front doors. She pulled the envelope from her bag, opened it, and began to read. The lunch crowd's loud chatter, Miranda Lambert's man-who-done-her-wrong lyrics blaring from overhead speakers, chairs scraping on the tile floor, and the cook's "order's up" shouts all faded away. The only sound was her own gasp. She returned to the first paragraph and read it again. "This can't be right."

"What? What can't be right?" Theo dropped into the chair next to hers. "Gut or bad?"

"Mr. Steadman wants to pay me eight hundred thousand dollars for the farm, to include all buildings, farm equipment, and livestock, minus any buggies and horses used to pull those buggies." Jocelyn let the sheets of paper slip through her fingers and land in her lap. "The offer excludes all household furnishings. It also excludes any pets."

Shaking his head, his eyebrows raised and forehead wrinkled, Theo whistled. "That's a humdinger of a price, to be sure."

"You suggested seven hundred thousand dollars. Which is more money than I could even fathom. Why would Mr. Steadman offer above the fair market value?"

"Can I read it?"

She scooped up the document and handed it over. "Be my guest."

Theo slipped on a pair of silver-framed reading glasses. No gasping, but Theo did grunt and wrinkle his nose a few times. Otherwise he didn't speak while perusing the long contract. Finally he raised his head and peered at her over his spectacles while returning the paperwork. "It's a mighty fine offer. Much better than what I got for my property."

Someone had taken advantage of Theo's desperate need to flee from the home he'd shared with his wife. The desire to give that person a large piece of her mind flooded Jocelyn.

"Don't look at me like that. It was my fault. No one else is to blame."

"It wasn't very kind of the buyer."

"Believe me, I did a gut job of hiding my true state of mind. He had no idea. He lowballed it, expecting me to dicker, and I didn't."

"How can I turn down an offer like this? It would pay all of Bonnie's medical bills. She'd be taken care of when I pass. We could put some of it into the district's medical insurance fund to replenish all we've taken from it. We could upgrade the electrical wiring in the shop."

Breathless, Jocelyn stopped, even as other ideas bombarded her.

"Or you could hang on to the farm, hire someone to work it with you so you have a steady income for years to come. Bonnie and her mann can live there and work it when you get older. You can live in the *dawdy haus* until you pass."

His dry tone poked a hole in Jocelyn's excitement. It drained away. "You have it all figured out, don't you?" Her tone was more snippy than she intended. "I pray for Gott to give Bonnie a mann, but it hasn't happened yet. It might never."

"Jocelyn, your order's ready."

Terri's bullfrog voice sliced through the thick tension. Waving her receipt in one hand, Jocelyn popped up. She grabbed the four large Styrofoam containers and thanked the diner owner. "I'd better get going. The girls will be starving by now."

"Theo, yours is up too."

His expression penitent, Theo rose as well. "My big nose got into your business again, didn't it?"

She'd invited him into her business, and now she didn't like his advice. "It's not so easy."

"I know." His soft eyes held a sweet kindness, and Jocelyn's throat clogged. His hand touched hers for the briefest second, then dropped. If only it could've stayed longer, held on longer. It had been forever since she'd felt a comforting touch. "Our seasons aren't exactly the same. I know that."

Jocelyn opened her mouth. "I—"

"Theo . . . Jocelyn." Only a few syllables, but the familiar voice from church services and Gmay meetings hung heavy and somehow accusing in the air.

Jocelyn squared her shoulders. No helping it now. She joined Theo in facing the dining room area crowded with red Naugahyde booths across from a long counter where customers sat on stools, hunched over full plates. Bart Plank, Jed Knepp, and Martin Hershberger sauntered into the foyer. All three Gmay elders had the same curious expressions.

Theo raised one hand and offered a half wave. "Hallo."

Was the pause that followed awkward, or was it simply the twenty-six years of being married to the same Plain man? Jocelyn had never stepped out in public with another man other than with family. Plain women in her Gmay didn't do that.

Courting couples did so privately.

She and Theo weren't courting. An odd sensation, like disappointment, took root.

The bishop pursed his lips. His glance seemed to drill holes in her heart. Jocelyn forced a smile. "Hallo." She edged toward the door. "Just picking up lunch for the *maed*."

"Uh-huh." He tapped a toothpick into his palm from the container next to the cash register. "And you, Theo?"

Theo held up his smaller white bag and a large drink. "Grabbing my lunch to-go."

"The diner is a popular place. Just about everyone from the Gmay comes here at least once a week."

Was that an admonition?

"Families do, anyway," Martin added. He had a sliver of something brown between his buck front teeth. "The youngies know how to court in private."

Definitely an admonition. Guilt slow-danced in Jocelyn's head. She pushed on the door with her elbow. In her haste, her tote bag's strap slipped from her shoulder. She grabbed it before it fell to the floor. Instead the Styrofoam box on top of her pile slid to one side, teetered, and fell.

Lettuce, sliced tomato, cucumber, green pepper, chunks of meat and cheese, bacon bits, and slices of hard-boiled eggs spilled onto the floor directly in front of the restaurant's double doors.

The door's bell dinged. An English woman stepped in the mess before Jocelyn could open her mouth. She slipped, slid, and squealed. Theo grabbed one arm. The man behind her grabbed the other. Her suntanned face snarled in disgust, and she righted. "Seriously?"

"Ach, I'm so sorry." Jocelyn bit back a groan. She squatted, set aside the other lunches, and went to work scooping her salad back into the container with her bare hands.

Theo snatched a wad of napkins from a dispenser on the counter. He knelt next to her. "Let me help."

"Nee, nee. Don't. Just let me." Wave after wave of embarrassment crashed over Jocelyn. Her heart beat so fiercely that her chest hurt. The heat was worse than any fever. She glanced up. The three district elders looked on with the same expressions that landed somewhere between concern and disbelief at what they were seeing. "Really, I don't need your help."

Theo's gaze met hers. His concerned expression faded to neutral. "Okay." He picked up his lunch and arose with the ease of a much younger man.

"Out of the way, gentlemen." Terri pushed a mop bucket on wheels between Bart and Martin. "I've got this. You all run along, scat."

Amazingly the four men did as they were told. Relief made Jocelyn's legs weak. Her knees hit the floor.

Which was worse? The surprised look on her bishop's face? Or the hurt one on Theo's?

The latter. Definitely the latter.

What did that say about her understanding of the Gmay's rules?

Chapter 23

*A*nywhere but here. Almost anywhere, Elijah hastily amended the thought. At least he wasn't standing on an auction platform with a microphone in his hand.

He set the last box of canned goods on the table, then squeezed between tables into the combination store's farmers market booth in the middle of downtown Lee's Gulch. Then he slid them back together. Still on the outside, Slowpoke woofed.

"Poor hund." Sadie plopped her basket of individually wrapped cookies on the first table. "He likes to sleep under canopy."

The girl's speech had improved so much at the English school, and she was as outspoken about all pets as she'd always been.

They'd already had this discussion twice. "No hunde allowed. The health department says so." Elijah directed his comments to Slowpoke as well.

A full-throated bark this time. It was bad enough that Slowpoke had been left behind while Elijah traveled the auction circuit for most of the month of May. Now this.

Elijah shrugged and threw his hands up. "Discuss it with the inspector, my friend. You too, Schweschder."

"Do you always talk to your hund like that?"

Her tone full of thinly veiled disdain, Kathryn slid Sadie's basket toward her and began to arrange a few of the cookies on the table. The woman had been as prickly as a full-grown cactus since that night a month ago at the farm. No wonder. Elijah had offended her with his too-honest words in the workshop. Even so, they had no choice but to work together today.

The sly look on Mom's face when she told him he'd have to go suggested that she might not like having tummy troubles, but she did love the idea of Elijah working in town at a market where Bonnie also would be selling her wares. Especially after having been out of town. If Mom gave any thought to how uncomfortable it might be for Kathryn and Elijah to share duties in the booth, she hadn't shown it.

"What other way would I talk to him?" That probably wasn't the best way to respond to the woman's question. After all, he'd given her reason to be angry with him. Still, lots of people talked to their dogs as if they understood—because they did. "This is the last box of canned goods. Shall I arrange them, or do you want to?"

"I'll do it." As the only Miller girl not currently down with a nasty stomach bug, Sadie was determined to be helpful. "Let me."

"Jah, let her."

So far Elijah hadn't run into Bonnie, but there was still plenty of time.

Sei so gut, Gott, let there be time.

And let me be up to the task.

Night after night of lying in his motel bed, listening to Grandpa snore, imagining the conversation. Asking the question. Getting the right answer.

Today was the day.

What if she said no? And why wouldn't she? Why would she

want to spend time with a man who couldn't carry on a simple conversation like a normal human being?

Stop it. One step at a time.

"I'll take care of the table, Sadie. Why don't you go get yourself a cruller and some chocolate milk?" He held out a few dollar bills. "Take Slowpoke with you. That will make him happy."

With a delighted whoop, Sadie pushed her thick-lensed glasses up her nose with one hand and took the money with the other. Her sweet tooth was notorious. She took off at a trot, Slowpoke following at her heels. This way Elijah would have something to do. He needed to keep busy. Sadie had learned to make change at school, and she loved helping out in the store. Still, Mom's instructions had been clear. Two adults should be in the booth at all times.

He slid a quart jar of bread-and-butter pickles across the table next to dill pickle spears, pickled beets, tomatoes, green beans, and an assortment of jams and jellies. All were made from produce grown in his mother's garden. The pickles were the bestsellers, just ahead of the strawberry jam.

The farmers market in Lee's Gulch was hopping with Plain and English shoppers alike, taking advantage of the Saturday gathering of artisans and farmers from across the region, buying everything from handcrafted jewelry to leather goods to fired ceramic pots to the fresh produce available the first week of June. A local bluegrass band made up of retirees, who strummed a banjo, a mandolin, and a fiddle, played with more enthusiasm than talent. Shoppers rewarded them with tips thrown into a banjo case.

Kathryn had already been in the booth when he and Sadie arrived. Her responses to his questions had been just short of snippy. Her pink cheeks, the way she rushed around arranging baskets of individually wrapped chocolate chip, oatmeal raisin, sugar, and peanut butter cookies, her head bent, clearly spoke of her discomfort.

Kelly Irvin

"Maybe we should put out some more of the banana bread and the zucchini bread." Elijah reached toward the box of baked goods on the back table at the same time Kathryn did. Their arms bumped. She backed away like she'd been burned. "Es dutt mer."

"It's okay."

Her face said differently.

"I know you didn't want to be here." Elijah dug for the words. It was like trying to rip the stump out of the ground when an old maple tree had died in their backyard. Painfully difficult, almost impossible. He wiped his forehead with his sleeve. Suddenly it felt like August in this particular booth. "I don't either."

"I'm happy to be here. It's my job." Kathryn slapped a set of Josie's handmade hot pads on the table next to place mats Sherrie had designed and sewn. "I'm sorry it's a hardship for you."

"It's not . . . I don't mind." Elijah wiped his damp palms on his pants. He grabbed a washrag and scrubbed the table. "Somebody set their coffee on the table. They spilled it and didn't clean up after themselves."

"I can handle this by myself."

"We never leave an employee alone. In case it gets busy. Or there's a question you can't answer."

"Or the person isn't capable of making change on his own."

"I can make change." True, Sadie did a better job than he did. Elijah rarely worked with money. His math skills, however, were good, the product of measuring, cutting, and fitting his wooden pieces. "I'd just rather you do it."

Because her people skills were better. He'd get flustered and count out the money wrong because he was nervous. Not because he couldn't do the math.

182

"Gut. I may be a girl, but I do plenty of math when baking. Ever tried to triple a recipe?"

Time to move on. "Mom sent a thermos of iced tea and sandwiches. Would you like some?"

"No, danki."

The temperature rose another ten degrees in the booth.

"Bruder, Bruder, look who I found." Sadie's excited shout likely could be heard four booths down. "It's Bonnie!"

Elijah turned. Sadie held hands with none other than Bonnie Yoder. The little girl smiled from ear to ear. So did Slowpoke, who immediately lay down at Bonnie's feet. Bonnie's smile was fairly wide too. She spoke first. "Hallo."

Elijah dropped a loaf of cranberry-raisin bread on the table. Bonnie wore a deep-purple dress. Purple was definitely her color. Elijah opened his mouth. A person should say something in response. For the life of him, nothing came to mind. He glanced at Kathryn. She was busy with an English woman who wanted assurance the jam was gluten-free and to know why there was no list of ingredients on the jar. No help there.

Bonnie's expression turned quizzical. "Are you all right?"

"Jah, Bruder, are you all right?" Sadie jumped around like a kid who needed a bathroom. "Mamm said Bonnie is your friend."

His face on fire, Elijah nodded. Mom had enlisted a little girl in her matchmaking schemes. She had no shame.

"Cat got your tongue?"

"Nee, Matilda the Cat would never take his tongue." Sadie frowned. "Do you have a cat?"

"I do. Her name is Puff."

"A gut cat name. Mine is Matilda the Cat."

This was ridiculous. Elijah shook his head.

"Laryngitis?"

"Nee, he talks gut." Sadie frowned. She let go of Bonnie's arm. She crawled under the table and popped up on Elijah's side. "I get you water. You need drink."

"Hallo." Finally, he got it out in a hoarse croak. "Hallo. I'm fine."

"So you're back."

"Jah."

Bonnie picked up the bread, then laid it so it completed a neat, straight row of baked goods. "You haven't been by the shop to see the display."

"Just got back."

"You'll need to restock. Your toys have sold well."

"Gut. That's gut." So good. He had a reason to return to the store to see Bonnie. "I will. I have a week before we go again."

"You're still not done?" The sweet kindness in her voice said what the words didn't. Bonnie knew how much Elijah dreaded calling auctions, and she understood. "Jason is still doing poorly?"

"He's back in the hospital."

"Ach, what happened?"

"The infection came back. The doctor said it's fairly common when an appendix bursts. It has some fancy name . . . perit-something. It means Jason has an abscess near his belly. They're pumping him full of antibiotics."

"That's awful. Is he going to be all right?"

"Doctor says jah. Dat says Gott's will be done. Dat and Caitlin are up there now."

"That's scary. It's gut, though, that there's so much family to help Caitlin out. And you can pitch in with the auctioneering."

That she could say that with a straight face said much about her. Elijah forced himself to nod.

"Now that you're stepping up to be an auctioneer, I'm surprised you don't want to sell your toys here in your family's booth." Kathryn's customer had left without buying the jam. She sidled closer to Elijah, then leaned in front of him to straighten a row of fruit pies. "You can support both businesses, and we can take care of the bookkeeping and carting the toys from your workshop."

Her emphasis on *we* was unmistakable.

"Elijah's a Homespun Handicrafts vendor, so we have them on display in *our* booth. They're selling well. Tourists are more likely to shop here in town." Bonnie's tone seemed affable, but a definite current ran through her words. "Feel free to stop by and take a gander. They'll make fun Christmas gifts for the kinner in your family. You might like one of my stuffies for yourself."

"I'm a little old for stuffed animals." Kathryn glowered. "Besides, my mamm makes them."

"Oh, sorry, I thought you were still in school."

That would make her fourteen. She was at least eighteen, maybe nineteen. What was going on here? "I made a commitment to Homespun Handicrafts." And its owners. Elijah edged away from Kathyrn. The family store had thrived without his contribution for years. "I'll start on some new pieces as soon as I can. Which ones have sold the best?"

Neither woman seemed to have heard him.

"Bonnie?"

The woman's gaze switched to him, no longer warm. "Stop by the shop later. Hannah has the inventory. You can get your report and whatever receipts you have coming."

Definitely snippy.

She sidestepped Slowpoke and stalked away.

In Elijah's late-night imagined encounters, their conversation had never gone like this. Every time he'd gathered his courage, spoken with ease, and asked the question. Made the invitation. Started the journey.

Sadie set a plastic cup of water on the table. "You make her mad?"

"Nee, I don't think so." Who knew? He was terrible at this. "Maybe."

"You go talk to her." Sadie pushed on him with two sticky hands. "I sell eppies."

She was more likely to eat them. "Mamm said I shouldn't leave—"

"Mamm say you need talk to Bonnie."

"I'll be right back."

"Wait a minute." Kathryn planted her hands on her hips. "I thought we weren't supposed to be alone in the booth."

"Not alone. I'm here." Sadie touched the metal cashbox on the table. "I make change gut."

"You're how old . . . ten . . . eleven?"

"Eleven. Big girl."

"I'll stay within eyeshot and earshot." Elijah squeezed Sadie's shoulder. "But Sadie's right. She's gut at making change. The customers like her too. She's a gut saleswoman."

Sadie beamed.

Ignoring Kathryn's disapproving scowl, Elijah slipped between the tables that lined the back of the booth. Of course Slowpoke immediately followed. "Stay."

If dogs could speak English, Slowpoke would've said, *"In your dreams."* His sharp bark didn't need translating. Elijah rolled his eyes. "Fine. Whatever."

Bonnie had moved on to a Cumberland County photographer's booth, where she sold her framed photos as well as greeting cards featuring them. Heart clanging in his chest, Elijah approached with all the care he'd use with a skittish horse. He picked up a framed photo of the Blue Ridge Mountains. His hands shook. He returned it to its spot. Words were in short supply. He cleared his throat. "You seem bent out of shape."

"Who, me?" Bonnie held up an eight-by-ten of two gorgeous Morgans in a pasture shrouded in fog. She showed it first to Elijah, then Slowpoke. "This would sell well in the shop, don't you think? Tourists would love them."

Slowpoke's tongue hung out the side of his mouth. He didn't seem impressed.

Words wanted to stick in his throat, but Elijah forced them out. "Are you mad at me?"

He sounded like a lovesick teenager.

Bonnie settled the photo on the table. She rolled on to the next booth featuring potted herbs and cacti. "My mamm wanted me to pick her up some fresh lavender. The dill smells so gut, doesn't it?"

This was ridiculous. He gulped a long breath, straightened his shoulders, and went for it. "Bonnie, look at me."

The force of the command surprised Elijah. If Bonnie's startled expression was any indication, her too. She moved away from the booth. Her rollator wheels bumped and shimmied over the uneven asphalt and concrete. Elijah kept pace.

"I'm not mad."

"You sure act mad."

"Why would I be angry? It's a free country. If you'd rather work in a booth with a teenager, it's no skin off my nose. I'm just a . . . business partner."

"Nee. You're not." Elijah huffed. A chasm opened up. He stood on the precipice. Now or never. "Not to me. Maybe to you, but not to me."

Bonnie's gaze skittered toward him, then back to the uneven pavement in front of them. "What are you saying?"

"I'm saying . . . I'm asking you to take a buggy ride with me."

She halted. Her hands gripped the rollator handles so tightly, her knuckles were white. "Why?"

"What do you mean, why?" Elijah's voice faltered. He swallowed hard. His heart pounded. *Don't blow it. Don't blow it.* "Why do you think? Why does a Plain man ask a Plain woman to take a buggy ride?"

Bonnie's cheeks had turned scarlet, but she met Elijah's gaze straight on. "When?"

"Tonight."

"Okay. Tonight."

Suddenly aware of the people surging around them, the prying stares from Plain booths, and the fact that he'd broken his promise to Kathryn, Elijah backed away. "Tonight."

He whirled and strode away, Slowpoke at his side, before Bonnie could change her mind.

Chapter 24

During a typical rumspringa, Bonnie would've been expected to sneak out the front door. These weren't typical circumstances. Number one, she was twenty-five years old, too old for something so ridiculous. Number two, her mother would be alone in the house. Number three, Mom would worry if she woke up and found Bonnie gone. Maybe she shouldn't go. Maybe this was a bad idea.

A Plain man needed a wife who could run a household and raise children. Someone who could get up with a baby at midnight, change his diaper, feed him, and put him back to bed without waking a hardworking husband.

The image of a toddler trotting in front of a racing buggy assailed Bonnie. How fast could she move to save that toddler?

Not fast enough.

Too late now. It would be hurtful to say yes and then back out. Elijah had gathered his courage and overcome his natural reticence to ask her on this ride. If she bailed, he might never try again.

"Mamm." She fumbled for the switch on the propane lamp on the bedstand next to her mother's bed. Clouds partially obscured the moon's light through the window in her mother's bedroom.

Darkness cloaked the room. The lamp clicked on. "Mamm, are you awake?"

"I am now." Squinting, one hand shielding her eyes, Mom sat up. "What's wrong? Are you sick?"

"Nee. I'm . . . I'm going out."

Mom leaned closer to peer at the battery-operated clock on her nightstand. "It's almost ten o'clock."

"I know."

"Where are you, I mean, why would you . . . ?" Her lips formed an O. Her eyes widened. "Oh, oh, why are you telling me, maedel? Get out there and go. It's Elijah, isn't it? Nee, don't tell me. We have to at least pretend—"

"Mamm, Mamm! I didn't want you to worry. I'm going now."

"Go, go, git." Mom slid down under the patchwork quilt that had been on the bed shared by her parents for as long as Bonnie could remember. She pulled it up to her chin. "I'm fine and dandy. No worries. I'm tuckered out. I'm sleeping."

Bonnie couldn't contain a chuckle. More of a hysterical giggle, truth be told. "Sweet dreams."

"Be careful. Be gut. Have fun."

Mom's voice followed Bonnie as she rolled into the hallway. She grabbed her bonnet from a hook by the front door and let herself out. A welcome evening breeze that swept away some of the June day's earlier heat greeted her.

Knowing this was a bad idea and taming her longing for such a night as this were two different things. She simply wanted what every Plain woman wanted. Was that too much to ask?

"Well, Gott?"

No answer. "Fine."

"Stop it already." Her voice quivered. Talking aloud to herself.

Now she really had gone around the bend, over the culvert, and into the ditch. "You're being ridiculous."

Flies buzzed around the porch bulb. The momma cat, sprawled on the swing's cushion, meowed, obviously annoyed at having her slumber interrupted. A mockingbird sang. The scent of the coral honeysuckle growing on the porch railing drifted over her.

Such a beautiful evening. The anticipation heightened with each passing second. This was it. Bonnie rubbed her breastbone with her palm. It ached. She hadn't been hurt. Not yet. This might be the start of something, but no one knew how it would end.

Least of all her. If only she could simply ease into it. Let the joy of the moment wash over her. Let it be the simple, time-honored ritual of a Plain boy taking a Plain girl for a ride. Nothing more. Nothing less.

The *clip-clop* of a horse's hooves sounded in the distance. The creak of the buggy wheels got louder. "Here we go." *Stop it!* Bonnie rolled down the ramp, suddenly filled with a sense of lightness and belonging. Of being like every other girl in every Plain community across the country. She'd waited a lot of years for this moment. "Just enjoy it. Live for today."

She was allowed to speak to the four corners of her world, even shout it from the barn loft and whisper it to the horses in the corral. "Just be."

Elijah pulled into the yard. He stopped the buggy a few feet from where she stood and immediately jumped down. He strode around the buggy before she could manage to greet him.

"Shall I lift you into the buggy, or should I just take your arm to steady you?"

"Hallo to you too."

His hands dropped. He halted. "Is it okay for me to ask?"

"Jah. I'd rather you'd ask, then have you put your hands on me without permission."

"Can you get up there by yourself?"

Unfortunately, no. Not anymore. "I could use a lift."

With a surprising ease, Elijah put both hands on her waist and lifted her into the buggy.

"Danki." Bonnie worked to keep her voice even. He wasn't a big man—shorter, slighter than his brothers—but he was strong. "Can you stick the rollator behind the seat?"

The porch light was weak, but the uncertainty on Elijah's face was still apparent. He picked up the rollator. "It might be better in the back."

"It collapses. Then you can slip it behind our seat."

"Ah. Okay." He lifted the rollator's padded seat, then let it close. He rubbed his nose. His forehead wrinkled. He pushed on the handles.

"Nee, put the seat up. There's a bar under the pouch. Just reach in there, feel for it, and pull it up."

He followed her instructions. His frown faded and turned into a smile. "Whew. Easy if you know what you're doing."

"Unless you have someone who uses one, you have no reason to know."

"Now I have someone." He sounded breathless. His face reddened. "I mean, I know someone, I know you—"

"I know what you mean."

He stowed the rollator and trotted around the buggy. A second later he was seated next to her. Close, but not too close. He snapped the reins. The buggy jolted.

Bonnie clasped her hands in her lap. She inhaled the dank evening air. Carol had peppered her with advice while they boxed up their wares at the market and carted them back to the store.

"He's so shy, you'll have to do the talking. Ask a lot of questions. Tell him about your day. Ask about his."

This was Elijah. He might be shy, but he'd worked up the nerve to ask her out. Now Bonnie had to return the favor and try to make him feel comfortable.

"I reckon you're glad to be home after being on the road for three weeks."

He nodded vigorously. "I am."

Two-word responses weren't helpful.

"I'm surprised Slowpoke didn't insist on coming with you."

"He tried, but I said nee. Sadie took pity on him. She was sitting on his rug with him, feeding him leftover baked pork chop when I drove away."

Sadie had been a girl on a mission at the farmers market. She'd offered to share her doughnut with Bonnie if she'd come to their booth "for a visit."

"She's a sweetheart. Should she still be up?"

"She's a night wanderer. Josie or Sherri probably already dragged her back to her bed."

"Gut. Gut." Bonnie peered into darkness that held towering pines, birch, oaks, maple—stands of trees that had been on this road before she was born and likely would be there when she passed from this earth. Nothing there to talk about. She ran her hands over the burgundy upholstery that matched swathes of carpet. "This is a nice buggy."

Lame, so very lame.

"It was Jason's way back when. He gave it to me when he got married." Elijah's voice warmed to the topic. He pointed at the cupholders. "Two cupholders. And there's space for lap blankets under the seat. There's a battery-operated fan. Should I turn it on?"

"I'm fine, but danki."

"It has a battery-operated heater, too, for wintertime." He gestured at the dashboard. "It even has a speedometer." He leaned forward and peered at it. "We're going twelve miles an hour."

"Gut to know."

The silence built for a few moments. Now what? Bonnie racked her brain. "Tell me what it was like out on the road. Did you call an auction?"

Elijah ducked his head. He snapped the reins.

Not a good topic. "What did you do, then?"

"Kept track of inventory. Moved sales items to the platform. Listened to Daadi snore. Thought about you."

Bonnie almost missed those last three words. Elijah's voice had petered out until it was barely a hoarse whisper. Taking a quick breath, she wrapped her fingers around her apron. "Say that again."

"Kept track—"

"Nee, that last part."

He cleared his throat. "I thought about you."

Maybe she should've talked about the weather. It was supposed to rain the next day. Farmers could always use rain. "What did you think?"

"I wondered if you would say jah." Elijah's gaze met Bonnie's, then bounced back to the gravel road illuminated by the buggy's battery-operated headlights. "I worried."

"Worried. Why?"

"About what to say." He ducked his head. "I'm no gut at this. At talking. I wish I was Toby or Declan. Or even Jason. Anybody but me."

"You're doing fine. I'm glad it's you and not one of your brieder. Or anyone else." The urge to squeeze his hand almost overcame Bonnie. Not for any physical reason. But because he was another human being who wanted desperately to be something he wasn't. "Don't say that. Don't ever say that."

Bonnie gave in to the impulse. She squeezed his hand and let go. "I like Elijah Miller, the quiet, thoughtful bruder. The one who works with his hands. The one who liked me enough to ask me to take a buggy ride with him. No one has ever done that before."

"Nee? That can't be right." Elijah pulled the buggy onto the shoulder of the road next to a wooden fence. Beyond it was a field of tall grass. He parked under an elm tree. Flies buzzed. The horse's tail whipped. Two chickadees chattered from the tree's lowest branch. "I've wanted to ask you forever."

"Then why didn't you?"

"I didn't know what I would say."

"Yet here we are. Talking."

"About what a dumkoph I am."

"Nee, talking about the fact that you were thinking about me." Bonnie worried her bonnet's ribbons. How much should a girl say on the first buggy ride? Carol and Ryan had talked for two hours. Then they kissed. Really, there was no rush. None whatsoever. Even so, Elijah had admitted something quite personal. Maybe Bonnie should too. "Fact is, I was thinking about you too."

"You were?"

"Don't sound so amazed."

"I didn't think you even remembered who I was until I came into the store that first time. Then I figured I was just another vendor. I've always liked you, but you never really gave me a sign you liked me. Except maybe a little bit that day at the frolic. With the big eppies."

"I remember you being kind when I was in grade school. So does Sophia. She said you pushed her wheelchair out to the ball field when she finally came back to school after the accident. We both agreed. You're worth waiting for."

Elijah turned in the seat. It was too dark to see his blue eyes under his hat's brim. "Really?" The amazement in his voice broke Bonnie's heart. He truly didn't know what a good man he was. "Don't answer that. I'll try to be worth it."

"You don't have to try. You just are."

"You're so nice. And so kind." His hand crept toward hers. Bonnie met him halfway. His fingers were warm. "And so pretty. I don't understand why some other man hasn't snapped you up."

"You see the world through the eyes of a nice, kind man." Bonnie concentrated on the feel of his calloused fingers on hers. Strong fingers. Rough skin. Tender heart. "Most men are practical. They want a fraa who can rototill the soil for a garden, who can do laundry, put up meat and vegetables, and nurse a baby all at once."

"You'll have help. Family. Your mann." Elijah tugged her closer. Bonnie went willingly. He let go of her hand and put his arm around her shoulders. "You wash dishes. You bake eppies. You sew. You make stuffies that bring joy to kinner. You keep the store's books. You run a store. That's a lot. More than a lot of folks who don't have SMA do. Tell me about the disease. I don't know anything."

He sounded winded. Like he'd just used up his entire store of words for the year. All for her. Bonnie obliged. "Do you know about the founder effect?"

"Jah. That's why we have more special kinner like Sadie."

"That's why we have more cases of rare diseases like spina bifida, dwarfism, maple syrup urine disease, and spinal muscular atrophy. SMA causes muscle weakness and atrophy—when the muscles shrink up."

She told him about learning to walk as a toddler, then losing that ability and not understanding why. "I was just a little thing. I could see my cousins walking, then running, skipping, hopping, jumping, but not me."

She explained about the surgery to straighten her spine and fuse it so it would stay that way. About the shots in her spine every four months and the pills that slowed the progression but couldn't stop it forever.

She lifted her skirt enough to show him her braces. "They help me lift my feet so I don't stumble so much."

"I reckon you can reach the Velcro piece so you can put the shoe on, but how do you get your socks on if you can't bend over?"

"Gut question. I'm so thankful for whoever it was who invented this handy-dandy sock aid. You stick the sock over it and then hang on to the strings while you stick your foot in and pull the sock on. It's genius."

"Where there's a will, there's a way."

"Exactly."

Elijah rubbed his fingers across her arm. "I lay in bed at night in our motel room staring at the ceiling, listening to Daadi snore, thinking about doing this."

"Me too," she whispered. "Only I was alone in my bedroom with Mamm down the hall, sleeping peacefully."

Then his lips brushed hers in the most fragile of kisses, so fleeting she might have imagined it. "Is that okay?"

"Jah." Bonnie kissed him back. Now she knew what Carol and Sophia meant. No one else in the whole world had ever done something so wonderful. Just Elijah and her. "It's okay."

Elijah sat back. He heaved a huge sigh. Like a runner who'd leaped over a mile-high obstacle.

"Why the sigh?"

"I want to remember this moment forever."

Bonnie leaned her head against his chest. She stared up at the star-studded sky. *Danki, Gott, danki.* Mom would say that God's timing was perfect, that everything happened according to God's plan. This felt like the beginning of something wonderful.

"Danki, Gott," she whispered. "Let it work out, sei so gut."

"What?" Elijah lifted her chin and stared into her face.

"Nothing. I've developed the habit of talking to myself."

"They say it's not a problem if you don't answer."

Bonnie squirmed. "Then I guess it's a problem."

"Ah. I see." Elijah chuckled. His arm tightened around her. "Don't worry. People think I'm weird because I talk to Slowpoke like he understands."

"Because he does."

"Of course he does."

He sounded so relaxed, so different from the anxious Elijah who came into her shop in hopes of selling his wares in April.

"Can I ask you a question?"

He shrugged. "Sure."

"I know this is just one buggy ride, but you did just kiss me, so I was wondering . . ." How could she ask this question without seeming full of herself? As if she knew what God's plan was? As if this was a sure thing? "Have you really, really thought about what it would be like to have a special friend who has a disease that takes away her mobility? A fraa who can't care for boplin on her own? Who might need a wheelchair one day? Who can't mow the yard or plant a garden on her own?"

Elijah was quiet for a long time. A pair of blue jays joined in the chatter with the chickadees. The horse tossed his head, flicked his tail at buzzing flies, and snorted. "Everybody has limitations. The vows say in sickness and in health, don't they? I reckon some things have to be taken on faith. One day at a time until Gott lets you see the bigger picture of His plan."

Add *wise* and *faithful* to Elijah's list of attributes. Naive too. "My dat would've liked you."

"I remember your dat. He used to come to the auctions when I was a kid. He was nice to me."

"He used to sit me on his lap in the evenings and tell me stories in front of the fireplace." Bonnie tucked her arms around her middle. As if they could substitute for her father's arms. "He always told me not to worry, that Gott had chosen Mamm and him to be my eldre. I was a gift from Gott to them. I know we're not supposed to feel special, but he always made me feel that way."

"You must miss him something awful."

"I do."

"My dat doesn't mean to, but he always makes me feel less than the rest of my brieder." Elijah's words revealed no bitterness. "Less than Toby or Jason or Declan and on down the line. If I have kinner—"

"When you have kinner."

"When I have kinner, I will make sure that each one knows he is who Gott wants him to be. He's made in Gott's image and when Gott made him, He said it is gut. Scripture says He will know a bopli's name before he's born. He'll know the number of hairs on his head. Gott doesn't think we're less-than."

"If I have kinner—"

"When you have kinner."

"When I have kinner there's a gut chance they could have SMA. How can a mamm with SMA take care of a bopli with the same disease?"

"You'll know exactly what to do, and you'll have help. Don't sound so sad." Elijah removed his arm from around her shoulders. Instead he took her hands in his and rubbed them as if to warm them. "I think you need a joke to cheer you up. I asked Declan and

Toby if I should tell you a joke. They said I should stick to being who I am."

"I reckon they're at least partly right." An electric current ran through Bonnie. Elijah's touch warmed not just her hands but her heart. "On the other hand, if you want to tell a joke, you should. Declan Miller doesn't corner the market on being funny any more than Toby Miller has an exclusive right to being the best Miller auctioneer."

Head bent, Elijah stopped rubbing. He said nothing. His face was hidden by his hat and the dark.

"Elijah? I didn't mean anything—"

"What do turkeys and teddy bears have in common?"

"I don't know. What do turkeys and teddy bears have in common?"

"They both have stuffing."

"That's bad." Yet Bonnie laughed. Joke tellers relied on people to laugh simply because a joke was so very bad. "Really bad."

"Hey! Everyone laughed when Declan told it at the supper table." Elijah's deep laugh rivaled the one Bonnie's father used to have. It was a rare commodity, one Bonnie wanted to hear more often. "I thought maybe you'd know because you stuff teddy bears all the time."

"Jah, but I don't think I've ever stuffed a turkey. My mamm does it." Occasionally. Mostly, they'd always gone to one of the onkels' house because a family of three didn't need a full-size turkey. Besides, giving thanks should be shared. "My aenti Frannie makes a good stuffing. She says it's the sage. I think it's the turkey broth she uses. It's very moist."

"But you've stuffed many animals, making many kinner happy. That's a gut thing."

"You have a way of finding the silver lining."

"Scripture says God can bring gut from all things."

"I keep telling myself that. We're going to Strasburg on Monday." She should tell him why. It was one thing for a man to imagine a life with a woman who had SMA, another to live it. "I'll be gone for at least two days. I'm getting tests done to see if there's been progression."

"Maybe when you get back we can try this again."

"I'd like that," she whispered, "but let's see how it goes."

"Nee." Elijah raised her hand to his lips and kissed it. "We'll see each other in a few days."

Bonnie shivered. "Gott willing."

Sei so gut, Gott, be willing.

Chapter 25

Hello, old friend, old foe. Bonnie paused on the sidewalk in front of the two-story, post-and-beam building that had housed the Center for Special Children in Strasburg since more than a decade before she was born. Her gaze traced the dormers and the little cupola on top, memorized the gray exterior and brown trim, the benches where she'd sat many times mulling her future in the shade of red maple, hawthorn, and box elder trees. Her future in those days hadn't included a Plain man with few words, big blue eyes, dimples, and blond hair that needed cutting. It wouldn't include this building much longer either.

Maybe one day, God willing, Elijah would go with her for her visits at the newly constructed clinic in Gordonsville.

Mom's hand rubbed her back. Swallowing the lump in her throat, Bonnie raised her face and let the hot June sun dry up the urge to cry. "Is it weird that I'll actually miss this place?" The clinic, built by Amish and Mennonite men in 1986, was being replaced by a much larger one in Gordonsville about seventy-five miles south of Strasburg. It would actually be a shorter drive from Virginia. "There have been plenty of days when I really hated this place."

"I suppose there's a sense of security in coming here." Mom

raised her face to the sun and smiled. "Change is hard. But everybody's talking about how amazing the new building is. So much more room. This old building was never intended to see this many patients, especially children who have grown into adults with all the treatments that research has provided."

Bonnie pushed forward toward the double doors. "In a way it's sad that there's such a need for these services. It seems like there are so many ways our physical body can go haywire."

"But it's a blessing that this place exists where so much research has been done and new treatments discovered." Mom was in a glass-half-full mood. "Plain and *Mennischt* boplin died of many of these genetic disorders before the clinic doctors started doing their research. We didn't know our Plain ways led to the founder effect."

"It seems almost cruel." Bonnie waited while her mother opened the door so she could pass through. "Scripture tells us to hold ourselves apart from the world. To not be conformed to the world's ways. We obey Scripture and only marry within our faith. So what happens? We end up with all kinds of awful, rare diseases."

"Bart could give a whole sermon on original sin in answer to that question." Mom led the way through the reception area. Check-in was quick. Bonnie was a regular. Mom picked a seat where they could see out the window and admire the stands of trees in the distance. "God doesn't cause these ailments. He allows them because a faith untested is a weak faith."

"Like the fact that you and Dat only have one bopli, and she has SMA3."

"Gott knew what He was doing. He gave His beloved kind to a couple who would love her with all their heart, just like He does."

They'd had this conversation more than once over the years. Mom's responses never wavered. Comfort could be found in that fact as well.

Twenty minutes later they were led into Dr. Newcomb's exam room, where they waited some more. It wasn't so bad. Photos of Amish farms, horses, and Virginia's Blue Ridge Mountains adorned walls painted a friendly eggshell blue. The air, which smelled lightly of cleansers, wasn't frigid the way it so often was in the medical buildings Bonnie had visited far too often growing up.

Mom pulled a copy of *Murder Simply Brewed* by Vannetta Chapman from her canvas tote and started reading. As a veteran of many doctor visits, she knew how to come prepared. Bonnie occupied herself counting squares on the tile floor. She was too tied up in knots to read at a time like this.

She shouldn't be, but she was. *Es dutt mer, Gott.* Bart said God never got tired of hearing those words. He wanted His children to come to Him, confess their sins, and beg for forgiveness. It gave Him a chance to show His mercy and grace. To say, "Go and sin no more."

That last part was the hard part. How many times had she laid her worries at the foot of the throne, only to pick them up again? And again. And again.

"Es dutt mer. I did it again, Gott."

"Hmm?" Pushing her glasses up her nose, Mom looked up. Her befuddled expression said she'd been deep into the story. "Did you say something?"

"Just apologizing."

"To whom?"

"Never mind."

Fortunately, at that moment Dr. Newcomb bounced through the door like she had loaded springs for legs. She had to be fifty-five or sixty. Her silver hair was so short that she could've been a boy except for the chunky turquoise jewelry and tortoise-shell glasses she favored.

"What's up, missy?" The neurologist positioned herself in front of a computer on a stand that went up or down depending on the height of its user. Being tall, she pulled it up. She entered a few keystrokes, then swiveled to smile at Bonnie and her mother. She always exuded good cheer. Always. No matter what day of the week or what Bonnie's problem might be. "I hear you're concerned about progression."

Bonnie explained in short order. Her doctor studied something on the computer screen. "You're due for your Spinraza injection today, so let's get that out of the way. Then you can see the Bobbsey Twins. We'll get Deb to test your grip strength." That's what Dr. Newcomb called the occupational therapist and the physical therapist, who operated as a team for the purpose of these visits. "Have you been doing your exercises?"

"I have."

"Any falls?"

The most hated of all the questions. It was a badge of honor to be able to say none. "Just one, and it was really stupid."

More nose wrinkling, this time along with a wrinkled forehead. "What happened?"

Bonnie recounted the series of unfortunate events that led to her sprawled on her back with her rollator on top of her and Slowpoke barking loudly.

"Let's try not to do that again." Dr. Newcomb rarely used her severe tone, but falls were one area where she reserved the right to chastise. Patients could end up with fractured bones, concussions, cuts, scratches, or worse. "Were you hurt?"

Only her dignity and, perhaps, her vanity. "No, just a little scratch on my wrist and some bruises on my arm."

Dr. Newcomb typed for several seconds without speaking. Finally, she looked up. The frown had disappeared. "Have you been wearing your ankle-foot orthoses?"

"She has." Mom answered for her. "She spends a lot of time on her feet at the shop."

"Any shortness of breath? Trouble sleeping?"

"No shortness of breath. The sleeping is the same."

Despite multiple muscle relaxants, her tightened hamstrings and calves never relaxed. Neither did the ones attached to her fused spine. Rolling over was hard. Then there were the headaches. Dr. Newcomb knew all of that.

"We'll do the respiratory testing as usual. Any UTIs?"

"No." Thankfully. The antibiotics needed to cure a urinary tract infection had their own set of challenges. "Not since before Christmas."

"Good. How are things going at the shop? Are you doing big business?" Dr. Newcomb peered over her reading glasses at Bonnie. "Are lots of vendors with disabilities lining up to sell their wares?"

"Even ones without disabilities." Mom's sly grin signaled what she was thinking about. "Even a young man."

"Mamm. Sei so gut!"

"Ah, someone special." Dr. Newcomb's smile held delight and approval. "This is getting exciting. I'd like nothing more than to one day receive a wedding invitation in the mail." The doctor studied the computer screen. "How's your appetite? You're down two pounds. Are you eating enough?"

"I'm eating plenty."

"She's always on the run—so to speak." Mom grimaced. "You know what I mean."

"I do." Bonnie hoisted herself to her feet. "I'd really like to get the shot over with."

A person never really got used to having a needle stuck into the spinal fluid around the spinal cord. The spinal tap usually led to a headache, backache, and occasionally vomiting. Still, the side effects were worth it if the medication staved off progression.

"Maybe you should see the dietician."

Dr. Newcomb was still on the weight-loss issue. No need. It was a fluke.

"I have all the printed materials she gave me. Besides, Mom is a gut cook." And she never stopped slipping a second helping onto Bonnie's plate every chance she got. "The garden will be full of vegetables soon. I eat salads, fruit, vegetables, all the healthy stuff. I'm gut."

"Okay. I'll stop by after you've been to PT, OT, and RT, and we'll talk again."

Fortunately there was no waiting in line for the injection. Forty-five minutes later Bonnie sat in the physical/occupational therapy room, her gaze focused on her hands. Maybe it was just her imagination. Maybe she'd had a bad day. Maybe today the strength test would show no change. Or better yet, maybe she'd grown stronger in some miraculous turn of events.

The occupational therapist, Deb Van Dyke, looked more like a high school girl with her long brown hair in a ponytail, her sandals, and the chewing gum. But she was all business. "I brought my trusty hand dynamometer. Remember, it'll feel like nothing moved. Just squeeze your hardest and let go."

She said this every single time, as if Bonnie would forget.

They repeated the familiar routine on both hands. Deb typed in her usual rapid-fire motion. Then there were the other manual tests of strength in her arms. "Okay." Deb swiveled in her chair and faced Bonnie. "You were right. There's been some deterioration in your grip strength, about two points down on both hands. I know that's not what you wanted to hear, but it's not unexpected."

That didn't help at all. Her grip strength had already been

poor. Now it was very poor. Why pray if a person never received the answer she wanted?

"Gott's will, not yours." The deacon's words during baptism class rang like an accusation in Bonnie's ears. Why give her a longing to have a baby if she could never care for one? She couldn't be sure she wouldn't drop this fragile creature.

She could have a baby. She simply couldn't take care of it the way other mothers did. Elijah said it didn't matter. He said that now, but what about later? How many buggy rides would it take before he began to see what yoking himself to a woman like her would mean?

A lifetime of caregiving. It was a selfish thing to do to Elijah.

Bonnie's throat ached at the thought. She wasn't a selfish person, but giving up on something so lovely so soon sent a fierce pain arching through her body.

That sweet kiss. A first kiss. A first buggy ride. With no second or third one? Surely God didn't ask that of her. Or maybe He did. Was this a test?

Oh, sei so gut, Gott, don't make Elijah my test.

Elijah could marry someone else, have a dozen children, and never look back. If Bonnie stopped it now. *Give me a sign, Gott. Could I have a sign?*

And what about the sewing? Her way of making a living? She avoided her mother's gaze.

"No worries, Bonnie. I'm taking care of the sewing. You have plenty to do with running the store and keeping the books."

Maybe, but the making of dolls and stuffed animals gave her joy.

That too, Gott, would You take that too?

Bonnie heaved a breath. "There's nothing to be done, I guess."

"In so many ways, you're doing great." Her tone filled with

compassion, Deb backed away from the computer stand. "Do you have any questions for me?"

"No. Thank you."

"If you ever need anything from me, any advice, any questions answered, you know where to find me." She never failed to say that. These people had such a heart for helping people like Bonnie navigate this disease. It took a special person to work at this clinic. "I'll turn you over to Jeanie."

The physical therapist, short and chubby with even shorter hair than Dr. Newcomb, was Deb's polar opposite physically. But she had that same deep well of compassion as her colleague. She did the usual push and pull of Bonnie's legs. The spasticity hadn't changed. Three kinds of muscle relaxants daily, and Bonnie's legs wouldn't bend the way they should. "Are you still doing your stretching exercises?"

"Every day. For all the good it does."

"Taking your pills?"

"Yes, ma'am, for all the good they do."

Jeanie smiled and said the same thing she always did. "Imagine how much worse the spasticity would be if you didn't do the stretches and take the pills. You don't have a lot of muscle spasms, and your hands and arms don't seem to be greatly affected. That's the good news."

She was right. Sometimes a grumpy bug infected Bonnie when she entered these familiar exam rooms. For a reason. When she first started coming to the clinic as a child, she'd labored under the naive illusion that they could fix her problem. They could make it so she could walk again. Maybe even play baseball or skip rope or jump up and spike a ball over the volleyball net.

The realization that the staffers could only help her manage the symptoms took its time sinking in—mostly because she was too young to understand and then too stubborn to believe it. She prayed every night for God to fix what the doctors couldn't.

That didn't happen either. God's will be done. That's what Mom and Dad always said when she asked about it. Finally she stopped asking.

"Have you been doing your neck and shoulder exercises?"

"Yes, when I have time."

Jeanie kept adding exercises until it would take half the day to do them all. "I noticed when you walked in that your shoulder curvature has worsened. The rollator and hunching over your sewing are taking a toll, I suspect. Try to do the exercises every day. And remind yourself to straighten up as much as you can when you're using the rollator."

Which wasn't much. Nobody liked being a twenty-five-year-old hunchback, but no amount of exercise would change it. "I do. I will."

Still seated, Jeanie rolled on her stool to the counter near windows that afforded them a view of the wooded lot next door to the clinic. She picked up a stopwatch. "Okay, my friend. Let's do the TUG." The TUG, short for Timed Up and Go. "Let's see how your gait's doing."

Bonnie excelled at the TUG. Always being in a hurry at the shop assured that. She sucked in air and prepared to give it her best shot. She had to stand up, walk ten feet, turn around, walk back, and sit down. This tested how fast she could safely do it. It also allowed a determination of whether she was a fall risk.

Which she was not. Emphatically not.

"Remember, no rush. Be safe. Okay: ready, set, go." Jeanie punched the stopwatch.

No rush. Ha!

Bonnie stood, pushed across the room to the piece of yellow

tape on the tile, turned, and hiked back. The second she sat, Jeanie stopped the watch.

Bonnie had learned early on that the goal was for patients to be able to get to the tape and back in seven seconds—the amount of time a pedestrian had to cross the street before a green light turned red. "How'd I do?"

"You've lost about two seconds." Jeanie sounded apologetic. "Your gait has a wobble in it that wasn't there four months ago."

"That's not possible." Bonnie closed her eyes against tears that burned. No crying. She opened them. "Let me do it again. I'm sure I can do better."

"Unfortunately, your legs will be tired after doing it once. Your time will be longer if we do that." Jeanie typed a few keystrokes. Then she turned, leaned forward on the stool, and planted her elbows on her thighs. The compassion on her face was almost too much to bear. "Dr. Newcomb made a note about your fall."

"It was silly. I tripped over a dog. It has nothing to do with weakness."

"With the progression we're seeing, it might be time to consider a wheelchair."

"No, no, absolutely not." Stifling a sob, Bonnie grabbed the rollator's handles and stood. "It was a stupid accident. No reason to act like it was a big deal. I'll exercise more. When I come back next time, I'll be stronger than ever."

Exercise didn't help. It didn't hurt. But the effect didn't last. No matter how hard she tried.

The rollator didn't allow for dramatic exits. Not waiting for her mother, Bonnie rolled from the room. If she tried to race out, she'd end up on the floor. And then in a wheelchair.

Chapter 26

*O*ut. Bonnie needed out. Too many patients in the clinic had something to cry about. She was blessed. She'd live a long life, God willing. She could still walk and feed herself and go to work at the shop five days a week. *Stop being a crybaby.*

The command did little to curb the tears that threatened. Instead of turning left and heading down the hallway to the respiratory therapist's exam room, Bonnie went right past the doctors' exam rooms and kept going until she smacked the panel that would open the doors and set her free from the building.

"Bonnie. Bonnie!"

Mom's voice calling after her wasn't enough to make Bonnie stop. She kept going until she reached Chet's van, parked at the edge of the parking lot. She knocked on the passenger door. The window hummed down. Chet sat up and rubbed his eyes. "Ready to go, my dear?"

"Wait, wait." Huffing and puffing, Mom marched up to the van. "You can't just leave like that, Dochder. You still have to see the RT. You were supposed to see Dr. Newcomb again."

"I've had enough for one day. Enough for a lifetime." Bonnie swallowed hard. The quiver would give her away. She gritted her teeth, breathed, and counted to five. "Let's go home. Sei so gut."

The severe lines around Mom's eyes and mouth eased. She patted Bonnie's arm. "I'll call Dr. Newcomb later. Right now, I think we need some ice cream before we get on the road. What do you say, Chet?"

The driver saluted. "Your wish is my command, Miss Jocelyn."

Mom helped Bonnie into the van and stowed the rollator in the back. They settled into their seats. Bonnie buckled her seat belt. She inhaled the pine air freshener Chet favored. She stared out the window, determined to corral any tears that attempted to escape.

"Dairy Queen okay with you?" Chet's concerned gaze met Bonnie's in the rearview mirror. "Or are you more in the mood for thirty-one original flavors?"

"DQ is fine." Mom answered when Bonnie didn't. "Thank you."

"You're welcome. I could use a Dilly Bar myself. And a cup of coffee."

"Did you ever wonder why Gott allows a person to have scoliosis and then a fused spine and then allows her to have weak hands so she keeps dropping stuff she can't bend over to pick up?" Bonnie stared at the passing scenery. An Italian restaurant, an elderly couple sitting at a bus stop, a car repair shop. People walking from store to store. Life went on. "What kind of sense of humor is that?"

"It's not intended to be funny. A person's character is honed by trials."

"When is it honed enough?"

"I don't know."

Those last words were spoken softly. Mom didn't often admit to not having an answer. Bonnie's trials were Mom's trials too. And she'd lost the man who'd vowed to spend the rest of his life with her. Had she known how short that time would be, would she still have said yes to being his wife?

Bonnie scooted around in her seat. "Es dutt mer. I'm being a big bopli. I know it, but I can't seem to help it. This place brings out the worst in me."

"A pity party is allowed as long as you don't stay there. You're allowed to vent for a minute, but then you have to get over it and get on with it." Mom squeezed Bonnie's hand. "We all have to let off steam, or we'll blow up. Right, Chet?"

Chet's gray, shaggy-haired head bounced in an enthusiastic nod. "Sometimes I get so irritated, I have to go out in my backyard and howl at the moon."

The image of the rotund man hitching up his pants and lumbering out to his backyard to howl like a wolf tickled Bonnie. She almost smiled. "Does it help?"

"Doesn't hurt. I'm just glad I live out in the boonies where I don't have any neighbors. They'd think they lived next to a lunatic."

What did Chet have to be irritated about? He was a retired teacher who carted Plain folks around in his van. He spouted poetry and sang songs. "Does your wife howl at the moon with you?"

"Nope, she left me a long time ago."

Left as in died? Or left as in divorced? Chet had never talked about his life, other than his love for teaching. Bonnie always asked how he was doing. He always said "fine" with a goofy grin so genuine, no way it hid a secret lament.

It seemed inconceivable that anyone would divorce a nice man like Chet. But then the English saw marriage differently than Plain people. "I'm sorry." Such pathetic words. The English language often seemed lacking in the words needed to express real emotion. Deutsch wasn't much better. "That must've been hard."

"It was for the best. I'm sure she's very happy with the principal from my last school, and I'm very happy with Misty and Peanuts, my Chihuahuas; my books; my movies; and my community theater." Chet tapped a snappy beat on the steering wheel. "She doesn't have to listen to my snoring, and I don't have to listen to her complaining. When I took those vows I thought it was forever. She thought differently. I can't control that."

A person really couldn't know until she walked a mile in a man's shoes, what he'd been through. "You never remarried?"

"Nope. I promised to love, honor, and cherish until death do us part in front of my God. There's no going back on that."

Which was why a person had to think long and hard about saddling someone with a lifetime of caregiving. No matter what a person said, he couldn't know what it was like to care for someone with progressively worsening weakness and mobility day after day, year after year.

Was Chet lonely? Dogs were good company but not the same as a wife. They should invite him to supper soon.

It wouldn't make up for his solitary life, but it was something. *Until death do us part.*

"What are you thinking about?" Mom nudged Bonnie with her elbow. "You keep rubbing your forehead. Do you have a headache?"

"Nee, I'm just thinking about a mistake I made."

"What mistake?"

She couldn't tell Mom about the kiss. The hand-holding. "Nothing. It's not worth talking about."

It was, but not to her mother.

Mom didn't seem convinced. "I have ibuprofen in my bag, if you need it."

"I'm gut." Bonnie would make the best of her situation. She always did. She had no choice.

※

Even a sweet, creamy, cold Peanut Buster Parfait couldn't erase the acrid taste in Jocelyn's mouth. A mother couldn't fix everything. But it would be nice to be able to fix a few things here and there.

She cast a glance at Bonnie. Her scowling daughter sat across the table in the Strasburg Dairy Queen, stabbing her plastic spoon into an Oreo Cookie Blizzard. Whatever was going through her head, she was done sharing her thoughts.

Likely tuned in to the unspoken tension between his two passengers, Chet had disappeared down the hallway to the men's room after consuming a Dilly Bar.

This wasn't the time to talk about the farm, Mr. Steadman's offer, and the future.

It would never be the right time to tell Bonnie that her mother was thinking about selling the home in which they'd lived her entire life.

Nor was it the time to share how Theo Beiler kept winding his way into Jocelyn's thoughts.

Stuck. She was simply stuck. She couldn't see her way forward. So much depended on what happened with Bonnie. For twenty-three years, Jocelyn had focused her energy on two people: her husband and Bonnie. Then, for the last two years, on Bonnie.

Her own needs weren't important.

Sell the farm. Don't sell. *Gott?*

"That was something about Chet's wife." Bonnie patted her lips with a napkin, her scowl fading. "I can't imagine how awful he felt. He's in limbo, really."

Thinking about someone else. That was always a good move.

"Jah, not like being a wittmann." The mere word brought to mind Theo's rugged, smiling face. With the big nose. Really his nose wasn't that big. In fact, it was perfect. Jocelyn tucked her smile in tight where it couldn't be seen. "A wittmann can remarry."

"Among Plain folks, he'd be *expected* to remarry." An actual smile gracing her face, Bonnie waved her spoon, flinging tiny drops of melted ice cream in the air, then pointed it at Jocelyn. "Same with a wittfraa."

She was making a definite effort to get past the day's events. Somehow Bonnie had managed to take the conversation with Chet and wind it around until it came back to Jocelyn. Had she somehow heard about the incident at the diner? Or had Bonnie acquired the ability to read minds?

Thank goodness no one could read minds. Theo had been on Jocelyn's far too often—like a pesky mosquito that she couldn't swat away. The thick silver hair, the teak eyes, the beefy shoulders. The lazy grin. *Stop it.*

Jocelyn took a quick bite of her parfait. So good, unless a person ate it too fast and got a brain freeze. Punishment for moving too fast. That could apply to many situations in life. "What's your point?"

"No point. Other than a wittfraa is expected to remarry." Bonnie fixed Jocelyn with an intent gaze that reminded Jocelyn of her own attempts to elicit information from Marlin when she knew he was keeping a secret from her. Usually about something important like the Christmas or birthday present for her he'd hidden somewhere in the house. Or sometimes the barn. "When you came back to the shop from the diner on Wednesday, you were in a tizzy."

Stand strong. "I'm never in a tizzy."

"Is it because of Mr. Steadman's offer?"

"Nee." *Yes. No. All of the above.*

"Then why won't you talk about it?"

Because if she did, it would become a real possibility. What if

Bonnie hated the idea? Even more daunting, what if she thought it was an excellent idea? If Marlin were here, what would he say?

If Marlin were here, none of this would be happening.

"I don't want to. Not yet."

Her eyes narrowed, Bonnie ate some more of her Blizzard. She licked her lips. "Rachelle Miller was at the diner that day, having lunch with Layla Troyer. They came into town together to get some material. Their boplin are growing like crazy, according to Rachelle."

"Really? It was super crowded at the diner, like it always is at lunchtime. I didn't see her."

"She saw you."

"Really?"

"Really. With Theo Beiler."

"I wasn't with him. Not *with him*, with him." Jocelyn's heart bucked like a horse spooked by a rattlesnake. Heat worse than a hot flash flooded her body. Her tongue twisted her words. "We ran into each other on the sidewalk. He was going to the diner. I was going to the diner. So we both walked in the same direction. That's all. Really."

"She said you were reading a bunch of papers." Bonnie laid her spoon on the table. She leaned back and crossed her arms. Her gaze skewered Jocelyn. "Did you show the offer to Theo? The one you refuse to share with me, your dochder, your family?"

"I was waiting for our order. It takes a while to get a bunch of orders that time of day."

"That's not an answer, Mamm."

"Bart and Martin and Jed stopped by to say hallo. I dropped my salad. Terri helped me clean it up."

"Mudder. What did Theo think of the offer?"

"You haven't said anything about your buggy ride with Elijah."

"Don't try to change the subject. What happened with Theo?"

Chet chose that moment to return to the table. "I took a walk around the block to stretch my legs. Figured you two needed a minute to get your bearings." He peered at Bonnie, then turned to Jocelyn. "I'd give you another minute, but if we don't get a move on, I'll be late taking Misty and Peanuts for their evening constitutional. They get a wee bit cantankerous if I mess with their schedule. As it is they'll be sitting at the door, waiting, with their legs crossed."

"I'm ready to go." Jocelyn stood. A feeling not unlike the one she used to get when the school bell rang on Friday afternoon swept over her. Free. She grabbed their trash and stepped away from the table. "I'm eager to get home."

"Me too. Very eager."

Jocelyn glanced back. Bonnie's expression said this conversation was far from over.

Chapter 27

*P*rayers answered. Elijah leaned against the wall in Jason's living room. His family sucked up all the rest of the space. The celebration of Jason's oldest boy's birthday had turned into a celebration of Jason's returning health. Working in the garden with Caitlin had added color to his pale face. He was still too skinny, according to their mother, but that wouldn't last long, considering the amount of sausage, cottage fries, corn on the cob, coleslaw, and cake and ice cream he'd consumed in the last few hours. Soon he'd be strong enough to take up his beloved microphone and call an auction.

Danki, Gott.

"Here, finish this cake." Declan offered Elijah a thick slab of two-layered chocolate cake with buttercream frosting. "My eyes are bigger than my stomach."

"I've already had a piece." Despite his words, Elijah took the plate. He wasn't a big fan of cake, but he did like a good frosting. "When have you ever filled that hollow leg of yours?"

"Since my fraa stacked my plate with a double serving of sausage and extra fries. She spoils me. She knows how much I love chocolate cake." Or any kind of cake. However at peace Bethel and

Declan seemed to be regarding his cancer, in remission for now, they both seemed inclined to celebrate life whenever the opportunity presented itself. Declan cocked his head toward the front door. "I know what you're thinking. Join me in my office."

The front porch in other words. Elijah followed his younger brother outside into an evening still hot and dank with humidity. A storm had hovered on the horizon all day, threatening but never breaking. A good thunder boomer would be a relief as June meandered its way toward July and midsummer. "What do you think I'm thinking?"

"I think you're thinking that you'll soon be off the hook. Despite the fact that we've done three mock auctions with all the kinner and their friends lined up as bidders, you're still hemming and hawing about calling an auction. Another week and there won't be any holding Jason back. He's chomping at the bit now."

"If there's no real need for me to do it, I don't see a problem with bowing out."

"Number one, Jason has the stamina of a newborn foal." Declan stopped a shiny new basketball that had sailed onto the porch. He tossed it back to birthday boy Zachary, who whirled and tossed it into his new portable basketball hoop. The other kids surrounded the ball, fighting for the rebound. "Number two, you keep saying you need to call an auction, but you never actually step up. You'll regret it."

"That's Dat's call. Maybe it wasn't meant to be."

"You've never insisted. And that's wishful thinking on your part." Declan's hand went to his throat as it so often did. "You've practiced and practiced. You've done every other job. You can't walk away now, not without testing your mettle."

Yes, he could. Couldn't he? "I won't be needed. It's as simple as that."

Declan swiped the fork from Elijah's plate. He stole a dollop of frosting, stuck it his mouth, closed his eyes, and savored it. After a few seconds of humming and smiling, he opened his eyes and held out the fork. "Don't you want to overcome your biggest fear? Prove to yourself that you can do it?"

Elijah took the fork. "To myself or everyone else?"

"Either. Both."

Elijah grabbed a canvas lawn chair with one hand. He slipped down the steps where he shook the chair open, then settled into it, his cake safely in his lap.

"No answer?" Declan chose to sit on the steps. "Or are you afraid to even think about it?"

"I took Bonnie for a buggy ride."

"Whoop!" Declan sat up and clapped. "Way to go."

A couple of the kids on the makeshift basketball court yelled their thanks and bowed. Declan laughed and clapped harder.

"Don't make fun."

"I'm not."

"I need to get my toy business going."

"Why? Was it a prerequisite to her going out with you? You have to sell your toys in her store or else?"

What went on between Bonnie and Elijah was personal. "Nee, don't be narrisch. I'm thinking of the future."

"The future?" Declan screwed up his face like he was thinking hard and it hurt something fierce. "You've taken one ride."

"Use your noggin, Bruder. Do you really think I can be gone six months out of the year if things go the way I hope they will with Bonnie?"

"Ah, ah, you mean because she's got SMA."

"Jah, that's what I mean."

"I don't even think of it. She's always used a walker or a rollator. It's just who she is."

"Which is the way a person should see it." Elijah set the plate in the grass next to his chair. Another bite of cake and he'd hurl. "But there are some things that are different because of it."

"Jah, jah, I can see that." Declan swatted a mosquito that had landed on Elijah's arm. "They like you better than me. You must be sweeter."

"There you are."

Dad's voice cut through the air before Elijah could respond to his brother's ridiculous statement. He craned his neck and looked back. Dad stomped down the steps. "Your fraa is looking to leave, Declan. Your bopli is fussing. She wants to put him to bed, I reckon."

"I'll bring the buggy around." Declan rose. He clapped Elijah on the shoulder. "You'll figure it out. If there's anything I can do to help, let me know."

He'd coached Elijah on his calling and how to talk to women. He'd covered all the important topics. "Danki."

Dad took a chair. "What were you two talking about so serious-like?"

"Not much."

"I'm not blind or deaf, Suh."

"I know that."

"It's true you could probably get away with staying home when Jason goes back out on the road, but you have to go."

"Why is that?"

"I'm sure Declan already told you. If you don't call an auction, you'll always feel like a failure."

No, that was Dad's litmus test for success, not Elijah's. Even so. "You're the one who keeps putting it off. I've been ready."

"I wanted to make sure you were truly ready."

"I have to get my business going."

"You know Declan decided at one time that he wanted his own business. Of course it was going to be an auctioneering business. But that all fell to the wayside when he got the cancer."

"I have my reasons for wanting to focus on my woodworking." More than one. "I don't have the right temperament for auctioneering, for one."

As if Dad didn't know that. Yet he continued to insist.

"Give it another few weeks. I truly believe that once you call an auction and do it well, you'll want to do it again. And again."

Maybe Dad *was* blind and deaf. Or simply didn't understand the one child he had who was different.

"I'll call that one auction." Elijah swiveled so he could see his father's face. "But I can tell you this now. One is all there will be."

"We'll see about that." Dad's chin jutted. He tapped one bent finger on his chair's arm. "You can't predict the future. Neither can I. Declan lost his voice and had to lay down his vocation so he could sell plants. I don't know why, but there it is." Dad tapped harder. He stared straight ahead. His ruddy complexion darkened. "Jason almost died from a burst appendix that spewed poison into his body. I don't know why he and Caitlin had to suffer through that season. But I do know that Scripture says Gott can bring gut from all things if we love Him with all our mind, heart, and soul. I just keep reminding myself of that. You should too."

It was the most words he'd ever uttered within Elijah's hearing. Only something weighing heavy on his heart could move Dad to speak of such things. A Plain man didn't. He plowed his way through, trusting in God's plan as demanded by his Plain faith.

Elijah should respond. No words came.

Dad stood. "It's getting late. We need to clean out the trailers tomorrow and start getting ready for the auctions next weekend. Don't stay out too late."

Again, no words. If his father knew Elijah was courting, he would likely be only too happy to encourage his son to stay out late.

Did God's plan for Elijah include Bonnie? Why give Elijah the gift of woodworking if not for him to use it? If God made everyone in His image, didn't that mean Elijah's shyness came from God?

Or was that a huge leap? Maybe the shyness came from Satan worming his way into Elijah, undermining his self-confidence and his ability to interact with other human beings?

Only one way to find out: keep putting one foot in front of the other.

Starting with hopping in his buggy and pointing it toward Bonnie Yoder's house.

Chapter 28

et him down easy. Such a thought was pride at its worse. Maybe Elijah was already looking for a way out. Sure, like he was the kind of man who kissed a woman and then dumped her. No, Bonnie would be the woman who kissed a man and then told him she'd changed her mind.

Chewing an already sore bottom lip, she lifted the living room curtain for the third time. He'd said he would come by this evening. He'd come.

Bonnie held the door open so she could roll through. The earlier heat of a fiercely sunny day had begun to fade. A lackadaisical breeze didn't help much. She paused on the porch to stare up at the inky night. The stars were just beginning to show themselves. Not a cloud marred the sky. A mockingbird chastised her from its perch on a beech tree branch. He would likely still be complaining when she finished her conversation with Elijah. They were like that.

Squeaky buggy wheels sounded in the distance.

"Okay, here we go." The cheesy meatloaf she'd eaten for supper sat like a brick in her stomach. "Be kind but be firm."

The mockingbird sang louder. "Hush now, he's here."

Elijah pulled up to the house and stopped. A second later he hopped down and trotted up the ramp. "Hey there. Ready?"

"I thought we might talk here."

Hand on the railing, he paused. "It's a beautiful night for a buggy ride."

Such a beautiful night and Bonnie was about to ruin it. "I wish things were different. I wish we could take a walk. Just you and me. No rollator."

Elijah edged closer. He put his hand over Bonnie's on the rollator handle. "I don't mind the rollator. Because of the rollator, you're able to get around. It gets you where you're going. As long as you're going the same direction as I am, I'm gut."

Such a perfect sentiment for this moment, for a walk. How would he feel when the rollator didn't do the trick anymore? "That's the thing—"

"What's going on?"

Bonnie cocked her head toward the swing. "Wouldn't you like to sit down?"

"I don't think so." He withdrew his hand. "What's going on?"

"I went to the clinic yesterday."

"I know. What'd they say?"

"I was right. My grip is weaker. A lot weaker."

"Your mamm's helping with the sewing. You've got it covered."

That one task, yes. But what about all the others as the weakness progressed? "My gait is worse too. Slower and more wobbly."

Elijah moved closer again. This time he slid his arm around her shoulders. "Es dutt mer. That wasn't what you wanted to hear."

"Nee, it wasn't. It surprised me." Bonnie eased away from him. She rolled to the porch railing. The mockingbird was well named. It seemed to mock her with its chatter. Right now she'd prefer a mourning dove. Its sad coo would be more fitting. "They started talking about a wheelchair. I got out of there."

"If you're safer using a wheelchair—"

"I don't *need* a wheelchair." The wind did nothing to cool Bonnie's warm face. Elijah didn't deserve her anger. Anger born of fear, frustration, and aggravation. "Not yet. I fell one time. And then it was just a fluke. So I'm a little slower. I'm fine."

For now. Until the next fall. The one that might cause a broken hip or shoulder. The one that would finally force the issue.

"Sophia uses a chair, and she's fine with it."

"She doesn't have a choice." If Sophia could hear Bonnie now, would she be hurt? No, she'd walked freely once. She ran, jumped, skipped, and played baseball. She understood how much it hurt to let go of what others did so easily, so naturally, so like breathing. Even toddlers did it. "I still do. For now, I still do."

Elijah edged toward the railing, so close his shoulder brushed hers. "Okay, no wheelchair. Not yet. So why won't you come for a ride with me?"

"Because it's coming."

"What's coming?"

"The hands that are less and less useful. The legs that are less and less dependable." Gritting her teeth, Bonnie counted stars. She swallowed against tears. "I'll have the store. I can run it the same way Sophia does. I know that. It'll be gut enough. It'll have to be gut enough."

"Nee." The muscle pulsed in Elijah's jaw. He shook his head hard. "Nee. You don't have to settle. People with wheelchairs don't settle. Sophia's getting married. It was announced at church last Sunday."

Sophia's revelations about her inability to have children were shared in confidence. "Every situation is different. Even among Plain women with disabilities."

Englischers wouldn't understand. English women had many dreams, among them marrying and having children. Plain women had that one dream. To marry and have children. They also had far fewer conveniences available to make caring for babies possible.

"Plain women have their faith and their family to make marriage and raising kinner work." Was there judgment in Elijah's observation? Or was it simply a statement of fact? "Whatever happens, you won't go through it alone."

A part of Bonnie wanted to frame that childish retort: *Easy for you to say.* In some ways it was easy. He couldn't know what it was like to struggle to accomplish simple movements. To turn over in bed. To even get in and out of bed. To put on socks. To hold an umbrella and push a rollator when it unexpectedly started to rain. To not be able to scramble for cover. "I know Gott must be disappointed in my lack of faith."

"Gott knows what's in a person's heart."

Which could be considered a double-edged sword. God saw her angst. He saw the bitterness she tried to hide from the people around her. He saw her determination to seem content with her lot. Rather than actually being content. "I'm supposed to bow to His will. When I was baptized and joined the faith, I embraced *Gelassenheit.* All He's seeing now is my hochmut. I want what I want. I'm questioning His plan. That's what He's seeing in my heart. You shouldn't be anywhere near me."

"Because He might strike you down with a bolt of lightning?" Elijah imbued his words with the merest hint of humor. "He'll come after me first."

"It's not funny."

"Nee, Bart would agree with you."

"And you?"

"I'm a grackle in a family of swans." Elijah leaned his forearms on the railing. He ducked his head as if he might pick an armful of pink roses so fragrant the scent almost overwhelmed. "I don't want to call auctions. I don't want to deal with strangers all day, six or eight days out of the month. I want to stay home in my workshop, making toys. I don't even want to talk to most people."

"There's nothing wrong with that."

He raised his head, but his hat still hid his face. "What do those sentences have in common? I don't want . . . I want . . . I don't want . . . I want . . . I don't. It's all about me." His voice grew hoarse and weary. "My family needs me. All my brieder and schweschdre are content to be part of the family businesses. Either auctions or the store. Except Declan, who had cancer and doesn't complain, even though all he ever wanted to be was an auctioneer. Then there's me, who wants nothing to do with any of it. How's that for hochmut and a complete lack of Gelassenheit?"

Bonnie sought words, but none came. A raccoon scampered across the grass in the distance. A barn owl hooted. Another answered.

"I'm trying so hard to make a way," Elijah whispered. "To make my own way. Is that wrong? Should I bow to my father's will? Is it my Father's will? How do I tell the difference between Dat's will and Gott's will? Either way, Scripture says to 'honor thy father and mother.'"

"These are all reasons for us to break off whatever this is. I hope you can see that." He'd made the argument for Bonnie so unexpectedly. Had she wanted him to talk her out of it? Maybe. Probably. Bonnie fought the urge to take Elijah's hand, to feel those calluses one more time and the strength of his grip. "A woman in a wheelchair can't take care of a house, a farm, kinner, while a man is away from home six months out of the year."

Elijah straightened. He met Bonnie's gaze. Emotions eddied in his face. "A powerful reason for me to make my own way. I want to be with you."

"Nee, I can't be your reason for going against your daed's wishes." Bonnie's voice caught and quivered. It deserted her when she most needed to stand resolute. "Nor can I encourage you, knowing what I know about SMA."

"Jason's home from the hospital. He's getting his strength back. He's raring to get on the platform again." Elijah's Adam's apple bobbed. His gaze shifted to her hands on the railing. He smoothed his fingers over hers. "I know you want to be independent. Can you forgive me for wanting to take care of you?"

"You just made my point." Bonnie scraped together the last remnants of her will to do the right thing—the right thing for this man who had no idea what taking care of her would mean. "Your daed wants you to live up to your family responsibilities. So do I. Faith, family, and community come first."

"You really mean that?"

No. "Jah. I do."

"I signed a contract."

"Bring in toys when you can." Bonnie drew away from him. She slammed the door on her true feelings. Time to assume her shop owner persona. "Certainly plan to make it your full-time job during the off-auction season."

Emotion fled from Elijah's face, replaced with a polite, neutral stare. "Gut plan." He tipped his hat to her. "I'd better get home. We have to clean out the trailers tomorrow. They need a gut scrubbing before we get back out on the road Thursday."

"Careful driving home."

That was an inane thing to say. Elijah drove a buggy most days. She never had. Bonnie plastered a smile on her face. "I hope all goes well on this trip."

In other words, she hoped he would overcome his fears and call an auction as well or better than his brothers.

He backed away, tipped his hat, turned, and was gone.

Taking with him all that Bonnie had ever wanted.

"It's better this way," she whispered.

The mockingbird disagreed. His song sounded just like a mourning dove's.

Chapter 29

F resh air, a shaded picnic table, a peanut butter schmear on homemade raisin bread for lunch, a cozy mystery, and the laughter of children climbing on a nearby playscape as background music. This sliver of Jocelyn's day couldn't get any better. A good mystery allowed her to shut out the worries that she shouldn't be carrying around with her. God must be so disappointed in her lack of faith in His plan. Another worry to add to the pile.

Without looking up from her book, Jocelyn found her travel mug of lemonade on the table and sipped. Bringing her lunch to the park had been a smart move. *Don't think, read.* Leave behind her worries about Bonnie's health. About her daughter's morose silence at the breakfast table this morning. The farm. Clyde Steadman's offer. Theo.

Theo.

Bonnie.

Theo.

The farm.

Ha. No matter where a person went, worries were sure to be there when she arrived. They were persistent like that.

Jocelyn set the mug down and picked up her apple.

Kelly Irvin

She could've eaten in the shop's back room, but then she would've missed the sunshine and listening to the kids yell, "Wheee!" as they whooshed down the slide. They didn't seem to care that the temperature crept upward toward the eighty-five-degree mark or that the sun warmed the playground equipment and threatened to leave them sunburned. To be carefree like them for even a few minutes would be a gift.

Pine Street Park was within walking distance of Main Street and the shop. The walk was good for Jocelyn too. It gave her time to work out the kinks in her shoulders and burned some calories after a morning seated behind the sewing machine.

"There you are."

Jocelyn didn't look up. No need. The voice, so like her father's, belonged to Uri. Gritting her teeth, she stuck her crocheted bookmark in the paperback and closed it. "How did you find me?" She located her smile and directed it at her brother. "Are you following me?"

At that moment, Theo came into her line of sight, ambling across the grass behind Uri. He had dirt stains on his pants. His shirt was missing a button. His hat had a dark sweat ring. He looked like a man who could use a woman to take care of him. Jocelyn grabbed a handful of corn chips and stuffed them in her mouth.

"Don't sound so happy to see me." Uri slid onto the bench across from her. He swiped one of her snickerdoodles. "I'm in town getting a part. I went looking for you at the shop. Bonnie said you were here."

"What did you need to see me about?"

"You're going to hurt my feelings if you keep talking that way."

"What way?"

"Like I only come to see you because I want something."

"More like because you want to tell me what to do."

234

"Ah, now I see why you're so surly."

"I'm not surly. I've never been surly in my life."

"I don't know about that." Theo plopped onto the bench next to Uri. "I might have seen a bit of surliness."

"You men always stick together don't you?" Jocelyn thumped her brother's hand just as he reached for another cookie. It seemed better than meeting Theo's gaze. She hadn't seen him since what had become known in her mind as the diner fiasco. "This is my lunch. Ask Frannie to pack one for you."

"Don't tell Frannie I said this, but your snickerdoodles are better."

"Don't you have alfalfa to cut? Why are you in town? Why are you looking for me?"

"I told you, I'm in town getting a part for the tedder. Theo came along for the ride since he can't do any work until we get it fixed."

"Did you get the part?"

"I did."

"Then shouldn't you be hightailing it out of town?"

"Theo mentioned you had a visit from a man named Clyde Steadman."

Anger descended from on high faster than a raptor hawk swooping in to capture a field mouse. Jocelyn glared at Theo. He busied himself tossing chip crumbs to a chickadee hopping in the sparse grass under a nearby poplar tree. "That's really not any of Theo's business."

"Don't get your nose out of joint. He just said the man came into the shop with that real estate agent." Uri helped himself to a drink from Jocelyn's travel mug. "You should've told me yourself. You should've come directly to me about it."

Jocelyn bit her lip. Uri was the oldest of her siblings. He was used to being in charge since their parents passed. Marlin used to mull over business with her brother all the time. Why hadn't she gone to him after this new development? *Pride.* Like Bonnie said, pride went before the fall. "I wanted to think about it." She reached for a placating tone. "I'm still trying to figure out how I feel about it."

"While you were thinking about it, I dropped into Logan Knox's office."

"Before talking to me about it?" Jocelyn used all her strength to keep angry words from breaking down her corral fences and trampling her brother. Counting to ten didn't even begin to do it. Marlin's smiling image came to her. Uri meant well. He knew more about land values and sales than she did. *Pride.* She exhaled. "And what did you find out?"

"He said he couldn't give me a copy of the offer because I'm not the owner of record, but he did give me what he called a 'high level' view of what Steadman is offering."

Jocelyn took a long drink of her lemonade. So much for a quiet lunch. Her stomach burned. Her indigestion was back. "And you think I should take it."

"I'd like to see the entire offer." Uri adopted the same placating tone. "I'd like to talk to Bart to see what he thinks. Maybe some other men in the Gmay."

It's my life. Mine and Bonnie's.

Jocelyn kept her lips pressed together. That was exactly Uri's point. She sneaked a peek at Theo. He nodded encouragingly. The rat. Maybe the raptor hawk would swoop down and get *him*. She pull the manila envelope from her canvas tote. Forcing a smile, she slid it across the table.

"I have to get back to the shop." She gathered the remains of her lunch and stuck them in her insulated bag. "When you get through kicking around his offer, you'll let me know what you recommend?"

Something like that. More than likely he'd tell her what he, her other brothers, and the elders had decided she should do.

"I will." Without opening the envelope, Uri stood and tucked it under his arm. "Do you want a ride back to the shop?"

"Nee. The walk will do me gut."

"Maybe it'll improve your disposition."

"There's nothing wrong with my disposition. I do get testy when a bruder comes along and eats my eppies and drinks my lemonade."

"For sure and for certain." Uri did an about-face and headed toward the street. After a few strides, he glanced back. "You coming, Theo?"

"Jah."

Theo hopped up, but he didn't take off after Uri. He leaned closer. "How would you like to go fishing with me on Sunday? It's our day off from church."

Fishing. Sunday. Day off.

An invitation. It was an invitation. From Theo. To Jocelyn.

"I, well, I, I guess. I mean, jah, jah."

He winked, backed away, whirled, and caught up with Uri in three long strides.

She was fifty years old and she was going on what could only be described as a date.

And a good-looking widower had winked at her.

Chapter 30

A noise in the kitchen at five thirty in the morning was unusual now that Dad no longer required breakfast at dawn. In the days when there'd been many chores to do, all three of them arose before dawn. Things were different now. Still rubbing the sleep from her eyes, Bonnie trotted into the kitchen to investigate. Her mother stood at the kitchen counter, her coffee cup in one hand and a pencil in the other.

"What are you doing?" Bonnie pushed her hair out of her eyes. "I'm an early riser and even I don't rise this early."

"I'm going fishing." Mom flashed her a "top that" smile. She managed to sound as if that wasn't the most astonishing utterance since telling Bonnie about the birds and the bees after she witnessed two horses doing their business in a nearby meadow in broad daylight in front of God and everybody. "I was just leaving you a note."

Fishing? That seemed highly unlikely. Mom was more of a you-catch-and-clean-it-and-she'll-fry-it kind of woman.

They'd often gone camping with aunts, uncles, and cousins when Bonnie was a child. Dad and Bonnie did the fishing, canoeing, kayaking, and swimming with the rest of the family while

Mom "kept house" back at the tent. Give her a book and a comfy canvas chair, and she was perfectly happy to enjoy the fresh air, sunshine, and sultry breeze.

Long ago and far away. Those days were so very long ago.

"Nee, you're not." Bonnie's eyebrows rose. Her nose wrinkled. "You hate fishing."

"I've been invited to go fishing, and I'm going." Jocelyn pushed aside the pencil and paper. She raised her chin and strode to the stove. She picked up the coffeepot and poured coffee into a thermos. "If you want me to put up your hair, I'll have to do it now. My ride is getting here around six."

Putting up Bonnie's hair started each morning with a ritual that prepared them both for the day ahead. As the strength in Bonnie's arms ebbed, she'd needed more and more help with her daily routine, especially in putting up such a large bundle of hair, but this seemed like a poor attempt to change the subject. She suppressed a smile. "Would your ride happen to be Theo?"

"Sit down. I'll get the comb and such. Do you have a clean, pressed *kapp*?"

"Of course I do." Bonnie braced herself long enough to pour a cup of coffee. "But it doesn't really matter. I'll be here by myself. No one will see. I can stick it in a ponytail and put a scarf around my head and be done with it."

Elijah and the other Miller men were out of town on the auction circuit. She didn't have to worry about running into him.

"Why are you such a gloomy Gilda these days? Elijah will be back before you know it."

Too often Mom could read her thoughts. "I'm not a gloomy Gilda. I'm not a gloomy anything." Bonnie added a dollop of milk to the coffee and an extra-large spoon of sugar—just in case she really did need sweetening. "I've been busy running the store, getting the books up-to-date, doing inventory, meeting with vendors. It's a full-time job."

"I feel bad about leaving you here alone." Mom's regretful tone matched her frown. "Maybe I should just stay home."

"Don't you dare. I have no intention of standing in the way of you getting on with your life."

Mom froze in the middle of the kitchen. "Is that what this is? Me getting on with my life? What would your dat think of that? Would he mind?"

Dad wasn't like that. He'd want a good man to fill his boots, to take care of his girls. On the other hand, the past two years had proven that they were capable of taking care of themselves. Together, they made a good team. The two of them. "You know he wouldn't."

"Do you mind?"

"Of course not." Her mother deserved to be happy. She was too young to be alone for the rest of her years. "I don't wish being alone on anyone, but least of all my mudder."

"I'll do your hair before I go."

"That's not necessary—"

"I'll be right back." She rushed from the room and returned a few minutes later. She carried the empty lard can on which Bonnie's prayer covering had been perched, filled with a comb, heavy-duty bobby pins, a hair tie, and a hairnet. She dumped the items on the table. "Sit."

"Mamm, it's fine."

"What if you want to pray while I'm gone? First Corinthians 11:5 says a woman who prays with her head uncovered is like a woman with a shaved head."

"I'm well aware of what First Corinthians says." Bonnie resisted the temptation to roll her eyes. She was twenty-five, after all. "I'll pray that you don't upchuck when you have to put a night crawler on a hook."

"I'm sure there'll be other thingamajigs I can use instead of live bait."

"You mean fishing lures?" Bonnie settled into a chair. She picked up the comb and handed it to her mother. "Nee, I think minnows would be a better choice for largemouth bass and channel catfish."

"Like you're an expert." The feel of the comb running through Bonnie's hair in long, even strokes was calming. A mother-daughter ritual that went back years. "When was the last time you went fishing?"

Four or five years. It had been that long since their last camping trip. Once Bonnie opened the store, she didn't have time anymore. Dad couldn't get away from his work on the farm. The older Bonnie got—and the weaker—the harder it was for her to participate in the fun. Dad insisted he didn't mind carrying her out to the dock and depositing her in the boat, canoe, or kayak. But she'd minded. It couldn't have been fun for him.

"You know, your dat loved spending time with you. He loved carrying you into the water and helping you float. He loved playing with you." Her mother's voice was choked with emotion. "He loved being your dat. He just wasn't the sort of man to say the words."

Most men, especially Plain men, weren't the sort.

"I loved it too."

"I should've pushed harder for us to go." Mom's voice quivered. "We don't realize how short time is until it's too late. I was selfish."

"You're the least selfish person I know."

"At the time all I could think of was how I didn't like sleeping on the ground, the mosquitoes, the flies, and snakes." Mom pulled Bonnie's hair into a ponytail. The hair tie snapped as she pulled it into place. "But what I remember now is the grilled fish and the coffee in the cool morning air."

"I remember Dat's tall tales. He always made it sound like he'd caught a whale-size catfish at the lake."

"His s'mores were always better than mine."

"Jah, but he always burned the hot dogs. You never did." Bonnie smiled at the memory. Her mother's gentle chuckle said she smiled too. "It was fun because we were together. I wish we'd gone more."

"It wasn't Gott's plan. I really shouldn't go today."

"You really should. Dat would've wanted it. He loved fishing."

"He loved fishing with you."

"And you loved grilling the bass or breading the catfish and deep-frying the chunks so we could dip them in your homemade cocktail sauce. The horseradish in that sauce cleared my nostrils every time." The memories were more sweet than bitter. They were to be guarded and cherished. "You loved chatting with the aenties and babysitting the little ones while they played on the playscapes."

"I did. You were the one who always had an excuse for not going."

Bonnie laid the napkin on the table. She picked up her coffee mug, then set it back down. "It was hard to see everyone swimming and canoeing and running around free."

"Do you think you'll ever come to terms with it?"

"You mean with Gott's plan for me? I don't know." A person could try—had to try. "I know I'm made in Gott's image, but I also know I have a stubborn streak a mile long. I want what I want. I feel like a three-year-old on the verge of a tantrum."

"Gott's gracious and merciful. He will work out what's best for you. But you have to love Him with—"

"All my heart, all my soul, and all my mind. I know."

"I think you do really well. You run a store. You go to work every day. You've made a place for other people who have disabilities to earn their keep. I don't see any limitations there."

"You know that's not where my limitations are. Don't pretend you don't, sei so gut."

Mom didn't respond. The seconds ticked by. She picked up bobby pins, one by one, eight in total. Then the net.

Bonnie touched her prayer cover. She couldn't see it, but years of the time-honored ritual assured her. The brilliant white prayer cover would be neat and her hair tidy. Her mom's nimble fingers would make sure.

"So you need help. I help you now. I put up your hair. I help with your bath. I take care of you. There's nothing wrong with that. Nothing at all."

A daughter didn't come out and say the obvious words: "What happens when you're not around anymore, Mamm?"

"I know. I won't live forever. But there will be others who'll help. Your mann's family. Your friends, like Opal."

"I know. I know."

So why did she worry?

Mom stepped back and surveyed her handiwork. "There. You're ready for prayer."

Better to enjoy this moment and let the future take care of itself. "I'll pray Theo doesn't regret asking a finicky woman to go fishing with him."

"Who said anything about Theo?"

So Mom wanted to play it that way. "Really? How many Plain bachelors are there in our Gmay?"

"One or two, I'm sure."

"Name them."

"You name them." Mom brushed a few stray hairs from Bonnie's shoulders. "I'll put the brush back. Do you need help with your socks and sneakers? I can bring them out."

"Mamm. I can put my own shoes on." She'd been doing it for years. With the help of a sock aid and an extended shoehorn. "There's no rush. I'll put them on later."

"I'm just trying to be helpful."

"Or feeling guilty about courting. Don't."

"I'm not. I don't—"

A knock at the back door put an end to the conversation. Her cheeks suddenly pink, Mom rushed to the counter. She picked up a cooler. "I'd better go."

"He could come in."

"We need to get on the road. The fish bite early in the morning."

"As if you would know." Bonnie couldn't contain a giggle. "Try not to shriek the first time you get a bite. You'll scare all the fish away in the entire state."

"I would never shriek." Mom lingered by the door, her hand on the knob. "You could go back to bed."

"You just finished putting my hair up."

"You could go visit Opal. Or just relax and read."

"Opal will be visiting her in-laws. Reading's your pastime." Bonnie flapped both hands. "Go, go, I'll be fine. I expect fresh fish for supper."

"Are you sure?"

"Go, scoot, before he changes his mind."

That possibility apparently hadn't occurred to Mom. The pink deepened to a rosy hue. She jerked open the door. "I'll be back."

"No rush."

Bonnie leaned to her left as far as she dared without falling out of the chair. Nope. She couldn't see who waited outside for her mother.

The door closed.

Bonnie laughed aloud. Her mother was courting.

Could this life getting any stranger?

Chapter 31

Wiggly, slick things. Jocelyn wasn't squeamish. She was a Plain woman, after all. She'd taken care of a baby sick with diarrhea and vomiting. She'd cleaned chicken coops and slaughtered chickens. Helped with butchering pigs, cattle, and deer. What was it about fish bait that bothered her? Smothering a shudder, she selected a minnow and attempted to attach it to her hook.

"That would probably go better if you opened your eyes." Chuckling, Theo took the minnow from Jocelyn. He held up the slender, flopping fish in one hand, the fish hook in the other. "One-two-three. Done." He let the fishing line drop. It swung gently. "I take it you haven't done much fishing."

"I've done plenty of fishing." Determined to ignore the closeness of her companion, Jocelyn sidestepped him. She traipsed to the gently rising bluff's edge that overlooked Cumberland State Forest's Winston Lake. Inhaling the scent of decaying leaves, wet earth, and fish, she cast her line into crystalline water only just now touched by tendrils of the dawning sun. "Okay, maybe not me personally, but I've grilled plenty of fresh fish over a Coleman stove at a campsite."

"Then by all means, let's catch some fish." Theo stepped within arm's reach. He cast his line, the zinging sound of it unwinding from the reel so forgotten yet so familiar. "I'm a big fan of catfish. Whoever catches the first fish has to clean it."

"Nee. Number one, it should be the other way around." Jocelyn slapped away the flies that had taken a decided interest in her hands since she forced herself to select a minnow from the bucket. "Number two, I don't clean fish. I cook them. That's the rule."

"Got it."

To her question of why he hadn't hired a van for the trip that took almost ninety minutes by buggy, he said part of the joy of fishing was enjoying the leisurely ride in the semi-cool of morning before the late June sun heated everything in its path. He was right. It had been quiet but not awkward. The creak of the buggy wheels, the *clip-clop* of the horse's hooves, the gradual lifting of darkness. If it hadn't been for Theo's closeness—which prompted butterflies to dance in her stomach—Jocelyn might have been tempted to take a nap.

Theo seemed to be enjoying the lake too. Did fishing not remind him of his wife? Had he gone fishing with his son? Everything about the thick, untamed stands of loblolly pines, oaks, and hickory trees stretching to the skies behind Jocelyn, the quacking of a group of ducks leisurely paddling across the water as an angular blue heron watched from the shallows, and the hint of sun on her face sent Jocelyn hurtling back to days gone by. How could this be a new beginning if everything reminded her of her past?

"It's all right."

"What's all right?"

Theo plopped onto one of the canvas chairs he'd lugged from the buggy. "Making new memories is hard when the old ones won't shut up."

"Do you have memories of fishing with your fraa?"

"I do. She was an avid fisherwoman and surprisingly competitive." Theo chuckled. "She was also a gut hunter. But on the flip side, she wasn't much of a cook. How's that for a switcheroo?"

"Did you tell her you didn't like her cooking?"

"I didn't have to. She was the first to admit she lacked attention to detail. Two teaspoons of baking soda became three of baking powder. A cup of milk became two cups. A teaspoon of cinnamon became a tablespoon."

"Maybe she needed glasses."

"Her eyesight was fine. She just didn't like cooking that much, so she was in a hurry to get it over with." He smacked a mosquito, leaving a splatter of blood on his arm near his rolled-up sleeve. "I was a little late on the draw for that one."

"You'll itch tonight."

"I'm willing to pay the price if it means some gut eating." A smile played across his craggy, tanned face. "And spending time with gut company."

He thought she was good company. The butterflies dancing in Jocelyn's stomach turned into the frantic flapping of a hundred sets of wings. "It doesn't bother you that she loved to fish and here you are fishing with someone else . . . another woman?"

The words hung in the air. They would've been better left unsaid. Mostly because fishing wasn't so bad. Not with Theo as company. Jocelyn had been so alone for so long. She had friends, cousins, aunts, sisters-in-law. She had no need for more of that kind of company.

She had Bonnie. Again, not that kind of company.

To feel like a woman. Fifty wasn't too old for that, no matter what her change-of-life body said. But not with just any man. With this man. Why, she couldn't say.

Nor would she admit it.

"Do you think your mann would object?"

"Nee, he'd be glad."

"Same with my fraa. She told me as much not long before she passed." Theo shifted in his chair. His gaze turned pensive, sought the lake and beyond. "I denied I would ever need or want another woman, but she knew. She was smart like that."

"Do you think it was better to have that chance to talk to her about what was coming?" Jocelyn settled into the other chair. It brought her closer to Theo than she would've dared in other circumstances. Lean a little to the left and she could touch him. "Or be like me, who woke up to find Marlin gone? He didn't suffer, but I did, much as I tried to be stoic and a stout believer."

"Neither is a cake walk, to be sure. Knowing she was leaving broke something in me." He cleared his throat. "But I've worked my way out of that darkness because Gott doesn't really give us a choice. He's probably wondering what has taken me so long."

"Nee, He knows how weak we are but also how fervently we love. He gave us that capacity. We grieve so hard because we love so much."

Theo smiled. He was the one who touched Jocelyn's arm. That first intentional touch. Over bait that had a fishy stink. Jocelyn smiled back.

At that moment, her rod arched, the reel spun. The line raced out.

"Whoa." She shrieked and leapt to her feet. "I've got one."

"You sure have." Theo sprang up. He reached for her rod, then backed up. "You've got it. Hang on to the rod. Don't let go. Reel it in."

He thought she could do it on her own. Good man. Still, it was easier said than done. The fish fought a valiant battle. Jocelyn reeled in her line. The fish spun it back out. Back and forth.

Until the fish tired. Jocelyn turned the lever until finally the mammoth catfish swung with only an occasional flop in the air.

"He's a monster!" Theo doffed his hat. "Gut job." He grabbed the line and swung the fish in so he could get him off the hook. It flipped and flopped. "He's a fighter, this one. I reckon he weighs at least fifteen pounds."

"I can't believe it. I did it. I caught a fish." Jocelyn dropped the rod. She clapped and danced a little jig. So dignified for an old widow woman. At least Bonnie hadn't been nearby to hear her mother's shriek. "I caught the first fish."

"Indeed you did." Grinning, Theo stuck the fish on a line he'd brought for that purpose with quick, efficient movements. It went back into the water for safekeeping. "You fibbed. You're a pro."

"Am not."

Theo grabbed her hands and pulled her closer. What little breath Jocelyn had left disappeared from her lungs in a whoosh. Her heart strayed from its normal rhythm, lost in the moment. Theo's teak eyes were alight with amusement and something else. Something Jocelyn recognized because she felt it too.

An ache for closeness. A need to draw near. To explore something new and sweet and special.

Jocelyn stood on her tiptoes. She leaned her head back. Theo came the rest of the way. His full lips were warm and soft. He framed her face with his hands. The kiss deepened.

Finally, he raised his head. His hands slid the length of her arms and clasped her hands. The lopsided grin reappeared. "I've been wanting to do that since that first day when you opened the kitchen door and looked at me like you'd found a rat snake in your chicken coop."

It took a minute for Jocelyn to respond. *Breathe, breathe.* She bit her lip to keep from crying. She heaved a long breath.

"What's the matter? Are you crying?" His smile disappeared. He let her hands drop. "Did I read you wrong? I thought—"

"Nee, you didn't read anything wrong." Jocelyn swallowed back tears. "I've just been so lonely. That sounds ridiculous, I know, with all the family I have and taking care of Bonnie, but I missed having someone this close. Mind you, not just anyone, but someone like you. Nee, you. There's something about you. I can't stop thinking about you."

Head down, she put her hand on his chest. Theo's heart pumped as hard as her own. His fingers touched her chin, gently forcing her to look up. "It's not ridiculous. Like you said, Gott made us this way, after all. Adam and Eve, man and woman. After Ellie died, I swore I'd never go through that again. Why would anyone want to take the chance of having his heart ripped out of his chest like that? This here, this right now, this is why."

He kissed her again, quicker, more gently this time, but a kiss full of promise. "Because there's a spark that explodes when we breathe the same air. Because we like to talk to hear each other's voices. Because I feel whole again when I hold your hand."

A man with words. Theo was a rare find. He could put a name on what he was feeling. And on what Jocelyn felt. She loved him for that.

Loved. No, no, it was far too early for such a pronouncement. They hardly knew each other. One fifteen-pound catfish did not love make.

Theo traced her cheek with his finger. "Say something."

"I think you'd better catch another fish because I'm planning to eat mine."

He laughed. "All fifteen pounds. Either you really like fish or you have a powerful hunger. A conversation for later, then. As

Kelly Irvin

long as you don't regret this." He touched her lips with his, then withdrew. "I sure don't."

"Nee, no regrets."

"Gut." He picked up her rod and handed it to her. "The two whoopie pies you packed for lunch say I catch the next fish."

"Plain folks don't wager." Now that the adrenaline of the fish catch had faded, Jocelyn's shoulders ached. She might have a pulled bicep. Even so, she tossed her line out over the water with a jaunty flick of her wrist. "However, we do win prizes. The prize for catching the next fish will be my pumpkin spice whoopie pies filled with cream cheese frosting."

"Fair enough. Of course, there's a chance you've scared the fish off with all your caterwauling over catching one measly catfish."

"Me? Caterwauling? Ha. You clapped."

The banter continued for a few minutes. Eventually quiet reigned. One thing was for sure. If Jocelyn caught the next fish, she would award the whoopie pies to Theo as a prize for best first kiss. Kisses. Her cheeks flamed at the thought.

No disrespect to Marlin. They'd been sixteen-year-old teenagers when he first asked her to take a buggy ride after a raucous singing one warm May evening. She'd made him wait almost three months for that first kiss. Sweet, fumbling, learning their way. Neither of them had a clue.

So sweet. Oh, Marlin. What would he say now? How much would she tell him at the next picnic lunch? All of it, of course.

"You got quiet all of a sudden." Theo's sideways glance held trepidation. "Second thoughts?"

So he wasn't as confident as he liked to act. "Nee, no second thoughts. Just a dusting of bittersweetness."

"Same here." He pulled in his line. The minnow was gone. "Some fish got lucky."

"At this rate, you'll never catch anything."

"Fishing is a lesson in patience, my friend."

So it was. Another half hour passed. No bites. Jocelyn's peanut butter toast at four in the morning failed her. Her stomach growled. Face warm, she ignored it.

"Maybe we should have an early lunch." Theo reeled in his line. "I could go for a sandwich about now. And another kiss. Or two, or three."

"Easy, there." The flaming heat that inundated her had nothing to do with a blazing sun now well into the sky. "It's not even eleven o'clock."

"So?" Theo guzzled half a bottle of water, then poured the rest over his face and neck. His faded cotton shirt turned a deeper shade of blue. "The meal rules don't apply when you're lakeside."

"Well, then." Jocelyn reeled in her own line, set aside her rod, and went to work laying out lunch on an old quilt perfectly suited for a bed of crunchy leaves. "I hope you like ham and cheddar cheese on sourdough."

"I do."

He liked ham-and-cheese sandwiches and kisses. So did she. What else might they have in common? Suddenly Jocelyn couldn't wait to find out.

Chapter 32

*S*peak up. Say something. Step up.

Elijah studied his dirty boots while his dad handed out an updated inventory list for the three-ring circus otherwise known as a retirement sale that would begin in fifteen minutes on the Eash farm outside of Hughesville, Maryland. They were selling everything before retiring to Pinecraft, Florida—even their winter clothes. In order to accommodate forty years' worth of accumulated belongings, the Millers were doing three simultaneous auctions: household goods, furniture, and appliances; farm equipment and tools; and livestock.

"Elijah, you'll spot for me for the household goods, appliances, and furniture." Toby studied the thick sheaf of papers for a second. He snatched a stubby pencil from behind one ear and used it to scratch a spot above his left eyebrow. "Emmett is coordinating the item lineup. Dat's got the livestock. Daadi has equipment and tools."

Once again Elijah wasn't one of the callers. His family had conspired to give him the easy way out, even while insisting he come on the road as a substitute for Jason. His brother would be well enough to resume his duties next week. In fact, he'd argued to come to this auction but had been overruled by his wife. The mixed message didn't help Elijah's state of mind. He should step up. Volunteer. Do what he came to do. So why didn't he?

It wasn't an either-or. He could still craft toys and sell them at Homespun Handicrafts.

No, that wasn't it. Elijah still wanted his own business. The thought of stepping onto the platform, mic in hand, still filled him with dread.

He still wanted Bonnie in his life in the worst way.

He couldn't pursue a new life on a foundation built on failure. He would see himself as a failure. Right or wrong, so would his family.

Speak up. Say something. Step up.

If this was to be his life, now was the time to prove it. To his father. His brothers. To his family. To himself.

"I'll do my best."

Elijah swiveled to see Daadi trudging up the trailer steps. Despite his stooped shoulders and arthritis-gnarled hands, he presented a commanding figure. Even so, something was missing in his usual take-charge tone. "What's wrong, Daadi?"

"My heart's doing that hippity-hop thing again."

That hippity-hop thing, otherwise known as atrial fibrillation, or A-fib, according to the doc. Grandpa kept postponing a visit to the cardiologist recommended by his doctor—much to Grandma's chagrin.

"Do you need to go to the ER?" Toby dropped the papers on the counter. "Elijah can take you. We'll get a volunteer to spot for me."

"Nee. It'll settle down on its own. It always does." Grandpa plopped onto a collapsible stool. "Calling the auction will take my mind off it."

"Nee. If you won't go to the ER, you need to rest." Elijah straightened his shoulders. He picked up the inventory. "I'll stand in for you."

Grandpa reached for the stack of papers. "It's not necessary—"

"Mammi will tan our hides if we let anything happen to you." Elijah batted Grandpa's hand away. Tucking his list under his arm, he sidestepped his brothers and headed for the door. "She didn't want you out here in the first place, and she was right. I've got this. You rest."

"Who put you in charge?" Grandpa's words chased Elijah down the steps. "Hey, I'm talking to you."

Elijah kept walking. Toby, Emmett, and Dad joined him. A sense of unity he'd never felt before swept over Elijah. *You can do this.* He summoned Declan's voice. *"You have a nice cadence for someone who's never called an auction."*

He could do this.

The three platforms with sound equipment had been spread across the fairgrounds in order to make room for the crowds and to lessen the overlap of the sound system they used for calling. The crowd thickened as they drew closer to the equipment and tools platform. Farmers in John Deere or Massey Ferguson caps mingled with Plain buyers in straw hats in the blazing June sun only a few feet from the steps. They parted as the Millers strode through. A few hailed Toby and Dad. They were well known among the perennial auction-goers.

No one knew Elijah. Looking neither left or right, he clomped up the stairs.

You can do this.

Nee, I can't.

Not alone.

It wasn't Declan's voice anymore. Elijah didn't need Declan. He couldn't rely on his own strength; that was obvious. He needed to rely on someone far more powerful.

Gott, You make all things possible. I need Your help. I can't do this alone.

I'm here. You're standing on solid rock. I have your right hand.

The iron claw that gripped his lungs eased. Elijah gulped in air like a man reaching dry ground after nearly drowning in swift-moving rapids. He stopped near the podium where the mic lay. Not yet. He didn't have to pick it up yet.

Instead, he focused on the list in his hand. At first the words swam as if they, too, were caught in the eddy and swell of river rapids. Then, miraculously, they righted themselves. An alfalfa mower, three generators, a tedder, a side delivery rake, a flatbed wagon, a propane-driven motorized baler, a hitch cart, a manure spreader, a corn picker, each with their own brief description. Everything a farmer needed to cut and bale alfalfa, to fluff and dry the hay, to sow and reap alfalfa, corn, rye, barley, and wheat on a 161-acre farm in south-central Maryland.

Elijah forced his gaze to the crowd, growing with every second that ticked by. He waited for the paralyzing fear to inundate him. The ice to encase his body even as sweat soaked his shirt and made his hands too slick to hold the mic. He waited for his mouth to dry and stomach cramps to send him to his knees doubled over.

None of that happened. He heaved another breath.

I'm here, Elijah. I'm here. You're not alone.

He picked up the mic. "Good morning, friends. *Guder mariye.* Welcome, bewillkumm! Let's not mess around, folks. Let's get down to business before it gets any hotter this fine summer morning. Are you ready?"

The crowd responded by clapping, whooping, and cheering.

No pressure. He loosened his grip on the mic. *Do it. Get it over with.*

"First up a Safford Bush Hog ten-foot hay tedder. Ground driven." The words came, slowing at first, then picking up speed. The folks closest to the platform had the best view of the piece of equipment used to fluff and turn newly cut alfalfa so the hay would dry evenly. "We'll start the bidding off at $1,500, which is on the low side. You know it. I know it. So let's get it rolling.

"Bid 1,500, 1,500. Bid 1,500. I've got 1,500, 2,000? Who'll give me 2,000? Bid 2,000? Bid 2,500. 2,500. Who wants in? Now 3,000. 3,000. Bid 3,000."

A Plain man stuck up his bid card for the first time. "Danki, friend. I've got $3,000. Bid 3,500? Bid 3,500?"

"$3,200!" A Plain man, with a toddler on one hip and two girls hanging on to his legs on either side, shouted it out.

"That's . . . that's okay." Elijah trod closer to the platform's edge. Despite obvious use, the tedder was in decent condition. Not new, but well cared for. "Come on, folks. Bid $3,500. Who'll give me 3,500?"

The newbie Plain man lifted his card.

"Bid 3,500. Bid 4,000."

"$3,750." The family man lifted his bid card with his free hand.

"Driving a hard bargain, aren't you?" Elijah pointed at the tedder. "This is a gut piece of equipment. Well cared for. Someone give me what it's worth. Bid 4,000."

So it went. Back and forth. In the end Family Man walked away with a new addition to his farm equipment at $4,200.

Almost exactly what Toby had written on the inventory as a target price. Sometimes they found just the right groove to make it happen. Now to build momentum. He grabbed his travel mug and gulped down a mouthful of water. His gaze caught Daadi sitting on the first row of bleachers. His grandfather raised his hand and flashed a thumbs-up. His grin said it all.

A-fib, my foot.

No matter. Elijah checked his list. Generators. Used generators were bargains almost every Plain home could use. They went quickly and for good prices. So did the side delivery rake, the hay-loader, a hitch cart, a manure spreader, on and on. Now his shirt was soaked in sweat. Not from nerves but a hard workout up and down the platform. Get through it. One item at a time. One sale at a time. This would never be his dream job, but he could do it. He was doing it.

One of the Eash sons, acting as Elijah's spotter, filled his travel mug twice. Steady water consumption was critical. A dry mouth made it difficult to keep up the pace. So did dehydration.

At noon they took a thirty-minute break for lunch. Elijah took a sack weighted down with two sets of cheeseburgers with everything on them and curly fries, a carrier heavy with two large ice-cold root beers supplied by the Eashes to the bleachers. He settled next to Grandpa. "I know what you did."

"You're crushing it up there, Enkel."

"Your heart is fine." Elijah partitioned out the food and drinks. "It's mean to make us worry about your health."

"My heart is feeling better. Its rhythm synced up right about the time you sold that tedder." Grandpa wiped the grease that dripped from his burger with a napkin. "Of course, it won't be so great after I eat this heart-attack-waiting-to-happen." Grinning, he took a huge bite and proceeded to chew happily.

"I could go get you a salad."

"Bite your tongue." Food muffled Grandpa's words. "Rabbit food."

Grandpa maintained that people his age had earned the right

to eat whatever they wanted. Besides, eating red meat, potatoes, and an endless supply of homemade bread and desserts hadn't killed him yet.

Elijah demolished most of his burger before he bothered to try again. A man worked up a powerful hunger calling an auction. "What made you think this time would end any different than the first one?"

"I didn't." Grandpa ripped open a ketchup packet. He squirted the contents all over his curly fries. "I prayed it would. I just knew you'd never get on with your life if you didn't get back on the platform. Sort of like falling off a horse. You have to get back on."

"Nothing like falling off a horse. Mostly no one sees you. Maybe just family."

"You know what I mean." Grease shone on Grandpa's lips. Crumbs from the bun nested in his beard. Elijah handed him a clean napkin. He waved it like a flag. "I know we've been hard on you. Your dat, your brieder. Me. It was wrong of us. There's nothing wrong with you. You are who you are. You shouldn't have to change on account of us. Gott made you who you are. To hear Bart tell it, Gott gives us each gifts. We're supposed to use them. The gift of strutting on a stage ain't yours. That don't make you less-than. It just makes you different. In fact, it means you're sticking by your church vows better than we are."

The heavy stone on Elijah's heart rolled off. "We're supposed to bow to the greater gut. To put our needs last. The family business needs me."

"We'll get by. Emmett will go to auctioneering school in the fall. Your *kossins* have shown an interest. Your onkel Leif doesn't object. We'll be fine."

"Dat doesn't think so."

"You leave your dat to me." Grandpa hid a burp behind

arthritis-riddled fingers. "He has gut intentions. Faith, family, community. He forgets he was the only one of his brieder—my seh, your onkels—to join me when I started the business."

"They didn't grow up in the business. You farmed when they were kinner." Elijah had heard all these reasons in the stories Grandpa told over the years. "Dat was the youngest. He wanted to be just like you."

"True, but I wanted all my buwe to join me. Partly because I wanted us to stay together as a family." Grandpa shrugged, then heaved a sigh. "But also because it would make it easier for the business to be successful. Joseph, Mark, and Leif couldn't see themselves on a platform, blabbing into a microphone in front of a crowd of strangers any more than you could. It wasn't just nee, it was NEE in all capital letters. Respectfully, of course. My buwe are gut men. Your mammi made sure of that."

"Why did you decide to start an auctioneering business when most Plain Gmay didn't allow it?"

"I saw a need, a void, and I knew it would be a gut way to pay the bills. Farming wasn't as profitable as it used to be." Grandpa stuck his trash into the greasy bag and shut it. "I knew my plot of a hundred acres wouldn't be enough farm for all my buwe to support their families. I needed something else to pass down to them."

"One of these days Dat will pass it down to his seh."

"Those who want the business. There's no sense in shoving a livelihood down your kinner's throats. Making them miserable isn't gut for business. Your onkels taught me that."

"I never thought to ask them."

"You should, next time you see them. They'll tell you. How you spend your life is important to Gott. He gave you gifts. He expects you to use them. Sometimes that means standing up for yourself."

"So that's why you pretended to be sick so I would get up there on the stage?"

"I don't want you to feel like a failure. Now it's up to you to do the rest."

For the first time in months, no clouds or fog obscured the road ahead.

"Hey, Elijah, it's time." Dad zigzagged through the crowd that was quickly returning. "I heard you did a decent job this morning. Which is gut. But there's no time to slow down."

That was Dad. Easy on the compliments. Which was fine. Elijah rose. He took Grandpa's trash and stuffed it in the bag. He'd toss everything on his way back to the platform. "I don't plan to slow down. I'll finish the auction." He sucked down the last of his root beer, then toasted his father with an empty cup. "Tomorrow I'm headed home."

"But we still have auctions in Mechanicsville and Bird-in-Hand."

"I'm going home, Dat." Elijah brushed past his father. "I have to start my life there."

"But—"

"Let him go, Charlie." Grandpa's voice held notes of pride and command. They were music to Elijah's ears. "I reckon there's a girl involved. Your fraa will be peeved if you stand in the way."

What might have been said after that didn't concern Elijah. He had work to do.

Chapter 33

*T*he Hershbergers must surely be fighting a bit of envy. No one would blame Lee's Gulch's other Plain-owned grocery store owners if they were miffed to see their customers crowding a competitor's business.

Bonnie surveyed the grocery cart she was using at the Kleins' Bent-and-Dent Store to hold her purchases and steady herself while leaving her rollator by the front doors. Noodles, taco shells, Tabasco sauce, ketchup, bar soap, flour, a dented can of jalapeños, tortilla chips only a few days past their "best by" date, and her favorite: a package of raspberries dipped in dark chocolate. On average prices were slashed 75 percent for items past their recommended-by dates or goods with damaged packaging. A regular grocery store couldn't compete.

Bonnie wouldn't buy many of the store's bulk items simply because her two-person family was too small to eat them quickly. Plus they had no need for packaged cookies, crackers, soups, desserts, or canned vegetables and fruits. Baking and cooking from scratch was so much better. Canning vegetables and fruits from the garden guaranteed fresh foods year-round.

All the same, shopping in such a festive atmosphere was fun.

The Kleins and their five children handed out free samples of crackers, cookies, candies, and flavored waters. The scent of fresh-buttered popcorn in red-striped bags dispensed from a portable cart floated in the air. They gave away coupons for another 25 percent off already bargain-basement prices. Shoppers won door prizes. They'd decorated with red, white, and blue balloons and streamers in honor of the upcoming Fourth of July celebration. Everyone seemed to be smiling.

Who wouldn't with row upon row of dented canned goods, jellies, jams, pancake mix, granola bars, cereal, spices, pickles, paper plates, chips, cereal, cookies, crackers, bottled water, canned meats, disposable diapers, coffee, juice, and more? A customer never knew what she would find on any given day. It depended on the latest load of banana boxes—a surprise medley even for the owners.

"You're gloomy again." Opal charged down the cleaning supplies aisle with Tucker sleeping in her cart. Her tummy was showing more these days. Her morning sickness gone, she exuded good humor. Annoyingly so. "How can you be so droopy in the middle of these bargains?"

She didn't give Bonnie a chance to respond. "Look what I found!" She held up a huge box of lactation cookies. "They're full of oatmeal, brewer's yeast, and flaxseed. They're supposed to help with milk supply. The whole box is only two dollars. And they're not expired. Yet."

Now it was Bonnie's turn to feel envy crowd her. She stuffed it back in its lockbox. "Nice. It's a little early for that, isn't it?"

"The box says they recommend starting in the thirty-fifth week. They'll keep." Opal squeezed the box into the cart alongside Tucker. He didn't budge. "I'm so glad he's sleeping. It's easier to shop with a sleeping bopli than a crying one."

Bonnie chomped down on the words that threatened to storm

the ramparts. *I wouldn't know.* It wasn't enough to not say these things. She shouldn't even think them. *Gott, forgive me. Help me do better. Show me how to live out the fruit of the Spirit.* "He's a gut bopli."

"He is. What did you find?"

Bonnie showed off her discoveries. Her total would be less than twelve dollars. "Can't beat that with a stick. I'd better go. I told Carol and Sophia I'd spell them so they can get a chance to see what all the fuss is about."

"Wait. I know it's hard for you to see my family growing." Opal's roundabout way of referring to being with child paid lip service to the Plain tradition of keeping such rites of passage private. "The fact is, you're the one who is standing in your own way." Her gaze swept the aisle. They were alone. "You need to get out of your own way."

"Easy for you to say." Bonnie snorted. Both she and Elijah had reason to go their separate ways. In the end it hadn't seemed that difficult for Elijah to acquiesce to Bonnie's decision not to court. He had his own challenge. A man who was gone six months out of the year would think twice about taking a wife who had special needs.

It might be that God had given Elijah a talent and a certain way of being that He expected Elijah to honor. And his family. Maybe it was a test. How did a person know? If Bonnie didn't know, how could she expect Elijah to know? "I'm doing the right thing by not saddling a man with my limitations."

"I say this with all the love in my heart: stop feeling sorry for yourself."

"I'm not. I've never felt sorry for myself. Resigned, maybe, but I don't host pity parties. I'm simply being realistic."

"I know it's easy for me to say—"

"Very easy."

"But you said yourself that your doctor said you could have boplin."

"Physically, jah, it's possible, but my doctor isn't Plain. She hasn't lived the way we live, not using convenience foods, disposable diapers, dishwashing machines, washers and dryers, microwaves, and vacuum cleaners." Bonnie ticked the items off on her fingers. "To name just a few. But that's beside the point. The question is, should a woman who can't take care of a bopli bring one into the world, forcing someone else to care for him?"

"I can think of one man, at least, who would jump at the chance."

"Because he has no idea what he would be getting himself into. We're not talking about just taking care of a bopli or boplin, but also his fraa." Bonnie stopped, heaved a sigh, and forced herself to slow down. "Besides, we're getting way ahead of ourselves. Why talk about having boplin when there's no talk of marriage?"

"Only because you put the kibosh on courting."

"I don't want to argue." Especially in the middle of the Bent-and-Dent Store. "Let it go, sei so gut."

"Me neither." Opal rushed around her cart. She hugged Bonnie around the neck. "I just want you to be happy."

"And not gloomy."

"Exactly."

"I'll do my best. I promise. Now I have to go. Sophia and Carol will think I forgot about them."

"It's nice of you to cover the store on your day off."

"I don't mind." If customers crowded the store, it would keep her from obsessing over her last conversation with Elijah. But that didn't seem likely. They were all at the Bent-and-Dent. "I have some bookwork to do anyway."

"Oh, there's my aenti Lena. I have to say hallo. I'll talk to you later."

And she was off. Bonnie pushed her cart down the aisle toward the bank of three registers. The Kleins were certainly optimistic about how much business they would do in Lee's Gulch. They'd moved to town from Millersburg only six months earlier when they bought the old dollar store and converted it into its new use. It turned out Lee's Gulch couldn't support four dollar stores. Three would be plenty.

The wait stretched. The cashiers were still learning to use the cash registers. Bonnie's cashier, obviously a Klein with his towhead, fair skin, and deep-blue eyes. When Bonnie finally made it to the head of the line, she edged to the side of her cart and started laying her items on the conveyor belt.

"Gut choices. I'm Neil Klein." Neil scanned the Tabasco sauce first. He grinned triumphantly. "Can I get your name for the door prize drawing? You'll get another 10 percent off the next time you come in."

Bonnie enthused over the offer and gave him her name. He rushed around the counter to bag her groceries. She glanced at the other registers. The customers were doing their own bagging. "I can get that."

"I like to help." His smile widened and his face reddened. "I'm new here in Lee's Gulch. Maybe I'll see you at church next Sunday."

"It seems likely." The redder his cheeks turned, the warmer Bonnie's became. "Welcome to Lee's Gulch."

Ignoring the line waiting at this register, Neil kept his hand on her cart as Bonnie pushed it toward the row near the front doors—and her rollator against the wall. One hand still gripping the cart handle, she reached for her rollator with the other and pulled it toward her. As she did, her gaze collided with Neil's. His expression turned puzzled. The exact moment realization hit home, he winced and let go of her cart.

It wouldn't be fair to judge him. It took most people a second to adjust to seeing a young person using a rollator. It didn't fit expectations. It was an anomaly—to able-bodied people. To the person with the disability, it just was.

"Danki for your help." Bonnie shot him her best smile. "You'd better get back to your register. Your customers are getting restless."

"Jah, jah, I should." Neil backed away, turned, and scurried back to his post.

Determined not to let his reaction spoil her day, Bonnie held on to her smile. She wedged her bags into the rollator's pouch and straightened. Squeezing between customers grabbing carts and those returning them, she edged toward the door.

That was, until a cart blocked her path. Elijah. Of all people. Bonnie paused. "Do you mind? I'm trying to leave."

"Not at all."

Despite his words, Elijah didn't move. His face had turned brick red. His hands had a death grip on his cart's handle.

Bonnie shot him a questioning look.

Elijah licked his lips. His forehead wrinkled. He opened his mouth, then closed it.

They were back to that day when he first came to the store. Bonnie had met him at the front door. He'd been speechless then too. Where was the man who'd kissed her not so long ago?

"I really need to get back to the store. Sophia and Carol would like to check out the bargains too."

Head bent, Elijah backed up and maneuvered so Bonnie could pass by. She started forward.

"Stop."

A single syllable delivered in a tone that couldn't be ignored. Bonnie paused again. "What is it?"

"We need to talk." Elijah met her gaze head-on. The confident Elijah had reemerged. "Now."

"I'll be at the store if you want to review your sales and pick up your check."

"I don't want to talk about toys. Or money."

"Okay. What then?"

"Us."

Bonnie surveyed the store. Carol's mother and Opal's aunt were in line at one of the registers. Neither of them tried to hide their interest in the obvious impasse playing out in front of them. Bonnie swallowed her "there isn't an us" response.

"Not here we don't."

"What if I bring you a sub sandwich for lunch?" Elijah nudged his cart closer. "Talking business over lunch is acceptable. We can define *business* as we see fit."

He sounded different. In charge. Certain of himself.

"I like mesquite chicken, American cheese on a whole wheat roll, with mustard and mayo. Lots of fixings, except no onion or jalapeños. Barbecue chips. Iced tea."

Elijah's thumbs-up was almost jaunty. "Do you need help with your bags?"

"Nee."

He touched the brim of his hat. "Until later."

Suddenly Bonnie had a powerful hunger.

Chapter 34

*I*t's so hot today. Your favorite time of year. I never understood why a farmer loved to sweat. I'm thankful for the shade myself." Jocelyn opened the cooler packed with ice. Chilled air brushed her sweat-dampened face. She extracted the Reuben sandwich and laid it on the threadbare quilt she'd spread under the oak tree next to Marlin's small, white gravestone. Sun, heat, driving rain, and cold had already weathered it. The simple text had faded. It looked as battered as she felt. "The Fourth of July fireworks display is tomorrow night. Uri wants me and Bonnie to go with him. I haven't gone in a while . . . not since you . . ."

She knew the Fourth of July was her dead husband's favorite holiday. Hot dogs, potato salad, coleslaw, baked beans, corn on the cob, cake, and homemade ice cream. It seemed likely Marlin loved the holiday more for its food and fireworks than a sense of patriotism for his people's adopted country. He loved to blow things up and he loved hot fudge sundaes.

This year she would go. It was time.

The daisies she'd planted during her first visit two years ago drooped. She grabbed an extra bottle of water and poured its contents over the flowers. "You're probably itching to know what's going on with Bonnie. I'll get to that, but I want to talk about something else first—after we eat."

Jocelyn took her time eating half the sandwich with the smaller portion of chips. The salad of juicy chunks of orange, apples, honeydew melon, grapes, and cherries hit the spot. It was too hot for coffee. She'd substituted Marlin's favorite cherry limeade. After a sip of a drink turned tart from the fruit that preceded it, she brushed crumbs from her apron.

A chickadee swooped down from the tree. It hopped closer, stopped, studied her.

"Help yourself." Jocelyn pinched a bit of bread from Marlin's half. He wouldn't mind. He was the one who hung the bird feeders in their backyard and filled them every week. "I'm not crazy, you know."

The chickadee trotted closer. He, she, it? Who knew? It snatched the bread and scurried away. "Good job. I'm just trying to muddle through like everyone else."

Muddle through without her North Star. He'd fallen from the sky without so much as a by-your-leave. "So there's this man who wants to buy the farm." Jocelyn ran through the story with a minimum of words. It could be that Marlin already knew all this, listening from his vantage point, high and lifted up. If she could be so bold as to assume he'd been given a green light at the pearly gates. The living hope. Or maybe he was so engrossed, sitting at the foot of the throne or listening to the prophets of old tell their stories, that he had no time for eavesdropping on his earthly loved ones. "And then there's this other man."

Her throat closed. How did she tell her beloved husband about this man who'd captured a piece of what was left of her shattered heart? That he'd sneaked past her defenses? That his smile and his touch had begun mending her heart, sewing it together with such a sweetness? Piece by tiny piece. It was a laborious process, one she never would've attempted on her own. That she'd been fighting his attention with every ounce of her world-weary body.

No, she wasn't crazy. Not in the least. "I really like Theo. I hope it doesn't hurt to hear that. I can't imagine it does. After all, Gott willing, you're seated next to Jesus at the right hand of the Father Himself. Our piddly mess down here probably seems ridiculous."

A breeze picked up. Raising her face to it, she closed her eyes. Tears threatened. Not tears of sorrow. More of a drab of melancholy for a time long gone that would never return. The memories had already faded. Marlin's touch. His warmth. His laugh. The light in his eyes when he reached for her.

"I'm lonely," she whispered. "But it's more than that, Marlin. He's a gut, gut man. What I feel for him is different. Because I'm different. I'm older. Wiser. Worn. Slower. The season is different. It's one you left before you could experience it. A winter season. I'm all the more lonely now because I had a tiny taste of what life could still be like. It's cruel. He didn't mean to be cruel, I know that, but it is. It makes no sense, but at times like this, I miss you more than you could possibly imagine. Because you always were my touchstone."

The breeze picked up. The rustling sound of leaves filled the air. She opened her eyes. Dappled sunlight touched her face—warm, soft—a second, then gone with the trembling of the tree's branches.

"I know. I know. Me too." Jocelyn opened the cooler again. This time she presented Marlin with a huge slice of two-layered carrot cake topped with cream cheese frosting. She added a single candle and lit it with a match. "*Froh gebortsdaag*, mann."

The candle's flame flickered but held. Jocelyn sang "Happy Birthday" softly, her voice hoarse with tears. When it came to the end, it was all she could do not to add that line she always sang to him: "And many more."

Carrot cake wasn't just Marlin's favorite. It was hers too. They'd discovered this early in their courting. One of the cakes at their wedding had been spice-carrot. Jocelyn blew out the candle. She began to eat, savoring every shared memory of twenty-six years of life in every bite. All the while she recounted the latest news about their daughter's health, Bonnie's certainty that she shouldn't marry, the possibility that Elijah Miller might change her mind, and all the nuances of that uncertain journey.

"And so that's it." Jocelyn slid the fork into a plastic bag along with the small paper plate and the rest of her trash. "That's everything." Despite her best effort, her voice quavered. The taste of spicy cake and smooth, sweet cream cheese lingered on her tongue, made bittersweet by what came next. "I'm not saying farewell. I'm saying it might be a while before I come back. There likely won't be any more Reuben sandwiches or brownies.

"It doesn't mean I love you any less." She rose onto her knees so she could brush away leaves that slumbered on the headstone. She kissed her fingers and pressed them to the stone. "I've only discovered that my heart has room to love another. Its capacity is almost frightening. Because loving is so nice, but it's also painful.

"Why do people stick their hearts out there again and again, only to have them pummeled and ripped to pieces? Tell me that, mann of mine."

One more kiss. Jocelyn wiped tears from her face. She gathered up her things, stood, and picked up the wicker basket. "Sweet repose. Until we see each other again, Gott willing."

The ache in her throat might never recede. With the breeze at her back, Jocelyn waved good-bye to the chickadee, now perched on a bough above Marlin's grave. "Take care of him, will you? Talk to him. Sing to him. Keep him company."

The thought that Marlin might be lonely too was almost too much to bear.

The chickadee chirped. It hopped along the branch as if it might follow her.

"Stay, stay with him. Sei so gut."

The bird's song sounded like sweet surrender.

"I'm not crazy," she reminded herself for the umpteenth time. She quickened her stride, kicking dirt clods as she navigated the winding path that led to the spot where she'd left her buggy. "Everyone grieves in their own way."

"Still talking to yourself, I see. Or hear."

Jocelyn raised her head. Theo leaned against his buggy. He straightened and smiled that silly lopsided grin. Those full lips that kissed so sweetly. She quickened her step. "How did you know where I was?"

"Frannie might have let drop at the breakfast table this morning that today would've been Marlin's birthday." Theo moved as if to meet Jocelyn in the path that passed by the gravestones of her Plain friends and family. "I know where I'd be, if it were possible, on Ellie's birthday."

"Do you visit her grave?"

Theo took the basket from her without asking. "I did when I lived in Berlin. After I came to Virginia, I realized I didn't have to physically visit her grave to feel close to her. She's in a cooling breeze, a bird's song, in the rain, and even the thunderstorms."

"So I'm not crazy."

"Not unless I am too."

They paused between her buggy and his. Jocelyn studied his

calloused fingers wrapped around the basket handle. "What are you doing here?"

"I didn't want to intrude on your time with your mann."

"Not here, here on the road. Here, with me."

Theo shoved his straw hat back with his free hand. The sun had deepened his tan and the crow's feet around his eyes. Their teak color seemed even lighter. "There's something I need to talk to you about."

The gravel in his voice said it wouldn't be good. This wasn't about another kiss. "I'm all ears."

Theo scooped up a maple leaf. He twirled it between two fingers. "You're the first woman I've even tried to get close to since Ellie passed. You're the only other woman I've ever kissed. And I didn't even kiss Ellie on our first date. That has to mean something."

"Same here. You sound troubled, as if it's a problem." Jocelyn stilled his hand. He offered her the leaf, brown and brittle from the heat. She took it. "What's going on?"

"It's Noah." Theo kicked at a clod of dirt with his boot. Emotions flitted across his tanned face. Frustration. Concern. Aggravation. Even a touch of despair. "He sent me a letter. He's taken a job working with a gut friend's dat. He's courting. He wants to know if and when I'm coming home."

Ah. Ah. A ginormous leap into a bottomless pit. "Are you . . . going home?"

"The funny thing is, this place, Virginia, Lee's Gulch . . ." Theo waved his hand in a gesture encompassing the Virginia landscape and Jocelyn. "It has started to feel like home. But Noah. He's my only suh. Ellie's suh. He's still finding his way. I feel as if I left him behind too soon."

His gaze skipped over her shoulder, touched the sky, then plummeted into the ground. "Sometimes it can't matter what the heart wants. Our kinner come first. Even when they're grown up. He's been through a lot. It seems that I have unfinished business in Berlin."

"I have a daughter who's been through a lot, so I understand your dilemma." Jocelyn hugged her arms to her chest. "I would . . . miss you. In case you were wondering."

Theo studied the horizon. "I thought of asking you to marry me. You could move to Berlin with me."

"First of all . . . first of all." Jocelyn struggled to corral her words. "First of all, we've only known each other three months. Not long enough to speak of marriage—"

"I know—"

"Let me finish. Second of all, I can't abandon Bonnie. I just said she needs me."

"I know, I know. That's why I didn't ask you."

"But you had to throw it out there."

"I'm grasping at straws."

"Jah, you are."

"Bonnie could come with us."

"Bonnie co-owns a store here. Her family and friends are here. The farthest she's ever been from her home is the Outer Banks. She loves to stare at the ocean."

"No ocean in Ohio."

"Nee."

"The thing is, I have to go to Berlin. I have to talk to him. See where we stand."

The fresh stitches in Jocelyn's heart gave way. "When?"

"Tomorrow."

"I see."

"If things turn out the way I hope they do, I'll be back with Noah."

"And if they don't?"

"We have to leave that to Gott. I don't have the right to ask, but I'm hoping you'll wait for me."

"Where would I go?"

"I was hoping—I have no right, I know—but I was hoping you'd wait a bit before you make a final decision on selling the farm."

"I can do that . . . for a few weeks." Jocelyn studied his face. She memorized his eyes and that big nose, not really so big, and his full lips. "Any more than that would be unfair to Mr. Steadman. He deserves an answer so he can move on."

They all needed to move on.

"I won't leave you hanging. If I can't come back, I'll send you a letter. I promise." Theo set the basket on the floor of Jocelyn's buggy. He took her hand. His was warm and big. It covered hers completely. "In the meantime, we have today. Let's ride around these country roads like teenagers on their rumspringa. How does that sound?"

If it meant Theo holding her hand for a little longer, the answer was yes. Jocelyn edged closer. She would pay for it later, but for now, how could she refuse? She stood on tiptoes and kissed his cheek. He leaned back and stared at her. "What was that for?"

"For giving me whatever time you're able."

He kissed her back. Longer and deeper.

"What was that for?"

"For not saying no. For understanding. For waiting."

"Let's go." Today might be all they had. It would have to be enough. "Time's a-wasting."

After making sure her horse was securely tethered and had plenty of grass within reach, they left her buggy where it was parked and took that ride in Theo's buggy.

Jocelyn took Theo's hand and held it for as long as she could.

Chapter 35

*S*lowpoke's expression gave new meaning to puppy-dog eyes. Elijah groaned. "Nee. The last time you went in the shop, Bonnie fell."

More sad eyes. A whimper. Slowpoke was good. Elijah held up the sub sandwich shop bag. "If you stay in the buggy, I'll give you half my sandwich. It's meatballs and Swiss cheese with ketchup and spicy mustard. Just how you like it. I'll even take the lettuce and tomato off your half."

Slowpoke plopped down in front of Homespun Handicrafts' door. He barked once. The dog drove a hard bargain.

"Fine. Fine. But you better mind your p's and q's. You stay out of her way."

Slowpoke huffed as if offended that Elijah felt the need to voice these concerns.

Elijah heaved a breath. He squared his shoulders. "Here we go."

As if on cue, Slowpoke moved aside, allowing Elijah to open the door. Of course, Puff appeared immediately. She didn't look happy to see Elijah, or maybe it was Slowpoke. "Howdy, Puff. We come in peace."

She stuck her nose in the air. Her tail swished. Then she was gone.

Bonnie stood behind the front corner, ringing up a college girl's purchase of a life-size sloth stuffie. Her purple-and-white tank top advertised her university, the sloth, her youth. They seemed engrossed in a conversation about fruit smoothies. The girl urged Bonnie to drink more of them with nutritional yeast, ground flax, and some other ingredients Elijah didn't recognize.

Of course Bonnie graciously took all this well-meaning information under advisement.

Then she glanced up. Saw Elijah. And stiffened. The college girl swiveled and peered at Elijah through purple-rimmed glasses. "What a cute dog! Can I pet him? I love dogs. My folks have a mutt that looks like him at home." She padded in flip-flops that smacked on the wooden floor over to Slowpoke. "Is he friendly?"

His tail whapping so fast it was almost invisible, Slowpoke nudged her hand with his nose. *Pet me, pet me.* "Very friendly."

Elijah stared at Bonnie while the college girl carried on an extended conversation with his dog. Bonnie cocked her head toward the hallway that led to the office-slash-workroom. "I'll be back in a minute."

"I hope you don't mind I let Slowpoke come in. He was about to have a conniption fit."

"He's always welcome." Did she really emphasize *he's* or was that Elijah's imagination? "You know that."

"Come on, hund. Let's get out of the way so this customer can finish up her purchase."

Fortunately the college girl took the hint. She let Slowpoke lick her fingers one more time, muttered a few sweet nothings in his misshapen ear, then headed back to the counter. Elijah spent the next five minutes pacing in the workroom, touching Bonnie's works-in-progress, ordering Slowpoke to pick a spot, lie down, and stay there, all the while thanking God that Bonnie's mother wasn't here. He hadn't even considered that she might be.

"Why didn't you sit down?" Bonnie rolled to a stop at the work-table. "I'm sorry I kept you waiting."

"Nervous, I guess." Even admitting he was nervous made for more nerves. Elijah motioned toward the bags. "I hope you're hungry. You know how big their subs are. I got you chips and a white chocolate macadamia nut eppy for dessert."

"Yum. I love their eppies." Bonnie maneuvered into a chair. "How much do I owe you?"

"Nothing. You don't invite a woman to lunch and make her pay." Courting was hard, but at least that rule was easy to understand. Elijah opened her bag and laid out the food. "It's no feast, but my mudder sometimes says any meal she doesn't have to cook is a feast in her eyes."

"With nine kinner, including five buwe, I can see how she would feel that way." Bonnie took a sip of her drink. If melted ice had turned it watery, her expression didn't register that fact. "You said we need to talk. About what?"

"I reckon you know." Elijah took a bite of his meatball sandwich. It felt like sawdust in his mouth. He took a long swig of root beer. The carbonation tickled his throat. He coughed.

"Are you all right?"

Slowpoke whimpered. The little beggar. Elijah tore off half his sandwich and laid it on the floor on top of a paper napkin. Slowpoke barked once appreciatively. He slunk across the floor, low on his belly, until he was close enough to snarf a bite.

"I'm fine."

"My mamm would be horrified to see you feed an expensive sandwich to a hund. She thinks scraps or dog food bought at the Bent-and-Dent are gut enough for pets."

"Mine too." Elijah ran his hand over Slowpoke's massive head. "Slowpoke's not a pet. He's a friend."

"Man's best friend."

"Woman's, too, if she lets him."

"I know you didn't come here to talk about hunde."

"Nee. After we talked the last time, I did a lot of thinking."

"Did it hurt?"

"Very funny. You and my bruder Declan, the jokesters."

"Did you come to any conclusions?"

Elijah wiped the ketchup from his mouth onto a napkin. He sipped his drink again. "I called an auction yesterday. The entire auction of farm equipment and tools for the Hershberger retirement sale."

"That's wunderbarr." A smile bloomed on Bonnie's face, then faded. "It is wunderbarr, isn't it?"

"It is." Elijah handed the rest of his sandwich to Slowpoke. The dog ignored the bread and went directly to the meatballs. "I can't be seen as a failure by those who don't understand who I am or what I want to be."

A flush of relief ran through him. That part of his life had ended. He could move on with no sense of remorse, loss, or feeling less-than.

"That's more than wunderbarr." Bonnie laid aside her sandwich. Her chips were untouched. "No one should ever make you feel less-than for simply being who you are. So you're shy. You're also smart, creative, and a hard worker. And faithful. I'm proud of you, that you recognize that."

"I don't know how smart or creative I am, but I work hard. I know my self-worth isn't measured by the same yardstick as my brieder. The qualities they need are different than the ones I need." If only those good traits were enough to convince Bonnie to take a chance on him. And herself. "Now, if only you would do the same for yourself."

"What do you mean?" Her expression turned quizzical. "No one tries to make me feel less-than. Just the opposite. They never stop telling me I can do anything I want to do."

"Except you."

She shook her head. Her cheeks reddened. "That's not what I do. I work hard at being realistic, to be content with who I am. It's different."

"Not from where I sit. You make yourself feel less-than." Elijah reached for her hand and recaptured it. The feeling of her skin against his ignited the words. They flamed out. "When I look at you I see a hard worker, a faithful Plain woman, a smart woman, a gut dochder, a gut friend, and a pretty woman. I'd be blessed to have someone like you in my life. For always and ever."

"Elijah." Head bent, eyes shiny with tears, Bonnie tugged her hand away. "You don't know what you'd be getting yourself into. I can't ask you to do it. I . . . care about you too much to allow that."

Her face set in firm lines, she pushed back her chair. "I'll get your report. It includes an inventory. Your toys are selling well. I think you'll be happy." Her tone was all business. "Now that you're home for gut, you can get busy and catch up with inventory. You'll need to restock just about everything. After you look it over, I'll give you a check for your share of the sales."

Elijah ignored the paperwork in her hand. She laid it in front of him. "Elijah, sei so gut. Let's be business partners. Friends, even."

"I don't want to be friends. I faced my fears on that platform. Then I told my dat I was done with auctioneering. I came home because all I wanted to do was see you and tell you. To celebrate my gut news with you. Then get to work on more toys to bring to your shop." Elijah stuffed his trash into the bag. He deposited his cookie next to hers, then stood. "All I'm asking is for you to give it a chance. To give me a chance. To give us a chance."

"You don't know what that really means. You have no clue." Her voice dropped to a whisper. "They're already talking about me using a wheelchair. Do you know my mamm puts my hair up for me because my arms aren't strong enough to do it myself? She cuts my toenails for me. Imagine being with a grown woman who can't cut her own toenails."

"Don't be so full of hochmut."

"Hochmut? There's nothing prideful about my attitude or my words." Bonnie's face turned a dusty rose. "I'm being realistic. What man wants to marry a woman who is so dependent on others for basic tasks?"

"You think you're the only person in the world who has these challenges?" Where did the words come from? The reasoning? Even Slowpoke looked impressed. The dog drew closer and laid his head on Elijah's knee. Elijah smoothed his fur. His hands shook, but his voice didn't. "All over the world, people who love each other take care of each other. In sickness and in health. You don't have the corner on that market. Look at Sophia. She's getting married. Full steam ahead. I heard that Carol is courting. My mamm used the word *besotted* about her beau. I had to look it up in the dictionary. It sounds like a word only used in the silly romances she reads."

Finally, he'd run out of words. Breathless, he gulped air. Slowpoke nudged his hand with his head. *Pet me, pet me.* It worked. Petting his dog soothed Elijah's frazzled nerves.

"Romance stories aren't silly."

"That's what you got out of my entire speech?"

"That, and you aren't the man who came into my shop a few months ago hardly able to look me in the eye, let alone give such a speech."

"That's a gut thing, isn't it?" Elijah leaned forward. He fixed his gaze on her face. "I want to be a better man. Not because I think there's something wrong with being reserved, but for you. I want you to look at me and see someone you can't imagine living without. Talk about hochmut."

"Not hochmut. It's because I care about you that I'm drawing the line." She grabbed her rollator and moved behind the desk. Putting space between them. "It's because I want you to have a happy, full life."

"If you really mean that, you'll at least try. Spend time with me. You'll see. It'll work. We'll make it work."

"I can't." She rolled away from the desk, headed toward the door. "I need to get back to work. It's Hannah's turn to have lunch. We've been busy. A load of seniors entered from an assisted-living center in Lynchburg. Every one of them bought something."

More distance. Talking business. Shop owner to vendor. The air had cooled to frosty.

"Bonnie."

"When you've looked over the report, let me know. I will cut you that check."

Elijah stood. He stepped into the aisle, blocking her escape. "Sei so gut, don't do this."

"Sei so gut, don't make it harder."

"Ahem." The sound of a throat clearing. He whirled. Carol stood in the doorway. Her gaze bounced from Bonnie to Elijah and back. "Sorry to interrupt. Moses Dalton is at the counter with a big box full of his mother's crib blankets. He wants to settle her accounts for her."

"I'll be right there." Bonnie moved forward. Elijah had no choice but to step aside. "Tell him I just need to pull his inventory."

"No rush, I'm sure." Carol pivoted on her crutches in a smooth

Kelly Irvin

move perfected from years of practice. "If you two have business to finish, I can handle Moses."

"No need," Bonnie called after her friend. "We're done here."

"Didn't sound that way to me." Carol's voice floated back, punctuated by the *thump* of her crutches against the wood floor. "Sounds like you need a do-over."

Chapter 36

*T*ime did not heal all wounds. Especially if a person kept picking at them. Ripping off the bandage. Rubbing the scab like a toddler with a skinned knee. Elijah squeezed a box of wooden puzzles into the back of the buggy next to another rocking horse made for a custom order. An English Homespun Handicrafts customer wanted a horse with a pink bridle, a pink bandanna around the horse's neck, and a pink saddle for her little girl's birthday. Elijah was glad to oblige, especially since it had to be delivered to the store before the child's third birthday this last week of July.

Today, in other words. He stepped back, wiped sweat from his face on his sleeve, and picked up his inventory. He snagged the pencil behind his ear and checked off the items on the list Bonnie had handed him the last time he was in the shop. She'd barely looked up. She paid more attention to some Tom, Dick, or Harry from the next town over.

He checked off the mower, the dollhouse, and the barn with a collection of farm animals. The tip of the pencil broke. His frustration at work.

Which could be true in other contexts as well. He'd pushed

Bonnie too hard and scared her off. Now he had to work his way back, removing one stone at a time from the wall she'd built around her.

He tossed the pencil into the box and threw the list on top. "Grrrrrr."

Slowpoke barked.

"I'm not growling at you. It's just hot and I'm tired."

Not because it was hot, but because he didn't sleep well. Too much on his mind. He slapped at a swarm of gnats drawn to his damp face. If only he could scatter unwelcome thoughts as easily.

"Who *are* you growling at?"

Sadie plodded on dirty, bare feet up to the buggy. Despite it being the middle of summer, the eleven-year-old wore her school backpack. Instead of books, the backpack held Matilda the Cat. Matilda seemed quite happy with her ride. Slowpoke ambled away. He and Matilda were not close friends. "Slowpoke only one here. You have imagin-nar-eee friend?"

Maybe. Maybe his dream of a family and a life with Bonnie was a product of his overactive imagination. "Nee, my imaginary friends moved to Lancaster County when I started school."

"Ach, mine come to school with me." Her almond-shaped eyes earnest, she pushed her dark-rimmed glasses up her flat nose with her index finger. "You miss yours?"

"Sometimes, but I have you and the rest of my brieder and schweschdre to keep me company."

"Why you growling like a mean hund, then?"

"Sometimes I get frustrated."

"Me too. Like when I can't make my hair stay in a bun. Or my sneakers won't stay tied."

Elijah pretended to peek under Sadie's prayer covering. Their sister Josie had put it up in a bun early that morning. She used extra bobby pins, knowing Sadie's running around, chasing animals, and climbing trees would likely knock it loose by the end of the day. "Your bun looks plenty gut to me." He made a show of peering at her sneakers. "Your shoes are tied. Gut job."

"Danki. I'm supposed to tell you something." She curtsied deeply, then proceeded to drop her backpack on the ground so she could dig around in a pocket on the front. Matilda apparently didn't like being disturbed. She wiggled from the bag, hopped out, and hightailed it for the house. Unperturbed, Sadie held out a plastic bag filled with crumbling oatmeal raisin cookies. She'd been known to stockpile them when Mom wasn't looking. "Want an eppy? I share."

"Nee. I'm gut, but I appreciate the offer." Elijah hid his smile. "What were you supposed to tell me? Does Mamm know you're eating her eppies?"

"Nee. Ach. That's what I was supposed to tell you."

"What?"

"Railing on the steps to the store is loose, and so is one of the boards on the steps. Mamm wants you to fix them before you go to town."

"Gut thing you figured it out." With the rest of the men away on the auction circuit, Elijah was in charge of all chores around the farm that Mom and the girls couldn't handle. Josie was handy with numbers and taking care of customers, but she didn't wield a hammer. Nor did Mom. Elijah tickled Sadie's neck in that spot that always made her giggle. "I won't tell Mamm you're hoarding the eppies again."

"Danki." Still giggling, she spun around twice, curtsied again, then trotted away on short legs.

Slowpoke returned in a leisurely trot. He liked Sadie, just not the company she kept. Elijah rolled his eyes at the finicky dog.

"Chicken. Matilda's not that bad and you know it. I have to get my tools and do some work for Mamm. Then we'll head out."

A few minutes later Elijah had the railing fixed and knelt to work on the loose board with Slowpoke overseeing from his spot on the shaded porch. Using an elbow, Mom pushed through the door carrying two glasses of what likely was iced tea. She loomed over Elijah. "I'm glad Sadie caught you before you headed to town."

Elijah straightened. His back complained so he stretched. "Railing's taken care of. I'll have the step done in a jiffy."

"No rush. Most of our customers come by in the morning before it gets too hot." Mom held out a glass. Elijah laid the hammer aside and took it. She offered him a smile. "I'm glad you haven't given up on Bonnie."

No rhyme or reason to the way his mother's mind worked. "I don't know what you're talking about."

The smile disappeared, replaced with a scowl. His mother plopped onto a nearby wooden bench next to a handwritten sign that read HANDCRAFTED BENCH $95. INQUIRE INSIDE. "Suh, I'm your mudder."

"And I'm a grown man." Elijah gulped down half of the tea. He set the glass aside. Perspiration trickled down his back and tickled his spine. He grabbed the hammer and pounded a nail into the loose board with more force than necessary.

"Pound away. I know you can hear me."

Mom's voice did carry over the hammering, but it seemed disrespectful to continue. With an exaggerated sigh, Elijah stopped.

"I figured you haven't given up if you're still visiting her at the shop."

"I'm a vendor at Homespun Handicrafts. I'm just restocking my wares."

"Uh-huh."

Elijah leaned back on his haunches. "I'm done here. I'd better get going."

"If she's the one for you, she'll come around."

"How do I know if she's *the* one?" Elijah rested his knees on the step. He pulled his hat off and wiped his forehead on his sleeve. "It's not like I have experience with such things."

"Her mamm and I talk."

Moms would be moms. No getting around it. "I'm sure you do, but it's talk you should keep to yourself."

"We compare notes. There's no harm in that."

The harm came in making plans and sticking their noses in other people's business, even when those people were their adult children—especially when they were their children. "Mamm, you have a problem. You need to sit with the deacon."

"I do *not* have a problem." The way his mother drew out the word signified Elijah had hit a nerve. "I care about my kinner. I want them to be happy."

"What about getting in the way of Gott's plan for your kinner?"

"I would never."

"Maybe you already have. Jocelyn too. You said yourself if Bonnie is the one, she'll come around."

"And she will. I just don't want you to miss it because you're busy being a dumkoph."

"I go to the shop. I take my toys. I say hallo. I smile. I eat muffins and drink kaffi." Elijah shoved the hammer and nails into his toolbox. "You know what she does?"

"Nee. What?"

"She smiles at the vendor from Burkeville who brought in a pile of poorly made wooden puzzles." Sure, she smiled at everyone who approached the counter—customers or vendors. Just less so with Elijah. "They spent twenty minutes talking about crossword puzzles and their favorite dictionaries."

"You sound peeved. Is it possible you were jealous because you don't like words?"

"I like words fine."

"As long as you don't have to use them."

"I barely get a nod when I come in the door and half a wave when I leave."

"Has it ever occurred to you that she may be regretting her decision to keep you at arm's length?"

That he should be so blessed. She could barely look at him. Elijah stood. "She sure has a funny way of showing it."

"She doesn't know how to walk back her words." Mom took the sign and propped it against the bench's arm. She patted the seat. "Sit with me. The shop is open all day. She'll be there until it closes."

"I don't know much about courting or women. Maybe I went about it all wrong." He sat at the other end of the bench. "Maybe I should take a hint and bow out."

"That's your hochmut talking."

"Nee, it's my heart talking. It's still sore from the last time she said nee."

"Have you lost your nerve, then?"

"I wish it were that simple. My heart won't leave me alone. It keeps saying I pushed too hard. That I should slow down and take my time. Give her time. Maybe I'll grow on her so much she won't be able to stop herself from wanting more than friendship."

"Huh." Mom contemplated her dishpan hands for a few seconds. "That's not a bad plan."

"That sounds an awful lot like you think I know what I'm doing."

"I wouldn't go that far, but you do surprise me."

"I'll take it. With all the other kinner you have, I'm surprised anything can surprise you."

"You don't give yourself enough credit." Mom scooted closer. Looking oh so satisfied with herself, she patted Elijah's arm. "I was surprised when you called an auction. I was surprised when you stood up to your dat. I'm surprised at how you stand up to me. You've grown up. You'll make a fine mann."

"I hope you're right."

"Are you ready for what that'll mean with Bonnie?"

No need to pretend he didn't know what she meant. "I am."

"You know we'll always be here to help out."

"Danki. If my plan works, I'll keep that in mind."

"When it works. From where I sit, it looks like you're well on your way." She stood, picked up his glass, and headed for the door. "I'd better get back to work. You'd better get into town. Remember, just bide your time and pick the right moment. Bonnie won't be able to resist."

"Gott willing."

"Gott willing."

Chapter 37

*B*onnie had stayed in the washtub far too long. Her fingers were as wrinkled as prunes. She didn't want to get out. The August heat pressed on her despite the cool bathwater. The dog days of summer. She held her breath, slid under the water, and hunkered there until she couldn't take it anymore. Sputtering, she burst from the water, splattering it over the sides and onto the pine floor.

"Are you ready to get out?" Mom hustled into the laundry-slash-mudroom. She had a towel under her arm, her pedicure bag in one hand, and a pair of scissors in the other. "What have you been doing? It looks like a flood hit in here."

"It's nice and cool."

Mom dropped the toiletries on the chair and held up the towel. "Let's get you out of there."

She'd been perfectly willing to acquiesce to Bonnie's hankering to have a lovely bath instead of a quick shower. Sometimes a woman simply needed to sit a spell in the bathtub, let the aches, pains, and worries float away. But Mom also couldn't hide her concern that Bonnie might fall getting in or out of the huge metal tub.

"Danki, Mamm. I know this is more work for you."

"I like a nice bath too. A shower just isn't the same." Mom

grasped one arm while Bonnie used her other hand to push herself up from the tub's side. "Besides, it's not like we're in a hurry. The big day isn't until tomorrow."

"I can't believe Sophia is getting married. I've known her since we used to make mud pies down at the pond and catch tadpoles to see if we could grow them into frogs."

"You graduated school together and got baptized the same Sunday."

"We opened a shop together."

"You did indeed. Just between you and me and the tub, I'm proud of you. Don't tell Bart I said that." Mom helped Bonnie step over the tub's side. She waited until she was steady on both feet, then wrapped the big towel around her. "I thought I would trim the dead ends on your hair and give your toes a look-see. It's been a while."

Bonnie studied her toenails. They were in need of a trim. "Some things don't change, I suppose. No matter how you long for it."

"I don't mind, Dochder."

"I do." At a bare minimum, a person ought to be able to trim her own toenails. Bonnie quickly dried off. "Isn't part of growing up becoming independent from your parents?"

Mom helped her don her nightgown. If she saw any irony in Bonnie's words, she didn't admit it.

"Didn't I mention you're a store owner? That's pretty independent." Her pleasure at her quick rebuttal evident in a tiny smile, Mom spread her tools on a clean hand towel on an old end table situated next to two chairs from their previous kitchen table set. "Have a seat. It'll give us a chance to catch up."

Aha. Mom was fishing for information. She'd likely heard about Elijah coming back from the auction circuit early, about them conversing in the Bent-and-Dent for all the world to see. She might even have heard about his regular visits to the store since then. To pick up his check and to replenish his wares. She couldn't know that those visits had been short and the conversation stilted. On her part. Elijah acted like nothing had happened, as if she'd said yes, like they were still courting.

He smiled. He complimented the shop's display. He ate muffins and drank coffee. He even petted Puff, much to Slowpoke's chagrin. Slowpoke took his cue from Elijah, nuzzling Bonnie's hand every chance he got, giving her kisses, guarding the door against intruders.

All in all, in every way, making her feel like a mean, ugly person for not caving. It took all her strength not to cave. She'd done the right thing. So why did she feel like the sun had died?

"Doing the right thing doesn't always feel good." Her dad's voice, deep and warm, sharing that tidbit of wisdom with her on a cold winter night in front of the fire after a particularly trying day at school, rang in her ears.

Bonnie lowered her head and stared at her wrinkled fingers. The familiar feel of Mom's stroking Bonnie's wet hair with a big-toothed comb soothed as it always did. She closed her eyes. "What are we catching up on?"

"Oh, just this and that."

"This and that. What a broad topic."

"Well, we could start with why you've been wandering around like a maedel who's lost her best friend. Did you and Opal or the girls at the store have a tiff?"

"Nee. I'm fine. We're fine. We're all fine." Bonnie opened her eyes. She tempered the retort with a respectful tone. Mom wasn't responsible for her frustration or her melancholy.

"You've been up and out of the house after dark. Does that mean what I think it means? If it does, you should be happier about it. I would be."

Her roundabout way of asking if Bonnie was courting.

"You know I have trouble sleeping. Sometimes I need a breath of fresh air. I need to tire myself out, I guess. I take a stroll down to the corral to check on the horses."

"In the dark. I hope you're not crazy enough to do that."

With a rollator. Her mother's unspoken words vibrated in the air. "I don't go far. I'm careful."

"You hit a rut in the road and you'll be flat on your face. You'll be there until morning, Dochder. Sei so gut, don't do it again."

"Fine, I won't. What do you really want to talk about?"

Mom laid aside the comb. She sat and proceeded to prop Bonnie's foot on her knee. The tight muscles in her hamstring and calf twinged. They didn't hurt, just complained a little. "As a matter of fact, there is something besides the courting we're both pretending isn't happening."

"Gut. Otherwise this will be a quick chat."

"Theo went back to Berlin."

Try as Mom might, she couldn't pull off the careless delivery of this news. "When?"

"Last month."

"Why didn't you say anything?"

"I didn't know what to say."

"So he's not coming back?"

"I don't know. He went to talk to his suh, Noah. He wants him to move here. But he hasn't come back, so . . ."

"If Noah said nee?"

Mamm picked up nail clippers. She raised her chin. "Then I don't think he's coming back."

"Es dutt mer."

"It's okay." Mamm studied Bonnie's toes as if she'd never seen them before. "He's doing the right thing. He's putting his suh first."

"You say that, but your face is so sad."

"I don't want to make you feel bad or uncomfortable."

"Nee, nee. Tell me, sei so gut."

Mamm clipped the nails with quick efficiency. She set aside the clippers and gently lowered Bonnie's leg. "I thought it was the beginning of something. It felt special."

"Like it felt with Dat?"

"Nee. Different."

"But nice."

"Very nice."

"His suh is a grown man. He's capable of living his own life." Bonnie kneaded the towel she'd lain over her lap, then tossed it in the dirty clothes pile. "Maybe he'll tell Theo it's time for him to go, live his own life."

"I don't know. Imagine if I told you I was marrying Theo and moving to Berlin, leaving you to live with Onkel Uri and Aenti Frannie. How would you feel?"

The lovely contentment born of a cool bath and familiar rituals dissipated. This was their home. The place where Bonnie had grown up. Where she'd sat on Dad's lap, first in front of a fire roasting marshmallows while he told tall tales, and later on the hay wagon, helping cut alfalfa. Where he'd taught her to ride a horse and then drive a pony cart. Where he'd held her when she cried—realizing she could no longer do either. Where he'd whispered calming, encouraging words while she endured rehab and PT after six hours of painful back surgery.

The last place she'd seen him. That evening they played checkers and talked trash. She beat him three out of four games, but Bonnie could never be sure that he didn't let her win—even though she was no longer a child.

How could she live without him and without her mother,

who'd taught Bonnie to cook, sew, and be a faithful, kind woman? "I'd say nee. I'd say don't go, sei so gut." She smoothed her soft cotton nightgown. "But that would be selfish of me, wouldn't it? I want you to be happy, to be loved."

"And I want the same for you, Dochder." Mom dried Bonnie's other foot with the hand towel. She picked up the clippers again. "It would be selfish of me to put my needs ahead of yours. You're my only dochder. This is your home. I won't take that from you."

"There has to be another way."

"Theo even considered asking me to marry him and that we all three move to Berlin."

"Me? Leave the store? Leave Carol and Opal and Sophia?" Bonnie waved her hands to encompass the laundry room, the house, the farm, Lee's Gulch, everything that had been home her entire life. "For Ohio. I can't imagine."

"I don't want you to imagine it." Mom's face, with its deepening lines around her mouth—smile lines—and crow's feet adorning her chestnut eyes behind glasses, was pensive. "Gott's will be done. If Noah agrees to come here, so be it. If he doesn't, then I'm happy to have known Theo."

Bonnie's foot jerked. Not because of this unexpected conversation, but because it tended to do that when someone touched it. The doctor called it hyper reflexes. "It's ridiculous, isn't it, how the first thought is always *It's not fair*? Like we're still kinner who didn't get the biggest piece of cake? You should have this time. You deserve this time."

"I had twenty-six wunderbarr years with your dat. More than I ever deserved." Mom bent her head over Bonnie's foot and went to work. "I'm an old woman. I'll learn to be content with what Gott gives me."

"You're not old. I know you've been lonely, and I hate it for

299

you. I can feel it in the way you look sometimes when you set the table with two plates. Or you fry too much bacon in the morning. The way you read your book on the porch in the evenings, but you never turn the page."

"It's only a season." Mom straightened. She leaned back in the chair. The clippers rested in her lap. "Gott blessed me with a mann I loved once. It would be greedy to ask for more. I didn't ask for it, so why should I hold it against Gott if it doesn't happen? I have to believe this is Gott's will."

"But if Theo comes back, then that's a sign, isn't it? We could pray for that."

"I think we're supposed to pray that Gott's will be done, not tell Him what that should be." Her smile wry, she removed her glasses and wiped the lenses on her apron. Mom always looked so much younger without them. Her dark-brown eyes squinted. "It's your turn, Dochder. It's your season for love."

Was it love she felt every time she saw Elijah? The possibilities that spun on tiptoes in her heart—despite knowing she couldn't offer him everything he deserved? The pain she felt at disappointing him? "How do you know that it's love you feel for Theo? Does it feel the same as when you were with Dat?"

Six months ago it wouldn't have been possible to even contemplate such a thought, let alone voice it. The words and the images didn't hurt. They held hope for something better. No more living in gray days and long nights.

"Like I said, it's different from the way I loved your dat. Not any less, mind you, or more, for that matter. Just different. Because I'm different. Older, wiser, more worn. Less naive. Less self-centered."

"How long did you and Dat court before he asked you to marry him?"

"Over two years."

"You've only known Theo for four and a half months."

"Believe me, I've noodled that fact for hours and days." Puzzlement mingled with a tempered joy flitted across her face. "I've never believed in love at first sight. We're taught to tread carefully. Wedding vows are unbreakable. Marriage is for life. It's sheer foolishness to jump into something so quickly."

"I hear a *but* in your voice."

"That's all well and gut when you're sixteen or seventeen, but at my age, a person recognizes that life is fleeting. I only have to think of how quickly we lost your dat to know how suddenly a life can end. I don't want to stand by and watch life pass me by if the chance presents itself. If it doesn't, then Gott's will be done."

Dad would've wanted a new life for Mom. He loved her so much that he would've wanted her to be happy. Not lonely. Not misty-eyed over a pile of bacon. "I wish I could be as faithful and obedient as you are."

"You're funny, Dochder. It's not easy for me. In my head, I'm kicking and screaming like a two-year-old who wants a candy bar for supper. I've had my time. I need to accept that. It's your turn."

"It's different for me."

"Because of your disease? Sometimes there are disabilities more limiting than the physical. They're disabilities we create ourselves by doubting that we can have the full lives others around us have."

"That's a noble thought. But until you've watched a friend, now a mudder, hold her bopli, feed him, carry him to his cradle, and lay him down, and mourned that you can't physically do the same thing, I don't think you can really understand my situation. Even you, who has lived with me my whole life and done things like help a grown woman get out of a bathtub, dress herself, cut her toenails, and help her put her socks and shoes on."

"English women pay people to cut their toenails."

Kelly Irvin

"It's different and you know it."

"I do. I just don't want you to cheat yourself out of a full life because you're afraid of being a burden. The man who loves you will care for you out of that love, not out of a sense of obligation or pity. Elijah strikes me as a man who would do that."

He would. He'd said as much. Somehow it made the choice that much harder. He was such a good man. Bonnie's heart ached to give him everything a good wife would. But especially children. Lots of children. "He's a very gut man. He deserves a full life with a fraa and kinner."

"So do you."

Mom stared at Bonnie. Bonnie stared back. Here they were, mother and daughter, but now also two women trying to figure out how to live, love, and work, and to support each other doing it.

"Elijah thinks he knows what it would be like, but he doesn't. He can't. Not really." Bonnie could share a lot with her mother, but not the way Elijah's kisses, his touch, drove all other thoughts from her mind, made her think something was possible when it wasn't. Not truly. "I know I've sent him mixed messages. When he's around me, I can't think straight. I say and do things I wouldn't normally say or do. I don't want us to be apart. When he leaves, I'm mortified because I think I've led him on. I know we can't be together. I finally told him we can't be more than friends and business associates. Period."

"You can say it all you want, but you can't stop how you feel. I can hear it in your voice and see it on your face. I reckon he can too. I reckon he's not giving up."

"He's not. He comes to the store and brings his toys and acts like everything is wunderbarr. It's almost annoying. I keep telling myself not to fall in love with him. It's not right. It's not fair. I tell myself to stick to the plan. Run the store. Be content. Enjoy my nieces and nephews."

302

"And yet you can't help yourself. You think you've got a plan for your life and it doesn't include Elijah Miller. It reminds me of your grandma Yoder. She passed away when you were too young to remember her. She was a firecracker. Your dat came by it naturally." Mom settled Bonnie's bare foot on the floor. "She used to tell him—and me—to go ahead and plan. Because you know what Gott does when He hears us planning?"

"What does He do?"

"He laughs."

"So you think He has something up His royal robe's sleeve?"

"Always. Theo thinks He does."

"I hope Theo's right."

"Me too. We'd better get to bed. Tomorrow is a big day."

For Sophia, who was brave enough to embrace the challenges the future would most certainly bring.

Gott, make me brave, sei so gut. Or send me a sign. Or share the plan. Give me something.

God was probably thinking about how bossy Bonnie was. *I said sei so gut. If You don't mind. I need to know, Gott.*

Chapter 38

The temptation to peek at the crowd gathered in the Hershbergers' barn gripped Bonnie. She gritted her teeth. Nope. Not doing it. Acting as one of Sophia's witnesses was an important, somber responsibility. Bonnie needed to focus on the matter at hand. She wasn't a moony-eyed teenager with a crush.

One of the witnesses stood at an angle between Bart and Matthew. He signed the vows, even though the groom was wearing his new hearing aids. Bart had said he wanted to make sure that there was no misunderstanding or not hearing these lifelong vows. Not that every Plain couple who got this far didn't know the vows by heart, having heard them hundreds of times during a lifetime of attending weddings.

Bart's voice droned on. Last night's cooling bath was a distant memory. The temperature approached ninety without a hint of a breeze. The air in the barn hung heavy with humidity. A baby whimpered. Sophia's great-grandfather snored gently from his bench seat on the front row. Sophia's cheeks were bright pink; the blue dress Bonnie and Carol had helped her sew made her cornflower-blue eyes all the more brilliant. She seemed on the verge of bursting with happiness.

This day couldn't get any better. A best friend marrying. *Danki, Gott, what a blessing. Danki for giving Sophia the desire of her heart.*

Dare Bonnie add a selfish PS to the prayer? Not today. After a fitful night with troubled dreams, she still couldn't see through the fog to her future. She shook a mental finger at herself. This was Sophia's long-awaited day.

Whatever Your plan is for me, Gott, I will do my best to accept it. Even if this is as good as my days get in the future.

The merest hint of a breeze found its way through the barn slats and touched Bonnie's face. Bits of dust and hay danced in the sunlight that entered the mammoth building by the same means. Light in the darkness.

Bow to God's will. He didn't ask so very much. Bonnie bit back a sigh. God was good. Scripture told her so. He could bring good from all circumstances. Even from SMA. Even from a car accident that left her best friend paralyzed. Even from spina bifida.

She sneaked a glimpse at Carol. Her friend beamed so hard that her cheeks surely hurt. Carol was as excited for Sophia as she would've been had it been her own wedding day. She was a good friend. They hadn't said so aloud, but they'd acknowledged that life would be different now. Sophia was the first to marry. Until she and Matthew decided to adopt, she would keep working at the store. Another blessing in a day of many.

Help me keep an attitude of gratitude, Gott, sei so gut.

Finally the last of the vows were spoken. Bart joined Sophia's small hands with Matthew's oversized, calloused hands and said the final words. A tall man who could use a few more pounds on his lanky body, Matthew pushed Sophia's chair back to the women's side. Wearing a grin that was his best feature, he joined his father and brothers on the men's side. Bonnie rolled to the third row, where her mom sat next to Aunt Frannie and her girls.

Just a quick gander. Bonnie cast her gaze across the crowded barn. More than one hundred fifty guests would attend the reception. Only about seventy-five fit in the barn for the church service.

Elijah was one of them. He sat toward the middle between Emmett and Declan. The rest of the Miller men filled the fourth row, a series of cookie-cutter faces with blue eyes and dimples, a bit of blond hair visible under their black hats, some with beards, others not.

Elijah's head came up. His gaze connected with Bonnie's. A hint of a smile. A soft throat clearing.

Bonnie dragged her gaze from Elijah's. Mom's eyebrows got a workout. "Jah, jah," Bonnie whispered. She sat at the end of the row and left the rollator by her side in the aisle.

"What are you looking at?" Mom whispered.

"Nothing."

"Didn't look like nothing."

They knelt for the benediction. Rose for a final hymn.

Then it was over.

"I'm to help with serving." Mom stood. "What are you doing?"

"Washing dishes for the lunch." Others would have shifts for the evening meal, which would be even more elaborate.

"After you eat at the *eck*, of course."

Bonnie would rather not. The tradition of the newlyweds reserving seats at their corner wedding table for their unmarried friends in order to pair up existing couples or matchmake new couples had long been a thorn in Bonnie's side. "We'll see. I'm not very hungry."

God's plan. God's timing. Bonnie almost groaned. *Sorry, Gott, I didn't mean to forget so quickly. Really.*

"Walk with us up to the house?"

Bonnie turned. With Matthew behind her and Carol at her side, Sophia beamed up at Bonnie. The question was delivered in a tremulous voice, but out of sheer joy, not tears. As brides went, Sophia was by far the most beautiful Bonnie had ever seen. And the happiest. She was so sure of herself, of her love for Matthew, and his for her. So positive, she was willing to take lifetime vows. In sickness and in health. Come what may for her and for Matthew. To be so certain. To have so much faith—not only in God, but in herself and in Matthew. "Of course."

Sophia reached out her hand. Bonnie took it. Sophia's fingers were cold. Bonnie rubbed them between her hands. "Congratulations." She glanced up at Matthew. "To both of you."

His grin stretching across his whiskerless face, Matthew nodded hard. "Danki."

He was a man of few words, but the joy inscribed on his plain face spoke for him.

Together they joined the stream of people chattering, laughing, and jostling their way from the barn into the blinding sunlight. Person after person stopped them to offer their congratulations. People from Lee's Gulch, but many who'd come from Lancaster County for the festivities. Many people Bonnie hadn't seen since the last wedding brought them to Virginia. Last fall? Or maybe in the spring.

Slowly they made their way up the paved road between the barn and the house. The hum of dozens of conversations and the high-pitched laughter of kids thrilled to race around after a three-hour service filled the air. The teenagers were already setting up the volleyball net.

Mom trotted ahead with Frannie and their friends. Bonnie and her group took their time wheeling over the road that the Hershbergers had paved from the barn to the house to accommodate Sophia's wheelchair. Within seconds, sweat slid down Bonnie's back, tickling her spine. Her hands were slick on the rollator handles. Perspiration dampened her face. They rolled up the ramp and stopped on the porch so Matthew could open the door.

"Matthew, you go ahead, I'm right behind you." Sophia signed the words even as she spoke them aloud. "I want to talk to my friends for a second."

Again Matthew nodded, but he signed a few words. Bonnie didn't know much American Sign Language, but she recognized the signs for *I love you*.

Sophia shot him a smile. "Right behind you."

He slipped inside.

"I want to thank you for being my friends." Sophia's face was damp with more than perspiration. This time her voice quavered through tears. "These past few years at the store have been so happy. If I'd never met Matthew, I could've gone on forever, content. Working with you two. You're like schweschdre. I have loved every minute of it."

"Aww, that's so sweet." Carol leaned a crutch against the railing so she could duck down for a hug. "But we're not going anywhere. This isn't farewell."

"Nee, but it does feel like the end of a season." Sophia patted her face with a handkerchief. "I feel like I ran ahead—I know how ridiculous that sounds. You can be this happy where you are. If anyone knows that, I do. But this is something so special. I want you to have it too. To have it all. Don't doubt it for a minute. Don't doubt yourself. That's it. That's all I wanted to say."

Wiping at her cheeks with the crumpled handkerchief, Sophia ducked her head and hiccupped a sob. "Don't mind me, I'm just a little emotional today."

"I can't imagine why." Laughing, Bonnie wheeled her rollator around so she could sit down to talk to Sophia without towering over her. "We promise to be happy, no matter what happens. You just said you would've been content with life as it was before you met Matthew. So can I. Marriage and a family would be icing on the cake, for sure and for certain, but I love my life right now."

Maybe if she said it enough, she would believe it. She'd been happy, content at least, until Elijah Miller stood at the shop's door, a box of toys in his arms, upending her world.

"Sure you do, but don't sell yourself short. You have the possibility of a wunderbarr life shared with another person you love so much, you can't imagine life without him. It fills you up until you could burst with happiness. I'm not exaggerating, I promise."

"It must be crazy wunderbarr—most people want to do it," Bonnie conceded. "But life can be gut even without marriage and a mann and the whole kit and kaboodle. Gott's plan is Gott's plan."

Her words sounded so faithful. God would be justified in smiting her on the spot. Fortunately, He was merciful and gracious. The sheer enormity of her happiness when Elijah had kissed her— and she kissed him right back—couldn't be denied. She wanted it. She wanted the whole kit and kaboodle. What did God have in mind for her? *Could I get a hint, Gott?*

"I think I might know the feeling you're talking about soon." Carol lowered her voice so much that Bonnie and Sophia had to lean forward to hear. "I think Ryan is going to ask me to marry him."

"I knew it." Sophia squealed. "I knew it."

"You did not."

"Did too. I saw him staring at you during church last week. He had that hang-hund expression on his face. He's a goner."

"Did not. Is not."

"Then what makes you think he's going to pop the question?" Bonnie inserted the question before the two friends could squabble more. "How could you even tell?"

"He wants to go for a buggy ride tonight, even though he got up before dawn to help set up here. When I told him I might be too tired, he said it would be a short ride, just long enough for us to talk about . . . things. That's how he put it: 'things.' His face got all red, and he kind of stuttered."

Another wedding loomed around the next curve. Happiness for her friends enveloped Bonnie. God was good and wise. Especially wise. He would do what was best for her friends and her—whether she liked it or not. She stifled a sigh. "That's wunderbarr. I can't wait until tomorrow. You can tell us all about it at the store."

The door opened. Sophia's mom stuck her head out. "There you are, Sophia. Your mann is sitting at the eck all by his lonesome." Despite her words, she smiled. "They'll be serving your table first. Get a move on. You maed too. Your seats are waiting for you."

"On our way." Carol grabbed her crutch. "Hold the door for us."

Bonnie moved aside to allow the bride to go first, then Carol.

"Bonnie, wait."

At this rate all the dishes from the first round of meals would be washed before she made it to the kitchen. It sounded like Elijah, just for a second. She swiveled, midday sun shining in her eyes. She squinted and put her hand to her forehead. Theo strode toward her. A younger man with the same lanky frame and loose-jointed gait accompanied him. "You're back."

What a silly thing to say. Stating the obvious.

"I'd like you to meet my suh." Theo mounted the steps. "This is Noah."

"You're here." *Seriously. Get a grip.* Noah had his dad's teak eyes and tanned face, but his was clean-shaven. His lopsided smile matched his father's without the lines. Bonnie nodded in his direction. "Bewillkumm to Lee's Gulch."

"Danki." Noah cocked his head toward Theo. "Dat has nothing but gut things to say about folks around here."

How much had Theo told his son about Bonnie's mother? About the farm? About Bonnie? The questions buzzed around her head like riled-up wasps. "We're a friendly bunch. Are you here for a visit or coming to stay?"

"That depends."

Bonnie waited for Theo to explain. The three-syllable response hung in the dank air. The pause grew awkward. "It was nice to meet you. I should get inside. The dirty dishes are piling up as we speak."

"Wait." Theo glanced around. He came a step closer. "Where might I find your mudder?"

In the kitchen filled with gossipy women or in the crowded living room serving plates mounded high with food. "She's serving today."

"Ah." Theo got her drift. "Are you hungry, Suh?"

Noah shrugged. "I could eat."

"We'll find a place to sit inside." Theo reached past Bonnie and pulled the door open. "We should all go inside before the folks out here spin an entire yarn around what we're talking about here on the porch."

Bonnie surveyed the yard. Men had gathered around picnic tables under the elms and oaks that shaded the house. Teenage servers placed pitchers of water, along with silverware rolled into paper napkins, on the tables. The hum of conversation had died down. The quiet was unsettling. "I guess folks don't have enough to do that they have to worry themselves about something that's none of their business."

"Some things never change." Theo chuckled. "They're probably already planning another wedding."

Kelly Irvin

"Yours or mine?"

The question came out before Bonnie's brain bothered to examine it for pitfalls. A single Plain woman did not have this conversation with a Plain man and his son. "Es dutt mer. Don't answer that."

This time Noah chuckled. He sounded just like his dad. "You certainly are direct. I like that. But I'm spoken for."

Relief whooshed through Bonnie. "I'll just go inside before I put my foot in my mouth again."

She scooted away as fast as her rollator would allow. The Beiler men's soft, kind laughter followed.

$\mathcal{T}$he plate filled with grilled chicken breast, two sausage links, potato salad, barbecue beans, corn on the cob, and a mammoth roll weighed at least five pounds. At least it felt that way in Jocelyn's hand. Its aroma no longer made her mouth water. Her elbows ached. So did her shoulders. She should've left the serving to the younger women, but the task allowed her to see and chat with the many visitors who'd come long distances for Sophia's wedding. That was half the fun of a social gathering.

The Hershbergers and friends had decorated the tables with white paper cloths. Every table featured a Mason jar filled with purple asters and golden mums. The place settings were white china on blue place mats with blue-and-white-checked napkins. A gorgeous three-layer cake with white frosting and red roses made from spun sugar occupied the spot of honor on the wedding table. It was one of four cakes of various flavors.

So pretty. So festive. Yet simple. It would be fun to do something similar for Bonnie. God willing. Someday.

Or even . . . No, she would not go there. Theo was gone. He might not come back. Probably wouldn't come back. If it were Jocelyn and she had to choose, she would choose Bonnie. It had to

Kelly Irvin

be. She respected Theo as a family man and a father. He had his priorities straight.

So get over it.

Jocelyn leaned in to place the overburdened plate on the table in front of a man who'd hung his black hat on the back of his chair. His silver hair was thick and unruly. And familiar.

He scooted his empty salad plate so it joined a bowl of fruit. Desserts would come later. His hands were big, fingers calloused. Familiar. No, it couldn't be. He was in Berlin. "Here you go. Enjoy. If you need more tea or water, wave down—"

"Danki." Theo swiveled and smiled up at her. He leaned closer. "I was hoping you'd be our server."

"He actually scoped it out." The young man sitting next to Theo leaned back in his chair. Jocelyn got a glimpse of his face. Spitting image of Theo. It had to be Noah. "I think more than one of the women serving were offended when he decided not to sit at her table."

The cascade of emotions made hard it to think, let alone speak. The tray in her other arm, filled with plates, teetered. Jocelyn steadied it. "I'm surprised."

"I can see that." Theo's baritone with its usual hint of amusement was just loud enough to be heard over the steady hum of conversation among the other men seated at the table. That included Uri and his sons. All of whom were waiting for their food. Theo cocked his head toward his companion. "This is my suh, Noah."

"I figured as much." Jocelyn hurried to set a plate in front of Noah. "It's nice to meet you. I'm glad you came. I have to serve this food before it gets cold."

"Later."

314

Only one word, but Theo's gaze promised so much more.

"That looks gut." Uri took his plate from her hands before she could set it down. "It's about time. What was Theo saying? I couldn't hear over the ruckus in this place."

"Nothing. Just introducing me to his suh."

"Uh-huh. I reckon you're glad to see them."

Jocelyn placed a plate in front of her nephew. "I'm glad to see all the visitors. I reckon you're glad he's back because he does more work than two of most men."

"Be that way." Uri scooped up a mound of potato salad and stuffed it in his mouth.

Good. She didn't have time for his idle talk. Jocelyn served nephew number two and headed back to the kitchen. She laid the tray on the counter. *Breathe, just breathe.*

"What's going on out there?" Elizabeth loaded more full plates onto the tray. "Your face is redder than Charlie's when he's been in the sun too long."

"Nothing. It's all gut."

"I saw Theo Beiler is back."

How that grapevine grew so fast was a mystery. "Jah."

"And his suh. How old is he?"

"Twenty-two, I think."

"Ah, hmm. Name?"

The wheels were turning so fast that they whirred in Jocelyn's ears. "Noah."

"If he looks anything like his dat, he'll catch a lot of attention from the girls. It's a shame my Josie is too young. She's only sixteen. But your niece Rose is eighteen, isn't she?"

Suddenly this matchmaking game turned Jocelyn's stomach. God's planning. God's timing. He didn't need meddlesome mothers sticking their noses in His plans. "Rose is helping the new teacher out at the school. She's not in any hurry to court."

"Ahh. You're not thinking about nudging him toward Bonnie, are you?" Elizabeth scowled as she slid another plate onto the tray. A sausage link rolled off. She plunked it back in its place with her gloved hand. "Oh no you don't. The sausage, I mean, not you. But surely you know how much Elijah cares for your dochder. He came back to town before the road trip ended last month, which was his way of telling his dat he was done with auctioneering."

"I heard something about that." Jocelyn was done picking apart the personal, private lives of the young people in her life. She had her own p's and q's to mind. "I better get this tray out there before the food gets cold and people go hungry."

"Jah, go, go." Elizabeth's scowl softened. "Make sure Theo Beiler gets an extra big piece of cake. I've heard the way to a man's heart is through his stomach."

Elizabeth heard and saw way too much.

By the time everyone in the shift had been served, Jocelyn's feet, knees, elbows, and shoulders were on fire. She'd be the last to admit it, but serving at an event of this size should be left to the youngies. A new round of servers flooded the kitchen to take over the second shift. *Danki, Gott.*

"I'm not that old," she muttered to herself as she hobbled out the door to the back porch. "Just a lot of mileage."

She stopped and raised her face to the afternoon breeze. The air was humid but not as warm as in the kitchen. The sun had retired behind a bank of clouds, lowering the temperature a few degrees. She rolled her shoulders, stretched first one arm and then the other. A pine rocker called her name. If she sat down now, she'd fall asleep.

"*Psst, psst.*"

Jocelyn craned her head. She surveyed the porch and yard. Saw nothing.

"*Psst*, over here."

Theo stuck his head out from the house's corner to her right. "Come here."

Jocelyn checked the vicinity. Most of the guests were around front. The grills and the wedding wagon were set up directly in front of the porch, but farther out so they wouldn't block the road and the smoke wouldn't drift into the open kitchen windows. Elijah and his brothers were all gathered around the grills. So were the Hershberger men, but they were so intent on talking and grilling, they wouldn't notice.

This was ridiculous. She was way too old. "Coming."

She whipped down the steps, trotted around the corner, and walked into Theo's outstretched arms. He hugged her hard. Jocelyn hugged back. "What are you doing back here?"

"Waiting for you. I heard some of the other servers talking about being glad the first shift was over. They were tuckered out. I figured you'd be done too."

"And you were sure I'd come out the back?"

"Nee. Just hoping. If you hadn't, I would've found another way. Or come to the house tonight. But then I thought you might be too tired and go to bed early."

He was talking fast. Like he was nervous or happy or both. "Why hoping?"

"I didn't want to wait until tonight to talk to you."

His hands ran up and down her arms. He touched her cheek. His gaze didn't waver from hers. Jocelyn's blood rushed in her ears. A chair. She might need a chair in case her legs gave out. "Where's Noah? What do you want to talk about?"

"I introduced him to Uri's seh. They're playing cornhole and volleyball and introducing him to some of the other folks his age. He's fine."

"So what did you want to talk about?"

"Come for a ride with me."

Escape from the wedding of one of Bonnie's best friends to go riding with a man. Teenagers did stuff like that. Not a middle-aged woman and widow. Yet the idea sent a sweet tremor of delight through Jocelyn. *Nee, be a grown-up.* "It's a wedding." She smoothed her damp, stained apron with shaking hands. She was sweaty. Not the best condition for a ride with Theo. Besides, ditching a social event, as her daughter would call it, was wrong. "So many guests, so many visitors."

"So many that you won't be missed for a short ride. We'll be back in time for the singing and games."

A ride with Theo versus making small talk with people she saw a few times a year. "I smell like barbecue."

"I like barbecue." Theo grabbed her hand and tugged her toward the old, rutted dirt road that led deeper into the Hershbergers' property. His buggy sat next to a barbed-wire fence that separated the road from a field of alfalfa. An ancient live oak shaded his horse, who was busy snacking on thick grass that hugged the road. The horse tossed his head and whinnied.

"I know. I'm here."

Theo helped Jocelyn into the buggy as if she hadn't climbed into one a thousand times in her life. The strange feeling of being cared for washed over her. Two minutes later, they were on the road. The buggy's wheels creaked and groaned with the hollows and ridges in the road. The clouds sank lower in the sky. The breeze had died. As if everyone and everything paused, breath held, waiting for what came next. Still, Theo didn't say a word. He kept his gaze trained on the road in front of them.

"Theo?"

"Hmm?"

"What are we doing? Are we running away? Did you have a stopping place in mind?"

Abruptly he pulled on the reins. The buggy halted. "I'm too old for this."

"Me too. Whatever this is."

"I wanted to do it right." Theo tied up the reins. He swiveled in his seat. "Only I couldn't figure out what that meant exactly. I feel ridiculous. Like I'm back in my twenty-year-old body."

"I know what you mean." Jocelyn gripped her hands in her lap. Her heart fluttered. Her breathing sounded loud in her ears. "At least I think I do. What are we talking about exactly?"

"You and me."

The flutter increased in velocity until Jocelyn's heart hurt. "Is Noah here to stay or just visiting?"

"He's on the hunt for a job here. He's got a room at the B and B in town for now."

"And the girl he was courting?"

"She'll come along when he gets settled. She's only eighteen. There's no rush."

Unless she felt about Noah the way Jocelyn felt about his father. Waiting might then seem impossible. Unadvisable. Almost painful. "Funny how we say that to our kinner, like we've forgotten how hard it is to wait when the heart is involved."

"Isn't that the truth?" Theo took off his hat. Squinting against the sun, he spun the hat round and round in his hands. "It's different for us. We've seen too much to pussyfoot around. You'd think we'd want to step carefully, not wanting to go through all that upheaval again."

"Instead we're chomping at the bit because we know how fleeting life can be." Jocelyn touched the hat. The spinning ceased. "We know we're not in charge. We know everything could change from one awful, heartbreaking moment to the next."

"Or it could go on and on in blessed contentment."

"Either way, it seems that spending that time together is so much better."

"As old, once-married people, we know these things."

"How did you convince Noah to move here?"

"It turns out it wasn't that hard." Theo heaved a sigh heavy with a mixture of relief and disbelief. He laid the hat aside. "He was waiting for me to make the first move. He missed having me close. Like I missed him. He was just too stiff-necked to admit it."

"Sort of like his father."

"I sought him out."

"Finally."

"Deciding to move was hard. He had a decent job there with gut people. But not his people. We talked and talked and talked until finally I told him it was up to him. That I would stay in Berlin and find a job there."

"He didn't want you to do that?"

Theo glanced toward Jocelyn, then away. "He knew how much it would cost me."

"Cost you?"

"I told him about you. About everything. He got up from his chair and left the restaurant." Theo's voice turned ragged. His gaze traveled to the open field. "I thought he was angry that I had another woman on my heart. I went after him. He said he was going back home to pack."

"I'm so glad." Swallowing against sudden tears, Jocelyn gripped her hands together. "For you and for him. A suh needs his daed."

"He's like your Bonnie. He doesn't want me to be alone. Especially since he's hoping to marry soon too."

"Too?"

"Like me."

The flutters turned into cartwheels. Jocelyn laid her hand on her chest. *Stay put, stay put.* She heaved a breath. *Easy, easy.* "What are you trying to say?"

"I'm saying I love you. I can't get you out of my mind. I don't want to. I want to be around you all the time." His gaze fixed on her face, Theo took Jocelyn's hands in his. "Will you marry me, sei so gut?"

Every jagged, broken piece of Jocelyn's heart found its new place in her chest until it was whole and complete again. A familiar rhythm, like an old friend, resumed. She slipped her hands from Theo's, placed them on either side of his face, and kissed his lips. "Jah."

"Jah? Jah." Theo covered her hands with his. He heaved a breath. "You said jah."

"You sound surprised."

"I wasn't sure you would. We haven't known each other very long."

"Not one muscle or bone in my body is saying stop, don't do it. My heart and my head are in agreement. There's only one other time I've . . ." Jocelyn stopped. Her heart squeezed. Tears threatened. Gulping air, she tried to tug her hands free. "There's only one other time I've been this certain about anything."

"Me too." Theo didn't let go. He kissed her gently. "The first time I proposed."

Jocelyn rested her forehead on Theo's. "The first time I was asked."

"I guess that means Ellie and Marlin approve." Theo's soft laugh held wonder. "Do you think Bonnie will?"

"I know she will."

"So you didn't sell the farm after all?"

"Nee. I told you I would wait and I did." Holding out for a second chance at love. "I'll call Mr. Steadman tomorrow to let him know I've made a decision. He and his wife will have to look for another place for their new start."

Theo heaved a breath and smiled. "Whew. I was afraid Uri and Bart would decide it was better to sell than to wait around for me to make up my mind. A bird in the hand, as it were. They would've been right."

"They both saw the wisdom in waiting if it meant keeping a Plain farm Plain rather than selling it to an English couple, however nice they might be." If they hadn't, Jocelyn had been prepared to dig in her heels and stand her ground. "Even Uri can admit he's wrong about something—once in a while."

"Uri only wants what is best for his schweschdre. His meddling is his way of showing his love." Theo dropped a kiss on Jocelyn's forehead. "How will Bonnie feel about me moving into the house you shared with her daed?"

"It'll be an adjustment." Jocelyn contemplated the sun sneaking between the clouds. "We may have to give her—and us—time to get used to the idea."

Time to paint and rearrange. To change some things to make

the home more Theo's and hers. Time to let Bonnie find room in their house and in her heart for Theo.

"I like the sound of that." Theo put his arm around her. "We'll wait to talk to Bart. Today's Sophia and Matthew's day."

"We'll have our day." Jocelyn leaned into him. His arm tightened. "As many days as Gott wills."

Chapter 40

One more pot. One more serving dish. One more ladle. Bonnie rested her forearms on the sink. She scratched her nose with her sudsy hand. It only made the itch worse. A few more pots and pans and she'd be done—with the lunch's dirty dishes. In plenty of time for the supper meal of roasted chicken and stuffing, mashed potatoes, noodles with brown butter and cheese, lettuce salad, beets, green beans, and watermelon. More cake, but also three kinds of pie. Every dish she'd washed would be dirtied again.

"Stop daydreaming, will you, and wash that casserole dish." Opal flapped a damp dish towel at Bonnie. "I have to finish up quick. I need to go to the bathroom pronto."

"Run along, go, don't wait. I'll dry it." Bonnie flicked a soap bubble at her friend, who was big enough now that she probably wouldn't do any running. Despite being six months pregnant, she'd done a full shift drying dishes while several other women had been recruited away from the job for other tasks as new folks were seated for lunch. Through it all, her dark-brown eyes sparkled with good humor. Her chestnut hair remained perfectly contained behind her prayer covering and her dress unwrinkled. "You should get off your feet, anyway. Have some cold tea. You look overheated."

Opal popped the bubble and sent another flying back at Bonnie. "Danki. I need to check on Tucker. If he naps much longer, he won't sleep tonight, and I need my sleep."

"Go. I'm gut." Between the warm water and the hot breeze wafting through the open kitchen windows, she was sweaty and her throat parched, but she enjoyed finishing a job strong. "Give him a kiss for me."

"Will do."

"I'll take that towel. You go see your bopli bu." Her mom tugged the dish towel from Opal. "I'm rested and ready for another round of work."

Hand on her lower back, Opal shuffled away as fast as her swollen feet could carry her.

Bonnie hadn't seen Mom approach. Her mother's face was overly pink as if she'd spent too much time in the sun, but a smile belied any discomfort from it. Bonnie handed over the casserole dish. "That was a smooth handoff."

"It's all about timing." Mom wiped the dish dry with quick, efficient swipes. "And energy. I just ate a piece of cake and drank a big glass of extra-strong, sun-brewed sweet tea."

Sugar and caffeine. That would do it. "I'm about done myself. They did the rest of the pots and pans in the wagon. Elizabeth is supervising so you can imagine how quickly they're moving. It's time for the next shift to take over here. Sarah, Harriet, and Hannah, if I remember right."

"Gut. I wanted to talk to you, anyway. You look like you need a cold drink yourself."

"I'll stick with lemonade. I don't need anything that will keep me awake tonight."

Mom strode away without responding. A minute later she returned with the three women in question. She tugged dry towels from the dwindling stack on the counter and handed them out. "The youngies are collecting the last of the dessert dishes, glasses, and silverware. They should be in shortly."

"We've got it from here, boss." Hannah, who had a dirt smudge on her sweaty forehead, gave Bonnie a thumbs-up. "We won the volleyball game. It was a gut time to make our getaway before the buwe ask for a rematch."

"No one was keeping score, of course." Bonnie plucked the towel from Hannah's hand, dried her own, and handed it back. "And you were the picture of gut sports."

"Absolutely."

Laughing, Bonnie followed her mother out the door to the back porch. As promised, she brought a large glass filled with lemonade and crushed ice for her.

Bonnie parked her rollator and sank into the nearest rocker. She rolled the cold glass across her forehead, once, twice. The scent of grilled chicken and sausage didn't appeal nearly as much as it had a few hours earlier. "It feels so gut to sit."

"Doesn't it, though?" Mom's rocking chair creaked under her weight. She leaned back and sent it rocking. "Although I'm so full of pent-up energy, I could plant a garden, bake ten pies, can a dozen jars of tomatoes, cut several acres of alfalfa, and still make supper."

"My, my, that tea was strong."

"It's not the tea." Mom rocked harder. "It's been an eventful afternoon."

"An eventful day. Matthew and Sophia got married. It doesn't get more eventful than a Plain wedding."

"Well . . ."

Bonnie swiveled in her chair to take a closer gander at her mother. Mom's pink cheeks had turned red. Her smile bloomed. She might burst into song any moment. "What's going on?"

Mom glanced at Bonnie, then out at the wedding wagon. She used a fingernail to scrape dried gravy from her apron.

"Mamm?"

"A Plain wedding makes for an eventful day, for sure and for certain." She rocked harder. "A man asking a woman to marry him that same day makes it even more eventful."

The words hung in the air. Bonnie plucked at them one by one, until she'd gathered them all together so she could understand their meaning. "Someone else is getting married?"

"Jah. Me." With a high-pitched laugh, Mom crossed her arms, then uncrossed them. "Theo asked me to marry him. I said jah. Are you mad at me?"

Shocked, but not surprised. Did that make any sense? Happy, but sad. Anxious, yet calm. "Not mad. Of course not mad." Bonnie gripped the rocker's arms. It was her turn to rock harder. "I'm happy for you."

That wasn't a lie. A person could be happy and sad at the same time.

"But?"

"No but. Even if it is soon. You've only known each other a few months. Part of that time he was in Berlin."

"I know, I know. We talked about it, but we've both been through this before." Mom's hands fluttered. She crossed her legs at the ankle, then uncrossed them. "We have experience with these feelings. We also know how short time can be."

"You've both also lost your spouses. You're both lonely."

"True, but that's not why he asked and I said jah." Frowning, she rocked harder. "Surely that's not what you're suggesting."

"Nee, nee. I'm simply wondering how can you be sure of that?"

"I just am."

How could anyone be that sure of anything?

"I don't want to get into how I know this is right and gut. It would be painful for both of us." Mom laid her hand on Bonnie's arm. "Trust me when I tell you I've never been more sure."

"So Theo and Noah will work the land?"

"Yah, starting right away." She stopped rocking. Her smile had returned. "Then when we get married, Theo will move in with us."

The memory of Dad sitting at the kitchen table, singing "Happy Birthday" to Bonnie on her tenth birthday, filled her mind's eye. Mom had baked her favorite German chocolate cake, along with carrot-spice cupcakes for Dad, just because. "Into Dat's house."

"He would be happy for me. And for you." Mom's voice turned ragged. "You know he would. He'd want to know you're taken care of."

"I think we've been doing a fairly gut job of taking care of ourselves."

"Gott didn't mean for people to be alone. That's why He created Eve from Adam's rib. He knew it wasn't gut for man to be alone. He needed a helpmate—"

"Mamm, seriously, you're quoting Genesis to me?" Bonnie snorted. It wasn't the Scripture itself. It was as familiar as the Lord's Prayer. As the Ten Commandments. "I understand in my head. It's my heart that's taking a minute to adjust. I want you to be happy. I also know how short life is."

Bonnie flung both her hands toward the sky and continued, "I know, but there's been so much change. To think of someone taking Dat's place—not just in the fields or the house but in your heart. It's hard."

She choked back a sob. The images of her dad's sunburned face, his grin, his thick, bushy beard, his muscle-bound arms that hugged hard and long, that picked her up with ease, whirled around in her brain. "It's just hard."

Mom popped from the rocker so fast the back smacked against the house. She swooped down and hugged Bonnie. "He's not replacing your dat. Your dat will always be your daed," she whispered. "I hope you and Theo can be friends. I'd be happy if you liked each other. That would be a blessing."

"I promise to try." Mom hugged her so tightly that Bonnie struggled to draw a breath. She disengaged. "If you promise to lay off the caffeine and sugar."

"I will, I will." Mom beamed. "But it's not the tea and the cake. It's this feeling. I never thought I'd feel this happy again."

"I'm happy for you."

"You could be even happier. You could feel like this."

"Here we go again."

"I heard Elijah asking where you were. One of the girls told him you were washing dishes. He couldn't very well stroll into the kitchen to talk to you." Mom clapped her hands as if applauding. "But I reckon he'll find you before the day is over. Promise me you'll consider what he has to say. Give him a chance."

"It's different. The situation is different."

"Only if you let it be."

"Look at me, Mamm. Really look."

"All I see is a stubborn, willful woman who underestimates herself and the man who will love her."

"Then you've switched your reading glasses for rose-colored lenses."

"Ha. I'm older, wiser, and more experienced. Take my advice. Give him a chance."

The screen door opened. Cindy Hershberger stuck her head out. "Josie was right. She said you were out here. Jocelyn, we could use another set of hands cutting pies and plating the slices, if you don't mind."

"Glad to help. I'm on my way."

Cindy disappeared inside. Mom headed toward the door. She paused, one hand on the frame. "Don't miss out, Dochder. If you do, you'll only have yourself to blame. Gott has placed an opportunity in front of you. But it's your choice whether you act on it. Tell me you'll at least think about it."

"I will. I promise."

"Come get a piece of pie."

"Maybe later."

She went inside. Bonnie stopped rocking. She sat perfectly still, trying to quiet the sudden vertigo. Her world spun out of control.

"Dat, I miss you," she whispered.

Chapter 41

A bouquet of feelings. Not the pretty bouquet of tulips or daisies. The one Bonnie carried in her heart held roses, but also dandelions, and mums, and thistles too. Thorns made clutching it painful. Happiness, uncertainty, anxiety, joy, even fear, opened their blooms. Everyone was getting married. Even her mother.

Bonnie pushed the rollator harder. The paved road had ended. She should go back to the wedding reception, but the laughter, the games, the singing, and the noise were too much. She couldn't think. She needed to sort out her feelings.

Happy. She was happy, deliriously happy, for Sophia. She'd be over the moon for Carol if all went as hoped later this evening. Her feelings about Mom and Theo refused to settle down in one basket. Her mother deserved to be happy. So did Theo. It had been two and a half years since Dad died. Bonnie tightened her grip on the rollator handles. She shoved the rollator over a bump in the rutted dirt road. The rollator rocked. She hung on. It settled.

Dad wouldn't mind. He would be glad. Bonnie should be

glad too. "I am glad," she whispered. "I'm just . . ." Just what? Scared?

Not scared. She wasn't a coward. She'd faced every challenge head-on her entire life.

Except one. The one with the dimples, blond hair, and a shy smile.

Oh, Elijah.

A strange man would live in Dad's house. He'd sit in Dad's chair at the breakfast table. He'd lounge in Dad's chair in the living room on winter nights, warming his feet by the fire while he read *The Budget* newspaper.

He'd sleep in Dad's bedroom.

Every nook and cranny of the house, once filled with her father's enormous presence, his sweaty scent, his laughter, his stern rebukes, his stories, would belong to another man.

However nice, kind, however much Theo loved Bonnie's mom, he would never be Dad.

Bonnie would face this new season with an obedient, willing heart.

The sun disappeared behind clouds that hovered just above the horizon. The day's heat had begun to dissipate. The oaks, maples, and poplars lining the road cast long shadows. A breeze heavy with rain yet to come dampened her face. She inhaled. The aroma of fresh-cut alfalfa wafted, mixing with a potpourri of wildflowers—coneflowers, purple dame's rockets, bee balm, and burdock. Bonnie rolled the names around on her tongue. Virginia's wildflowers were wonderful in their variety, colors, and hardiness. She could take a note from their example.

The rollator twisted left, then right. The ruts deepened. Bonnie clutched the handles and straightened it. Her shoulders ached. Her legs dragged.

Time to turn around. She didn't even know where this road led. *Go figure.*

I get it, Gott. I don't have to know. Faith is following even when I can't see the destination. Easy for You to say.

The rollator plunged downward, twisted, rocked. Bonnie lost her grip. The rollator toppled. Bonnie followed.

In that split second, her brain registered what was coming. *You're falling. Stop it. Catch yourself.* She threw out her arms.

Falling, falling. It took forever, yet only seconds, to fall.

She smashed into the sunbaked dirt face down.

The thud registered. The *oomph* as the air left her lungs. The jolt. The smack of her face against the rocky dirt.

Get up. She needed a minute. A minute to breathe. To take stock. Her nose hurt. Her poor nose always took a beating in falls. Her knees burned. Her arms were okay. Maybe not. Her wrists hurt.

Get up.

She shifted and tried to rise on her hands and knees. Like a baby learning to crawl.

Her left wrist screamed with pain. The right one wasn't too happy either.

"Ach, ach." She panted. *Easy, breathe through it, in, out.* She had plenty of experience dealing with pain. And with getting up after a fall. None of it good. "Nee."

Bonnie stretched back and lowered herself to the ground. *Give it a second.*

The minutes ticked by.

Come on. You can do it. The rollator rested on its side, within reach. If she could get to it, she could propel it upright, and use it to pull herself up.

Okay, she had a plan. She gritted her teeth and tried again, this time on her forearms. She dragged herself to the rollator. Once there, she shoved it over. Pain shot through her wrist.

Ignoring it, she pulled herself up until her forearms settled on the rollator's seat. "Come on, come on, up, up, up."

Her legs, as usual, did nothing helpful. She could rise on her knees, but her calves and hamstrings refused to work together to get her onto her feet. Frustration rocked her. "Gott, why? Sei so gut, why?"

She knew the answer. It had been the same since the first time she voiced the question. It was the equivalent of a father telling his child, "Because I said so" or "It's for your own good."

Exhausted, she laid her head on the seat and closed her eyes. "So now what, Gott?"

Eventually someone would miss her. Mom would come looking for her. She'd be mad. *"You know better! Did you hit your head? Are you all right?"* All the same questions, all the same concern and worry. Mom didn't deserve these trials.

Bonnie tried again. Same result.

I'm sorry, Mamm. I'm sorry, Gott.

Maybe if she could reach a tree, she could use a branch to pull herself up far enough to get her legs under her. Bonnie straightened. She eyed the selection along the road. They were old trees that towered far above her. Not a single low-hanging bough.

Come on, Gott.

She laid her head down again. Titmice and bluebirds bickered in the trees. A hawk soared overhead. At least it wasn't a vulture. Bonnie half snorted, half laughed, but she didn't sob. Crickets started their nightly chorus practice. Bullfrogs joined in.

Darkness crept along the road, night falling.

It was almost peaceful. Her breathing evened. Her heart slowed.

Hochmut. Pride went before a fall.

I know I'm a willful, ungrateful woman, Gott. Forgive me for being so full of myself. For wanting to do it all on my own. For not wanting anyone's help. For asking for Your help as a last resort. For whining because I don't like the answer. For being selfish. For refusing help when it was offered. Sei so gut, forgive me.

A dog barked. And barked. Louder and louder. Closer and closer.

Bonnie sat up. Stray dogs were common in these parts. People somehow thought they were being kind by dropping off their unwanted dogs "in the country" or "on a farm." Because farmers needed dogs? Because dogs could fend for themselves in the country? The rationalizations made no sense.

Let it be friendly, sei so gut, Gott.

The barking got louder, more insistent. Bonnie tensed. She had nothing with which to defend herself. Not even a stick.

Eyes glowed in the growing twilight.

"Hey, pooch, hey, pooch." Maybe if she talked to it, it would see that she was no threat, just a silly person who'd gone and gotten herself in a pickle in the middle of the road. "I'm a friend, not a foe. I promise."

It came closer. The bark softened, turned into a *woof, woof.*

A woof that sounded familiar. Bonnie peered into the dusk. The dog was big with a muscular body. A pit bull. Her heart thrummed. Not every pit bull was mean. They got a bad rap, according to her dad. Blame the owners, not the poor dogs, he always said. "Hey, pooch."

"Woof, woof."

Realization dawned.

"Slowpoke? Is that you?" The adrenaline faded so fast, Bonnie's body went limp. Purple dots danced on her periphery. A rush of relief cascaded through her. "Slowpoke, you found me, you beautiful hund."

Slowpoke bounded toward her. He covered her with sloppy, wet kisses, all the while professing his concern with whines deep in his throat. Bonnie hugged his neck in return. He might be beautiful, but he also had stinky breath that smelled like rancid meat. "It's okay. I'm fine, I'm fine."

"Bonnie! Bonnie?"

Shouts reverberated through the dusk. One voice. Elijah's. *Danki, Gott.* "Here! I'm here!"

A second later Elijah's figure came into sight down the road. He ran toward her. "Bonnie, are you all right?"

"I'm okay. I'm fine. Now that this beautiful hund found me."

Elijah didn't slow down until he was almost on top of her. He plowed to a stop and dropped to his knees. "You fell? Obviously, you fell. Did you hit your head? Are you hurt?"

"Nee, I'm fine, I'm fine."

Scowling, his face dark with fear, Elijah nudged Slowpoke out of his way. The dog hunkered down within reach, as if guarding them both. Elijah touched her cheeks, her crumpled prayer covering, her shoulders, her arms. "You sure you didn't hit your head? You must be delusional if you think Slowpoke's beautiful."

Delusional with relief. Bonnie drew a shaky breath. "He's the most handsome hund in the whole state of Virginia."

And Elijah was the most handsome man in the country.

Elijah gently tugged her into his arms. Bonnie leaned against him and breathed in his man smell. His heart pounded in her ear. His breathing had a hitch in it. She patted his chest. "I'm okay, I promise. I'm just so glad you found me."

He pulled away and stared down at her. "What are you doing out here?"

"Walking. I needed to get away. To think."

"By yourself?"

"I'm not that far from the house." She couldn't be. It took her forever to walk on smooth terrain, let alone a rocky road.

"Nee, you're not."

But too far for a woman with SMA using a rollator. The thought didn't sting. It was a simple fact. She could take a walk. Alone. During the day on a smooth, flat stretch of asphalt road or cement sidewalk. "I had a lot on my mind."

"Like what?"

"What a hypocrite I am. What a coward."

"Harsh words. I would argue you aren't either."

"I see Mamm getting on with her life. And I'm too scared to even court, let alone commit my heart and soul." She held her throbbing wrist to her chest and closed her eyes for a second. "I want to help you, but I don't want you or anyone else to help me. I'm ridiculous. I'm sorry."

"You're not ridiculous. You're human." Elijah touched her cheek. His gaze met hers. "I'd like to think we can meet somewhere in the middle. I won't jump in to do things for you, if you'll promise me to ask for help and accept it when you do need it."

"Agreed."

He touched her arm. "Are you hurt?"

"My wrist. I think it may be broken." She held it out.

Elijah took it in his hands. He stared at the scraped, dirty heel of her hand. Then he bent his head and kissed her wrist.

"Es dutt mer. I shouldn't have come out here on my own," Bonnie whispered as she ran her free hand over his thick blond hair. "Where's your hat?"

"It fell off when I started running." He kissed each finger, one by one. "What about your other wrist? Is it hurt?"

Bonnie held it out. "It's sore, maybe sprained."

Elijah dispensed kisses there as well. "We need to get you up to the house. The Hershbergers will have a first aid kit."

"In a minute." Bonnie kissed his cheeks and his neck. "What made you come out here?"

"I couldn't find you. Nobody seemed to know where you were." Elijah shifted so Bonnie could lean against him again. "Carol thought you went home, but Opal said no. I said I had to ask you a question about my stuff at the shop. They were both grinning at me when I asked, like they didn't believe me."

"I'm sure they didn't, since you were telling a bald-faced lie."

"I did want to ask you a question about the shop. Hmm, what was it?" He scrunched up his face as if thinking hard. Then he snapped his fingers. "I know what it was. Did you mind closing for the day for the wedding?"

"I didn't mind at all, and that's a very weak excuse of a question."

"Slowpoke was whining and carrying on like he'd lost his best friend. I didn't want to ask your mamm or Sophia. I felt funny asking anyone. It was like something an English man would do, like putting up a big billboard advertising my feelings—"

"Our feelings. That we're courting."

"Are we?"

God had spoken clearly. Stop stumbling around in the dark. Stop striking out on her own. Stop being so proud. It had nothing to do with having a disability. God wanted all His children to trust Him. To be willing to show weakness. *In Your weakness I am strong.* Trust. Trust God. Trust Elijah. "We are. Es dutt mer I made it so hard. My pride got in the way. I can't promise it won't again, but I'll do my best."

"Whew. Gut. I'm glad we cleared that up. I was afraid I was

courting all by myself." More kisses. "Is that what you came out here to think about? You and me?"

"Theo proposed. Mamm said jah."

Elijah stuck his arm around her. "And you don't know how to feel about it."

"I'm happy for her, but it's still hard to imagine this other man living in my dat's house."

"I've only talked to Theo a few times. I don't know him, really."

"He's nice. Kind. A gut dat, according to Mamm, and a gut man."

"But not your dat."

"Nee."

"Change is coming."

"It is, but I know it can be gut. Sophia is so happy. Carol has Ryan. They're taking chances. They're trusting Gott's plan. Mamm's trusting Gott's plan even after losing Dat so suddenly. She's not afraid to try again. I'm not a coward—"

"I could've told you that. If Sophia can do it, if Carol can do it, so can you."

"I know." Bonnie raised her head and slid her good arm around Elijah's neck. He met her halfway.

More than a kiss. A promise.

When they parted, Elijah smiled. "We'll take it slowly. You have a lot of change to deal with right now. I can wait. Just know I'm not going anywhere."

"Danki. Me neither."

"Let's get you back to the house."

Elijah hopped to his feet. With ease he scooped Bonnie up and sat her on the rollator's seat. "Would you like a ride, my friend?"

There was no shame in it. He was her friend, her partner, her future husband. He would care for her and she would care for him. "I would like it very much."

Letting someone else take care of her wasn't a sign of weakness. It didn't mean she couldn't hold up her end. It simply meant she was loved.

Chapter 42

*S*ticky cotton candy sweet on her tongue, Bonnie craned her head to see past a cluster of overall-clad farmers who'd paused in front of the auction platform to watch Toby Miller ply his trade. Elijah's brother was in his element with three English women and one English man waging a fierce bidding war over a handmade, king-size Broken Star quilt. The Center for Special Children would see a nice chunk of money for this one item. There were hundreds more pieces from outdoor furniture to tractors to sewing machines to toys to fresh eggs donated for the express purpose of helping the clinic accomplish its mission of serving all patients with genetic diseases, regardless of whether they had insurance or the ability to pay.

Theo and Uri had split the cost of hiring a van to travel to the auction in Leola, Pennsylvania. It was the closest fundraiser for the clinic and one of three for which the Miller brothers would do the calling this year.

Bonnie pressed her hand to her forehead, shielding her eyes from the blinding June sun. It didn't help. Times like this, she missed her rollator. Using a wheelchair had many perks, but not being able to see over people who failed to notice that they blocked her view was not one of them. She didn't have enough strength in her arms to move the chair any distance by herself. The Center for Special Children was working on getting her an electric chair adapted to run on battery power. It would give her so much more freedom. Getting used to a wheelchair had been hard. Another lesson in giving up control, in relying on God and her family. In asking for help. Hard lessons.

"Gotcha." Her chair started to move. Bonnie swiveled and looked up. Rachelle Miller, Toby's wife, had commandeered her chair. "Excuse me. Coming through. Excuse me. Thank you. Thank you."

The crowd parted. Within seconds Bonnie was parked in front of the bleachers alongside Judah and Robbie King, who sat in their chairs. Their sister Claire lounged on the front row, her walker parked in front of her, half a dozen of her friends on either side. They joined in a rousing "bewillkumm," the loudest coming from little Sadie Miller and her best friend Jonah Lapp.

"Danki, danki." Bonnie shot Rachelle a grateful smile. "For your help."

"You're welcome. We like to have a cheerleading section for our auctioneers." She grinned. Marriage to Toby suited her. The former schoolteacher's figure had filled out after having two babies. Her cheeks were red in the toasty sun. Her eyes sparkled every time she shot a glance at the stage. "The more the merrier. Where are your mamm and Theo?"

"They went to look at a sofa. Ours is falling apart. It's been repaired one time too many."

Although getting a large piece of furniture home to Lee's Gulch would be a challenge. More likely they would find another way to support the clinic. Mom simply liked to shop. She would spend all day purchasing smaller items that would add up to a nice "donation."

Although she nodded, Rachelle didn't seem to be paying much attention to Bonnie's words. Her gaze skipped over Bonnie's head, scanning the crowd. No doubt she wondered about Elijah but was too polite to ask. Unlike her mother-in-law, Elizabeth, who hemmed and hawed about it every time she came into the shop—which was far more often than she had before her son started courting one of its co-owners.

Everyone had to know the couple had been courting for almost a year. A wonderful, lovely time of growing closer; snatches of conversations and kisses in the shop workroom; long, rambling rides in the buggy; and picnics by the creek. So perfect. So why didn't Elijah take the next step? Did he still have doubts? Surely not. What held him back? *Why, Gott?*

"Well, look who's coming our way."

Bonnie followed Rachelle's gaze. Elijah strode along the edge of the crowd, a cardboard box under one arm and a tall reusable cup in his other hand. He seemed intent on studying the mass of people milling in front of the platform.

"Hey, Elijah!" Rachelle cupped her hands around her mouth. "Elijah! Over here!"

Heat infused Bonnie's face. Rachelle might not be Elizabeth's blood relative, but she seemed to be cut from the same cloth. She squeezed Bonnie's shoulder. *"Gern gschehme."*

What could Bonnie say? "Danki."

"No worries." She held out her hand. "Would you like me to take the stick?"

Bonnie gave the cotton candy stick to her. Rachelle took it and, in exchange, gave Bonnie a baby wipe. Always prepared. Bonnie thanked her and took care of her sticky hands while Rachelle traipsed toward a metal barrel trash can at the end of the bleachers. Very strategic withdrawal.

The cheering section was less circumspect. They chorused a welcome to Elijah. His fair skin turned radish red. He ducked his head. "Hallo."

"Bruder, Bruder!" Sadie hopped down from the bleacher and ran to Elijah. "What's in the box? Is it for me?"

"Nee." Elijah squatted, laid the box next to Bonnie's wheelchair, and hugged his little sister. "It's a present for someone else."

"Who? I'm your schweschder. I need present."

"Not this time." He smiled at Bonnie over Sadie's head. "This is for grown-up people."

Sadie's round face lit up. She whirled and threw herself at Bonnie for another hug. Bonnie returned the favor. The little girl was a warm ball of chunkiness. She smelled of caramel corn and chocolate milk. "My bruder got you a present. I help you open it."

"Not this time." Elijah gently lifted the girl from Bonnie's lap. He carried her to the bleachers and settled her next to Rachelle, who had a knowing grin on her face. "I'll be back later. I can give you a piggyback ride to the van."

"Jah, jah, jah," Sadie sang. "And bring me present."

He laughed. He looked happy. And so handsome. *Breathe.*

Bonnie couldn't contain her smile. "So what *is* in the box? Is it a present?"

For me?

"Nee, just odds and ends."

"You bid on a box of odds and ends?"

"Jason was auctioning off a bunch of the mystery boxes—you know the ones you can bid on sight unseen. Sometimes they're full of treasures. Sometimes they're full of junk."

"How much did you spend on this box of junk?"

"Three whole dollars."

"And did you find any treasures?"

"We'll find out later." Elijah set the box on her lap before she could protest. "Let's take it to my family's van. I don't want to carry it around all afternoon."

We'll. That sounded promising. The box didn't feel too heavy. The flaps were tightly folded. Her curiosity piqued, Bonnie grabbed a flap. "Let's just take a quick look."

"Nee. No peeking."

"Why?"

"Because I said so."

Without a backward glance at the Miller/King contingent, Elijah took control of Bonnie's wheelchair. He wheeled her along the narrow path between the crowd and the bleachers toward the fairgrounds exhibit hall food court.

Bonnie pointed to the plastic chairs and tables near the long row of food booths with their neon-green paper signs advertising barbecued chicken, pork sandwiches, soft pretzels, homemade doughnuts, fruit skewers, ice cream, pizza, and much more. "We could sit over there and look through it."

Elijah bent closer to be heard over the steady roar of hundreds of people all talking at once. "You're like a little kid. It's just a box of junk."

"Or a box of treasure. You said so yourself."

He didn't stop at the only open table.

"Hey, we were supposed to sit—"

"Never said that."

"But I'm hungry. I want a cheeseburger and fries."

"It's only eleven o'clock. By the time we drop the box off and come back, it'll be time to eat."

"You're being weird."

"Nee. I'm being the adult."

"Ha. Since when?"

"Funny, funny."

He pushed Bonnie's chair through the throngs of people gathered in front of massive displays of household goods, crafts, toys, donated appliances, and produce. The ways people and businesses found to support the clinic never ceased to amaze Bonnie.

A good ten minutes later, they approached the long line of vehicles parked in the overflow parking lot. Like Bonnie's family, the Millers not associated with the auctioneering business had hired a van to drive them from Virginia to Leola that morning. They'd arrived too late for close parking. It was halfway down the row.

"Here we are." Elijah parked Bonnie's chair behind the van's back end. He wiped his face on his sleeve. "It's really warmed up since we got here."

He made no move to open the back doors.

Bonnie patted the box. "Put it away so we can go back. Those french fries are calling my name."

Elijah slapped his hat back on his head. "We should open it first."

"But you just said—"

"I changed my mind. Go on, open it."

Bonnie shook her head and rolled her eyes. Sometimes Elijah brought out the teenager in her. "You really are being weird."

He shrugged. "Heatstroke. It must be eighty-five degrees."

The allure of these boxes was the unknown. Once Bonnie's dad bought one and found a rare first edition of a Louisa May Alcott book that Mom still treasured. Sometimes a box held nothing more than plastic ice trays and Dollar Store trinkets.

It took some doing, but Bonnie finally pulled out all four flaps.

A pair of rooster salt-and-pepper shakers lay nestled in a small red, blue, and purple crib quilt on top. "My mamm will love the shakers." She examined the quilt's tiny, even stitches. Made with love. "Talk about treasures. This alone is worth far more than three dollars. It'll be a perfect gift for a bopli born in winter."

Elijah took both items. "For future conversation . . . and use. What else is in there?"

Sewing shears, a pack of Uno! cards, a package of clothespins, another of ink pens, a box of birthday cards, a cake tin, a pie server, a complete set of dominoes, three crossword puzzle books, and a *First Baptist Church of Leola Women's Cookbook of Potluck Recipes*.

"Not bad. These are all useful items worth a lot more than three dollars." She grinned at Elijah. He grinned back, looking supremely pleased with himself. Bonnie started to close the flaps. "I think we can chalk this one up as treasure."

"Don't close it up yet." Elijah put his hand on hers. "You're sure there's nothing else in there? Nothing at all?"

"I don't think so." Bonnie tugged her hand free. She rummaged through the items, digging to the bottom. "Oh, jah. Some pot holders. A box of toothpicks. A Niagara Falls refrigerator magnet. I think that's it."

"Are you sure?"

Perplexed, Bonnie ran her gaze over the box's contents. She pulled out a rumpled piece of paper from under the cookbook. "Except for this. It's probably a receipt."

"Maybe."

Bonnie unfolded the pale-blue paper. Not a receipt. The neat penciled script seemed familiar. It read:

Dear Bonnie,

Will you marry me?

Love,

Elijah

Tears blurred Bonnie's vision. She blinked and reread the simple words. After all this time, it didn't seem possible. Was it really happening? The paper fluttered to the ground. She lifted her gaze to Elijah.

His hands hung at his sides. Hope danced with uncertainty in his face. He cleared his throat. "I've been trying to find a way to ask you for days. I wasn't sure—"

"Wasn't sure I'd say jah?"

His Adam's apple bobbed. He nodded.

"For a smart man, you can be so dumb."

"That doesn't sound like jah."

The letter was sweet, but the question she'd waited so long to hear needed to be spoken. Shaking her head, Bonnie pointed at the paper that had landed face down in the grass. "Maybe you should try again."

Elijah straightened. He swiveled left, then right. They were alone in a sea of vehicles under a cloudless Pennsylvania sky. The crowd's noise was a distant murmur. Not even a bird uttered a peep. Elijah dropped to both knees. He took Bonnie's hands in his. His blue eyes were brilliant in the morning sun. "Will you marry me?"

"Jah. Of course I will."

He gasped. His dimples reappeared. He jumped to his feet. "Jah, you said jah."

The folks at the livestock auction could probably hear his shout.

"I did. I thought you'd never ask." Bonnie smiled up at him. "Why are you so surprised?"

"I didn't know if it was too soon. I was afraid you'd use the wheelchair as an excuse—"

"I haven't offered it as an excuse for anything else, have I?" Bonnie began using the chair after her fall the previous summer. With one broken wrist and the other sprained, she couldn't use the rollator so she'd made the switch. She simply never went back. "I can beat Sophia in wheelchair races now, and it makes for a nice lap for the boplin."

For Opal's baby, Esther, and for Sophia's soon-to-be-adopted son, Caleb. Carol's baby was due in the fall. Bonnie was an honorary aunt to all of them.

"We said we'd go slow. It'll be a year in August. I figured that was pretty slow, but maybe your definition is different."

"I'm so relieved. I was beginning to think you'd never ask."

"Ach, seriously?" Elijah shoved his hat back. His expression bewildered, he shook his head. "You could've said something."

"The man does the asking."

"I've been so happy, I didn't want to spoil things by moving too fast. These past ten months have been the best days of my life." He knelt again and took her hands in his. "I'm working full time in my workshop. Homespun Handicrafts is doing well. Your mom and Theo are happy. You're happy, aren't you?"

Amazingly happy. The changes had been swift and relentless, yet surmountable. Hannah now worked full time in the store. A new employee, who also used a wheelchair, had taken over Sophia's duties. Not that Sophia played any less of a role in the business end of owning a shop. Same with Carol. They loved Homespun Handicrafts as much as Bonnie did.

Having Theo living in the house had turned out to be far less difficult than Bonnie had imagined. He made Mom laugh. He knew when to be quiet and when to talk. He smiled often and rarely complained. He simply fit. "I'm very happy. You make me happy."

Elijah's smile grew—if that were possible. He leaned in. Finally, he kissed her. The moment she'd been waiting for. A kiss to seal the promise. He tasted of cherry limeade and sweet joy.

As the kiss deepened, Bonnie let go of all the uncertainty, the fears, the what-ifs. The space filled with promises made, joy, and the certainty of two who would become one. They would face the what-ifs together.

When they finally broke apart, Bonnie clasped Elijah's face in her hands. "Elijah Miller, did you lure me out here to the van so we could kiss and make out like youngies?"

His aw-shucks grin grew. "Since we never got to do this as youngies, I thought it was about time."

"Seriously, though, why here at an auction? Why not some place private?"

"Because I found my courage at an auction. If I could stand in front of a crowd holding a mic and call an auction, I figured I could summon the courage to ask you the most important question of my life here."

"Makes sense." In a guy sort of way. All about bravery and courage. Such a simple question. "I think."

More kisses. More murmured words of love followed.

After a while, Bonnie leaned back. "It's perfect. So perfect."

It wouldn't always be perfect. Life would get in the way. Her health. The challenges of childbearing for a woman with SMA weren't for the faint of heart. Bonnie picked up the crib quilt. She held the soft material to her cheek. "Do you wonder what our bopli will look like? I hope he has your dimples."

"I hope he has your heart." Elijah held out his hand. Bonnie gave him the quilt. "Come what may, we'll be a family."

"Like I said, you're a smart man."

Elijah laid the quilt in the box. He closed the flaps and picked it up.

"Hey, that's my box."

"I bought it at auction."

"And you gave it to me." Bonnie nodded at the paper still lying in the grass. "I want my piece of paper in case I need to prove you asked me. No backing out now."

"Like I'd try." Elijah scooped up the paper and handed it to her. She took it, but he didn't let go. They both held on. Seconds ticked by. The unspoken words flew back and forth. "It belongs to both of us."

"For now and forever." Bonnie let go. "Slip it in the box with our other treasures."

"Gladly."

True treasures had nothing to do with pot holders, cookbooks, or refrigerator magnets. Time was theirs to treasure. Bonnie intended to do just that for all the days of their lives—however many that might be.

Discussion Questions

1. Elijah is a shy man in a family of extroverts. His dad expects him to join the family business as an auctioneer. The thought of standing up in front of a crowd makes Elijah feel physically ill. Have you ever been in a similar situation where family or friends expected you to do something you didn't feel comfortable doing? What did you do? What advice do you have for someone like Elijah?

2. Shy or introverted people are often mistaken for being unfriendly or "stuck up." Have you ever thought someone was unfriendly, only to find he or she simply had a hard time making conversation or meeting new people? How can considering this possibility change the way you approach new people?

3. Do you consider yourself an introvert or an extrovert? Why? How does that facet of your personality affect how you treat other people? Your choice of occupation? Your recreational choices and hobbies?

4. Do you think Elijah should push beyond his comfort zone and meet his family's expectations for all the brothers to join the family business? Why or why not?

5. The mainstream world sees women, marriage, and family differently from how the Amish see them. Amish women have one goal in life: to marry and have a family. Do you find this limiting, or do you see redeeming value in it? Or some of both? Even if it's not right for you, can you respect it?

6. An Amish woman living with a debilitating disease, Bonnie worries that she'll never have the chance to be a wife and mother. Then Elijah comes calling. Suddenly her greatest wish is a real possibility. Put yourself in her shoes. As you thought about your disease's effect on your ability to have children and care for them, what would you decide to do? What advice might you give Bonnie if she asked?

7. Theo and Jocelyn have known each other for only a short time, but sparks fly for the widower and the widow. They're falling in love. Do you think it's possible to fall in love so quickly? How do you feel about "love at first sight"? What advice would you give Jocelyn?

8. Theo decides he must return to Berlin to reconnect with his son. Knowing she would put Bonnie ahead of her own needs, Jocelyn agrees with his decision. How do you feel about single parents putting their children in front of their own needs? Does it make a difference that Bonnie and Noah are adults? Or that Bonnie has a progressive, debilitating disease? Why?

9. The Amish embrace children with all kinds of disabilities and diseases as "special children," as "gifts from God." Many people with disabilities in the mainstream world prefer not to be seen as "special." They simply want to be accepted for who they are. Do you find the use of the word *special* objectionable? Why or why not? If you do not have

a disability, can you see why someone who has one might object?

10. Bonnie ponders whether people sometimes have disabilities that can't be seen—whether they be physical, mental, emotional, or even spiritual—making it hard for others to understand them or relate to them. What do you think of this possibility? Do you see one of them in yourself or someone close to you? How do you handle it?

Acknowledgments

I find it hard to believe we've already arrived at book three in the Amish Calling series. My original intent to explore the impact of the founder effect on Amish communities took me on an unexpectedly difficult journey. Each book took me deeper into self-examination of my own life as a person living with disability and disease, while delving into how others perceive these issues—both Amish and non-Amish folks. It's a discussion fraught with sometimes fragile, sometimes fierce emotions. As often happens with the stories I write, these discussions enriched my life and the books. They taught me to take care with assumptions and to leave room for differences of opinion.

I'm so thankful to HarperCollins Christian Publishing and its Zondervan imprint for giving me room to pursue these stories and for publishing them. It's an uneasy publishing world in which we live and work. I never take it for granted.

The story as it appears in this book would not exist if it weren't for the dedicated, exquisitely kind, but firm editing of Becky Monds and Julee Schwarzburg's line editing. Thanks for your patience. My thanks to the marketing, public relations, and editing team at HCCP as well. You're the definition of team players.

Acknowledgments

As always, my thanks to my agent, Julie Gwinn, for practical advice and talking me down from the ledges on those gray, uncertain days. You make me smile.

To my husband, Tim, no words could begin to express what your support means to me in this writing journey.

Finally, to my Amish romance readers, many who've followed and supported me for more than ten years through the publication of twenty-five books and a dozen novellas, thank you from the bottom of my heart. Your kindness and prayers mean so much to me.

God bless each and every one of you.

About the Author

Photo by Tim Irvin

Kelly Irvin is a bestselling, award-winning author of over thirty novels and stories. A retired public relations professional, Kelly lives with her husband, Tim, in San Antonio. They have two children, four grandchildren, and an ornery cat.

Visit her online at KellyIrvin.com
Instagram: @kelly_irvin
Facebook: @Kelly.Irvin.Author
X: @Kelly_S_Irvin

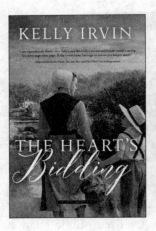

Enjoy more stories by Kelly Irvin in the Amish Blessings series

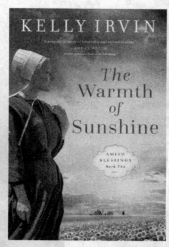

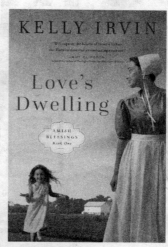

Available in print, e-book, and audio